"KISS ME THE WAY A BRIDE SHOULD KISS HER HUSBAND!"

The Baron pulled Savannah roughly to him. She managed to turn her face away and laugh. "Excellency, do you want me to appear disheveled in public?"

Despite the rocking of the carriage, the Baron did not loose his grip. "You will not appear disheveled if you remain still." The tone of his voice made this statement sound not like advice but like an order.

His mouth bore down hard upon hers, bending her backward; her arms were pinned beneath her. His mouth moved lower and he seized her tender skin between his teeth. Each time she struggled, he bit her harder.

At length the carriage slowed and he released her. "After tonight you will not resist me again," he promised her. *"Your first lesson in your marital duties will be so thorough it may leave you marked for life."*

HELEN JEAN BURN

SAVANNAH

PLAYBOY
PAPERBACKS

For my children:
Angela
Claudia
Melissa
James
and
Robert
and for Chris, who was there
in the beginning

SAVANNAH

Copyright © 1981 by Helen Jean Burn

Cover illustration copyright © 1981 by PEI Books, Inc.

Published simultaneously in the United States and Canada by Playboy Paperbacks, New York, New York. Printed in the United States of America. Library of Congress Catalog Card Number: 81-47260. First edition.

Books are available at quantity discounts for promotional and industrial use. For further information, write to Premium Sales, Playboy Paperbacks, 1633 Broadway, New York, New York 10019.

ISBN: 0-872-16908-1

First printing October 1981.

1

The mother superior's colorless old face was radiant. "Savannah," she said, "I have received a letter from your father. Sit down, child."

In the past a summons to Mother Dominica's office meant Savannah had broken another rule, so the reverend mother's words were a relief. She slid into the chair.

The elderly nun nodded approvingly toward the letter before she put it down and turned to the girl. She was very nearly smiling. "He tells me you are to be a baroness, your betrothed is descended from a very ancient family, and he has great wealth!"

Savannah said nothing. She'd gotten a letter, too. In it her father said Maman was on the way to Switzerland from Brazil to get her. There was mention of going home by way of Paris for the trousseau. He, like the mother superior, referred to the marriage as if it were a victory for Savannah—which she found puzzling, since she'd done nothing whatever to achieve it.

Mother Dominica, in an uncharacteristic gesture of tenderness, took the girl's face in her hands. "God has blessed you, my dear. You have the face of an angel. You will be able to do much good in the world."

Savannah, unaccustomed to praise, felt at a loss for a response. She didn't much like her looks and tried to think about them as little as possible. Unfashionably slender and taller than her classmates, she was the only girl in the whole school who had red hair. Her skin was much too pale and her eyes—well, she kept hoping they'd turn out to be deep blue after all; but her friend Jocelyn said they were the color of amethysts, and the other girls enjoyed telling her they were purple. Fortunately, Savannah never cried. Well, almost never. For some reason she felt like crying now, and kept her face down.

The reverend mother reached out and gently lifted her chin. "What is it, my child?"

"The Baron . . . he's not . . . *young.*"

"A man in the prime of life?" She smiled reassuringly. "He will be wise, understanding, and patient. In view of your temperament, I would say that is exactly what is required."

No doubt the mother superior was thinking of all the trouble Savannah had gotten into in her nine years at the convent. She was cursed by a tendency toward wild impulses. Apparently it was more important than ever to stifle them; lately the nuns had been repeatedly harping on the fact that she was no longer a child, talking as if sixteen were quite on the brink of the grave. She was just beginning to sense what being a child no longer might mean: no more death-defying circus acts like the one that had made it necessary for the gardener to rescue her by ladder from the fingertip hold she was rapidly losing on the edge of the chapel roof. No more snatching the toupee from the visiting bishop's bald head and arranging for it to be served to him under a covered dish at luncheon. No more laughter; just these stupid infuriating tears.

The old nun closed her eyes and folded her hands. "Let us thank our Lord for His marvelous goodness."

Savannah looked up, able at last to focus her dismay. "But I didn't choose this man!"

"Naturally. Are you competent to make so momentous a decision? Your father loves you dearly, so he has done it for you."

"But Jocelyn says—"

Even though Mother Dominica clasped her hands around the cross she wore on a chain from her belt, she was not successful in suppressing the disapproval in her tone. "I have told you before that your friendship with that English girl is quite inappropriate. Her father is a member of the House of *Commons*. A liberal member! Her life will be very different from yours."

"I don't see why."

"Because, child, you are Portuguese."

"My father is a North American and my mother is French!"

"But you are marrying into the Portuguese nobility."

Risking impertinence, she persisted. "He's Brazilian."

"Brazilian Portuguese, Savannah. The Brazil part is a geographic accident. The Portuguese, like the Spanish, are Iberians. I am sure you recall the history of the Iberian peninsula? Then you understand why their attitude toward women is far more Moorish than European. An attitude which is, incidentally, entirely in keeping with Holy Scripture. You will be completely protected from the world, and of course you will lack nothing the world's wealth can provide." Mother Dominica's dry hand stroked a strand of coppery hair from Savannah's face. "Remember, God will never punish you for obedience to those He has placed in authority over you—your confessor, your father, your husband." She embraced the girl tenderly, enveloping her in the pungent odor of holy incense and bringing tears afresh to her eyes. Then in a voice uncharacteristically strained she murmured, "Bend, Savannah. Bend! Or you will be broken."

A few days later her mother arrived, packed her up, and trundled her off to Paris for a month of shopping. By the end of the first week Savannah was exhausted from the endless fittings. Whenever she complained about the clothes, her mother, who was French, would say, "But *chérie*, it is *le dernier cri!*" That meant the newest thing—literally, the last cry, which Savannah, as she surveyed these 1896 fashions, felt sure was a shriek of pain.

Her complaints did no good. One day they were in a cluttered workroom where the wedding gown was being made. Maman had proudly shown the proprietress the Baron's photograph, and all the women had sighed over this distinguished-looking man with the pointed beard and imperious eyes. Savannah stood wearing the heavy garment of ivory satin covered with filigrees of hand-stitched seed pearls; the veil under her tiara was like the clouds in a holy picture. The circle of women caught their breath as she turned slowly before them; then Maman told her to walk across the room to make certain she could move without stepping on the train. She crossed the floor littered with pins and bits of lace, and stopped dead before the three hinged mirrors against the wall. Looking from one image of herself to the others, she was stricken by the thought: *I am going to be married, I will be some man's wife, and I don't even know him.* . . . The three startled reflections before her formed a triptych of terror; and the fear she saw for the first time in that moment never went away. Yet each time she tried to talk about it, her mother changed the subject.

Through all of this Savannah kept awakening before dawn, just as if she could still hear the convent bell for matins; only now she opened her eyes to darkness in strange places—in railway compartments, stuffy hotel rooms, and the stateroom of an ocean liner.

One morning, after two weeks at sea, Savannah submitted to a long-stifled impulse and got up before dawn. Moving in the dimness quietly lest she awaken her mother in the adjoining stateroom, she found her embroidered bedroom slippers and her mauve challis robe. Then she threw a cashmere shawl over her long hair, peered through the adjoining doorway to make certain Maman was sleeping soundly, and moved silently into the passage.

Outside the first-class cabins the promenade deck was deserted. She stood at the rail and watched the sky turn a paler shade of gray above the dreary ocean, savoring the delicious feeling of having escaped the rules for a few moments. She'd get into trouble for it later; she always did. But that never diminished the pleasure.

The wind blew fitfully, scattering foam along the swells. Closing her eyes, she made an effort to imagine the world, and this liner crawling over it. The ship, in her mind's eye, was the model in the window of the steamer office in Hâvre; two black funnels, three white decks with ventilators stuck here and there like macaroni; and propped against the wheelhouse a meticulously lettered card which said *Esperança—Latest Design Twin Screw Steamship with All Electric Lighting*.

And the world Savannah pictured was the globe in Sister Cécile's geography classroom. In her imagination now the toy ship moved over the painted globe, south from Hâvre past rose-colored Portugal and the sand-yellow shoulder of Africa. It wound among the islands, Madeira and the Cape Verdes, all of them small rosy pieces of Portugal, although Sister said they were the tips of submerged mountains. Then, crossing the fine black line that said *Tropic of Cancer*, it turned slowly westward to Brazil.

She turned from the rail to find the sailors working their way toward her. Each day, before the passengers awakened, they washed the decks, scrubbed the ship's white walls, waxed the hardwood railings, and polished the brass fixtures up and down the companionways. They were barefoot, their white duck pants rolled to the knees. Some of them had taken off their double-breasted jackets and turned up their shirt sleeves, baring their strong young arms to the sea wind.

Savannah watched them, standing like a new girl at school, like one who longs to play but doesn't know anybody's name, until she was surrounded by sailors. It struck her suddenly that she shouldn't go about unchaperoned, and that being on deck in a wrapper and slippers was definitely not done.

Holding her shawl close, she started toward the passage, but a muscular young sailor barred her way. He grinned at her and said, "Hey, girl, you like to sleep with me? I give you very much good time." She stepped aside; he stepped with her. The others laughed. The shawl had fallen to her shoulders. As her hair lifted in the wind, he gripped it and drew her toward him. The others murmured warnings, but he didn't stop. He said, "I take care of you good, what you say?" She pressed both hands against his chest, but he didn't move. He gripped her so closely she could see nothing but his mouth grinning; she could smell sweat, garlic, and tobacco. It was the feeling of being unable to escape from the odor that made her angry. Her temper flared and she struck him in the face. He laughed and held her closer, even though a scarlet ribbon of blood crept from one nostril toward his swelling upper lip.

Then she heard a voice behind her speaking Portuguese in a tone of command. The sailor's features paled and as the color drained from his face she felt the strength ebb from his grip. He backed away, but not in time to avoid the hand that grasped his shirtfront. The voice, beside her now, continued speaking in that tone of authority. Free now to turn, she saw the passenger named Manco, the one who always wore black, a high-collared suit without lapels that made him look like a priest on business. At the rim of her vision she perceived the circle of sailors falling back, murmuring apologies, bowing to him. The one who'd held her looked terrified. Manco spoke again. The sailor nodded emphatically. When the hand gripping his shirt released him he fell to his knees at Savannah's feet, saying, *"Desculpe, senhorita! . . .* Forgive me!" But his eyes were fixed on the passenger's face; when Manco nodded, the sailor got to his feet and fled with the others down the companionway.

Manco gripped her arm just as her knees failed her. She rested against him a moment, breathing as if she'd just learned how and needed practice. It was always this way: She never knew until a crisis had passed that she'd been frightened, not until she was safely down from the chapel roof or until the bishop, gibbering with rage, was packed into his carriage under a skewed toupée; then, invariably, she'd begin to shiver like a steeple made of pudding. Now, with Manco's help, she walked unsteadily to the rail and stood there a moment, wondering if the pounding of her heart and the tremors that shook her body were the fault of that sailor—or of this man whose arm was protecting her now. He said, "Did he hurt you?"

"No. He was only teasing, I'm sure." Embarrassed, she drew away from him a little, glancing at him covertly as she moved. She'd watched him during the voyage. He was always alone, dining apart from the others, never conversing with anyone, walking on the deck with long soundless strides, all in black like a three-dimensional shadow. But until now she had never seen him close up. His eyes were dark, almond-shaped, and tilted at the outer corners. His hair—long, but tied back —and the narrow moustache forming a parenthesis at each corner of his mouth were so black they looked iridescent, like a bird's wing. Yet his skin was not dark, it was a pale bronze. Perhaps he was a South American Indian, but with Spanish or Portuguese blood, because he was very tall. He was far handsomer than any priest, or any other man she'd ever seen.

Now he had taken her arm again and was saying she'd better let him see her to her cabin. Of course, that was not done either. "No, thank you, I just need to get my bearings here for a moment," she said. Together they stared at the waves far below until Savannah said, "Why is the sea a different color today?"

"That's the Amazon."

She looked at him. "But aren't we still a long way from Brazil?"

"It takes the ocean a long time to absorb the river. Even a hundred, and sometimes two hundred miles at sea, the Amazon remains distinct." He looked beyond her toward the west where, above the dark mass of clouds on the horizon, lightning flashed. He told her that the river flows four thousand miles. It starts in the Andes, only a hundred miles from the Pacific, and travels across the whole of South America. He spoke quietly but his voice was so resonant she heard him clearly above the hissing sea and the rush of wind. He said, "It carries the snows of the mountains, the vegetation of millions of square miles of jungle, and the mud of a half-dozen countries . . . along with the blood of dead men and the tears of their women."

She turned to gaze at him. His eyes were utterly black, without a trace of light in them, yet they seemed to burn. She said, "Blood?"

He sighed, still looking far into the distance. "While we stand here, men are dying where this water comes from." He turned to her suddenly. "I hope I haven't distressed you."

It was difficult to concentrate; his eyes seemed to impale her.

He smiled. "You are very beautiful." His eyes softened. He said, "You mustn't blame that sailor. And of course," he went on, "you were alone."

"But I must be alone sometimes, or I get all muddled. And anyway, I think etiquette is so stupid. Maman is forever preaching at me about the things done and not done."

He stared into the ocean. "Among the jungle tribes the women always stay close to one another. They eat together, work together, swim in the river together. They do it because there is an unwritten law that any woman found alone in the forest is fair game. She can be attacked, not just by one man, but by all the men." He looked back at her. "So you see, your mother's etiquette may be more widespread than you realize."

She shuddered. "That's horrible." She saw that his hands on the rail were slender and well formed, the hands of a gentleman. Yet his treatment of the sailors had not been gentle.

He sighed. "Unfortunately, the remedy for brute force is more brute force, or at least the fear of it. At any rate, I recommend that you no longer walk alone." He stepped back from the rail.

She held out her hand. "I'm Savannah St. James. Thank you very much for helping me." Did she imagine it, or had her name startled him? Not startled; he hadn't moved, she'd seen a change. His eyes had narrowed, intensified. She said, "Perhaps in Manáos you will visit us."

She'd never seen such laughter. "That is most unlikely," he said and added with a slight ironic bow, "Baroness."

Stiffly she said, "I am not a baroness." She didn't add the other part; she didn't say *yet*. How did he know who she was?

But he wasn't listening; he'd turned back to the bronze waves. He said, "Did you know, the jungle peoples say there are spirits in the river? The one they fear most is the *boiuna,* who takes the form of an anaconda to scent and seek out girls who are becoming women. Then he crushes and devours them. When is the wedding?" he added.

She turned away, her hands busy with the shawl. It twisted in the breeze as she shook her hair free and wrapped the garment more firmly about her.

"Are you not looking forward to your marriage?"

She turned toward the west, where beyond the clouds the huge river sprawled, reaching its twisted limbs deep into the continent. "It's odd," she said, "but I can't remember Manáos. I've been at school so long, it's like going home to a completely foreign place. I'm not even sure I can still speak Portuguese."

He walked around to stand in front of her. She didn't want

to look at him, to encounter the full force of that burning scrutiny, but he lifted her chin gently and looked into her eyes. He said softly, *"A senhorita não responde."*

"I don't have to answer you."

He frowned and shook his head as if to free himself of something. "No, you don't." Then he stepped back, bowed slightly, said, "Senhorita," and was gone.

2

Veronique St. James was awake, but she remained in her berth. She was fifty years old and had made this ocean crossing many times. Still she'd never gotten used to it, never gotten over the seasickness that confined her to bed and made the faintest odor of food a torment. Nor had she gotten used to the sudden change of climate. Going from her native Paris in the snow of December to the humid midsummer December of the tropics struck her as utter madness. But the Amazon region was madness itself, a place where—although the temperature scarcely varied all year—people persisted in talking of seasons. Seasons! From December to June it rained every day and the river rose. Then the rest of the year, called quite absurdly "the dry season," it rained only every other day and the river fell.

Veronique was resigned. At least she was no longer poor. Being in Paris again, seeing the narrow streets of closely packed houses, made her sharply aware of her good fortune. Had she spent her life in France, she'd be somebody's cook now. Or worse. Years ago if she'd gone to a gypsy to have her fortune told and the woman had gazed into her crystal ball and said, "You will have many servants and much money, your home will be a mansion with a broad veranda and white pillars," Veronique would have called her a fraud and demanded her money back. And if the woman had said, "You will live a thousand miles up the Amazon River in the deepest heart of the South American jungle," Veronique would have called a gendarme and had the fortuneteller locked up in a madhouse. Yet all this had happened.

Soon the *Esperança* would leave the ocean and start up the river for the more tranquil six-day journey to Manáos. Then over tea in her garden she would tell her friends the fashion news of Paris. No one was wearing bustles now; the shoulder was everything, everything! Oh, yes, and the newest hair style: a high bun called a "teapot handle," with crimped curls on the forehead.

She ought to have had Savannah's hair cut and crimped, but she was afraid His Excellency the Baron would be angry. He was deeply traditional. The girl's hair had never known scissors; it fell below her waist. And the copper color! Savannah was beautiful, Veronique decided. Exquisitely, aristocratically fair. She'd quite grown up in the convent.

The trousseau filled the stateroom, eight trunks stacked against the walls because Veronique couldn't bear to ship them in the hold. Gorgeous dresses, hats, wrappers, undergarments, all in the height of fashion. Veronique was content; she had done well by the child.

Now she was startled by the sound of footsteps outside Savannah's cabin. She called, "*Chérie*—is that you?" In a moment Savannah stood in the doorway connecting the cabins, abominably dressed and looking wind-blown.

Whenever Veronique was upset, her English deserted her. "*Mon dieu*," she moaned. At the same time she waved feebly in the direction of Savannah's wrapper in disbelief.

"Maman, I'm quite all right."

"All right?" She sat up in bed. "Are you seen? What will be said? Even properly dressed, a girl who is—what is *bien élevée?*"

"Well brought up." Savannah had heard it all before.

"Well brought up, such a girl does not go about alone! Never!"

"Only in Brazil, Maman." She reached behind Veronique, rearranging the pillows, then she helped her to lie back and began straightening the covers.

Veronique sniffed, her sharp nose looking increasingly pinched. "In Brazil. In Portugal. In Spain. In all the truly civilized countries of the world. You wish to live in a country where women straddle bicycles while wearing plaid woolen underdrawers, yes?" She smoothed the sheet across her lap. "In any case, you no longer go about unchaperoned. I instruct the purser to lock your cabin door. Then you leave only through my stateroom and with my permission."

Savannah sank into the boudoir chair and began brushing her hair. *Lord*, she thought, *teach me to be patient. I am a monster of ill temper and ingratitude. I have no right to be angry; her concern for me is justified. If Senhor Manco hadn't been there—*

Veronique tugged at the ruffled sleeves of her gown. "I must fulfill my responsibility. A man expects his fiancée's mother to be able to account for every hour of her daughter's life! And quite rightly."

Savannah paused, her brush in midair. "I thought—" she began, but she broke off, swept by rage. "Why don't you sprinkle me with lavender, wrap me in tissue paper, and keep me locked in a trunk until the wedding?"

Veronique was becoming upset again, but she deliberately lowered her voice; one must not forget the servants. "Have you no shame? If the Baron knew what you do this morning, he is appalled!"

Savannah had been listening to lectures of this sort for six weeks, but she'd had enough vexation for one morning; her patience was exhausted. She clattered the hairbrush down on the vanity. "The Baron!" she cried. "I'm tired of hearing about the Baron! I mean, you talk about him all the time, but you never *tell* me anything!"

Veronique, startled by the outburst, regarded her warily. "What is this nonsense?"

Savannah turned toward Veronique, the angry starch quite gone from her spine. "Maman, what is he *like?*"

"I have told you. He is a man of great distinction, a man of refined tastes, in the first rank of society wherever he goes. In Manáos you will not be lonely, I assure you of this. Soon—"

"Do you know what that Andrada woman said to me last night at dinner? She raised her glass to me and said, 'To the senhorita's health.' And I said, 'Thank you, but my health is superb, I am never ill.' And she said, 'Excellent. Then perhaps the senhorita will live longer than the Baron's other wives!'"

Veronique's fists clenched on the sheet. "That fishmonger! She is jealous because she desires to marry her own daughter to him, to catch in her own net the most wealthy man of Brazil!"

Savannah crossed to the bed and sat down beside her mother. "Why did all his other wives die?"

Veronique waved as if warding off insects. "Two, only two! The first died in childbirth, leaving him Porfirio. And the second of a fever, leaving him Esmeralda. Both are disappointments to him. The son drinks himself to death and the daughter longs to take the veil. Then what becomes of the houses, the estates, the business enterprises? The Baron needs a family, *chérie.* Is that not simple? Is that not natural?"

Veronique patted her hand reassuringly. "Get dressed now, child. It's time for breakfast. The doctor will be here soon. Wear the yellow muslin."

Savannah sighed, but obediently went to open one of the trunks. Assailed by the fragrance of lavender, she pulled away the tissue from the muslin dress. It looked so fragile, with tiny golden primroses on a lemon-colored background, the fabric gathered into delicate tucks with inserts of lace. But the muslin was backed by stiffened linen and forced into shape by sixteen whalebone stays stitched into the bodice. It was formidable enough to restrain a maniac, and she hated it.

Savannah returned to her own cabin and closed the door. She laid the muslin on the berth and hung her wrapper on a hook. As she began to wash, she caught sight of the necklace her friend Jocelyn had given her as a going-away present. What good times they used to have, and how desperately she missed her! Late at night they used a stolen lamp to read together under the bedcovers; Jocelyn's cousin Freddy, who went to Oxford, sent them boxes of bonbons or tins of short-bread biscuits with false-bottom layers for the books—lurid forbidden novels. If only she could tell Jocelyn about the sailor, then perhaps she could stop this infernal quaking. They used to talk about things like that. They found reading the love scenes in those books Freddy sent gave them a strange and rather delicious tremor.

She dried herself and took from the dressing table drawer a watered silk chemise, and found her matching pair of white silk knickerbockers with lace ruffles. Her trousseau lingerie had been made by the nuns. She was embarrassed at the time; being measured for knickers was rather alarming. Now she found it comforting to trace with her finger the rows of tiny stitches, remembering their tranquil faces as they worked listening to a novice read from *The Lives of the Saints*. She knew, too late, that she loved them. Yes, even the mother superior, who was so much like Maman, lecturing about what is and is not done.

All those years in the convent she thought she was miserable, homesick with longing for a place she could not remember; now she was homesick for the convent. Was this what being no longer a child meant? Always longing for the place you couldn't be and being so mixed up all the time, part of you wanting something terribly and part of you fearing it? *Bend*, Mother Dominica had said. But now, struggling to fasten the last of the two dozen hooks up the back of the yellow muslin and tugging at the stiff high-standing collar, she thought: *However am I to bend in all these whalebone stays?*

3

When the knock at the stateroom door was answered by a plaintive *"Entrez!"* from Veronique, the ship's doctor came into the room. Duncan Haversham was a stout Englishman with a remarkable white moustache. "Well, well, senhora— you're looking fit as a fiddle this morning!" Since he said that every day regardless of her condition, Veronique was convinced the man was an idiot. Savannah, however, liked him very much. Everything he said was outrageous, but he never bored her.

While Savannah used the tortoiseshell hairpins to fasten her hair into a knot, Dr. Haversham (singing something from Gilbert and Sullivan that began "Life's a pudding full of plums") gave Veronique a spoonful of green liquid. It was the same medicine he gave her every day, solemnly promising it would have her dancing the can-can by suppertime. Then he bowed extravagantly to Savannah and requested the inestimable pleasure of her company at breakfast. Veronique, her face still clenched from the bitter draught, waved them away pleading, "And Doctor, see that she eats."

"I shall indeed, dear lady. I am convinced that the science of tropical medicine would be advanced one hundred years by the simple expedient of introducing the hearty English breakfast—steaming porridge, hot buttered scones, kippers—"

"Please," the patient groaned.

Dr. Haversham took Savannah's arm and closed the door behind them. As he steered her along the promenade toward the dining room, humming cheerily, he was casting diagnostic glances at her face. "Do I detect signs of melancholia?" He stopped to feel her forehead and take her pulse. "No doubt about it. Clear case of rampant boredom. Have you tried the stereopticon in the Ladies' Saloon? All seven wonders of the world, hand-painted on glass. Take one every four hours and you'll be right as rain."

Savannah sighed. "What I really need is for people to stop treating me like an imbecile."

He chuckled. "Impossible. Quite out of the question.

Everybody knows all really nice girls are by very definition imbeciles."

The dining room was ready for the first-class passengers. The tables were laid with damask linen and a full service of Limoges china, while against the walls of mahogany and old rose tapestry, waiters in black stood beside steaming silver urns of coffee. Dr. Haversham guided Savannah to a large table by the windows and ordered two of everything: chilled grapefruit, sausage, omelet, potatoes, fillet of sole, and an assortment of hot breads.

After the waiter filled their cups, Savannah said, "Doctor, are you married?"

"Heavens, no. Free as a bird."

The coffee was too hot to drink. She held the cup, feeling its warmth and inhaling the strong fragrance. "I'd like that," she said.

"Wouldn't do. Knocking about the world? Wouldn't do at all, missy."

"You're saying I couldn't look after myself, aren't you?"

"I'm saying woman is a delicate creature. Needs a protected environment."

Savannah wondered if these waiters moving about the room as if they were trying to be invisible were the same young men as the sailors on deck. Did they cast off their white ducks, put on black suits, and stop being sailors? Was one of them . . . ? "Maybe I do need looking after," she said. "Maybe I'm an imbecile after all."

"Nonsense. You just need your breakfast." He took the cup from her and poured cream into it. "Now, what shall we discuss? The Dreyfus case? The novels of Feodor Dostoevsky? What are your views on the gold standard?"

She stared into the café au lait. "What do you think of Senhor Manco?"

"Don't think of him at all."

"Is he an Indian?"

"Most assuredly. Inca, no doubt. From the Andes. Built for breathing at fifteen thousand feet. Superb specimens, those fellows. Only other place in the world you find the same sort of men is the Himalayas. Different heart rate, metabolism, lung capacity. Supermen, that's what they are. Impervious to cold."

"Then what's he doing in the jungle?"

Haversham chuckled. "Tell you what he's *not* doing. He's not building a railroad. Can't be done. So the man must be a crook. His railroad scheme's a front of some kind. Probably uses the railroad story to cover his trips." He leaned closer. "My guess is the man's a professional gambler. He's in the Men's Smoking Lounge every night."

"Are you saying he is dishonest?"

He shrugged. "All I'm saying is, he wins. He wins so much you'll get folks who swear he reads minds." He chuckled again. "More likely he's got a marked deck."

The doctor turned, having caught sight of someone across the room at the entrance. "It's that American newspaper chap."

Savannah turned to look, observing as she did that the other passengers were carefully ignoring the cripple hobbling into the dining room. Quietly she asked, "What's the matter with him?"

"Infantile paralysis. Miracle he's walking at all, poor soul. Probably in a great deal of pain, but always cheerful; you can't get him to complain. Mind if he joins us?"

She watched the man labor across the room, his powerful arms and shoulders withered to thin, twisted legs, like mismatched parts joined by accident. Yet he was dressed with care, his light brown hair, moustache, and beard neatly trimmed. Almost a handsome face, but lined. She said, "How old do you suppose he is?"

"Middle twenties. Looks older, of course. Thing like that'll do it."

During his introduction to Savannah, Will Patterson stood with most of his weight on what appeared to be the better leg and braced himself against the vacant chair where, she saw, his knuckles showed white and his fingers were tremulous with effort. He sat down with evident relief across from her.

Haversham said, "Miss St. James and I have been discussing Gilbert and Sullivan."

Savannah said, "The doctor likes a song that says 'Life's a pudding full of plums.' "

Patterson began to sing softly. " 'Care's a canker that benumbs. . . .' " And the doctor chimed in, his spoon keeping time on a water goblet:

> " 'Wherefore waste our elocution
> On impossible solution?
> Life's a pleasant institution,
> Let us take it as it comes!' "

When the song was done, Savannah asked Patterson, "What brings you to the Amazon?"

The doctor chuckled. "I warn you, if you say 'the salubrious climate,' I'll have you committed."

Will shook his head. "Hardly the climate. Although we've got swamps and fevers back home too."

Savannah asked, "And where is your home?"

"I'm from Baltimore." But before she could ask any more questions, the chief steward approached the doctor and whispered to him. Haversham put his napkin on the table. "Seems a passenger in second class decided to become a mother halfway through the sole." He looked ruefully at Savannah's half-full plate. "May take a bit of time, missy. Shall I take you back first?"

Patterson said he'd be happy to escort her to her cabin. She watched the doctor follow the chief steward from the room and turned to find Will Patterson smiling at her. She liked the way he smiled; his eyes were very blue and marked by deep laugh lines. Still, she wished the nuns had taught her a little less geography and more Polite Conversation with Disconcerting Strangers. She said, "In the war, did Maryland side with the North or the South?"

He shrugged. "We were never able to make up our minds. It was a costly indecision. Both sides kept blowing up our railroads, Baltimore was put under martial law, and the mayor got thrown into prison."

She said, "My father was a Confederate. After the war he went to Brazil to avoid being Reconstructed."

The waiter brought Will's eggs. In the silence she wished she could think of something more to say, something light-hearted and appropriately imbecilic. But all she could think of was what a terrible shame it was . . . this nice, good-looking young man with the boyish squint. At last she said, "Life's not a pudding, is it?"

He laughed. "No, indeed not. But it won't do to say so."

"Why? Why does everybody pretend? Why don't people say what they really think? Wouldn't the world be better?"

"Certainly not. It would be a nightmare. Politeness and small talk are all that keep us from continual misery." She couldn't tell if he was serious or teasing her. He nodded in the direction of an overdressed woman several tables away. "Take that woman, for instance. What do you think of her?"

Savannah leaned closer to him. "I think she's got a face like a rice pudding, and her squeezed-up little eyes are the raisins."

"Very well. If I were to stand up and shout across the room, 'You look like a rice pudding!' she would cry out, 'Silence, you freak! You don't belong here, you're an offense, you shouldn't be allowed in public!'" He spoke softly, without a trace of bitterness. He smiled. "You see? It would be miserable."

She nodded. Then finding the sadness in his eyes too painful to look at, she stared into her cup. "I don't believe that's what she's thinking."

"Yes, it is. People find it very hard to look at me. The more kindhearted they are, the harder it is. What they don't know is that a lot of the time, I don't really mind being this way. It's made me experience life more intensely. It's rather like sneaking downstairs to a party for the grownups, a place you've no right to be. The candles glow for you, the silver gleams, the flowers give off an intoxicating fragrance the invited guests never notice."

Savannah looked up. "I understand; I feel the same way—because I'm not supposed to be allowed in public either." She arranged her silverware in a neat row on the tablecloth. "You see, I'm right. You're not pretending, you're telling me what you really think." She pushed her silverware aside. "Please don't stop."

"Well, I meant to live a secluded life, to stay indoors and write books. I've got a house in Baltimore, a good brick house on a quiet square. In the back there's a walled garden." He drew lines on the damask with his butter knife. "The study's at the back, with big windows, floor to ceiling, looking out on the garden."

"It sounds very nice."

"Yes, it is. But when I settled down there, I found I couldn't write. I didn't know anything. I'd grown up in an artificial environment, no more like the real world than a hothouse is like the Amazon jungle. My father'd had me tutored; when I went to college, the coachman pushed me from classroom to classroom in a wheeled chair. Special arrangements were always being made for me. When I told Father I was determined to earn my bread, I was elected to the railroad's board of directors. Not a taxing job, but lucrative.

"Then I announced my intention of becoming a journalist. Next day the editor of the Baltimore *Sun* invited me to write book reviews for him."

She smiled. "What an odd coincidence."

"Yes. But I'm not proud: I accepted. From book reviews I went on to reporting, hopping on and off trolley cars to cover fires and things. Hard work, but much more satisfying than being wheeled about."

"And now you've been to Europe."

"England and France. I sent home dispatches about the Botanical Gardens at Kew and the new Velodromes, the cycling arenas in Paris. Americans love to read about Europeans. I suppose it makes good tea-table conversation to know that the Prince de Sagan mounts his two-wheeler wearing a black velvet suit and white kid gloves. Anyway, the articles earned enough to pay for this trip. I've been chattering like a monkey. I'd better take you back."

On the promenade Savannah moved slowly, trying not to see the excess motion his walking required. The sky burned down on the ship, and all around them the ocean lay dazzling under the sun. She said, "Are you going to write about the Amazon?"

"Yes, some dispatches and perhaps a travel book."

They'd reached the entrance to the passageway. She stopped and offered him her hand. "I've enjoyed our conversation, Mr. Patterson."

"Shouldn't I take you to your cabin?"

"No, this is far enough. Thank you." He turned away, stiff with dignity. "Mr. Patterson, may I say what I mean?" He paused, holding the rail along the wall. "My mother considers interesting young men a danger to my reputation."

A smile lit his eyes. Then, his arms hard at work, he moved away along the promenade. It had been a strange smile. Wistful. He seemed to be looking at her across a chasm, as if she were on a stage and he were in the audience. Or as if she were at the grownups' party and he were looking down at her from the stairs.

4

Under the awning on the afterdeck the passengers were playing quoits. They seemed determined to ignore the midafternoon heat. The men, in dark jackets, wore their hats throughout the game. And the women, wearing full-skirted dresses of gabardine or serge, and small straw hats covered with velvet bows and flowers, kept their gloves on even when taking their turns.

Out of the wind on the sheltered side of the promenade Will Patterson sat in a deck chair. He opened his leatherbound journal and began to write.

We are nearing the mouth of the Amazon, a great maw two hundred miles wide and full of islands. One of them, Marajó, is larger than Switzerland. Our route lies to the south of Marajó, for the channels to the north are uncharted. They constantly change their courses under the violence of the tidal bore, a wave ten to fifteen feet high which, when the tide turns, roars upriver five hundred miles. It tears small boats from their moorings, rips docks away, and at times crushes riverside houses like heaps of lucifer matchsticks. Echoing the sound it makes, the natives call it the *pororoca*.

A young lady is pacing the promenade, swathed in netting, although we have not yet come to the famous clouds of Amazon mosquitoes. A mulatto girl in maid's uniform follows her back and forth; a sloe-eyed girl with skin the color of café au lait, she walks gracefully as if bearing an invisible burden on her head.

Customs here are quite unlike ours. Brazil freed its slaves only eight years ago, the last nation in this hemisphere to do so, and I have been told the institution has not yet been fully erased. It is, of course, inappropriate for a visitor to pass judgment; I merely note these facts. And this one also: Brazilian women of good family seem cloistered. But I digress.

Today the sea is full of vegetation. Gulls wheel about the ship uttering harsh cries. It is very near; I feel it. Tonight we enter the ship channel and in the morning we will anchor at the first Amazon port. Tomorrow I shall see for myself the greatest, most mysterious and deadly jungle in the world.

Savannah threw herself into the chair beside Will's, pulling the gloves from her hands and tugging irritably at the veiling around her wide-brimmed hat. She said, "Maman is mortally terrified the tropical sun will ruin my complexion. I think if she detects one freckle on me anywhere, she'll pack me off to a leper colony and go into mourning." Then, seeing him close his journal and place it with his books, she said, "I'm sorry, I didn't realize you were working."

"It's quite all right, I've finished for now." Looking at her in this light he was struck by an impression of extreme fragility. Her lips were coral-colored and the shadows at the inner corners of her eyes shone faintly lavender. Her skin seemed transparent; he felt he could see clear to the throbbing pulses, to the delicacy of her bones. The more he looked, the more helpless he became. He saw beneath the skin an astonishing network of veins, some blue, some a fine tracery of red, like the brushwork on trees in Japanese paintings. The strand of hair loosened from the beige netting of her hat was the color of new copper wire. He could think of nothing to say to her. At last he forced himself to look away, to stare at the ocean. He said, "You're not playing quoits?"

She looked depressed. "The other passengers are not our sort. Whatever that means." Another silence.

The deck chairs were close together. Will tried not to look at their legs stretched side by side before them. "I've read almost everything ever written about the Amazon," he said at last. "Do you realize how vast it is? That if this jungle were in North America it would cover almost the whole United States? And the river itself would flow all the way from San Francisco to New York? It's hardly been explored at all." *I'm boring her,* he thought. *She's not much more than a child; she has no idea she is so beautiful.* But he couldn't stop talking. "When I was a little boy I used to pore over maps of the Amazon. It reminded me then of my mother's silver meat platter—you know, the kind that has channels shaped like the branches of a tree to drain all the juices down to one end. The main course of the river is a great sea with many tributaries flowing into it, great rivers themselves, some of them more than a thousand miles long, and all colors—brown, blue, white, even black. I used to fall asleep reciting the names of the tributaries . . . Pará, Xingu, Madeira, Tapajós, Putumayo, Marañón, Ucayali, Japurá, Branco, Urubamba." It occurred to him that he was making a fool of himself. He said, "It's just that I've wanted to come here for such a long time."

She smiled. "I hope you find something worth writing about."

"No doubt of that. I can always describe Manáos, the 'Paris of the Jungle,' the fabulously wealthy white city in the heart of the Amazon. And for the ladies, I'll describe your wedding." He said it as a reminder to himself, to quell the thought: *If a man could sleep with this girl in his arms, if a man could cherish her and care for her. . . .*

He opened his journal dramatically, his pen ready. "I'll say, 'This correspondent conversed with the bride prior to the nuptials. She was gotten up like a beekeeper and appeared quite ready to bolt at the merest mention of the ceremony.' "

Not looking up, she said, "Is it true that in the United States people marry for love alone?"

"Yes, it is. That explains our shocking divorce rate."

"You aren't serious, are you?"

"No. I'm entirely in favor of love. Are you in love with the Baron do Rio Mar?" Savannah sank deeper into the deck chair and mashed her hat down over her eyes. He was dismayed, the man in him ashamed of the correspondent; and the shame was compounded with his feeling of loss, of being bereft of something he had never possessed outside of dreams, dreams in which his legs were always straight. Softly he said, "I'm sorry. I shouldn't have said that."

She gazed dully at the sea. "I just feel . . . the way you did in your house in Baltimore. I don't know anything. I don't even have any opinions—just feelings. . . ."

"You're still very young."

"I know. But people treat me as though my feelings are abnormal. As though any normal girl would be happy and there's something wrong with me, but it's temporary, I'm just having a little spell of some kind—a rather shameful condition not to be discussed."

After a moment he cleared his throat and said, "I suppose you ought to be talking about this to your parents."

"My mother thinks it's all the fault of the nuns, that I have had an imperfect education. And my father—I've scarcely seen him. He's not well. A recurring fever. He came to Lausanne once, last year, in the spring. But I didn't know about any of this then."

She told him of her father's visit to the convent. He'd spent a few minutes in Mother Dominica's study; then Savannah had been sent for. She was surprised; she scarcely remembered him. A frail man, like a poet; not fatherly-looking at all. He may have been glad to see her; she couldn't be certain—he did not embrace her. When she raised her face to his, the lips he pressed on her forehead were hot and dry. Mother Dominica had loosened Savannah's hair, combed it, and braided it anew in one plait down her back. Then, with the other girls watching excitedly from the upper windows, she and her father had left.

They drove through the streets of Lausanne in a carriage,

not stopping anywhere except a photographer's. The man, a German, put her between a potted palm and a fake stone balustrade. Then, while a clamp held her head still, he darted in and out of the black cloth over his camera until he had immortalized her in a half-dozen poses. Her father meanwhile paced nervously in the background, giving instructions. Then he took her back to the convent in time for tea.

After he drove away she could remember nothing he'd said to her, only that he spoke English with an accent. Not like Jocelyn's. And not like Hester, the girl from Philadelphia. So that night in the dormitory after the nuns were gone, Savannah entertained her friends with a recitation of "The Boy Stood on the Burning Deck"—in Georgia English. Still, their delighted laughter could not assuage her inexplicable desolation.

She watched the gulls fluttering around the smokestacks. "Maman says the Baron's house in Manáos is a palace. It takes up an entire city block, not counting the acres of gardens at the back. Over the staircase there's an enormous gilt frame hanging empty, waiting for my portrait to be painted. The engraved medallion says *Dona Savannah, Baroness do Rio Mar.*" She sat up and tossed her hat aside. "For all I know I may love him very dearly. He may be cheerful and kind, like Dr. Haversham. Or he may be like you, somebody I can talk to honestly, about anything." She turned and looked at him intently. "That's possible, isn't it?"

What could he say?

"On the other hand," she said, "it is also possible that he is none of these things. He may reek of garlic." She gripped the arms of her chair. "In that case I shall have to refuse him."

"Wouldn't it be better to tell your family how you feel?"

"They don't seem to care. I suppose I shall simply have to insist upon my rights." Will looked away. The clouds on the western horizon had darkened. "Of course," she went on, "I'd better find out what they are first, hadn't I? Do you know anything about the law?"

"You are a minor." He looked away from her intense stare. "In the eyes of the law children have no rights at all; I mean, the laws are designed to protect them—"

"As if they were imbeciles?" She was silent a moment. "In that case, if I do not wish to marry the Baron, I shall have to run away and learn to use a typewriting machine." She put her hands in her lap and studied her fingers doubtfully. "Do you happen to know the passage from Manáos to—say, Paris?"

"It's thirty pounds."

"Is that a lot of money?"

He nodded. "If you were trying to earn it on a typewriter, it would take years." He did not utter his heart's sigh: I will sell my father's stock for you, and my house, and all my books. . . . She continued to stare at her fingers, so he leaned forward until she looked at him. "There's nothing wrong with you, Savannah. Your feelings are perfectly normal. All you need to do is be . . . persuasive. Be very mature and logical." He stopped; he knew he'd allowed himself to interfere in something that was none of his business.

Her relief eased his guilt. "I will," she said. "I'll tell them I need more time. That's a perfectly logical request, isn't it?"

The players of quoits had fled the violent heat of the afternoon. In the passageway Manuela stood watching. When Savannah looked up, the maid nodded.

She looked at Will ruefully. "We could have been friends all this time. I've seen you every day since we left Hâvre, but I always looked away."

He wanted to touch her, but he didn't. "That just means you're tender-hearted."

"No." She shrugged impatiently. "It means I'm a terrible coward."

He watched her walk toward the passage, her yellow dress pressed to her body by the wind. A man would be a fool to let her go. he thought, a man with legs would follow her. The whole length of the Amazon and all its tributaries.

5

Maman was feeling better. She said the knowledge that this was their last day upon this formidable ocean had eased her *mal de mer*. Veronique took some broth, while Savannah worked with her sketchpad. She drew Veronique's worn face, feeling a vague sadness at the way the dark hair, center-parted and swept back, was streaked with gray. How terrible it must be to have nothing to look forward to but another season's fashions. Manuela worked about the stateroom and the tiny bath, where she was filling the copper tub. "Maman," Savannah said in French, "please send Manuela away. I want to talk to you."

As if she hadn't heard, Veronique yawned. "The moment I

have my bath I rest. You also ought to lie down. Perhaps then I am well enough to go to dinner this evening. Tonight, you know, is the celebration for crossing the equator. Dr. Haversham dresses himself as King Neptune. Such a bag of winds, that one!"

Savannah touched her arm. "Please, can't we talk?"

Draping herself in her wrapper, Veronique said, "Have you written to Mother Dominica? Then do so. Use the form in the etiquette manual. Thank her for her thousand kindnesses to you across the years. You may work at the writing desk in the Ladies' Saloon, then bring to me the letter for correction."

"Enchanting. When I'm done may I look at the Seven Wonders of the World, hand-painted on glass?"

From the bath Veronique said, "Very well, if you wish. I will send Manuela to find you when I am finish."

The Ladies' Saloon was a large room with windows to the promenade. Almost every inch of space was filled with furniture, most of it overstuffed and hung with fringes. The Turkey carpet was itself carpeted, covered with smaller, unmatched scatter rugs.

As Savannah entered, she saw a half-dozen women sitting about, all of them with busy mouths and busy hands, embroidering, fanning themselves, talking, poking in the candy dishes. She sat down at a writing desk by the window and helped herself to the stationery.

Dear Jocelyn,

I miss you most awfully. I keep writing you letters in my mind and then changing them so Mother Dominica can read them. I am such a ninny it took me all these weeks (how many is it now? 6?) to realize I could send it to Freddy and ask him to send it to you in one of his boxes with false bottoms.

Only now I don't know where to begin. We spent 4 weeks in Paris. It was awful, shopping every day and getting fitted. We didn't even go sightseeing except to the cemetery to put flowers on my Aunt Madelyn's grave. It was raining and cold. Then we had to drag trunks of clothing and other things Maman had bought, cheeses and pots of jam and packets of things you can't get in Brazil, across town to the train. Then we traveled to Hâvre and spent two nights there and then we got on the boat.

Now we've been two weeks on the ocean. The wedding is to be January 7th with a dinner for 300 after, only I can't imagine myself getting married. I feel as though I have aged 10 years since I saw you. I never knew the world was like this.

I must end this letter soon and put it away. I can't let my mother see it because she is, I have discovered, a genuine fossil and I wish she could meet your father and find out that civilization isn't built on a foundation of whalebone stays.

I wasn't going to tell you this, but I think I came very close to getting molested because I went out on deck in my wrapper before anybody else was awake. Luckily I was rescued by one of the first-class passengers, a marvelously handsome man. I know that sounds like something from one of those novels Freddy sent us, but this man is dark as a sheik and moody, and fortunately for me the sailors who had me surrounded seemed frightened to death of him, so they ran away. I will try to draw his picture for you sometime. He is tall and very slender and moves like an acrobat, without making a sound—he seems to carry his own silence about with him. He is some kind of Indian (Inca, the ship's doctor says). I suppose I must have a man to look after me, but is it wrong to want him to be magnificent? I am very proud; I wish to be oppressed by a god. Not by a—well, there's no sense getting into that subject. I can't begin to tell you how unhappy I am. Please burn this letter.

Write me in Manáos. Make it sound as if you just decided to see how I am. If you say anything personal or refer to what I've said, do it in lemon juice around the margins. I won't hold it over a candle until it's been read by whoever will be reading my mail now. And be sure to tell me where you'll be when term ends. I have no idea what's going to happen.

Thank you for all the good times we had.

Love,
Van

Though it was not yet nightfall, the Saloon had darkened. Gusts of wind whispered in the passageway and the windowpanes rattled as rain spattered against the glass. Folding Jocelyn's letter small, Savannah placed it inside an envelope addressed to Frederick Estyn, Oriel College, Oxford, England.

She tucked the whole packet into the back of her sketchpad, all the while rejoicing grimly that she was not the crying kind. Then she forced herself to write a brief formal note to Mother Dominica. By the time that was done, she felt dreadfully nettled. Now that a storm was moaning about the ship, the women sitting in the Saloon were uttering little yelps with every clap of thunder.

When lightning brightened the windows, Savannah saw the ragged wisps of cloud nearest the sea scudding above a huge wave that loomed higher than the railing of the promenade. She decided she preferred the storm to the company of shrieking ladies. The writing desk had a small drawer, so she locked her sketchpad up and put the key on her necklace with the single pearl, Jocelyn's going-away gift.

Pausing at the entrance to the deck while her eyes adjusted to the gloom, she began to discern the wild movement in the surrounding dark. It was as if the whole world were adrift and howling. The sea was streaked and boiling, the green ocean at war with the brown river. Above, the sky seemed in panic, the clouds fleeing pell-mell toward the horizon. Lightning ripped through smoke-black vapors, and, a single heartbeat later, thunder roared about the ship and echoed away to clatter around the horizon.

She stepped on deck in a moaning lull, only to be struck full force by the wind and the stiff curtain of rain that lashed the ship. By the time she'd fought her way down the length of the promenade she was drenched and laughing, feeling exultant; it was as if these elemental shenanigans had been produced for the purpose of draining away her frustration.

As she rounded the wheelhouse and tried to cross the foredeck, a blast of wind flattened her against the wall. She braced herself and watched the steamer wallowing in a valley surrounded by live liquid mountains, moving in ranks upon the *Esperança*, then melting and falling down in dark fluid avalanches. As Savannah watched fascinated, a huge wave poised above the bow, its top curling a moment before it picked up speed and crashed upon the ship.

Her feet were knocked from under her. With the foredeck canting at a crazy pitch, she slid downhill and slammed into the rail. She wasn't hurt, just astonished, for the yards of sodden yellow muslin blunted her impact on the metal railing. But she couldn't get up. The swift ebbing of the wave pulled her heavy dress seaward. Meanwhile the deck lost its tilt, leveled, and tipped the other way. The hissing foam loosened its hold, eddied about her, changed direction, and began to flow across the deck, pulling her back the way she'd come.

Gripping the rail post with all her strength, she lay there trying to decide what to do, when the lightning revealed another wall of water looming above the bow. During a moment that seemed endless she watched a ridge of foam hiss slowly along the peak. Drops broke away and fell down the slope faster and faster until the whole top of the wave began to curl, rounding toward the glassy surface that was moving upward toward the peak.

A moment later the chill avalanche pounded her body, choked her mouth and nostrils with the taste of salt and seaweed, ripped her hands from the rail, and flung her down the promenade toward the stern of the ship. When it drained away, Manco had her in his arms.

In the brief level moment between waves he carried her into the athwartship passage behind the wheelhouse, where he put her down in a gloomy darkness, for the *Esperança*'s electric lights had failed. Bracing himself in the entrance to the narrow corridor, he wrapped his short cloak around her quaking shoulders and held her close to him. While the ship pitched, he stood immobile, and Savannah, feeling his grip upon her body, was speechless with surprise. How had he found her? How had he known? She rested against him, wondering why his body felt so warm. Had he a fever? Or was this the altered bodily function the doctor had talked about?

When her eyes adjusted to the dimness she lifted her face from his black broadcloth shoulder and looked up at him. He was watching the storm; looking in his eyes, she saw the lightning reflected. Rivulets of rain ran down his cheek. She watched a single tearlike drop pause in the narrow moustache that framed the corners of his mouth. All his flesh seemed taut and firm; there was no softness anywhere; even his lips looked lean and tense. Still, while she shivered, he was radiant.

He smelled of damp wool and spices—cinnamon, perhaps, or cloves. She tried to breathe in unison with him, but it took effort, for his breathing seemed deeper and slower than hers. Dimly she sensed that he was experiencing the storm as acutely as she was experiencing him; he was perceiving it with all his senses. She wondered if this spectacle of natural violence was a religious experience for him. Did his people fall upon their knees before the sky?

She turned toward the sea and found the fluid mountains had worn down to rolling hills. The lightning had stopped.

The sky looked cleaner, brighter; and the air smelled like fresh laundry. She, too, felt spent, but profoundly calm. Safe . . . as if nothing could ever frighten her again, so long as Manco held her in his arms. At the same time she felt a great hunger, a longing of such intensity that she yearned to cry out. But she didn't know what it was she hungered for.

In the distance the thunder murmured, growing fainter. Manco pulled his cloak from her shoulders and released her. He did not smile, yet his eyes seemed warm, as if they'd shared something no one else could know. She started to speak, but he gently placed his fingers on her lips. Then he lifted her chin and kissed her eyes. When she opened them he was gone.

6

Savannah found her cabin door bolted; she was forced to enter by way of the other stateroom. Veronique was reclining on a chaise. For the first time in two weeks she was fully dressed. Perhaps the garment, a mutton-sleeved black taffeta trimmed with appliquéd black velvet roses, had been chosen to match her mood; she was very angry. She silenced Savannah's greeting. "So, how is this you write letters? Manuela finds you disappear! And now you are in the rain, look at this muslin!"

Savannah weighed the possible results of explaining she'd nearly got washed overboard, and decided not to. She said, "It was a terrible storm."

"But who in the right mind goes out in the tempest? Remove at once your things! You will dress for dinner in the emerald silk. I myself arise from the bed to chaperone you."

Savannah dried herself absently, while Manuela took the dripping muslin away and closed the stateroom door behind her. Savannah stood indecisively by the chaise in her damp underclothing. Manco's presence still enveloped her; he was more vividly present to her than Veronique. What had happened to her in this last hour? It was as if a door had opened. Even though she remained on the threshold, she'd glimpsed through the portal undreamed of possibilities. She decided it made no difference what she wore to dinner.

They were silent while she took out the emerald silk from one of the trunks and carried it into her cabin. As she stepped out of her damp underthings and put on dry ones, she closed her eyes and felt his arms around her. A moment later she said, "I'm sorry to have upset you, Maman, but we truly must talk. Now, without delay."

"We talk. *Certainement*, we talk. But only when you are properly dressed."

There were twenty-four buttons in the bodice of the dress and twelve on each sleeve where the fabric fit snugly on the forearm before it flared above the elbow. Doggedly she did them one after another, but the right wrist was hopeless, since her left hand was so clumsy; she went to Veronique to get that done. After that Maman led her to the vanity and began doing her hair, brushing it out and braiding it swiftly. Savannah closed her eyes again. When Veronique was done, the braid coiled up and down the back of Savannah's head in an elegant figure eight. As a final touch she attached to the top a soft bow of emerald surah. Savannah nodded to her reflection in the hand mirror. "Thank you, Maman. Now can we talk?"

Veronique sighed. Savannah followed her across the room, and they sat down at the tea table. "It is time now you begin to behave like a baroness," Veronique told her.

Savannah reminded herself that she must be very mature, very logical. She stood and moved to the porthole, walking bravely in her twenty yards of emerald silk, while the fullness fishtailed behind her. Casually opening the draperies to look upon the ocean, she said, "I really don't want to be a baroness." The rain had stopped, but the sky was dark and the waves heaved and fell in long turbulent swells. Where had he gone?

Veronique said complacently, "I understand, *chérie*. It is a little frightening, but quickly you will learn your responsibilities. And I will be there to help you. The Baron has an excellent staff. Only earn their respect and they serve you well."

"Maman, I don't want their respect. I don't want a staff. And I don't want to live in a palace. I've just gotten out of school; I want to be free for a little while, to have a life with no bells ringing." It was what she'd made up her mind to say, yet now it seemed a lie; it was no longer the real reason at all.

Veronique smiled reassuringly. "Of course, I understand. And so also does the Baron. He has planned the most marvelous honeymoon trip! You will love it, believe me."

I'm making a mess of it, Savannah thought, and rubbed her

forehead, as if that would summon up the logic she required. But it was no use. All she really wanted to say was his name. She closed her eyes, thinking *Manco* like a prayer, and after a moment she said, "I've simply got to have more time."

Veronique went to her. Taking her hands, she smiled warmly. "When you see the Baron you will say to me, 'Maman, why did you not tell me he is so handsome, so courtly, so generous! Must we wait so long for the wedding? I am in love!'" She put her arm around Savannah's waist and drew her back to the chaise; but then, looking quizzically at her troubled face, she said, "Don't tell me you do not wish to be in love."

"Yes, I want to be in love. But what if I don't love the Baron?"

"But you will!" Veronique sighed. "Anyway, it is of no real importance. Love is a childhood disorder. The fortunate outgrow it before it ruins their lives."

Savannah began pacing again. "That isn't true, I know that isn't true."

Veronique lay back against her cushions. "Well, *chérie,* you are an ignorant girl—"

"Then why did you remove me from school before I'd finished?"

"The ignorance you possess, no school can cure."

"What else can I be but ignorant? You drill me in etiquette, but tell me nothing I really need to know."

"How is this so?" She raised upturned palms. "Ask. Ask whatever you desire."

Savannah sat in the brocade chair. Now that the moment had come, she no longer knew how to begin. Should she say: "Maman; men frighten me"? Yes, even Manco frightened her —the power she felt in his body. Yet at the same time she longed for it.

She said, "Tell me about marriage."

"*Mon dieu,* what have we been discussing all these weeks?"

"I mean tell me about going to bed."

Veronique's gesture cast the question aside.

"A virtuous woman does not enjoy the bed of marriage. Nor does she object to it, because it is her duty. She simply endures it in silence, without complaint. Fortunately in Manáos there are many brothels." Savannah leaned forward, and in response to her puzzled look Veronique added, "Brazilian women boast of this. They say: 'My husband is such a man he must go to the Contessa's Palace three times a week!'"

"I don't know what you're talking about."

"A brothel. A place where women sell their bodies. Besides, the Baron is nearly fifty. You are very fortunate."

The rug seemed to writhe beneath her feet. She said, "I think I would rather be a nun. An orphanage, even nursing—"

Veronique laughed. "My child, you are not the—what is the word? The 'type'!" she rooted among the leftovers on the tea tray. "You have no idea of the hardness of life. You have the easy time, everything is given to you. And have you any idea what happens to the *vieille fille*, the old maid? When your father dies, what happens to you, eh? The life of a governess! A domestic! You become somebody's cook! To prevent this we achieve for you a marriage to one of the richest men in South America, and you complain because you want a life without appointments!" She moved to the vanity and began arranging her hair. With a sigh of exasperation, she placed two small diamond studs in her ears. "You are silly," she said. "You exaggerate. You take yourself much too seriously. A case of nerves, nothing more. You will adjust."

"Doesn't it matter at all to you if I'm *happy?*"

Veronique threw up her hands. "Of course we want you to be happy! Unfortunately you are too inexperienced to understand what is best for you." She turned from the mirror. "You will marry the Baron, Savannah. Whether or not that makes you what you call 'happy' is your own affair." Savannah lifted her hands and let them fall. Veronique examined her jewel box, selected three hairpins crusted with diamonds and onyx, and set them artfully into her coiffure. "It is out of our hands. Papers have been signed. It is now a legal matter."

Savannah smoothed the fabric of her skirt, trying to erase the folds she had put there. "What would happen if I said no in the cathedral?"

"That would be madness, Savannah. And in Brazil families of the first rank know how to treat such behavior." She stood to give her toilette a final appraisal. "When we get to Manáos remind me—since you have interest in the labors of the nunneries—I must take you to visit the mental asylum." She turned to Savannah. "I think you will find the experience most educational."

All through dinner and the silly spectacle of King Neptune's initiation of newcomers to the equator, Savannah remained quiet. Once, Veronique whispered approvingly: "Now you behave like a baroness!" But that night, she awakened drenched with terror and lay in her berth trying to think of something else. Vespers in the convent chapel. The mountains. Manco's laughter.

7

The *Esperança* sped through the night. It was long past midnight and calm now, all trace of the storm gone. The moon, looking enormous at this latitude, spread a gleaming path upon the water. Wide as a sea, the estuary of the Amazon lay still in the moonlight. The jungle was a black line on the horizon.

Manco stood on the foredeck, his eyes fixed upon the darkness. He'd been playing cards and had no idea how much money he'd won. Not as much as he had taken at Paris or Monte Carlo, but a satisfactory sum. His pockets were full of British pounds, American dollars, French francs, Brazilian milreis, and shares of Bolivian mining stock. In all, a good night's work. And necessary. Repeating rifles were expensive, even when purchased in hundred lots. So was the oil to keep them working in the rainy season. And of course the ammunition. It was all in the hold, in crates bearing the respectable names of equipment manufacturers in Manchester, Glasgow, and Cologne, crates labeled *high-pressure boiler gauges, corrugated metallic valves, hoisting gear,* and *steel hausers* ("one-third the weight, one-fourth the cost, and far more durable than hemp")—crates that appeared appropriate to the building of a railroad in the jungle.

He'd been trying not to think of Savannah. It was one thing to nourish the spirit with loveliness, to marvel at this manifestation of exquisite vitality. But quite another matter to be haunted by her, by the sight of her laughing as the wave tumbled her along the deck. . . . He forced himself to gaze into the night, willing his attention far away, far beyond the moon's path and the distant rim of trees, far up the river, westward, where it was not yet moonrise.

There at this moment Tomás—his pupil, friend, and comrade—would be moving toward the rubber landing named Concepción. Tomás, little more than a boy, a dark-eyed boy of the forest, a boy who ought to have been fishing or climbing trees in search of honey. A boy who in another time would not have need for so much courage.

* * *

Tomás dipped his paddle soundlessly, moving through the low-lying mist. Now that darkness brooded over the jungle, the water was warmer than the air and the river steamed. Behind him the other men in his canoe lifted and plunged their leaf-shaped paddles, working swiftly and in silence. Farther back, lost in the fog, three other canoes followed. Tomás paused, kneeling in the prow, his paddle uplifted. As the next canoe slid by, trailing mist, he signaled it to stop beside him. Together they drifted in the shallows, waiting.

Tomás thought how glad he was the rains were coming. Low water is the worst of times, for the shrunken river teems with death, with the crocodile who floats like a log, his blunt snout almost submerged until he raises it, his jaws agape; and the great eel whose jolt stuns even the crocodile, drowning him; and the multitudinous swift piranha whose snapping bite is so fastidious they will leave a man's skeleton fully clothed.

When the last two canoes appeared, Tomás dipped his paddle, steering through the overhanging foliage of the bank into an *igarapé*, a canoe path. This took them deep into the jungle behind the Concepción landing, where circling trails called estradas looped many miles among the scattered rubber trees.

Tomás and his men moored the canoes and set out on foot, walking nearly all night along the estradas. Mindano, who was of the Hacha tribe, went first, his eyes keen in the darkness, his machete cutting away the tangled lianas. Fording streams, they moved slowly and with great care, murmuring, "Sleep, piranha, do not awaken." And when they waded through the swamps they stopped from time to time to pull leeches from their legs with a mixture of tobacco and urine.

Along the estradas they found twelve palm-thatch huts, widely separated. There, isolated from one another, the tappers lived.

To each tapper they came upon, Tomás said: "We are Manconistas; do you want to come with us?" And always the men said: Yes. They were starving and weakened by fever, but they got to their feet and followed. Only two asked to be carried.

On the way back Tomás and his men hacked deep cuts into the rubber trees, killing them with their machetes. Then, at the canoes, Tomás divided the party. Into the first two boats he put his best fighting men; into the others he put the tappers with men to paddle. Then he led the way back down the *igarapé*.

At its mouth he sent the tappers downriver, where beyond

the great bend a steam launch waited. He watched them slip away into the mist, the sick men clinging to the thwarts while the others paddled toward the swift midstream current.

Now, he said softly, we will attack the landing.

At low water the Concepción landing lay on a raw bluff above the shrunken river, its dock standing high on pilings made of hardwood trunks. Beyond, the buildings spread against the wall of forest where a palm rose above the other trees, swaying alone, black against the graying eastern sky.

Avoiding the dock, Tomás and his men moved downstream thirty yards and beached the canoes. Tomás motioned the boy Riccu to guard them, then he and the others moved across the sand and climbed the bank.

A lamp burned in the cookhouse, but the other buildings, the house of the manager, the storage shed, the store, and the guards' bunkhouse, where armed men wrapped in mosquito netting slept in hammocks on the wide veranda, were all in darkness.

Tomás led the way to the shed. A soft snoring came from the hammock slung across the entrance. Tomás nodded to Mindaro, whose father had been a shaman—a magician. Mindaro drew carefully from the pouch at his side a thorn tipped with curare. The guard was dead within a minute and the wound that remained looked like the bite of a small vampire bat.

The lock wrenched easily from the shed's rotting door. Inside they struck matches and found a dozen captives. One, marked many times with the lash, was dead and covered with ants. They freed the rest, but two of them, their eyes burning with fever, were too weak to walk and had to be left behind. Five men, a small girl, a woman, and two boys followed Tomás and his men back to the river and were helped aboard the canoes.

Now Mindaro climbed a tree at the edge of the clearing. The boy Riccu followed with the arrow quiver and the matches. Mindaro, using a man-tall bow, fired flaming brands onto the thatched roofs. In a moment flames snatched at the sky.

Tomás ran along the dock to where the Concepción launch was moored, but he could not cast it away; it was chained and padlocked. He leaped into the boat and, using his machete, cut a hole in the bottom, just as shots pricked the timbers of the dock. Climbing from the launch, he saw guards running

from the bunkhouse. Some knelt, firing their rifles. Riccu fell
from the tree. Mindaro dropped to the ground and was cut
down. At the rim of the bluff one of the prisoners they'd left
behind crawled toward the canoes. Tomás swung the rifle
from his back and began firing. By the time the sick man slid
down the bank to the water's edge, Tomás had hit two of the
guards, but one of them kept coming.

Tomás turned and ran back along the dock, waving the
loaded canoes away. Guards now crested the bluff, firing.
Tomás saw the canoes backing toward the deeper water, saw
them turn, saw his men begin to paddle violently through the
shot-spattered water. He ran toward the end of the dock,
poised, ready to spring into the teeming river. Then a bolo
whistled through the air, its weighted thongs whipping around
his legs and flinging him to the warm planking, thudding now
with the tread of running men.

He watched the canoes ease into the midstream current
while beyond, from the other bank, a toucan shrilled, awakening the howler monkeys' roar.

8

Aboard the *Esperança* the passengers awakened to find themselves some eighty miles inland, with a city of 40,000 inhabi-
tants outside their portholes. Its name was A Cidade de Nossa
Senhora do Belem do Gran Pará—"The City of Our Lady of
Bethlehem on the Great River." Since only shallow-draft vessels could approach the quay, the ship anchored a half mile
off shore. While the captain awaited his clearance, no one left
the *Esperança*, nor was any other craft allowed to approach
them, except for the port officials.

Will Patterson, eager to begin exploring his first jungle city,
watched the shoreline. Pará, as they called it, looked flat, a
jumble of white buildings with red tile roofs, broken here and
there by a church dome or the tower of some municipal
building. Beyond, the jungle circled uninterruptedly, for here
in the Amazon there were no roads but the water, and the
widest and best-paved street must always end at that verdant
wall.

Dr. Haversham came on deck, and Will asked him about
the delay.

"Bureaucracy!" he cried. "Nonsense in quintuplicate! The

health authorities, after they make you cool your heels for a few hours, come on board and say: 'Have you any diseases?' To which we solemnly reply: 'We're in the pink!' And they, looking frightened, say: 'Is it contagious?' Then upon our earnest declarations that it is not, they wave their papers joyfully, kiss us on both cheeks, and permit us ashore to catch their smallpox and dysentery!"

Haversham sat down next to Will and together they watched the flat-bottomed barges plying back and forth between the seagoing vessels and the wharves.

Will began to feel guilty for not working, and turned his attention to his journal. But he couldn't force himself to write. The spectacle of this tropical port entranced him.

Native canoes skimmed across the harbor. They were broad and low, skimming along a river famed for its predators. The men in them looked Indian, African, and Portuguese—blended to result in every shade of complexion from pale bronze to blue-black. And to all this they added a mixture of clothing: striped cotton pants, the vest from a discarded three-piece business suit, a necklace of teeth or claws, and a broad-brimmed hat made of woven palm fiber. The overall effect made Will think of the center ring of a circus, full of exotic, colorful, and heart-stopping bravado.

Savannah was all in white today and defended from the sunshine by a ruffled parasol. She walked the deck slowly, Manuela following a few steps behind. When Haversham went looking for a waiter to bring them coffee, she dropped her parasol as she passed Will's chair. Stooping to retrieve it she handed him a letter. "Please mail it," she whispered, and moved on. He slipped the envelope into the back of his journal, trying not to wonder about Mr. Frederick Estyn of Oxford University.

Savannah paced, with Manuela trailing behind. From time to time she flung herself into a lounge chair away from the other passengers, trying to force herself to sketch the harbor, the ships, the native canoes, the wheeling gulls; but everything looked wrong and she kept scratching it out.

It seemed to her the vegetation on the shore was menacing, a luxuriant and almost violent growth creeping, climbing, entwining, striving to cover everything. It forced its way out through the cracks in the masonry, clung to the ledges of the stairways, draped itself along the top of walls. The trees themselves were weighted down with it: Parasitic vines encompassed the very tallest of them. The giant feathery palms swayed above the highest buildings, moved by a wind that scarcely touched the foliage below. She watched it, beginning to feel that the forest was alive, that if her eyes were acute enough they could see it moving, advancing, clutching at the city. She thought that if it could, it would strangle them all.

She felt confused, her thoughts like pieces of a puzzle that wouldn't fit into place. How desperately she needed to talk with a friend. But how could she begin to tell anyone about her feelings—a baffling mix of love and terror?

Of the two, the terror was easier to understand. She'd felt it when the sailor barred her way. She felt it whenever Maman began to talk about the marriage. She'd even seen it, this terror; it was in her reflection when she tried on the wedding dress. Most of all she felt it overwhelming her when she began to understand that Maman simply would not take her seriously, no matter how reasonable she tried to be.

Perhaps she was in the grip of some enchantment, for this morning she'd found herself parodying the holiest worship: She'd gone about the ship pausing at the places where she'd seen Manco as if they were the Stations of the Cross. She'd touched the rail where his hand rested, longing to kiss it like a sacred relic. And in the arthwartship passage behind the wheelhouse she'd had to fight the impulse to fall upon her knees where he'd held her in his arms.

Where was he now? Had he gone ashore unseen? Or was he sleeping behind one of these curtained portholes? She knew nothing of him, not even where his cabin was. He might be a criminal, he might be the Devil himself, he might have a wife somewhere, he might leave the ship for good here at Pará, he might never again speak to her or touch her. Did he hold her in his arms on the threshold of that open door and show her a glimpse of infinite possibilities only to enhance her despair? Did he come into her life just long enough to show her what freedom was, so that from this time on she must carry with her the recognition of her imprisonment?

Or was it the other way around? Was all this a temptation thrown into her path to keep her from doing what was right? Her dreams were filled with horrors, with serpents. Was that a warning of everlasting damnation?

And the thing is, she would have said to Jocelyn if Jocelyn had been beside her, *the thing is* I don't care. *If he is Satan, then Hell would be Heaven for me.*

* * *

"What are those initials?" As he and the doctor drank their coffee on deck, Will had noted the letters everywhere, on the small flags flown by the cargo lighters, on the bow of a trim white yacht nearby, on the walls of the warehouses along the piers. Scarlet letters on a black background: *RMR.*

"Rio Mar Rubber," Haversham said.

"So he's in the rubber business?"

The doctor chuckled. "He is the rubber business. All the others function at his pleasure. He controls traffic on the river. Works several tributaries himself. Leases the rest. Got his own army and navy. A bloody Chinese warlord.

"Know what the Brazilians call this jungle? The *selva.* Like the Latin word for trees. But take a peek in your Portuguese dictionary and see what the adjective *selvagem* means. Not just woodsy: it means savage." He pointed toward the west. "When you go upriver, you're going into frontier country, like your own western plains, my boy. The Brazilians just overthrew their monarchy in 1889. This republic is a mere seven years old. It's a huge country, so even if it had gotten itself organized, the government at Rio de Janeiro is very far away. Weeks away, in fact."

Just then one of the ship's officers summoned the doctor to the captain's quarters because the health officials had come aboard. Haversham said to Will, "We'll be cleared in a jiffy now, my boy. Chuck down some quinine before you go ashore!"

A few minutes later the native canoes waiting a short distance from the *Esperança* swarmed in upon the ship. They were loaded to the thwarts with produce for sale to the passengers—masses of flowers, stems of bananas and woven palm fiber baskets of oranges, trays of decorated cakes, stacks of native pottery, and bundles of crude rubber overshoes made by repeatedly coating the foot with latex and letting it dry hard enough to wear. The vendors climbed up the ship's stairway, their arms full and bundles on their heads, and began to push their way among the passengers who were attempting to disembark.

Will, waiting until the crowd had thinned, continued making notes and watching from his deck chair. Because of this, he saw the strange thing that occurred when Manco came on deck. Afterward he thought about it, trying to define what had happened. He was certain the other passengers saw nothing. It was the natives, the vendors who turned, touched one another and nodded, drew back to let him pass, lowered their eyes, pulled their straw hats from their heads and stood with them twisted in their hands. One of them, an emaciated man the color of cinnamon and so thin the veins coiled like cords along his limbs, bent his head and held out his basket of oranges. Manco refused but, pausing, murmured something. The man's eyes filled with tears above his toothless smile. Manco touched his shoulder and moved on. Walking in the smooth effortless way Will envied, he swung down the companionway.

When Savannah went to her cabin she found it full of flowers: a basket of orange blossoms so tall it was placed on the floor; a hamper full of orchids in all imaginable colors—mauve, lavender, ivory, scarlet, crimson, copper, gold; and other blossoms so strange she had no idea what they were. And one large blood-colored flower lay on her pillow. Their scent was breathtaking, heavily sweet.

Manuela was arranging fresh towels over the washstand. Savannah said, "What is all this?"

"There is a card in the passion flower." Manuela nodded toward a vase filled with complex rose-colored blossoms. Inside the envelope an engraved card decorated with a crest said: *Luíz Alvarez e Costa, Baron do Rio Mar.* And written across the middle in an emphatic black hand: *Welcome to Brazil.* Savannah sighed.

Manuela said, "What dress you wear to Pará?"

"I'm not permitted ashore."

The girl's dark eyes remained expressionless. "Then I may go now, senhorita?"

Savannah nodded. A moment later there was a knock at her door. Since it remained bolted, she answered by way of Veronique's stateroom. A sailor in a smart white uniform with the initials RMR in scarlet on his sleeve handed her a large package. Veronique came in from her bath just as Savannah closed the door, and followed her when she carried the box into her cabin. Veronique said nothing. She looked around the room at the flowers, then at the package. Removing the wrapping, Savannah found a large white music box, the top beautifully painted with a Watteau-like scene of shepherdesses being serenaded by musicians playing lutes. She turned the key. With melodious ticking plunks the box played "La Paloma." She slammed the lid down to shut it off.

Veronique snorted in disgust. *"Pàuvre petite,"* she said sarcastically. "So miserable a life we give you! Nothing but presents!"

9

After leaving Pará they traveled another 150 miles before reaching the Amazon proper. The Bay of Marajó was so wide they might still have been at sea, with nothing to look at but a distant smudge of shoreline hour after hour. But then they began to discern breaks in the shore, ragged indentations marking the presence of coves, rivers, and small streams. The next day they awakened to find themselves between banks of dense vegetation, lush creepers entangling hundred-foot trees that stood in the water on great buttressed roots. The channel was at times so narrow the foliage clawed the ship. No matter how intently she watched from the rail, Savannah could not see into the forest. It was impenetrable, the brilliant green of the shoreline darkening at once into a verdant blackness.

Manco had not left the ship for good at Pará, but had returned at evening. She was so overjoyed to see him mounting the companionway toward the promenade deck that she stood in his path, her hands restless with longing to touch him. He seemed distracted, unseeing; he passed by her and went on. At other times, however, she found him watching her. She'd lift her eyes from her sketchpad to find he'd walked silently into view and stood looking at her, his dark eyes burning. Sometimes at dinner she felt his gaze transfix her like a shaft and, her fork in midair, she returned his look while the world fell away from their locked glance. Yet he did not speak to her or touch her. At night she lay in bed aching for him, at times willing her heart to stop long enough for her to hear his almost soundless step as he prowled the deck in the darkness. Sometimes she thought she would sell her soul for one more moment in his arms. She determined to fling herself upon him and confess her misery, but when next she saw him her resolve melted under his scrutiny. At times she made absurd vows, especially to Jude, the Saint of the Impossible. She prayed: *Let him kiss me once more and I will go into the jungle as a missionary for the rest of my life.* But if the saint heard, he chose not to intervene in her behalf. So she watched the endless maze of river channels, preferring the enchanted purgatory of never arriving in Manáos to the journey's end and separation from her anguish.

Each day of that six-day journey to Manáos more gifts appeared. Savannah never knew if they were stored aboard the ship or picked up at the river towns along the way or sent over from the large white yacht that followed the *Esperança* upriver. But each day there were more. A clock crusty with pearls and amethysts. A comb, brush, and mirror made of carved ivory and engraved gold. A large silk hammock hung with tassels. Notes in that emphatic hand: *One day closer, my love*. And flowers, always the flowers, with orchids the most abundant of them all . . . orchids that looked to Savannah like dozens of discolored hungry mouths.

As they traveled, the heat intensified. The passengers spent most of their time on deck. Veronique, recovered from her seasickness, took over the duty of watching Savannah. Having learned that Will Patterson came from a wealthy mercantile family in the States, she had decided he was a perfectly charming young man and—in view of his unfortunate handicap—perfectly harmless as well. So while Veronique gossiped with a carefully selected coterie of fellow passengers under the striped awning of the afterdeck, she permitted Will and Savannah to talk to each other.

They spent the long airless afternoons wherever the deck offered shade, Will in a lounge chair with his journal and his books, and Savannah in her white silk hammock, hung for her by the purser's assistant between two of the awning supports. The hammock was very large, its width maintained by crosswise supports at each end. She sat in a heap of pillows with her sketchpad and pencil, rocking slowly, as she formulated a long, secret, and perhaps unmailable letter to Jocelyn.

Don't ever come to the Amazon, Joss, it's awful. The heat is indescribable! I keep saying to myself, In Switzerland it's almost Christmas. But Switzerland is five thousand miles away. Joss, have I ever told you how much last Christmas meant to me? You can't imagine how I felt all those years at the convent when everybody went home but me. Last year at your family's was really my very first true Christmas that I can remember, and I'm so glad you got the idea for me to stop eating and frighten Mother Dominica into letting me go home

with you to recover my appetite. I'll remember that holiday for ever and ever! I loved your house and I loved
your family and I just loved everything about your
life. I loved being able to eat whenever I felt like it, and
being able to wander off into one of those long galleries
hung with old tapestries to read a book on a window
seat without having to account for the way I was spending my time. And that day we spent in London with
your father and his beautiful lady friend—Countess
what?—going through the snow to see the palm trees
in the Botanic Gardens at Kew and then to tea at
Claridge's. It was all of it the best time I ever had.
Here I must be on my good behavior every single second—I'm watched like a potential murderess. And on
a ship I can't possibly escape from! What on earth
will it be like when I get to Manáos?

10

The Brazilians call the main Amazon channel the Rio Mar,
the River Sea, because it is hundreds of feet deep and so wide
in places the far shore is invisible. It rises and falls with the
ocean tides. The *Esperança*, avoiding the powerful midstream
current, hugged the shore, or wound among islands, so to the
passengers it seemed that the jungle was their perpetual horizon, cutting off escape.

On the aft deck Will watched Savannah nibble at the end of
her pencil and stare unhappily at the overgrown river bank.
He marveled at the slenderness of her throat in its high-
standing lace collar. Where the ruffled sleeve of her dress
ended, her wrist was thin as a child's. Eventually she sighed,
then turned to him and asked, "How is your travel diary
coming along?"

"Badly. I can't describe this place. Everything I write seems
like an exaggeration. I think that's what the Amazon is, an
immense exaggeration. No one back home will believe it. How
can I tell them the catfish in this river are ten feet long and eat
children?"

"Would you let me read what you've written?"

The smile lines around his blue eyes deepened. "Only if you
let me see your drawings."

She frowned and looked away, then sighed and turned back to him. "Only some of them."

"Fair enough."

She climbed from her hammock and knelt beside his chair, opening her sketchpad. He was astonished. He saw careful representations of the riverbank towns, a jumble of huts dotting the bluffs above the high water line, looking in danger of being strangled by the foliage. There were many practice studies of the trees, done in hard pencil with exquisite detail. Dr. Haversham's jovial eyes and extravagant moustache leaped from one page; on another, Veronique glowered. He found himself murmuring "Marvelous" over every drawing, but she insisted on pointing out their faults. At last he said, "You can forget about trying to learn to typewrite." He made her turn back to a sketch of a river town. "You could sell things like this to magazines." She stood up impatiently. "I mean it, Savannah. Each time they buy one of my dispatches, they pay some artist to do line drawings to illustrate it. Do those over in ink and let me submit them with my articles." She stood there frowning at him. Quietly he said, "It would be passage money."

She flung herself back into the hammock, pushing the toe of her high-buttoned white boot against the deck to make it swing. After a moment she said, "It's no use. I can't get away. I'm not even sure I want to now."

He watched her, puzzled. "Are you saying you no longer object to getting married?"

"No. I'm saying I don't want to leave Brazil."

The awkward silence between them was broken when the doctor joined them. While he and Will chatted, Savannah went in search of a waiter to bring them cool drinks.

Will's confusion over her reluctance to use her talent to earn an escape from Brazil cleared up when he found her sketchpad lying open where she'd dropped it in the hammock. The pages she hadn't wanted him to see were covered with pictures of Manco.

Manco striding, standing, leaning at the rail wrapped in his wind-blown poncho. His hands. His face again and again from every angle. But more—something Will himself had failed to see. Behind the cold mask, behind the vaguely Oriental features and the implacably guarded Amerind gaze, Manco was an inferno.

He closed the pad and made it a point to be hard at work on his journal when she returned with the drinks.

Close to shore we can smell the damp earth of the forest floor. It is the smell of death, of decomposing vegetation, falling trees, rotting flesh. On board the ship the women stroll the deck under their white parasols, beings of lace, ruffles, and the fragrance of flowers. They are like the butterflies that flicker in multi-colored flames along the banks. ...

He shuddered. Why was the sight of beauty so painful in this violent setting? It seemed in dreadful jeopardy, as if the verdant inferno that surrounded them would reach out to devour such loveliness. The *selva* was rich, vibrant with irresistible life; but it was the richness of decay.

He forced himself to take up his pen.

The selva is not a sensory experience, something the pen of a reporter can record. It is an event of the mind. Its force is felt as a profound psychic shock. The Amazon stirs me to violent responses—awe and terror, fascination and dread. And these spill from my pen. Well, I shall let them. On the next draft they will be carefully expunged. Shall I call my book *All Passion Deleted*?

Will smiled in spite of himself. Even his pain was fruitful. Watching Savannah, he felt his senses quicken. He was perceiving everything with a new-found intensity. Even his anguish. And he drew a grim satisfaction from the realization that the greater his dismay, the more his journal grew. The work was his penance for the crime of self-delusion. Misled by her pity or her need, he had been guilty of the inexcusable extravagance of hope. But that was gone now; he knew better.

It wasn't her engagement, for the thought of this luminous girl married to a man of fifty was too bizarre to be taken seriously. No, the source of Will's despair lay in himself, in his difference from other men. Especially in his difference from a man like Manco. Since childhood Will had watched the way men moved, the placement of their feet, the length of their strides, the smooth swing of arm and hand; he was a connoisseur of the art of motion. And he'd found in the extraordinary grace of Manco his most prized example. *If I could be whole*, he thought, *that is the way I'd wish to be.* Lean and agile, like the man who was the object of Savannah's obsessive scrutiny ... and now, of Will's as well.

11

There were some two dozen men in the Smoking Lounge, sitting about on the brown leather chairs. Under the slowly rotating fans they were reading the papers and magazines brought on board at Pará. Smoke from their Turkish cigarettes, their long black Havana cigars, and their polished meerschaum pipes lay over the room in uneven layers, barely disturbed by the movement of the fan. Four of the men played poker at a table covered in dark green baize. Others watched the game while waiters moved among them with trays of drinks.

"Can't be done," Haversham said. "Bound to end in failure."

Will sipped his whiskey, watching for Manco to appear. He said, "It may not be economical, but I doubt that it's impossible."

The doctor leaned forward in his Morris chair. "It is here. Chap tried it. Ten, fifteen years ago. Wanted to lay track through the forest to bypass the nineteen rapids on the Madeira. Lost twenty-five percent of his work force." He puffed his pipe reflectively. "Higher casualty rate than most wars. And he had a crack team. Yankees. Veterans from the railroad building in your West. They could cut their way through fifteen hundred feet of forest in a day. But that was up north."

Will gestured for a refill. "What was the problem?"

"The nature of this jungle. Saw your way through a ruddy hardwood trunk, but the blasted monster won't fall. Held in place by the lianas—tangled vines that go up as high as the trees themselves—hundred, two hundred feet. Then there're the insects. They gave up after seven years of work. Got only four miles of track laid."

Will watched the doctor relight his pipe. "Then what is Senhor Manco doing with a shipment of railroad equipment? I've seen the ship's manifest. Boiler gauges. Hoisting gear."

Haversham winked. "If you could find an excuse to travel back and forth lightening the purses of everybody foolish enough to sit down at a poker table with you, would you want to be bothered with the ruddy jungle?"

Will pulled a guidebook from his pocket and handed it to

the doctor. "Drill me on the exchange, will you? I'm having trouble making it stick in my head."

Haversham obliged. "What's a milreis?"

"A thousand reis."

"And how much is a reis?"

Will frowned. "I told you I couldn't get it to stick."

Haversham shook his pipe for emphasis. "It takes eighteen reis to make one of your pennies. Just remember, you've got to pay a thousand reis if you want to order a beer."

"I don't. They serve it warm. And besides, it's only six cents back home." He took the guidebook back and did some figuring on the margin. "So last night when Manco pulled in a pot containing ten thousand milreis—"

"He'd won well over a thousand pounds. Some fifty-five hundred dollars."

Will hadn't dreamed so much money was at stake. Yet not even when gathering in great heaps of the stuff did Manco seem to enjoy the game. It looked more like work, for he played with intense concentration. He drank little and never smoked. Sitting motionless by the hour, his hooded, deep-set eyes watching the faces of his opponents, he appeared to be waiting for prey. No turn of the game moved him to gladness or despair; or if it did, he concealed it. He was a man in perfect control of himself, a man who could sleep like a cat, on ledges.

Yet as Will watched Manco's long fingers shuffling and reshuffling the cards each night, he was impressed anew by the suppressed tension behind the surface stillness, a banked excitement.

Attempts to engage him in conversation during chance encounters on the deck were useless; Manco was not rude, but he answered in monosyllables and moved on. So Will decided to join the poker game.

The moment Manco appeared in the doorway, Will got up and started toward the green baize table. When Haversham saw Will limp across the room and lower himself into an empty chair, he followed and leaned close to him. "Old chap, I think you'll find the game a bit stiff for the likes of us. How about some backgammon?" Will smiled and winked reassuringly, but Haversham was insistent. "Brazilians play poker in deadly earnest, my boy. Their late emperor loved the game, and so they approach it like some crazy religion."

"I'll be all right, Doctor. We Yanks are pretty fierce poker players too."

Shaking his head and mumbling with concern, Haversham went back to his chair. In the meantime, Manco had seated himself and won a draw for the deal. He shuffled and began to deal five card draw. After half an hour two players left, their wallets empty. Will held his own by betting cautiously. He'd begun to enjoy himself when one of the Brazilians demanded a new deck.

Manco nodded and a waiter placed a fresh pack of cards on the table. On the next two hands Will and the fourth man, who said little, folded early while Manco and the other player raised and called each other. Manco won both times, once with a pair of jacks and once with three deuces. In each case his opponent had a better hand, but under the steady onslaught of Manco's betting, he'd backed down. The man had been losing heavily, and he angrily waved the spectators to stand back. Two hands later he ordered a glass-front picture removed from the wall behind his chair. On the next deal Will saw the Brazilian's tension ease as he squinted through the cigar smoke at his cards. He opened with a show of casualness and kept putting his hand down and picking it up again as if debating whether to throw it in. Manco gazed at him a moment, then folded. Will did too. The man cursed and threw down a full house, adding something menacing Will couldn't understand. Manco answered quietly. The Brazilian said something to the other player and, without bothering to collect the small ante left on the table, the two of them left talking angrily to each other.

Manco spoke to Will in English. "Do you also think me a cheat?"

"No. I think you are a careful observer of the human species."

"You are too, my friend."

"Then we will watch each other. Deal."

Will enjoyed the game. An atmosphere of acute intelligence permeated Manco's play. Watching him, Will could sense the careful checking of the probabilities, the review of cards that had been played, the calculation of odds and percentages. It was an interesting hour, and at the end of it Will was still holding his own. At last Manco said, "What do you drink?"

"Whiskey."

When the drinks were brought, Manco put the cards aside.

Will knew the Indian's face well enough now to say, "Had enough?"

With a trace of amusement playing about the edges of his eyes, Manco said, "Where did you learn to play poker?"

"In bed." One of the black eyebrows lifted slightly. Will picked up the deck and shuffled idly, turning up four aces, four kings, four queens. "I used to play alone, many hours at a time. I'd deal a whole tableful of hands and develop a character for each opponent. Then, during each one's play, I would assume his identity: the reckless man who plays to forget a sorrow, the bored heir who takes chances because it's stimulating, the embezzler who must win and return the stolen cash by morning or blow out his brains with a Derringer." Manco's head lifted in a silent laugh. Will watched him. "Which one are you, Senhor Manco?"

"A man who looks upon the game as an investment." He got up. "And playing with you, friend, promises no profit." He bowed slightly, and left the room. Watching him move with that effortless grace, Will suddenly realized what Manco reminded him of: An El Greco figure, lean and fanatic. The gleam in those hooded eyes was the burning of some lunatic dream. Will ached to know what it was.

12

Tomás closed his eyes against the sun coming in through the palm-thatch roof of the shed. He could not remember how long ago he had attacked the landing.

It was harder to concentrate in the light. And he must concentrate. Manco had taught him how to do it. He need only remember.

The first time was the hardest; nothing would ever again be so hard. He was ten years old and he had been swimming when the most terrible fish of the river had attacked him. The candiru is small, only an inch or two long, and very thin. But it is covered with tiny swept-back quills, and it enters the most secret places of the body. Manco had had to cut the candiru out of Tomás's flesh.

Everything was white in the mission hospital and Manco, who was then called Brother Esteban, bent over him wearing a white robe. Everything was white but Manco's dark face, his dark fervent eyes. He told Tomás of the Tibetan lamas who could, through the power of their minds, watch the outcome of a battle many miles away. He told him of the holy men of India who walk on burning coals and feel nothing. He said, "Imagine it, Tomás. Imagine this is a ritual you have chosen to prove your courage. When you pass this test you will enter the secret company of warriors. Your arrows will be touched with magic and you will fear nothing. You will swim mountain rivers choked with ice. You will wrestle the jaguar himself to the ground. And you will feel nothing but your exultation."

Manco's hands had been swift. Tomás had not cried out.

Now he remembered a river choked with ice, a swift tumultuous torrent foaming and leaping before him. As he plunged into the stream the roar of the rapids pounded in his head. He opened his eyes under water, seeing nothing but a boiling light. He felt the numbing chill creep through his body obliterating everything but the strong throbbing of his heart and the burning breath of his lungs bellowing in and out, in and out.

He did not feel the thongs cutting the flesh of his wrists where they had hung him. He did not feel the vermin in his wounds. He did not feel the lash of knotted tapir hide.

And he told them nothing.

It grew dark, and light, and dark again. Rain fell, drumming incessantly on the ground, on the building, on the leaves. It was no longer possible to tell day from night. And it was no longer possible for Tomás to be absent from his body. The pain inhabited him. It had become all there was to him, his whole being, his identity. He was a litany of pain, loud, ceaseless, monotonous. Yet sometimes it diminished; for a brief time he slept. He lived to sleep.

But the men always came back. He was the instrument upon which they played. At their hands the music of his pain swelled, rang from him in long screaming. But he said no words. He did not say the name "Manco."

He hated them at first, and the hatred gave him strength. But no more; now when he became aware of them he knew it would be terrible for a time, but when they were tired he would sleep. And perhaps, one time, he would not awaken. He would return to the earth, to the river, and be at peace.

At length they moved him. They bound him and threw him into a canoe, where he lay on the bottom under a heavy cover. Soon the heat, the burning of his wounds, became unbearable. His moaning made them tear the cover off and strike him with their rifle butts. Then he was still. When he awakened he heard and felt the river roaring under him. She took his pain too; she drew it from his body and dragged it toward the sea, toward Manco. Then she brought the rain and washed him, she made him cool once more. And she murmured to him while he slept. She said, *Tomás, Tomás, listen to me: I am the Tears of the Moon.*

That was the river's name in the language of Manco's people. The tears of the moon weeping for her love, the sun. They worshiped Intí, the sun, our father; and Pacha Mama, Lady Earth, who is our mother.

Tomás prayed. *I cannot wait for Manco to set me free. Take me now, Tears of the Moon. Let me sink as a stone or a tree; drag me away to the sea.* But she did not.

A room with walls, a roof through which the sun did not shine, a floor without the river under it, a room filled with the voices of men.

"Who has done this? Who is responsible?"

"Gomez. At Concepción."

"Disgusting. He is a beast. Punish him."

"How, Excellency?"

"Do to him as he has done to this man. And see that no prisoner is treated in this manner again. Such a waste, a stupid waste! How can he speak when he is dying of so many wounds? I cannot bear stupidity."

"What shall we do with him, Excellency?"

"Now you must make him speak before he dies."

After a time Tomás cried out: "Candiru. Manco, the candiru, take away the candiru."

"Manco? What is that?"

"A name, Excellency."

"Do you know this name? Any of you?"

"There was a priest. Some trouble in Bolivia."

"Yes, Master, he's right. Trouble in the mines. Tried to free the miners. Defrocked, and wanted for murder."

"It is also the name of a gambler. On the steamers and at the river ports. Very lucky. They say he reads minds."

"Is that not also the name of the man who thinks he can build a railroad in the jungle? Bypassing the Devil's Cauldron on the Escondido so that the rubber from the headwaters can be shipped out and not dragged around the rapids? Esteban Manco, Excellency, that is his name."

"Good, I hope you are right, for then we will know our enemy is a madman. But whatever he is, find him. Bring him to me. Let it be known the Baron do Rio Mar wants him and will pay well, for I want him very quickly. And in the meantime you will hire more guards for my landings."

"And this one?"

"He has more to tell us. See if you can make him well. Then perhaps we will begin again. But carefully this time, so he will live. Until I no longer need him."

13

It was their last night on the *Esperança*. Haversham would remain with the ship and, after a short time in port, go on to Iquitos, Peru, another 1,300 miles upriver. The others would disembark in Manáos tomorrow.

Now that they were nearly a thousand miles from the Atlantic, there was no evening breeze. The daily rainstorm left them hot and miserable. And Savannah was afflicted with restlessness. She kept leaping from her chair, taking a turn about the deck, and flinging herself down again. She wished it were over, that they'd arrived and she'd delivered her speech to her father, and had been disowned or thrown into the street or locked up in the madhouse.

She said, "What time is it?"

Will snapped open his pocket watch and tilted the face toward the lighted passageway. "Quarter past nine."

Twelve hours more. Savannah got up and began crossing the afterdeck, back and forth, snatches of conversation rising and falling away from her like the whining mosquitoes. She would never be able to sleep tonight, not unless she exhausted herself with walking.

She walked down the promenade, but in the stillness of the night, even there she could hear the murmur of their conversation. Why couldn't they be still?

Pacing the deck through bands of moonlight and shadow, she watched the dark forest, imagining giant predators creeping, coiling, and flying through the night.

Manco was standing on the foredeck in the shadow of the wheelhouse. His unease had deepened during the journey upriver. He'd felt it since before the *Esperança* anchored at

Pará. When he went ashore there, he'd tried to contact Manáos, but as usual, the telegraph line was out of order. He knew there'd been trouble. He felt it as a dull pain in the heart. Watching the moon's path shimmer like a dagger in the river, he wondered who had been lost. Riccu? Mindaro? Tomás? The aching of his heart intensified. *Soon*, he thought. *I will be there soon. We will not be defeated. Like the river we will rise and cleanse the forest. We will rise and destroy that life may begin anew. Even if the liberating flood is made of our tears.*

Twelve more hours, Savannah thought. But what then? Why couldn't the ship have been enchanted, never to arrive? Then perhaps, sometime in that endless journey, she could have learned the meaning of his brooding gaze. He no longer spoke to her. Not even in her dreams. But at least there she felt the warmth of his body, the weight of his hands upon her.

Was he sleeping now? She tried to imagine the dark eyes closed, the strong hands limp upon the sheet; but it was impossible. She could not envision him slack or unguarded or helpless.

One thing she knew: He was the Baron's enemy. When she'd told him her name, something in him had tensed, and at once he had begun to speak of the terrible spirit who crushes and devours. While the others had told her things would be all right, Manco had told her she was in danger. And he was right. Her heart, her mind, her body, her intuition, everything told her she was in the grip of something dreadful. When Veronique learned that Savannah had told Manuela to stop following her about like a shadow, she had paled swiftly, and sunk into a chair. In a vicious whisper she'd said, "You will conduct yourself properly, you will be civil to Manuela, you will appreciate the gifts—for if you do not, the Baron will be displeased." Savannah had laughed and said the Baron was not on board the ship. But Veronique had hissed, "Don't you know you are being watched? Don't you know he receives a full account of everything you do?" As if to give point to Maman's warning, the next gift card said: *I count the hours —Luíz.*

Perhaps what drew her to Manco was his knowledge, the sense that he alone understood that she was already trapped.

She paused at the foredeck railing, struck by the beauty of the night, the dazzling moonlight, the dark rim of forest, and the great calm river. In the distance a faint breeze touched the tallest palms. She loosened her hair, wanting to be cooled by that breath of wind. Then she turned to find him standing in the shadow, a dark form still as a statue, a radiant god of night whose eyes were touched by moonlight. The rising wind lifted her hair; it floated about her like sea grass. He came to her slowly and touched her hair as if distracted by it.

She said, "Have you enchanted me? Are you a magician?"

He sighed. "If I were, I would open the doors of all the prisons." Then, smiling, he said, "And I would spirit you away from the *boiuna*."

With both hands he caught her hair and held her face like a chalice. A soft moan broke from him and he kissed her, a long kiss that drained the strength from her body, but he held her so close to him she had no need of strength. Then suddenly he released her and turned away as if something had seized him. He gripped the rail with both hands and gazed into the night. "But I am not a magician. I am a man."

"Then why do you avoid me?"

"I must."

"Because I am engaged?"

"Because I have no time for you. Or for myself."

She watched his face for some sign, a message, anything. She saw the jaw clench and the eyes burning under their heavy lids. At last she said, "I don't understand."

He reached for her and drew her to him, not kissing her now, but comforting her as he would a child. "I know. And it has nothing to do with you. It's been going on four hundred years. It may never end."

She felt, through his dark coat, the warmth of his body against her cheek. "If the Baron is your enemy"—she turned to look at him—"then he will be my enemy too."

"Do not offend him."

"I'm not afraid."

Shaking his head, he said, "Laughing at storms is quite another thing. Nature is benevolent compared with man."

Her hands clenched on the rail. "I will not marry him. Nothing they do will make me marry him."

Reaching out, he stroked her hair. "His cruelty exceeds all bounds, but he provides well for his son and daughter. There are men like that, *conquistadores* who will not hesitate to murder for profit, but who care deeply for their families. I think you will be safe so long as you do what is expected of you."

"I've never been any good at that."

"You must. Smile and wear those dresses put on your back by the blood of the rubber tappers . . . and go to the cathedral to pray for the sins of the world."

She pulled away. "How can you say such things? I thought you understood."

Drawing her close again, he said, "Who ever promised us we could have what we desire?" He raised his face toward the moon. "My people say the moon loves the sun, but their union would destroy the world, so they must keep to different places in the sky. The moon's grief is so great that her tears have formed this river."

"And what about the sun? Doesn't he grieve?"

"Yes, but he does not weep. He labors, and the sweat of his labor is our gold." He lifted her face. "At Manáos Cathedral there is a good priest. Go to him, Savannah. He will help you do what must be done."

"You mean, help me accept my lot in life? No, thank you."

He touched her cheek. " 'Behold, thou art fair, O my love, behold, thou art fair, our bed of love is the green grass. . .' "

She said, "If I cannot marry someone I love, I would rather become a nun and never know what—what any of that means." He nodded, but said nothing.

"Where will you be? Will you be in Manáos? I need to know." When he failed to answer she said, "I need to know if you are hearing the same bells I hear. I need to know whether the rain is falling on you when it falls on me."

Though his laughter made no sound it was dazzling in the moonlight. He took her hands and held them to his lips, smiling and looking at her as if he would save the memory for some other time. "You make me forget the pain."

He turned her toward the rail and stood beside her while in the still night the waves slipped softly past the bow. "When my business in Manáos is finished I will be far away, in the *selva*. But the river will always touch us."

Thousands of miles of river. Her eyes filled. "How will I ever find you?"

"You will not find me."

"I will. I must."

"No. If we meet again, we will be enemies."

He turned quickly and walked away into the shadows. She was left alone, clinging to the rail while her tears fell into the dark river.

14

The *Esperança* steamed through the black waters of the Amazon tributary called the Rio Negro. It was a sunless morning. Shreds of mist were woven like gauze among the trees and snared in the hollows of the bank. In the distance a gash of color lay above the tallest palms, where the blue, gold, and green dome of the Manáos opera house rose incongruously above the jungle.

Savannah had been packed for hours. At Veronique's insistence she'd worn one of her most elaborate outfits, a gown of shirred lavender peau de soie with ruffles everywhere. The matching parasol was covered with ruffles of lavender chiffon, and her broad-brimmed hat was made of stiffened purple lace trimmed with velvet violets. As she stood on the foredeck watching for Manáos, with a light wind blowing across the ship, she was a mass of fluttering.

Now that the city was almost in view, the first-class passengers stood along the promenade with their luggage stacked around them. Just as it had been at Pará and all the other river towns, here at Manáos the ship would anchor off shore; in spite of the great volume of shipping, dock facilities were inadequate for oceangoing vessels.

Will was finding the dampness of the Amazon climate painful; aching in every joint, he'd taken to using his cane. Together he and Savannah watched the tiled dome of the opera house gleaming above the trees. Then, the city appeared, looking as if it had been thrown chock-a-block into a clearing on the edge of the river. The water was low, so the wharf pilings stood high, and beyond the block-long warehouse emblazoned *RMR* the town rose as the land itself lifted gently toward the encircling forest. As Will watched he began to discern broad cobblestoned avenues edged with palms, mango, and giant silk-cotton trees. The large official-looking buildings were white marble, but the walls of the Italianate cathedral were stucco tinted blue. Savannah was struck by the way the jungle rimmed the paved streets and marble buildings; she saw it as a snare drawn tight.

Will hung his walking stick on the rail and began leafing through his guidebook. Savannah stared at the ivory cane handle, carved to look like a dog's head. He said, "Population, forty thousand. That's about the size of your namesake city in Georgia."

He turned a page. " 'Manáos, called the White City in the Jungle, is the capital of Amazonas, the largest state in the Brazilian Republic. Amazonas is five times the size of Texas.' "

It really isn't white, she thought. It's got red tile roofs and blue stucco. And black water and green jungle. She looked at the river, some forty feet below. Who could believe in a black river? As if to answer her thought, Will read, " 'The river is dark because of decaying vegetation.' "

The sun was beginning to burn through the haze and she could see that behind his fair beard he looked pale. She touched his cane on the rail. "How do you put it out of your mind when you're in misery?"

"Work. The great panacea. You ought to get out your sketchpad and draw the opera house."

"I can't. My hands are shaking." She sighed raggedly and pulled her hat down closer to her eyes. "Let's go sit down. We're likely to be here half the morning."

The Baron do Rio Mar had awakened early, as was his habit. He set great store upon discipline—for his household, his enterprises, even Nature herself. And of course for himself. He had deliberately developed an ability to thrive on little sleep; he worked late each night and always rose before dawn. The early morning hours were the time he did his best thinking, when he analyzed the progress of his interests and contemplated his plans. This morning, however, his routine was disrupted.

He'd been sitting in his study at the back of the Palácio, his leather chair drawn close to the fire of aromatic cedar logs which counteracted the damp chill of early morning. Its radiance warmed even the distant corners of the high-ceilinged room. Now, beyond the deep red Turkey carpet, the parquet flooring of inlaid rosewood and jacaranda reflected the flames as if Hell itself glowed directly beneath the room.

Of middle height and powerfully built, the Baron felt himself to be, at fifty, at the height of his powers. His dark hair waved back from his forehead, the gray streaks like brushstrokes, and his meticulously trimmed Prince Albert beard and moustache seemed made of iron. His hands were well formed, the fingernails long and carefully manicured.

He paused over a page of *The Meditations of Marcus Aurelius*, contemplating a passage: "Let no act be done without a purpose, nor otherwise than according to the perfect principles of art." Of course, he thought. That was why stupidity and senseless brutality were so offensive to him; they lacked both essentials, purpose and art. And of the two, he gave primacy to art. Life itself was for him an art.

He was widely read and widely traveled; a connoisseur. He felt it necessary to affirm this even here at Manáos, where the climate required a great effort to sustain a life of elegance. What the climate called for was a spartan life: bare wood floors, walls of louvered doors to admit whatever breeze might blow, wide verandas. But this the Baron resisted. His house was a replica of an Italian palace, fit for a Medici, and filled with the finest furniture money could buy. He was determined that although the rubber business forced him to live in Manáos, rather than on his sugar plantation in Pernambuco or the coffee fazenda in São Paulo, it would never force him to live without elegance.

Dom Luíz looked up as Eustacio Moraes, captain of the Baron's yacht, arrived and begged leave to report to the master. He put aside his book and poured himself a cup of *café preto*, black Brazilian coffee grown at his own fazenda. Eustacio nervously smoothed his white uniform. "Your Grace," he said, "the *Esperança* is entering the harbor now. I pulled ahead at dawn to bring you word."

Dom Luíz sipped from the Sèvres cup. His glance strayed to the photograph on the mantel, to the slim, boyish girl whose eyes looked firmly into the camera and who appeared about to speak, to say something amusing. "Tell me of the senhorita, Eustacio."

"Excellency, permit me to say that the young lady is extraordinarily beautiful."

The Baron's gray eyes narrowed, while at the same time the pupils expanded almost imperceptibly. "And how does she spend her time on shipboard?"

"She watches the scenery and draws upon a sketching pad."

Dom Luíz nodded. "And my gifts?"

"All delivered, Your Grace. She caused the hammock to be hung on the afterdeck and spent her afternoons there."

"And her companions?"

"Her mother. The ship's elderly doctor. A crippled gringo journalist. Manuela reports that the girl and her mother are at odds. There are quarrels."

The Baron took another sip of coffee and dried his moustache with delicate strokes of his lace handkerchief, stirring a faint odor of attar of roses in the room. "A mark in her favor, Eustacio. I myself cannot abide the mother. Anything further?"

"Manuela says the mother was forced to have the purser lock the girl's cabin door. She has a tendency to walk the deck alone. In the mother's view the girl is . . . I believe the word used was 'headstrong.' "

The Baron nodded with satisfaction. "You know my Arabian mare, Semiramis?" He left his chair and walked to the tall window that looked out toward the gardens and the distant stable. "She is spirited, yet utterly obedient. And to me alone; she will have no other rider. But had you seen her when I bought her as a yearling, you would have despaired. It took months to break her." He walked back to his chair, his heels ringing on the polished floor. "Now the touch of my hand and the sound of my voice are the delights of her existence. Training like that, Eustacio, is a fine art. It demands absolute implacability, absolute self-mastery, for you must never relent. You cannot let the beauty of the animal, nor her anguish, soften you for an instant."

Eustacio moved his feet uneasily on the carpet. "She is magnificent, Excellency. And may I take this opportunity to wish you every joy on your honeymoon?"

Dom Luíz's moustache flicked in a wry smile. "It may well be a labor of love, Eustacio. But the rewards will come. Months later, perhaps. But they will come." After a pause he said, "Thank you, Eustacio. You may go." But when the yacht captain's hand touched the ornate brass door handle, the Baron stopped him. "One more thing. At Pará did you chance to hear of an anarchist by the name of Manco?"

Eustacio's forehead creased. "No, Your Grace. Only the gambler of that name who is aboard the *Esperança*."

Although the Baron did not move, he flushed slightly. He said, "On your way out, tell Raoul I wish to see the chief of police here in this room in less than fifteen minutes."

From deck chairs on the promenade Savannah and Will watched the Manáos dock. Under the high pilings of the wharf, a mass of native canoes clustered like a school of minnows. All were filled to overflowing with fruits, painted gourds, woven hats and baskets, masses of flowers, rubber shoes, trays of iced cakes.

Crowds of people waiting to greet the voyagers milled about the dock area. Men in white linen suits and tropical helmets; other men wearing dark business suits and straw hats; all of them carrying their black umbrellas like a badge that said: *Inhabitant of Amazonas.* Other men moved importantly through the crowd: customs officials in white uniforms. There were armed men, too: several dozen policemen and a group of soldiers. There were few women. Wearing white and carrying white parasols, they strolled about, looking toward the ship and talking to each other.

Apparently there was another woman present, too, but out of sight in the carriage stopped near the edge of the dock. It was a smart closed brougham, black and gleaming with gold trim. The coachman, in livery the color of old gold, was having difficulty keeping the matched grays still amid the milling crowd; they bobbed the golden feathers on their heads and shook the harness as their hooves stamped upon the paving. From the carriage window, where the dark gray drapes were nearly closed, a graceful hand waved a white handkerchief.

Will caught sight of Dr. Haversham and called him over. "Are they afraid we're in the pink?"

"No, that's all done. Seems now they're looking for a criminal. The chief of police himself is coming aboard to look at the passenger list." He frowned in the direction of the dock. "Hallo, that must be him now."

As they watched, a steam launch with a Gatling gun mounted on the prow headed toward the ship. On the launch's bridge a stocky officer braced his legs. His white uniform with its rows of insignia and golden epaulets made him look like the admiral in a comic opera. Beyond him Savannah saw the curtains part at the carriage window. Suddenly there was movement there. Savannah blinked and looked more carefully, but her eyes had not deceived her: It was a monkey. Swiftly the creature darted up onto the carriage roof, scampered over the top to the coachman, climbed to his shoulder, and perched upon his tall hat. At that moment the mass of native canoes laden with produce began to move. En masse the orange-blossom and banana armada advanced upon the *Esperança.*

On the steam launch the admiral–police chief blew a whistle furiously. He was ignored. Other policemen on the launch drew their pistols and fired into the air. The vendors continued to advance. The passengers were enthralled, especially when an officer manned the Gatling gun. He did not fire, but began to swivel back and forth, taking menacing aim first one way, then another.

Savannah's attention, however, was distracted. She looked toward the *Esperança*'s bow and saw Manco standing at the rail, his eyes fixed upon the dock where, at the window of the carriage, the graceful hand fluttered its lace handkerchief. He turned his back on the city and strode away, across the foredeck toward the river side of the ship. Savannah, unnoticed by the others, stepped back from the rail and ran toward the bow. As she rounded the wheelhouse she saw Manco at the rail on the far side. He paused, glancing along the deck toward the nearest lifeboat, then down at the black leather case in his hand. Then he dropped the case at his feet, slipped out of his shoes, and ripped off his black coat. Naked from the waist up, he swung up onto the rail, poised a moment while he drew a breath that lifted his shoulders and expanded his ribcage . . . and dived like a thrown spear into the distant river.

By the time Savannah got her legs working again, he'd disappeared in the black waves. Long moments passed while, scarcely breathing, she watched the water. There was no sign but her imagined glimpses of piranha in the murky depths. At her feet she found his shoes, the small black portmanteau, and the coat she'd leaned her cheek against when he held her in his arms.

She gathered up his things and carried them around to the promenade companionway. When she found her own hand luggage in the heap of baggage at the stair, she put the coat and shoes inside her carpetbag and fastened to its strap the handle of the leather case. Then she moved back to her place at the rail.

The harbor was a shambles. Overturned canoes, straw hats, and rubber overshoes bobbed like corks in the water. A tray of iced cakes slowly foundered in the wake of the police boat. The deck was littered with debris, with battered fruit and wicker baskets. And the police chief, alternately shaking his fists in the air and picking flower petals off his uniform, stamped back and forth on the bridge screaming Portuguese obscenities.

It took two hours for the police to search the *Esperança*. Eventually the passengers were permitted to step one at a time into the cargo lighters under the angry scrutiny of the officials. Edward St. James was waiting in his gig, an open two-wheeled carriage drawn by a single horse. Veronique had fussed herself into a frenzy over the delay and the hazards of transporting the trousseau from the ship to the wharf in a barge. When she learned the Baron had been detained by urgent business and they would not see him until the evening, she chose to ride in the luggage wagon.

Savannah, facing her father during the drive through the city, tried to recall the opening sentence of her speech. It seemed impossible to concentrate; over and over in her mind's eye she saw Manco pause, draw breath, and dive into the Negro.

Speaking in that soft drawling accent she remembered, her father started in on a tour: told her of the city's cultural events, the concerts in the parks, the sidewalk cafés where string quartets played Mozart, and the grand opening of the opera house, planned for the eve of her wedding.

She determined to begin and reached out to take his hand when her attention was arrested. At the side entrance of a large townhouse on the edge of the commercial district, she saw the black and gold carriage. Twisting in her seat, she read the gilded plaque by the building's main entrance. It said:

THE CONTESSA'S PALACE
Accommodation—French Style

15

The Contessa, watching from a window in her private sitting room, smiled. "She's exquisite."

"Who?"

"The St. James girl."

"I hope your interest is not professional."

She laughed. "Of course it is. And why not? Each day virgins are more difficult to obtain. And a natural redhead! A pearl of great price, my friend. Her first night's earnings would finance a revolution!"

Manco was not amused. The narrow moustache at the corners of his mouth framed lips tense with anger. The frown seemed in keeping with his garments: He was dressed in the long cassock of a priest. He had surfaced near the city's dockside market and walked to the Contessa's under a six-foot stack of palm fiber baskets, selling several of them along the way.

"Besides," the Contessa said, "it's a better fate than walking into the arms of Rio Mar. Do you not agree?" She turned from the window and crossed to a full-length pier glass. The room she saw framing her image had been furnished to complement her coloring. The pale gray walls and carpeting, the silver brocade draperies and upholstery, the Louis XIV furniture in antique white all seemed extensions of her costume, a gown of silver moiré taffeta and a hat of dove-gray felt trimmed with egret feathers. Everything matched or blended with her complexion, fair as the face of a china doll, and with her hair, which in the muted light of this room looked silver. This, combined with the slenderness of her figure and the fact that her face was almost free of lines, made her a woman of uncertain age. If she'd chosen to dye her hair, she might have passed for a young girl, except for her eyes. They'd seen too much of the world, and she concealed them behind tinted spectacles the color of smoke.

As she began removing her hat, the small gray monkey she'd been fondling climbed onto her shoulder and did his best to interfere by snatching the hatpins from her fingers and reinserting them all askew. "That's enough, Coco," she said irritably, pulling him away. Chattering in protest, he snatched the hat from her head, ran with it into a corner, and, turning it upside down, crawled inside. "Little demon," she said, and sat down across from Manco.

"Did you become acquainted with her on shipboard?" Seeing the frown around his dark eyes deepen, she laughed. "Your silences are more informative than the speech of most men. Champagne?" He shook his head, so she poured herself a glass of Cordon Rouge and raised it to him. "Here's to enchantment!" He watched her as he would watch a card player, trying to discern whether her mockery concealed some motive. She reassured him. "I am quite sincere, my friend. My interest in this redhead is the highest of compliments. After all, I am a connoisseur."

Manco got up from the brocade sofa and walked to the fireplace. The ormolu clock said half past twelve. He leaned against the mantel.

Smiling, she said, "How fortunate that your disapproval of my enterprise does not extend to my financial services."

"You know I do not judge you. Your friendship is invaluable. And I know you don't mean half of what you say."

"Nevertheless, my dear Esteban, you misunderstand the nature of my calling. As far as I'm concerned, the Contessa's

Palace is a theater—a stage with an audience of paying customers. Most of what they pay for is enchantment. An illusion. I enable men to act out their fantasies." She smiled again. "As for the drama's climax, that is a ballet. A pas de deux. In truth it is simply another performance. A skillful courtesan is always a superb actress. I respect my girls; I permit none of them to be mistreated; and they are free to leave whenever they choose. None of those things can be said about an arranged marriage to Rio Mar, and no amount of ceremony in the cathedral will make it anything other than the grossest kind of prostitution."

Manco studied her with increased interest. "I believe this is the first time I have seen you angry."

She ran a finger around the rim of her goblet. "Each of us has a raw nerve somewhere. Yours is inflamed by oppression, mine by hypocrisy." She put her glass on the table beside her chair. "Until this incident today, was your trip successful?"

He nodded. "I got everything I went for. Even the explosives. But I didn't want them on a passenger steamer, so I sent them ahead on a coal ship, under sail. They're coming up by launch from Pará."

"And the money?"

"I converted most of my winnings to diamonds in Amsterdam."

He drew a leather pouch from the pocket of his cassock. "The only money left on board in my bag was what I'd won since leaving Hâvre."

"How much was that?"

"I never count money."

"Perhaps those fools haven't found it. I'll send one of the girls."

"It is of no importance. A few thousand pounds."

She lifted her eyes in mock despair. "You're still a priest at heart, aren't you?"

He tossed the pouch of diamonds into her lap. "I'll need medicines. And food."

"When?" She rose and opened the wall safe behind her mirror.

He paused. "I can't leave until I find Tomás."

She'd put the pouch away and was counting out a bundle of bills, but she stopped and looked at him. "Esteban, you must forget Tomás. It's been eight days. He must be dead."

Manco passed a hand across his forehead. "He is not dead."

"You cannot know that."

"But I do."

"Because they were waiting for you?" She shrugged. "Every tapper you have freed knows the name of the Liberator. It was only a matter of time." She crossed the room and tumbled Coco out of her hat, tugging the brim back into shape and covertly watching Manco all the while.

Manco said, "If Rio Mar knew one of my men had been taken alive, would he not want to question him himself?"

"Not necessarily. Yet he wouldn't want some ignorant landing manager in charge. He would have him questioned by someone clever. One of the 'palace guard.' "

Manco walked over to the window. The house itself was quiet now at midday, but from the street below came the sound of carriage wheels, the cries of men selling lottery tickets, the din of peddlers clacking small sticks between the fingers of one hand to draw attention to their wares. "We have no one inside the Palácio?"

She shook her head. "He has no need of hired help. He has a houseful of loyal half-breeds. A regular dynasty, two full generations of them, borne to him by his black and Indian servants." Seeing the tension in his stance, she went to stand beside him at the window. "Esteban, please forget Tomás. He himself would tell you this. As soon as the guns are aboard your launch you must go. I'll see to the medicine at once."

But as she turned to leave, there was a knock. She opened the door and, after a whispered conversation, closed it and leaned against the frame. Coco plucked at her skirt and, distractedly, she picked him up and caressed him. Manco was watching. After a moment she said, "They found the guns."

"On the ship?"

"No, ashore. They're in the Customs Warehouse."

To her surprise he smiled like a man who'd just been dealt an excellent hand.

The gig stopped. Edward St. James said, "Welcome to Arcadia, Miss Savannah." She caught her breath at the two-storied white mansion with tall columns across the front. "The grounds are smaller, naturally. But the interior is as close to the original as memory and my bank account could make it. Come." She refused his offer to carry her carpetbag, so he took her arm and led her up the steps. Pausing at the top, he said, "Of course, back home this front gallery had a broad vista, a wide avenue of oaks running all the way down to the river of which you are the namesake. And the old homestead was backed by a great orchard ... where one night in 1864 your grandmama buried a trunk containing the family silver."

A row of servants lined the foyer, maids in gray cotton dresses with frilly caps and starched white aprons, and an elderly black butler in a white coat. St. James took Savannah's hand in his soft grasp. "Unfortunately, the press of business necessitates my return to the office. Cicero—" The butler stepped forward. "Cicero will show you to your room. You will no doubt wish to rest and refresh yourself in preparation for the evening. The Baron will dine with us *en famille,* and I am certain your maman's repast will require all the stamina we can muster." He kissed her on the forehead and she followed Cicero upstairs.

Her room was on the right-hand side of the upper hallway and at the back of the house. It was a corner room, the windows on one side overlooking a cobbled side street. Across the back were high French doors opening onto an upper gallery where wisteria hung along the eaves. Beyond, she saw a walled garden where graveled paths wound among blossoming trees. The room was large and furnished with antiques. Her bed was a canopied four-poster, draped with mosquito netting. Through a half-opened door she could see her bath, a footed tub and a washbasin with a matching china pitcher. Turning to find Cicero standing at attention like a soldier on guard duty, she said, "Thank you, Cicero. I don't need anything now."

His accent was very much like her father's. "Missy, if you wants to rest, I recommend you shuts the doahs. They's gonna be a fracas when Miz St. James git home and find we's havin' company fo' dinna. She like to spend two, three days gittin' ready."

He looked older than her father. She said, "Did you come to Brazil to keep from being Reconstructed?"

"No'm. He come fetch me when he build this house. I 'member the old place right good."

The groan of wagon wheels on the driveway announced the arrival of the luggage. Cicero excused himself and closed her door.

Manco's case was locked. She took his coat and shoes from her carpetbag, rolled them as small as she could, and put them inside one of the pillowcases under her white cotton bedspread; then she dropped the locked case behind the bathtub. By then the trousseau was arriving, trunk after trunk being carried into the room by the servants. Veronique, looking harried, ordered Manuela to unpack them all and iron the wrinkles out of every last thing before she hung them up. Then, rolling her eyes and sighing heavily, Veronique went off to see to the evening's dinner. Clearly, there'd be no restful time this afternoon for any of the servants.

Cicero saw that Savannah got a tray of tea and sandwiches for lunch. After that she hung her hammock between two flowering trees in the walled garden and lay there waiting for her father to return, firming up her speech to him and trying not to listen to the clatter and shrieking coming from the kitchen, until the late afternoon rain drove her indoors.

Her father found her in the library looking at a family Bible with all the names and dates of birth and death inscribed on the flyleaf. He chided her, saying their guests would be arriving soon. But Savannah said, "Why didn't you keep it up? You didn't add my name."

He sank into an old pine rocker near his desk. Looking tired and pale, he said, "There seemed no point; everything was gone."

"May I?" He shrugged. She took the book to his desk and dipped a pen in the inkwell. She wrote: *Savannah St. James, born 31st January, 1880*. "Was I born in this Arcadia?"

His voice was faint with exhaustion. "No, I hadn't built it. You were born downriver, at Pará."

"And when did Aunt Madelyn die?"

"Six years ago."

She added Madelyn's death. "And Maman and you were married . . . ?"

He yawned, and apologized, adding, "Eighteen seventy-nine."

She'd barely finished adding *Veronique Mercier, of Paris*, when Cicero came into the room. He'd brought her father a drink filled with ice. After he'd set the tray down on a table near the rocker, he opened the shutters, saying softly as he passed her, "You best git upstairs, missy, or you be in big trouble!" She nodded, but after he left she looked down at the Bible again. "I can't imagine it, you know."

St. James took a long drink, put down the glass, and leaned back in the chair, his eyes closed. "Can't imagine what?"

"Seeing the Baron's name here. I can't imagine myself married to a fifty-year-old man I don't even know."

He took another drink. "In another hour you'll know him."

She went to him and knelt down at his side. "Why couldn't

you have waited until I got home? Why couldn't you have told me first so we could talk it over? It's my life! Can't you see how I feel?" His forehead was damp with perspiration and he'd grown so pale the circles around his eyes stood out like stains. She said, "Father, are you ill?"

He lifted his hand and let it fall to his knee. "No cause for alarm. Benign tertian malaria, they call it. The attacks come every two or three days. Enervating, but not necessarily fatal, unless complications develop." He opened his eyes. "But it explains my haste to settle you in life. A prudent marriage is the only guarantee a woman has." Shivering, he reached for the shawl draped across the back of his chair. She helped him wrap it around his shoulders.

"I had no idea you were so sick, Father. I didn't mean to trouble you. But I see now—it's all the more reason for me to stay here and look after you. Maman isn't—I mean, I could help you. I write a good hand. Maybe in your business I might—"

He shook his head. "Rio Mar Rubber is not in need of additional employees, and a well-born woman's place—"

"I thought you were in banking."

"I am indeed, child. I am the treasurer of the company, charged with responsibility for overseas investments."

"We can talk tomorrow, when you're feeling better," she said. "Shall I call Cicero? Shouldn't you go to bed?"

"No, no. It will pass. Now you really must prepare yourself to greet our guests. Dom Luíz sets great store on punctuality." As she shut the door, she saw him racked by a fit of shivering.

16

Dom Luíz mounted the wide stairway of the Palácio, pausing a moment on the landing where the gilt frame entitled DONA SAVANNAH hung empty. *Soon*, he thought; *less than an hour now*.

He was glad the photographs had shown a spare, athletic girl. The long, almost gaunt oval of the face, the direct cool gaze, the slim body: a Botticelli woman.

If the girl herself fulfilled the promise of her photographs, he would in gratitude name their first son after Botticelli.

Alessandro. Sandro Aurélio. And one day he would take the boy to Florence and show him the paintings of his namesake.

The Baron's bath had been prepared. The pink Carrara marble tub was deeply sunken: He bathed like a Roman. Dropping his clothing, he stepped into the water, steaming with the scent of herbs. Juana, who was thirty-five but still beautiful, bent gracefully to collect his garments. Then she waited in the alcove, watching to see if he needed anything.

Savannah was like virgin clay crying for his molding hand. She must, he determined, move gracefully—even if he had to have her trained for years like a ballerina. He must allocate sufficient time to her training, quickly, before the soporific effects of motherhood impaired her malleability. Pregnant and nursing women, he had found, were unresponsive—as stolid and ruminant as cattle.

Unfortunately there was little time. He must have another heir quickly, now that he knew Porfirio was hopeless. It was not the drinking, nor his dreaminess, his inability to cope with business matters; others, pretentious bookkeepers like Edward St. James, could be paid to keep accounts. It was, rather, Porfirio's tragic impotence.

His horror at the boy's tendency was an enigma even to himself. His response, some months ago, on finding his heir prone under the body of his manservant had been devoid of reason. Dom Luíz had beaten him personally, whipped him until the blood flowed. He had nearly killed him, but some instinct stayed his hand. Then he'd watched while the servant was castrated and thrown into the river.

Later he was ashamed of his rage. He'd tried to save Porfirio, sending the best women he had to the boy's bed, but it was hopeless. By then the negotiations to obtain Porfirio a bride were well along. Dom Luíz had thought it might be amusing to marry his son to the St. James child. Certainly there was good blood there; the children would be fair-skinned and aristocratic-looking. In the depth of the Baron's despair, the girl's photographs arrived. From that moment the problem was solved: His own virility was not in question. When he had another heir he would dispose of Porfirio. If thine eye offend thee, Scripture said, pluck it out. Meanwhile there was this anarchist to dispose of so that he could devote his full attention to a possibly arduous, but fruitful honeymoon.

Juana had laid out his formal dinner clothing and stood ready to assist him. He said, "Get Raoul and the others. I want them all." When he came out of his dressing room, they were waiting for him: six strong young men in dark business suits. João, the oldest, was Porfirio's bodyguard. Dom Luíz said, "Is he sober?"

"Yes, Master. I have not left him these past two days. Juana is dressing him now." João was Juana's brother, the two of them having been conceived by the housekeeper Ana in Pernambuco. Jaime and Ignacio were mestizos; both had inherited the high cheekbones and warm copper coloring of their mother, who was a beautiful Shipibo Indian. Nero, who had from childhood been bodyguard to Dona Esmeralda, Baron's only daughter, was black, broad-nosed, full-lipped, mute and faithful; badly frightened at the age of twelve, he hadn't spoken since. Mario, the youngest, was a quadroon, three-quarters white and so fair he could have passed for Portuguese. Then there was Raoul, half Chinese, with dark gleaming hair and skin the color of antique ivory. Raoul was the most valuable of the lot; he thought like his father.

Dom Luíz suppressed a smile and turned to the jewel case on the chest of drawers, but as he selected the diamond studs for his shirt he watched the six men reflected in the large mirror before him. He felt a rush of pride. Their strength was the embodiment of his sexual vitality. There was no limit to his power; his fecundity, like the *selva*'s was inexhaustible. After he'd slipped his arms into the tailed jacket Jaime held for him, he said, "You may approach." One by one they kissed his ring, a three-carat black diamond set in silver. Then he seated himself in the tall red velvet chair beside which Juana had left his glass of sherry.

"I am no longer angry," he said. "Since I had instructed you to give the operation the appearance of official action, there was nothing you could do when the police mishandled the arrest." After Ignacio struck a match for the Baron's black Bahia cigar and stepped back, he continued. "And by tracking down the shipment listed on the ship's manifest, Raoul has given us a delicious bit of bait. Now we must, with care and precision, set the trap."

"Your Grace," Raoul said, "we have already tripled the guard on the Customs Warehouse."

Dom Luíz's steel-gray eyes were patient. "Could not even our stupid police chief do as much? Do you take this anarchist for an idiot? Why should he so foolishly jeopardize himself?"

Mario, who was prone to excitement, said, "He's no fool, and he outnumbers us. The rabble in the streets and on the river come to his aid. He could send a mob upon the ware-house—"

Ignacio frowned. "Then we would lose him and his guns as well."

Dom Luíz ignored them, keeping his gaze on Raoul, who said, "Then we must move the guns, but still devise to trap him there."

The Baron smiled. Raoul went on. "After dark tonight—"

"No, my son. In daylight. Now." On the driveway below the windows, the Baron's carriage halted. He rose and drew the watch from his pocket. "What shipment did we have aboard the *Esperança?*"

Raoul answered. "Petrol for Dom Porfirio's motor car. Twelve casks of wine from Portugal. Four hundred rose-bushes and the English boxwood hedges. Danish butter, cheeses—"

Dom Luíz raised his hand from the doorway. "Fill the anarchist's crates with sand and put his guns and ammunition under the roots of the hedge and rosebushes. Then bring them here, in open wagons, slowly through the streets. Now, Raoul, while it is still light. Then, when the warehouse has been stormed and our enemy finds that we have tricked him . . . he will come to us himself in search of rosebushes."

Savannah heard the carriage arrive. Footsteps sounded on the front steps and crossed the gallery; then the empty carriage rattled away. She had dutifully bathed and dressed, put-ting on the mauve chiffon evening dress Maman had laid out. Then, since dinner demanded Maman's attention, she'd been allowed to do her own hair. Before she'd gotten into the tub, she'd piled it up with combs; now it hung in moist tangles around her face and down the back of her neck. She decided to leave it that way. Perhaps if she looked sufficiently untidy, the Baron would lose interest in her and her problem would be solved.

A church bell rang, reverberating in the evening air. Where was Manco now? She must go downstairs. On the other hand, maybe she should be unpunctual as well as untidy. But in a few minutes Maman sent a kitchen maid to call her, and there was nothing to do but go down.

Hearing her step, the Baron left the drawing room and stood in the foyer. When she caught sight of him she stopped, still halfway up the staircase. There was no mistaking him. His eyes were the color of ashes and his pointed beard looked metallic. The eyes widened, then narrowed, and he turned back toward her father to nod briefly in approval. Then he mounted the stairs and took her hand. "Welcome, Senhorita Savannah." He lifted her fingers to his lips, fixing his cold gaze upon her. His gray eyes seemed to draw her into their depths. and as she watched them a chill spread upward from the middle of her body toward her throat. "We have been waiting for you most anxiously, my dear. Your photographs did not begin to do you justice." His Portuguese accent was soft and his voice was smooth and rich as honey, but without its sweetness.

"Savannah, have you lost your tongue?" That was Veronique, who seemed fascinated by her daughter's coiffure, but laughed nervously and said, "She is overcome, Dom Luíz."

Savannah, like an actress struggling to remember her lines, opened her mouth. "*Boa tarde*, Senhor Baron."

The young man standing with her father in the drawing room doorway said, "No, no! Not Portuguese! My father have decreed, for the senhorita all speak the English!" He was dressed like the Baron in white tie and tails, but he'd added a scarlet cummerbund and a large red flower in his buttonhole. He shifted his glass of champagne to his left hand and reached out to greet her. Breaking away from the Baron, she took Porfirio's hand. She said, "Does this decree apply throughout South America or only in Brazil?"

He kissed her hand and said, "Throughout the states of Amazonas and Pará of Brazil, I think." She liked his dark liquid eyes and his childlike, anxious smile, and when they moved into the drawing room she contrived to sit beside him. The Baron remained standing. He took a glass of claret from Cicero's tray and leaned upon the mantelpiece watching her.

Noting the absence of the Baron's daughter, Veronique said, "I had no idea Dona Esmeralda had gone already."

Dom Luíz did not look at her, but rather continued to examine Savannah. "It is a girlish whim. The novitiate is sufficiently long for her to outgrow it."

Porfirio waved his empty glass, but Cicero did not respond. Seeing his eyes, round as the eyes of a child who finds some adult ruling incomprehensible, Savannah asked him to tell her all about Manáos. When dinner was announced, she took Porfirio's arm. Her father almost spoke, but the Baron shook his head and offered his arm to Veronique.

The crystal chandelier cast a soft prismatic light upon the room, and in the shadows four servants stood ready to wait

upon them. As the meal progressed Savannah saw a new side
to Veronique: She was a gourmet cook. In a few hours she'd
created a meal so remarkable there was little time for conversation, except to exclaim over the dishes. There were so many
courses that Savannah lost count. The fish, under its mush-
rooms and sherry sauce, looked whole, but had in fact been
boned, sliced, fried in a delicate batter, and reassembled on
the plate complete with head and tail. The fish was followed
by stuffed birds; these two looked whole but had their bones
removed. And after that there was a roast. Beef, Veronique
said, braised in Port.

Savannah, after years of porridge, barley soup, and pots of
stew all served with boiling cups of tea, passed nothing up and
by the end of the last entrée felt as stuffed as the poor boneless birds. Then to her dismay dessert arrived: individual swan
boats made of sweet pastry frosted white and filled with coffee-
flavored mousse covered with whipped cream and shavings of
milk chocolate made to look like dark feathers in the swans'
down.

Another source of her dismay was the wines. When they'd
taken their places, they had found a row of glasses upturned,
and as the meal progressed they'd been filled one after another. Chablis with the oysters, Amontillado with the soup,
Sauterne with the fish; then two more red wines and another
white, followed by champagne with the dessert and cognac
with the coffee. By then the world had taken on an indistinct
glow, and she heard the conversation of the others like the
furry-edged cooing of the doves on the convent roof. She
found herself smiling at everyone, and she had to resist a
mighty impulse to invite the servants to sit down for a glass of
cognac.

After coffee had been handed around a second time, the
men were offered cigars. At that Veronique rose to leave.
Seeing that Savannah had not risen also, Maman said, "Savannah, will you join me in the drawing room?"

"No, thank you, Maman." She smiled around in the silence,
but she had the impression her smile was on crooked.

Her father said, "Miss Savannah, you will leave the gentlemen to smoke their cigars now."

She put her elbow on the table and propped her chin in her
cupped hand. "It's lovely here. I don't ever want to leave."

St. James frowned, but the Baron intervened. "My child, in
themselves these formalities may appear meaningless, but
upon reflection you will see it is our cultivated manners which

separate us from the barbarous classes of society." She felt him grasp her by the waist and lift her to her feet. Though powerful, he was not tall, and her eyes were nearly level with his. She raised her chin. "Then no doubt I should have been born a savage, for I dislike formalities." But he led her from the room and put her down in a loveseat in the drawing room, where she immediately fell asleep.

The next thing she remembered was Maman taking her upstairs to bed and scolding her furiously while getting her into her nightgown.

17

Sometime later she was awakened. Her mind was murky and her body numb. There was a sound beyond the mosquito netting of her bed. Gradually in the dim light from the lamp on her vanity she discerned someone standing in the room. It was the Baron. "Do not be alarmed," he said. "I wished to be certain you are well. And I have not as yet given you your gift of the day."

Lying in bed made her feel vulnerable, so despite the dizziness she forced herself to get up and face him. He took a velvet case from his pocket, opened it, and held it out to her. "These are for you, my dear."

On a background of black velvet lay a necklace of diamonds and amethysts, set in gold. The stones caught the lamplight and burned with intense, concentrated fire.

"I would like to see them on you." He removed the necklace from its case. "Lift up your hair." She felt his cool hands at the back of her neck, working the clasp. There was no fumbling, no awkwardness. In a moment he had removed her chain and its single pearl and fastened on the diamonds. He withdrew his hands. She looked down. The necklace rested on the bodice of her nightgown. She reached to straighten one of the stones, when Dom Luíz pushed her hand away. Untying the drawstring at the neck of her gown, he placed his hands on her shoulders and slowly pulled the nightgown down until the necklace lay upon her bare skin, just above her breasts. She trembled. He did not take his hands away, but leaned forward and kissed her shoulder. His beard rasped against her flesh.

She felt weak and giddy.

He lifted his head and looked into her eyes. Placing one hand under her chin, he leaned forward, his mouth slightly open, pressing his parted lips against her mouth. He drew back and smiled. "You do not know about kisses. I shall teach you." His fingers had begun to stray. "I shall tune you, little one. I shall play you like a fine instrument." His voice grew hoarse. He slid his hands from her shoulders and drew the gown down all the way until it fell at her feet. Back a step, he gazed slowly down and up again. His voice now soft as a sigh, he murmured, "Beyond imagination. Magnificent!" Savannah was transfixed, frozen, helpless. He loosened her hair and arranged it, draping a strand along one shoulder and coiling the longest tendrils around her left thigh. "My Venus," he sighed, "blown in from the sea." When he reached his hands to her again, moving them slowly over her body, over her shoulders and her breasts, down beyond her waist, beyond her belly, she threw back her head and cried, "No, you must stop, please don't do this." Then he touched her most private place and she recoiled; her hand flew out and struck him hard across the face.

Instantly he clutched her hair with one hand and dragged her head backward until her body arched against him. Close to her face he said through grinding teeth, "You will never raise your hand to me again. Never! Do you understand?" He twisted her body back and down until she moaned. Slowly he released his hold. Calm now, no trace of anger in his honeyed voice, he said, "There is no need for your lessons to be painful, my dear, unless you choose. It is up to you."

Once again he kissed her. She stood like a statue while cold hands caressed her back, her buttocks, her loins. "Good," he said. "Much better." Tremors ran the length of her. But she did not move. "Still," he said, drawing back, "you do not deserve this necklace. Later perhaps, if you learn your lessons well." Deftly he unclasped the catch and dropped the diamonds into their box. "We will see how you behave tomorrow."

When he'd closed the door behind him she sank to the floor. Hunched and shivering, she moaned and rocked herself and cried. But after a time she stopped and struggled to get hold of herself. Her head was clearer now, but she could not forget his touch. Her flesh crawled with it. She went into the bath and washed her face, trying not to catch sight of her image in the mirror, for she felt that if she looked at herself just once, she would be ill.

The house was quiet now. She locked the French windows, turned the key in her door, and put a table against it. Then she put her nightgown on again and got into bed. She fell asleep sitting straight up in the corner against the wall, wearing Manco's coat and holding his locked case in her arms.

The Baron was smoking the last cigar of the day. It was one o'clock in the morning. He had enjoyed the evening.

How like Madelyn she was. Even for blood relatives, such a resemblance was uncanny, far more than he'd seen in the photographs. It was the coloring, the hair of burnished copper and the eyes like amethysts; and the way she carried her head—like an Egyptian queen.

He'd almost forgotten the pain of losing Madelyn; he'd almost forgotten the way she made him feel . . . helpless in the face of her implacable hatred. Yet, after all these years, how marvelously it was working out. A second chance, now that he was older, wiser, and more implacable himself. This time he would not be carried away, either by passion or by rage.

Raoul knocked softly on the bedroom door and entered the firelit room. Dom Luíz sat in the high-backed Spanish chair by the hearth. It was unusual for him to be disturbed at this hour. He looked up. "How did it go?"

"Badly, Excellency. I did not wish to interrupt your evening."

"Then tell me now."

Raoul's face, smooth as an ivory carving, betrayed no feeling, but his voice was very low. "In the confusion at the dock today your cargo was not unloaded from the Esperança. When I insisted that Your Excellency urgently desired to have the shrubbery planted at once. . . ." Dom Luíz drummed his long nails on the wooden arm of his chair. Raoul ran his fingers through his straight black hair. "To get the shrubs unloaded, I was forced to round up our own men. Gardeners, mostly. The rest are upriver guarding the landings. By the time we'd gotten the cargo ashore, it had grown dark. I considered waiting until daylight, but I disliked the look of the streets around the dock. Some religious procession with fireworks and holy relics, with sufficient noise and confusion to mask an attack on the warehouse. I felt certain the guns would not be safe there through the night. And with that pageant going on, there'd be witnesses enough to accomplish your purpose."

"And?"

"Two blocks from the warehouse we found an oxcart with a broken axle blocking the street. A drunken mob of masked dancers began snatching at the bushes, carrying them on their heads and throwing them about. Then someone uncovered a gun." The Baron's lips grew white behind his beard. "Within two or three minutes all four of our wagons had been overturned and pillaged. They made off with the guns and ammunition and left your shrubbery all over the street."

Dom Luíz threw his cigar into the fire. "Your ignorance astounds me. But then, your mother was a pagan." Raoul's cheeks flushed, but he said nothing. "Do you not know there are no religious festivals on December twenty-third? The *festa* is tomorrow night, Christmas Eve, after the midnight Mass." He drummed upon his armchair again. "What kind of guns were they?"

"The latest British army rifles, Lee-Enfields and Lee-Metfords. Magazine, with ten cartridges."

"And we were not even astute enough to damage them before we let him have them back. How many were there?"

"Three hundred, Excellency."

"Three hundred?" He leaped from his chair, crossed the room, and returned to stare into the fire. At last he said, "What is this madman planning? A war?"

Raoul sighed heavily. "Your Grace, there is more. They got Nero." The Baron had taken another cigar from the box on the mantel. Now he stopped with it halfway to his mouth. Raoul cleared his throat and went on. "I don't know how it happened. I was in the first wagon and he was at the rear. When it was all over, he was gone. I reported the kidnapping to the police at once so we could search—"

Dom Luíz flung out his arm, striking Raoul backhanded and knocking his head back so forcibly that Raoul nearly lost his footing; but he righted himself and stood looking at the hearth. His hands hung limp at his sides, not clenched into fists; but the color had risen in his cheeks.

A muscle quivered near the Baron's right eye. "Idiot! Now all the world will know." He'd broken the fresh cigar; he threw it into the flames. "I have overestimated you, Raoul. You are just as stupid as the others. He's tricked us twice in a single day." But as he turned from the fire he began to laugh. "He's got himself a prisoner who can't talk, a mute! They can torture him till Hell freezes. Mother of God, that's marvelous!" Raoul raised his eyes to stare at his father; then he blinked slowly and looked away. Dom Luíz said, "I see I shall have to take personal charge if this matter is to be cared for properly, though God knows this is scarcely the time. Have we gotten the reports from upriver?"

"Bartolomeu has just arrived."

"I'll see him myself. In the study."

Bartolomeu hadn't slept or eaten or bathed. He stood in the high-ceilinged room, not on the carpet, but just off the edge of it, twisting his palm-fiber hat and shifting his feet in an effort to hide the marks his rubber shoes had made on the gleaming floor. He studied the parquetry, inlaid patterns of yellow, brown, and deep red woods. He wondered how it had been made, all the tiny pieces, and so smooth.

Dom Luíz sat behind his immense rosewood desk. "Well, Bartolomeu?"

Now that he had permission to speak, the words he'd been rehearsing during his three-day trip downriver seemed to tumble over one another in an effort to escape. "Senhor Baron, at every *seringal* it is the same. A Sunday comes when the manager has the store open for trading and the launch ready to bring the rubber to Manáos, but not one *seringueiro* comes. So the manager and his men go looking for them, but they do not find them. Their huts are deserted. Every tapper is gone."

The polished thumbnail of the Baron's right hand moved restlessly, twisting his black ring, but his voice remained calm. "They will appear. The *selva* will give them back to me. When they take to the river, we will find them." He leaned forward, fixing his glittering eyes on the man before him. "And when that happens, Bartolomeu, I want their experience to be a lesson for every other tapper on the Amazon. I am angry, Bartolomeu. Do you hear? Spread the word wherever you go. Their punishment will be a work of art. It will become a legend told at night around the campfires of every tributary, every canoe path . . . a legend ensuring that no one ever again will flee the estradas of the Baron do Rio Mar. In the meantime, the rains have begun. This means we need not feed them through the wet season. When the rains end and my trees can once again be tapped, I will gather more workers. Give Raoul a list of the landings in need of tappers and the number required at each of them." Bartolomeu moistened his cracked lips to speak, but Dom Luíz did not stop. "There must be hundreds of Indian villages we have not found. And the drought in Ceará increases. Men are hungry there. My representatives will promise them good wages, and they will come to me—do not fear, Bartolomeu." Dom Luíz waved him away.

As Bartolomeu closed the door behind him, Dom Luíz became aware of Raoul standing silently nearby. "Leave me," he said. Juana had moved noiselessly into the room and was building up the fire. He told her to bring him coffee, then for the rest of the night he smoked, deep in thought, his eyes fixed upon the map. At dawn he called Raoul in and said, "What do we know of the Rio Escondido?"

"Only that it is useless. The *selva* there is full of headhunters. One man, a Colombian, tried to set up an estrada there. He kept finding his tappers' torsos. The rest he never found. And even if he'd succeeded in gathering the rubber, his costs would have been prohibitive. Every boat must be unloaded and carried around the rapids they call the Devil's Cauldron."

Dom Luíz stared at the map through a veil of smoke. "Look. The map is incomplete there, but it appears the upper reaches of the Rio Maranhas veer close to the headwaters of the Escondido. . . . Did you not say there was a rumor that this Manco—"

Raoul nodded. "That he was trying to build a railroad there."

"Wire Rio at once. Say there is a well-armed insurrection here. We need weapons on a par with his." Dom Luíz was up and pacing. "Have St. James transfer sufficient funds to London. I want five hundred British rifles on the next ship out."

Dom Luíz went to his bedroom, but he was not tired. He sent for one of the kitchen girls and took her to his bed. An hour later he had Semiramis saddled.

The sapopema tree stands on roots so large and tangled and so high above the ground that whole rooms are formed, with walls, doors, and windows. So, as the Baron eased Semiramis into a gallop down a long gallery of jungle beyond his gardens, he was unaware that someone had been waiting for him. The man stepped so suddenly from the sapopema tree and into the path of Semiramis that she shied and nearly threw her master.

Dom Luíz reined in and held her until she stopped wheeling and came to rest, then he looked at the intruder angrily. A *caboclo*. The word meant copper-colored. He was half naked, of course, and barefoot. But this man was tall; a tall Indian is a contradiction in terms. And the moustache framing his mouth . . . Indians are not hairy. The Baron mockingly doffed his broad-brimmed hat. "Have I the honor to address Senhor Manco?"

"You have something of mine."

"And you are trespassing."

Manco laughed. "Spoken like a true *conquistador*, Baron. Take it and it is yours! I want Tomás. You will release him at once, and in good condition."

The Baron smiled. "Why should I do that? Are you proposing an exchange? I am not interested. I will break your man before you break mine. Or has that mulatto already talked for you?"

"An exchange requires items of comparable value. I am not so foolish as to believe that a man responsible for the death of whole villages—whole tribes—would be willing to deal in single lives . . . even the life of a natural son. No: I propose an exchange of something I value for something you value. An Indian for a warehouse." Dom Luíz watched him, not masking his distaste. High above them, where the straight trunks branched out into the forest canopy, monkeys chattered among the leaves. Manco said, "Unfortunately, you have a number of warehouses, separated by thousands of miles of river. It will be difficult for you to know which one is in jeopardy. And since they are all full . . . I suggest you see that Tomás is free by midnight tonight." Manco turned his back upon him. Before he'd gone two steps, Dom Luíz had drawn the pistol he wore when riding, but he barely got it free of its holster. There was no sound, but he dropped the gun, his hand impaled by a slender dart fired by an unseen blowgun.

Manco said, "The *selva* is a dangerous place for those who do not belong here. I suggest you get that attended to quickly, or you may lose an arm."

Dom Luíz slashed Semiramis's flanks with his spurs.

18

The men came no more to the room with walls and a floor without the river under it. Instead, an old Indian woman tended Tomás. She was not of his people, but she spoke Tupi, which many Indians of the forest understand, just as those of the mountains all understand Manco's language, the speech of the Inca people.

This woman bathed his body with infusions of plants, wrapped his wounds in leaves, fed him tea made of the bark of trees. To the worst places she applied hot oil from the copaiba palm. It stopped the pain. Soon he began to eat the farinha gruel she prepared for him, and he was able to get up from the floor and lie in the hammock she brought. Now whenever he opened his eyes she was sitting in a corner of the room on a low stool. In the hottest part of the day she fanned him with palm leaves.

He said, "Old woman, why are you doing this?" She did not answer. She bent over a clay pot filled with leaves, using a stone to bruise them. She wore a faded dress of cotton. Mission clothes. Was this a mission? Sometimes the rubber shippers took them over, drove out the priests, and enslaved all the Indians. Once he thought he heard the whistle of a steamer. He said, "Old woman, where am I?" She poured hot water over the leaves and stirred them with care. He said, "Is this a mission?"

After a time she said, "You will drink this now."

He did as she said. Then he said, "I want meat."

He watched her leave. She knocked on the heavy wooden door. The covering of a small barred opening slid back and a man looked in. Then the door was unlocked and opened a few inches. She went through and the door was closed and locked again. He never saw the guard's face.

Tomás got up from the hammock and examined the room. The floor was stone and the walls were solid hardwood. The one window was very high. He could see nothing there but sky through the bars. It was day and the sky was clear. He smelled the *selva*. The heavy scent of rotting foliage was nearby. And he smelled something else. Dung. Hay. Horses.

The old woman returned with meat. Not tapir or capibara or even manatee. No; it was white man's meat, the flesh of cow. He ate it anyway. He knew he would need his strength. He knew the men would return.

After he ate, he rested again. The woman awakened him from time to time to change the medicine on his wounds. They were healing well; there was almost no pain now. While she worked he heard the thunder and the incessant drumming of the evening rain. He lay still with his eyes closed, but he could not sleep. He heard the guards outside his door. He heard them cough, spit, talk to each other, and sometimes snore against the wall. And he heard the whinny of horses, heard them snuffle in their sleep. He tried to count the number of guards, to isolate their voices, to recognize which ones left and which ones came to relieve them. He could not; there were too many.

He tried not to think, but as more days passed and his strength grew, fear deepened in his heart. The *selva* and the rivers were too vast: Manco would never find him. The men would return and torture him and make him well and torture him again.

Once again he searched the cell, looking this time for something with which to destroy himself. There was nothing. He made up his mind to die. He would not eat again, no matter what they did to him. Like an old man of the tribe, he would lie down, close his eyes, and not move until he died.

But that night, as he lay sleepless with fear, he heard the uru bird crying repeatedly from the forest and his heart leaped with gladness for what the Indians know and the white men do not: The uru bird never sings at night. Manco had found him.

Yet the anguish of Tomás had not yet ended. The next morning the men returned. With them was an old one, a man with a gray, pointed beard and bandages around his right hand. This man, smiling in a way that showed his teeth, told Tomás in great detail of all the things that would be done to him if he did not tell them everything about Manco and the Rio Escondido. By the time they left him, all the old wounds were open again.

Savannah awakened trembling. She'd had a frightening dream. She was walking along a cobbled street, carrying schoolbooks. She must have been very small, because the people she passed were all much taller than she was. A servant, a black girl in maid's uniform, followed her, but had stopped to talk to a young man. Savannah heard them laughing together behind her. Then suddenly someone or something very dark reached out from a doorway and grabbed her. Everything was black and she could not scream. She felt certain she was going to die.

Awake now, she shook her mind free of the nightmare. She'd had it before, many times. But not for several years; it had stopped sometime during her early years at the convent. It doubtless had come back now because yesterday she'd been thinking about her life, and . . . the memory of last night struck her like a blow.

The table was still across the door into the hall, but she did not feel safe. She put Manco's coat and bag away once more, made the bed, and got dressed. Her head ached and she had a terrible taste in her mouth. No sound came from the house. She sat on her bed and waited.

Gradually she began to hear noises from the city, the shriek of a steamboat on the river, the screech of rusty axles on wagons, a church bell. Later she heard the cries and clacking sticks of the vendor who came along the street, bringing fresh produce to the kitchen doors of the houses. At last she heard Cicero's slow step in the upper hallway. She unlocked her door and asked him if her father was awake.

"Yas'm, but he be leavin' soon fo' business, directly he have his coffee. Miz St. James still sleepin'. Yo'all wants some breakfast?"

She shook her head and went downstairs. Her father was in the dining room, sitting at the table drinking his coffee and reading a newspaper. He looked up coldly as she drew a chair close to him and sat down. He said, "I see you have recovered from your inebriation. I hope you are fully aware of the scandalousness of your behavior and are prepared with ample apologies."

"He came to my room and took my clothes off!"

His face, always pale, turned ashen. She began to tell him more, but he waved for silence and ordered the maid standing near the sideboard to leave the room. He watched the girl close the door into the kitchen, then turned to Savannah. "How dare you?" His voice was quiet, but he was trembling with anger. "How dare you say such a shocking thing?"

"It's true! He said he'd come to give me a necklace, but then he—" Her head hurt worse than ever, her body felt clammy, and she was afraid she was going to be sick. Swallowing hard to control her nausea, she told him everything she could remember. He kept shaking his head and interrupted her repeatedly, taking issue with her story at several points. When she came to the end, he looked at her with disgust. "I had no idea your response to alcohol was so excessive. We shall see to it that you do not have access to spirits again. Frankly, I find your erotic fancies—"

Her voice rising, she cried, "It happened! It happened exactly as I told you!"

"Hush, do you hear me? You will not attract the attention of the entire household to your aberrations, is that clear?"

She reached for his hand, but he drew it away. She said, "Surely you saw him leave the room. I have no idea what time it was, but certainly he was gone for some minutes—"

Dryly he said, "Even a nobleman must respond to the call of nature from time to time."

"He came to my room. He did exactly as I have told you."

Even his smile was sarcastic. "Then perhaps you'll be good enough to produce this diamond necklace."

"He took it away!"

"I see." He stood and folded his newspaper neatly. "Miss Savannah, I find your behavior appalling. If you are not suffering from deranged sensibilities, then you are guilty of an even worse crime—slander. To malign a generous benefactor with such accusations. . . ."

She stood in his path. "All right, don't believe me! I don't care!"

For a moment they stared at each other; then he turned away. He walked to a window and looked out. His fists were clenched at his sides and he was breathing with difficulty. She saw his hands relax. When he turned around again, he was smiling. He moved to her side and put his arm around her. He threw up his hands in dismay. "Forgive me, my child. I have perhaps been unduly harsh. I can see you are not feeling well. No doubt the change of climate has been taxing to your constitution. Rest, and your maman's excellent cuisine—"

"He makes me sick. He's disgusting. And he frightens me."

He drew her toward the foyer. Cicero stood waiting with a straw hat and an umbrella. Beyond the opened door she saw the gig stopped in the drive. In a new tone of voice St. James said, "A marvelous day. Where else can you have a picnic supper and a game of croquet on Christmas Eve? The formal gardens at the Palácio will astonish you, my dear!"

He bent to kiss her forehead, but she said, "Didn't you hear? I'm not going anywhere that man is."

"Cicero, Miss Savannah is quite exhausted. She'll spend the morning in her room until I return. See that she's not disturbed." He rested his hand on her shoulder. "You rest now, you hear? There'll be fireworks and a pageant after midnight Mass."

Cicero opened the door from her room to the upper gallery and hung her hammock where she could look over the garden. There, she was protected from the side street, for the end of the gallery was blocked by a wall to ensure privacy. But near the garden wall, at the corner where the lower gallery began, a gnarled stem of wisteria grew out of the ground and climbed across the back of the house. After Cicero brought her coffee and some aspirin and she'd begun to feel better, she lay in the hammock watching the clusters of wisteria blossoms hanging above her like bunches of pale lavender grapes. She recalled what Will had said: Get out your sketchpad; work is the great panacea.

But her misery was too deep. Clearly she would get no more help from her father than she had from Veronique. That meant the idea of running away was no longer a vague speculation. What had Will told her about the passage money? How long would it take the *Esperança* to sail all the way up the Amazon to Peru and return? If Dr. Haversham would help her get on board . . . no, he'd said it wouldn't do for a woman to go knocking about the world.

She felt betrayed by everybody, by those shipboard acquaintances who wished her well, by her parents who didn't seem to care, and most of all by Manco. He alone was not afraid of the Baron, he alone knew the evil here, so his leaving her to this fate was the deepest and most painful abandonment.

Beyond the garden wall, beyond the other trees and houses, the jungle rose against the sky, an impenetrable wall of green above which vultures fluttered like black flags. Gradually she became aware of a voice, a man's voice singing. How long had it been going on, unnoticed? The house was still, now that the clatter of breakfast pot-cleaning had ended; but someone was ironing there by the woodburning stove, for Savannah smelled the sharp scent of hot fabric. The man, wherever he was, sang in English. Might it be the gardener? She sat up to look, but there was no one in sight in the garden. Then she caught a few words, a phrase, something about the tears of the moon.

Springing out of the hammock, she leaned over the gallery railing, twisting her body outward in order to see the side street. Shuffling along the cobblestones there was a blind man. White cane, battered cup, smoke-blackened spectacles showing under the brim of his ragged hat, and a small gray monkey on his shoulder. The main stem of the wisteria was sturdy. She got down to the top of the garden wall and knelt to look more closely at the man, her pounding heart far ahead of her senses. It was Manco.

The wall was high, but she jumped anyway, landing on all fours on the cobblestones. Hearing the thud she made, he turned, rattling his cup in her direction and saying, "Alms? Alms?" Tapping the cane along the paving he came toward her and she got up to meet him, oblivious of the stinging impact on her hands and knees. Her impulse to throw herself into his arms was checked when he pulled the monkey from his shoulder and held it out to her. "You like my monkey, senhor or senhorita? You give Coco money for the song?"

There was no one in sight, but the shuttered windows of the houses along the street could hide watching eyes. She took the monkey in her arms and petted him. She said softly, "I was afraid you'd gone and I'd never see you." Coco watched her curiously, blinking his small eyes and making swift nervous gestures, taking the tiny cap from his head and slipping it back on again with the chin strap in place. He wore a sleeveless vest trimmed with tiny beads and braiding. As she looked down at him, a tear fell on his little vest and rolled along its edge.

Manco whispered, "Are you well?"

She shook her head, but couldn't find the words to tell him of her fear and anguish, so she said, "I have your things. How can I return them to you?"

"It's not important, unless they put you in jeopardy." He adjusted the brim of his hat with the hand holding his cup, covertly glancing along the garden wall. "Leave them in the wisteria there. I'll have someone pick them up after dark."

She could not read the expression of his eyes, but watching his mouth, she saw him bite his lip. She said, "Please, please take me away from here. I can't bear it—"

Coco had crawled out of her embrace and swung down her skirt to the ground. He'd seen the shoe she left behind when she fell; he scampered over and picked it up, turning it one way and another. Manco said, "I need your help. Will you do something for me?"

A carriage passed and turned the corner. Over the rattle of the wheels she said, "Of course."

"I need you to search the Baron's palace for a prisoner. Look for locked rooms, guards outside certain doors, outbuildings, the cellar. Ask to see the kitchens, food storage rooms, the wine cellar. See if a tray of food is prepared, anything that might indicate the presence of a prisoner."

"Missy Savannah!" It was Cicero. He was standing on the upper gallery near her empty hammock with her luncheon tray in his hands. He had not raised his voice; it was an urgent whisper. Perhaps Maman was nearby.

"I'm coming," she said, "but the monkey has my shoe."

Manco tapped his cane. "Coco! Where is monkey, senhorita?" Coco was sitting on the shoe, scratching himself and grinning. Savannah touched Manco's arm and, while Cicero watched by craning his body past the gallery wall, led the blind man toward Coco, saying, "I'm afraid he'll bite me. Make him give me my shoe." Together they reached down to pull the monkey away and get her shoe back on her foot and as they did she whispered, "A special prisoner or just anyone?"

"A young Indian, short and stocky, hair cut straight across the forehead, Tomás. Take no risks. Only look. Do not endanger yourself." Their hands touched.

Cicero leaned over the railing, his wrinkled old face tense. He whispered harshly, "How you git down here? How you gonna git back?" He set the tray down and paced helplessly along the gallery.

She touched the blind man's arm again. "Senhor, can you help me? I need to climb this wall." She led him over to it. He felt the stones, reaching up to measure the height. Then he formed his hands into a stirrup and lifted her high enough to reach the top. Cicero helped her up the last part of the wisteria, and when Maman came onto the gallery with an armload of freshly ironed sheets, Savannah was swinging languidly in her hammock.

When Father came home at midday, she said she'd thought it over and had decided a picnic at the Palácio would be enchanting.

19

At three in the afternoon Manáos had awakened from its midday *sesta*. It had rained intermittently, but now the sun glared upon the city's steaming avenues. The giant palms, cottonwoods, and eucalyptus trees were still, for there was no breeze to stir the humid air. Despite the heat the streets were filled with vehicles: hansom cabs, barouches, phaetons. And along the sidewalks crowds of people moved. Savannah, riding with her parents in the gig, was struck by the languor of their movements; unlike the people on the streets of Paris, the residents of Manáos sauntered along as if the day would never end.

Sketchpad in hand, she watched the buildings pass, the Grand Hotel Internacional, the impressive Bank of Manáos, the pale stucco structures washed in pastel shades—mauve trimmed with purple, pink with rose, sky blue with moss green. She saw every imaginable sort of shop: diamond sellers, hat and shoe emporiums, French modistes, bookstores, sweet shops. And drinking places: There seemed to be more of these than anything else.

Savannah peered out the window, and her attention was caught by a group of gaily clad women lounging in doorways and leaning out from the upper windows of a building. Savannah said, "Are those Gypsies?" Indeed, they were dressed the part, with stars spangling their gaudy dresses, jewelry twined about their bare arms and throats, and paint upon their faces.

Veronique sniffed. "No, not Gypsies."

As the gig passed the open doorway of a saloon, one of these women waved, laughing. Her teeth glittered; they'd been set with diamonds. Edward said, "Those are women of easy virtue, my dear."

The Palácio do Rio Mar, like all of Manáos, had been cleared from the jungle. It was, however, the largest residence, the one farthest removed from the heart of town, and hence the one closest to the *selva*. It faced the city; a fence of spear-shaped wrought-iron palings separated it from the street. As the gig circled the carriage drive, St. James, pleased by his daughter's keen interest, explained that it was a Renaissance palace of imported granite and marble.

Savannah, already at work on the floor plan in her head, made mental note of the resemblances to Greek temples she'd seen in history books. A flight of wide stone steps rose to a portico where fluted pillars supported a triangular pediment covered with sculpture. Above and beyond that, the roof swelled into a dome with wings two stories high on each side. There were statues everywhere, at the ends of the stone walls that flanked the steps, at the corners of the pediment and the roof, and stuck here and there among the shrubs around the circular drive.

As they entered, she saw that the foyer was overwhelming, more than two stories high and topped by the dome where, around a circular window that showed the sky, painted cupids looked down at her. On three sides of the entrance hall, marble pillars supported an upper balcony; then, at the back, a broad stairway came down from above in two, joined, and split again to reach the black and white tile floor of the foyer separately. Footmen in scarlet livery, kneebreeches, and white stockings stared unblinkingly ahead. She thought they looked like something out of "Cinderella."

The Baron, dressed this time in white linen with a ruffled shirt, was coming down the stairway. Porfirio followed, looking breathless and adjusting his sky-blue cummerbund. "*Mon dieu*," Veronique murmured, "we're early." Then louder: "You see, *chérie*, is it not as I have told you? Is it not a palace fit for any king?"

The Baron kissed Savannah's hand, looking into her eyes meaningfully as he said, "Welcome. I trust you slept well last night?"

Porfirio also greeted her with a kiss. He looked a bit worn, his olive complexion sallow around the eyes; but his eyes— deep brown with flecks of gold, like velvet by candlelight— glowed at seeing her.

By concentrating, she managed not to shudder when the Baron took her arm and drew her toward the back of the house. The others followed, speaking of the weather.

Tall doors across the back of the house opened to a veranda running the length of the building. Marble steps ran down into the gardens. The Baron said, "This is the loggia," and led her to a grouping of white chairs of cane and wicker, overhung with plants and caged songbirds.

Savannah walked to the balustrade. The gardens lifted gently toward the forest some half-mile away. The pathways made geometric designs. There were fountains sparkling in the sunshine and peacocks strutting; they paused from time to time as if listening to something. "What do you think of our home?" the Baron asked her.

"I can't wait to see it all."

Fortunately Veronique insisted on accompanying them on the tour of the upper floor. Veronique chattered constantly, drawing Savannah's attention to the paintings, the Venetian mirrors, the crystal chandeliers, the china, porcelain, and silver objects. Dom Luíz opened a door. "This is Dona Esmeralda's room." Though large, it was bare and white, like a nun's cell. Veronique picked up a small framed photograph of a young woman with a cloud of dark hair and wide, dark eyes. Savannah said, "Is this Esmeralda?"

"No," the Baron said. "That was her mother." Seeing Savannah watching him, he said, "I have been widowed twice. It is difficult to find strength in a woman. And I am demanding. So I outlive them."

As he led them to his Spanish bedroom, Maman said, "Savannah, you are not to open every door we pass. Regarding the closets is rude."

Savannah said, "What is this door?" The Baron smiled and showed them his marble bath. "And this one?" she said.

He opened the carved mahogany door and they stepped onto a small balcony above the nave of the family chapel. "This enables the Master to hear Mass without leaving his bedroom." The little church was almost dark. Savannah made out the altar, where three candles burned; the rest was lost in darkness.

"Now," she said, "I wish to see the kitchen."

The tour of the lower floor took a long time and proved fruitless. She saw not one kitchen, but three, each specializing in something, pastry or meat, or soup and salads, and there were nearly two dozen kitchen workers. She saw the storage rooms where garlic, onions, figs, and cheeses hung from the ceiling, fastened there with cords specially treated to repel ants; and the dusky cellars where wine was stored. She saw nothing she'd been looking for and, passing back through the kitchens again, she found it impossible to believe that these servants cranking churns of ices or spreading heaps of frosting could be conspirators. She said, "Now I want to explore the gardens."

Veronique, complaining of fatigue, went off to the loggia for a cool drink, so the two of them went on alone, through the offices where several young men in dark business suits were working. The Baron introduced her to Raoul, but simply recited the names of the others and moved on. In his study with its polished floor, high-backed velvet chairs, deep-red carpet, and heavy matching drapes, she felt ill at ease. The room seemed menacing; it reeked of the Baron. They moved on through the shrouded music room—unused, he said, in Esme's absence—to the greenhouse where he grew his orchids.

It was as if they'd stepped into the jungle. Some of the plants grew to the green glass ceiling two stories above. In the dim light she began to discern flowers that burned in the gloom around them, scarlet and crimson, gold, deep orange. His face dark and fervent, the Baron began explaining the orchid to her, showing her the lips, the ovaries. He spoke of fertility, cross-pollination, cross-breeding, inbreeding. He bent so close to her she could smell his breath, the scent of those black cigars. She moved away.

"Look here," he said. She saw on the thick trunk of the palm in front of them a pattern of blotches, diamond-shaped and golden. It was a snake. He grasped the creature with both hands. It was thick as his arm. He drew more and more of it from the tree until he held the entire length, some eight or nine feet; then he draped it around her body. Eyes glazed, she stood frozen, waiting. She felt the weight of the snake's body across the back of her shoulders and the chill spreading as it moved along the back of her neck. The triangular head waved back and forth across her breast, its forked tongue reaching out into the air. Determined to die with dignity, she murmured: "Is this the anaconda?"

He laughed. "Of course not. This is the boa, a fraction of the size of an anaconda, and quite harmless to humans. I would no more have an anaconda here than I would a crocodile." He took the boa's head and unwound the snake from Savannah's body, holding it a moment before allowing it to twine around the palm once more. "This boa is useful. It keeps the house free of rodents, but eats nothing we eat. For me, everything must be either useful or beautiful." His hands when he caressed her throat were as chill as the touch of the boa. "You, my love, are both." He pressed his mouth against her lips.

She broke away from him, careful to laugh. "But I haven't seen the gardens."

He caught her and pulled her close to him again. "How like Madelyn you are—but in a tight little bud. I shall make you bloom."

Revulsion overwhelmed her. With a cry she pulled back from him and stood shuddering, her face averted.

Numbly she looked out through the greenhouse wall and saw the others lounging on the loggia, the green glass giving them the tint of algae on a fishpond. She found the door, and the Baron followed her outside. When she got to the wicker chairs, she said, "I would like to see the gardens."

Dom Luíz sank into a chair. "Porfirio will conduct the next tour. I am going to smoke a cigar."

While the house had bored her and the greenhouse had repelled her, she found the gardens enchanting. Although the touch of that chill hand on her throat stayed with her, gradually she relaxed and enjoyed the walk. Beyond the orderly and classical patterns of the pathways near the house, whimsy set in. There was a boat lake like a black mirror, where swans drifted. Porfirio said his father had the water piped in from the Rio Negro because black water was free of mosquitoes. Near the lake there were two buildings, a Moorish bandstand with pointed arches and an onion-shaped dome, and a pavilion like a Greek temple.

Savannah got lost in the topiary maze; she had to keep calling Porfirio's name until he could find her and lead her out.

He led her across a dainty arched bridge that spanned an artificial *igarapé*, and coming into a grassy clearing screened by trees, he threw himself down to rest. When he closed his eyes, she opened her sketch pad. She conscientiously drew everything she'd seen, the plan of each floor of the Palácio, the layout of the gardens, the placement of the pavilion, the lake, and the bandstand. But it was hopeless; she hadn't found what Manco was looking for. It could be anywhere; there were acres and acres of grounds. Could she take Porfirio into her confidence?

He seemed no part of Manco's enmity with the Baron. In fact, he struck Savannah as being incapable of cruelty. He seemed timid, eager to please, as trusting and vulnerable as the monkey Coco. She watched him as he rested and tried to imagine saying to him: "A prisoner is being held here; help me find him." In her mind Porfirio's velvet eyes grew sad as he shrugged his shoulders helplessly.

She closed her pad and found him watching her. He smiled and took her hand. "Senhorita Savannah, I am very much happy you come to be with us here." She turned away. Beyond the rim of shrubbery the forest rose, still now. Even the gardeners they'd met at every turn seemed to have vanished; she no longer heard their shears. Porfirio said, "You no be afraid of my father. He like very much make you happy. Always he try to make my sister smile."

"And you?" she asked. He frowned. "I mean," she said, "does he not wish you to be happy too?"

He swept his eyes along the wall of eucalyptus and clipped crotons. "No," he said softly, "all my father wish is for me to be a man."

"I know. They always want us to grow up so quickly."

He sighed. "It is very much difficult to make the parent happy. I am always fail. I cannot help this; it is my nature."

"What does he want you to be? I mean, what kind of man?"

He pulled handfuls of grass blades and scattered them. "The man of business. Like Raoul. To know always the price of rubber."

"The mother superior used to tell me: 'You have the ability to do what is expected; ask God to heal your resistance.' "

He nodded. "Yes, is true. You know something? Promise you tell no one?" She promised. He leaned closer, and she could smell alcohol. "I do no like the rubber. It stink very bad."

She smiled at him. "Maybe we should run away. You'd like my friends in England."

He looked around and whispered, "Do not say these thing. Please, no again." After a pause he went on. "You live here in the Palácio and my father buy you everything you wish." Seeing her frown, he took her hand. "Do no make him angry. He have very bad angry times, he much hurt people." He got up and helped her to her feet. "Now we play croquet, yes?"

But a bell had begun to ring. That meant it was time for the picnic supper.

20

Tables and chairs had been brought out to the pavilion. There was one long table, and at the smaller tables footmen stood ready to serve food in covered silver dishes.

During the meal the Baron seldom took his eyes from Savannah, watching the tilt of her head as she turned from the table to see the swans mirrored in the black water of the lake.

Still preoccupied with her mission, Savannah fiddled with her napkin. She had not seen the stable. Perhaps there. . . . she met his eyes again. "Do you have horses?"

"Yes. Several of them. Do you like to ride?"

"I'd love to learn. May I see the stable?"

"Not today. Ah, the music is beginning."

Twilight was descending. Dimly across the lake they could see the musicians moving into place in the Moorish bandstand. Everyone left the table and moved to more comfortable chairs. Dom Luíz drew his chair close to Savannah's and put his arm possessively around her shoulder, arranging it so that his limp hand fell close to her breast. She nibbled another cake, casting about for a way to escape. How long would the concert of Viennese waltzes last? The swans, gathering to roost, drifted along the edge of the lake.

Savannah sprang to her feet and took a handful of cakes from a tray. The Baron said, "You do not care for Strauss?"

"I wish to feed the swans," she said, and walked down the steps of the pavilion.

The Baron followed her. At the bank she knelt and tossed the cakes toward the gathering swans. Then, as she stood up, she lost her balance and fell into the shallow water.

As Veronique came running to the bank, loudly scolding her and saying they must go to Mass yet tonight, the Baron helped Savannah to her feet. Looking irritably at Veronique, he said, "It is unnecessary to disrupt the concert." He beckoned to a footman. "Escort the senhorita to the house and have the maids dry her clothes." Savannah had the footman bring her sketchpad from the pavilion; then she followed him to the Palácio.

Upstairs in Esmeralda's room Savannah sat by the fire in her chemise and knickers while a maid wrung out her dress and petticoats in the bathroom. It seemed to take a long time. She got up restlessly, glancing in at the maid, who apparently had chosen to wash the clothing in the tub.

From the windows she could see the gardens, the distant lake, the candlelit pavilion, and the bandstand. And off to one side she saw in the fast-darkening foliage the roof of a long building.

She paced the austere room. What had Porfirio said? "My sister go into the convent to pray all time for the immortal soul of her mother." Savannah looked again at the small framed picture. Esmeralda would not have been permitted to take with her to the convent this photograph of her mother, whose eyes looked to Savannah like those of a madwoman. Why did her immortal soul require ceaseless prayers? Had she killed someone? Had she killed herself?

At last the maid brought her things from the bathroom, hung them on a rack before the fireplace to dry, and left the room. Savannah waited a minute or two, then hid her drawing things under Esmeralda's mattress and walked barefoot in her underwear into the upper hall. She prowled the bedrooms once more, examining the windows for ledges, vines, rain gutters, hoping to make use of her experience with the convent chapel roof. The chapel. . . .

It was necessary to stand on the balcony off the Baron's bedroom for several moments while her eyes grew accustomed to the darkness of the small nave. At length the flicker of the three altar candles revealed the choir stall directly beneath her. Climbing over the railing, she lowered herself as far as she could and jumped to the padded pew.

She took a candle from its holder and explored the chapel. The doors leading into the house were locked, but the heavy doors to the front drive were only locked from inside. She went out that way, extinguishing the candle.

She kept to the shadows of the shrubbery all the way to the stable, losing her bearings only once. She found, then, that if she climbed a tree, she could look out across the gardens to the house and the lake, and find the proper route again. It was now very dark.

The doors of the stable were open and filled with light. She saw a long passage with stalls on each side. Her bare feet made no sound, but the horses bent their heads over the stall doors to watch her run, crouched, into the building. At the far end there was an intersecting passage. As she peered around the corner, she saw a man coming toward her with a bag of grain on his shoulder. Bent under its weight, he hadn't seen her. She vaulted into an empty stall and lay on the damp hay. When he'd gone, she climbed out and went in the direction he'd come from, keeping close to the tack hanging on the wall. The passage ended in another corridor. To the left she saw a room filled with bags of feed. On her right a man sat by a door that had been bolted shut and padlocked. He was snoring, his chair tipped back against the wall, and across his knees lay a rifle. Manco had said that was all he needed to know. Her job was done.

But as she started back toward the stalls she heard a voice, coming closer, passing the horses and singing a Brazilian cowboy song, the one that tells the bull how beautiful he is:

> O boi sirigado,
> O meu boi bonito . . .

By the time the singer got to the passage, she'd hidden herself among the bags of grain. His steps drew very near, then the light went out and she heard the door of the feed room closed and locked.

After he'd gone away, she sat up, wondering what to do. The room was completely dark and she couldn't remember what it had looked like. From the passage came the sound of the guard's intermittent snore. And something else: an odd scrabbling sound nearby. When the scrabbling stopped and something ran across her leg she knew at once it was a rat; leaping to her feet she climbed the bags of feed, clawing at the walls.

She found a window, high up, near the ceiling. Piling the sacks higher, she was able to reach it. It wasn't locked, but the frame, swollen from the dampness, was stuck fast. The thought of spending the night in the company of rats kept her working until she'd broken most of her fingernails. Then she heard the crack of thunder. She stood up and watched. Over the nearby wall of jungle, lightning flashed. Turning to face the room she saw, in the flicker of the storm, tools hanging along the opposite wall. Working in the intermittent flashes, she pried the window open and dropped to the ground.

She ran all the way to the chapel. As she neared the house, large raindrops began to fall and she could hear the picnickers and footmen hurrying up the path and across the loggia into the Palácio. Still, she worked her way back through the chapel carefully. She took her candle back to its place on the altar and checked herself for bits of hay. By the time she'd stood on the back of the last pew in the choir stall and, after several failures, jumped high enough to grasp the balcony, she heard them calling her name in the second-floor rooms. She pulled herself up and over the railing. When the Baron opened the carved mahogany door, she was kneeling on the balcony, deep in prayer. She fluttered her eyelids at the influx of light from his bedroom, said one more Hail Mary, crossed herself, and stood up in her damp chemise and knickers.

He said, "You select odd times and places for your devotions." Beyond him in the room Veronique buckled at the sight of her underwear and had to be assisted to a chair.

Savannah said, "Forgive my indecent attire. I hadn't realized how dreadfully I've missed the convent. This is the hour for complin, you know. The nuns always sing the responses at complin. Their voices were so sweet. Do you think the acoustics are better in a small chapel?"

"I suggest you clothe yourself at once," her father said brusquely.

Savannah walked past them all and closed the door of Esmeralda's room behind her. She allowed herself a moment to lean against the wall, gathering her strength. Then she took up her freshly ironed clothing and her sketchpad, and brought everything into the bath. After she'd gotten dressed, she drew the stable floor plan. Then she tore out all the drawings she'd done for Manco, folded them as small as possible, wrapped them in a handkerchief, and stuck it in the pocket of her dress. By then Maman was rapping on the door. Opening it, Savannah said, "Do the back of this, will you? Did you bring my mantilla? And Maman, is there time for you to fix my hair before we leave for the cathedral?"

The first thing Savannah did when she knelt in the pew was to give earnest thanks for her deliverance; and she vowed never, never to set foot in the Palácio again. Then she sat back to enjoy the Mass.

The cathedral was beautiful. It was all so familiar: the strong scent of burning incense, the sonorous organ, the voices of the choir. Even the idiotic smiles of the images' painted faces seemed dear to her, like old friends. She was exhausted from the day's exertions and from her sleepless night; the well-known phrases of the service lulled her into a state of relaxation, despite the fact that the Baron was sitting next to her. At least here she was safe from the touch of his hands.

But she must not close her eyes, for the church was filled, every pew taken and many people standing in the back and along the sides. Manco might be here. Would he be the blind man tonight? A friar in a hooded robe? He might appear at any moment. She must recognize him instantly, no matter what disguise he wore; she must reach into her pocket and pass the handkerchief to him without attracting attention.

She lived through those imagined seconds again and again while the priest delivered a sermon on the City of God. He spoke of people going hungry while others groaned from over-indulgence, of marble buildings concealing open cesspools, of fortunes drenched with blood. Then he spoke of Jesus's feeding the multitudes and healing the sick and comforting the bereft. She wondered if this was the priest Manco had spoken of. She bent close to Maman and asked her his name; it was Father Antonio. He seemed neither young nor old, and although his voice wasn't loud or dramatic, each word rang clearly through the cathedral. Holiness, that was the word he made her think of. His sermon seemed to ache with grief for the world's failure to follow Jesus into the City of God.

It took several minutes to get up the aisle and out the opened doors. She saw no one she thought was Manco. She decided that when she got home, she'd put the drawings in the wisteria vine.

The street between the church and the Cathedral Plaza was packed with people. The Baron's carriage had been sent for, but the coachman couldn't maneuver his horses through the crowd. While they waited on the steps, the *festa* pageant appeared around a corner and began moving slowly past the church. The Baron, cursing under his breath, grabbed her arm and began to lead her back inside, but she resisted. "I want to see it," she said and pressed forward toward the street.

A band came first, the men resplendent in green and gold uniforms. Dancers followed, wearing giant paper heads and scattering confetti. There were more bands, drums, guitars, gourds, and rattling sticks; and men on stilts, and people dressed in animal costumes, including a cardboard bull with garlands in its horns and four pairs of human feet. From time to time the paraders danced with the bystanders, taking them from the crowd and pulling them into the street. Then a murmur rose among the spectators as the climax of the pageant, the crèche, appeared.

It was a complete nativity scene built upon a wagon, with live animals and a stall filled with hay, and the Holy Family and Wise Men and even angels perched shakily above the Christ Child's crib. As the wagon neared the church steps, it lurched to a stop while Father Antonio, who had made his way through the crowd, blessed and sprinkled it with holy water. Just as he finished, one of the angels climbed down. It was not a child, but a stocky dwarf in a white nightgown. He left his perch above the cradle and swung over the wagon wheel to the street. He ran to Savannah and took hold of her dress, singing out "*Bela! Bela como Maria!*"

Veronique, who was closest to her, clutched vainly at Savannah's arm. The crowd helped the dwarf draw her to the wagon and lifted her up into the arms of the Wise Men. The original Madonna leaped cheerfully into the crowd and began dancing with a papier-mâché horse. The dwarf threw a blue cape around Savannah, pulled the pins from her coiffure so the hair cascaded over her shoulders, and crowned her with a gilt tiara. When he stepped away, the spectators cheered. Hauling at the traces, the six dray horses got the wheels to turn, and the wagon groaned away over the cobblestones.

And then she saw Joseph, kneeling by the crib in a coarse brown hooded robe and a stained beard of cotton wadding. It was Manco.

His hand moved from the edge of the cradle and covered hers. Together they bent to adore the doll lying in the straw. He said, "You are all right? I was afraid for you. I cursed myself for asking. . . ."

Savannah felt overwhelmed by an astounding physical sensation that set the blood throbbing in her veins. It was the same tremendous rush of life that came each time he was near; she wanted it never to stop. She raised her eyes to his and saw, in the shadow of his hood, that he felt it too. His eyes seemed to drink the sight of her and, where his cloak lay open, she saw a pulse beating in his throat. She said, "I think I found him, in the stable. I made drawings of the buildings and the grounds." She placed the packet in his hand.

The pageant had turned into the plaza; she saw Ignacio and Jaime shouldering their way through a score of dancers whose heads were topped with high stacks of fruit, oranges and pineapples, bananas and grapes. She said, "What would you have done if I hadn't been in front of the church?"

"We'd have taken you from your carriage." His hand tightened over hers. "If all goes well, I will be gone tomorrow."

The two mestizos, in their incongruous dark business suits, were getting closer to the wagon, but a phalanx of dancers intercepted them, lighting Roman candles and strings of firecrackers.

"But you must take me with you," Savannah said.

He scowled at the china face of the Christ Child; its half-opened eyelids fluttered as the cart moved. "There is no way I can take you."

"You can do anything you want." She gestured toward the cardboard bull, who'd somehow wrapped himself around Jaime and Ignacio.

What would I do with you in the *selva?* You are not an Indian woman. You cannot run all night carrying a torch down an unmarked trail through the forest. You cannot paddle a canoe up the rapids. You cannot build a shelter from the rain or weave yourself a garment or make flour from manioc or fish with a spear." He glanced around him, at the angels and the Wise Men and the dancers in the street. "And if I hid you away in one of these river towns, have you any idea how many people might die, just so that I might hold you in my arms from time to time?" He bent toward the crib and pressed his lips to her hand as the wagon stopped. "Take care, Savannah," he murmured. The Wise Men swung her down to the street, where the displaced Madonna waited. Savannah relinquished her cape and crown. She watched the hooded form of Joseph until the crèche rounded a corner and disappeared, leaving her to Ignacio and Jaime. Yielding numbly to them, she allowed herself to be led to the Baron's carriage.

The bars of Manáos never closèd. All night the glasses clinked, the dice rattled, pianos plunked and guitars twanged, and coins rang upon the marble tabletops and the long mahogany bars.

During this night, however, there were other sounds. A series of explosions jarred the dock area. When the smoke had drifted off across the Rio Negro, the block-long Rio Mar Rubber Warehouse was a heap of evil-smelling rubble.

Twenty minutes later, while the Baron and his assistants were looking at the wreckage, a dozen men came out of the jungle behind the Palácio. They ran directly to the prisoner's cell, bound the two guards outside the door and one other who came running, and broke open the door. Tomás was in a corner of the room. When Manco saw the boy's wounds, his eyes filled with tears. Gently he picked him up and carried him in his arms back to the *selva*.

When Dom Luíz returned he found Nero, unharmed, in the prisoner's place. The Baron picked up a riding crop from a heap of tack in the corridor and raged back and forth in the cell, slashing the crop against his boot. "How did they know where to look? Did you tell them?" Nero shook his head.

Raoul said, "Did they hurt you? Did they try to make you speak?" Nero signified they had not. "Where were you kept?"

Using a pebble on the stone floor, Nero drew a picture of a launch. He had been, the whole time, somewhere on the river. And no, he hadn't recognized any of his captors.

The Baron paused in his fretful pacing and looked around him grimly. He said, "There is a traitor here."

Until dawn they cruised the river, but Nero could not find the launch he'd been aboard.

21

Cicero awakened her with coffee. He said, "Wake up, missy, it's Christmas!" When she sat up and took the hot china cup in her hands, he opened the doors to the gallery. "They was lots goin' on last night. Whole city in a uproar!" She nodded, remembering the pageant—and Manco's lips on her hand. "Can't figure how they done it, settin' the whole place afire at once."

Now she smelled it, a choking pall smothering the town. "What is that awful odor?"

"Tha's rubber. Burnin' rubber. Whole Rio Mar Warehouse went up in smoke last night. They say it look like tarnation itself down there."

Now she recalled hearing sounds in the night. Thinking it was more fireworks, she'd gone back to sleep. "Was anybody hurt?"

"They say not. But I hate to see ol' Massa Baron today." He rolled his stained eyes at her. "He be 'turr'ble mad, you bet!" He took the coffee cup. "You git right up now, you hear? We gots a tree and ever'thin', jes' like back home."

Apparently there were no pine trees in the Amazon. The Christmas tree in the drawing room had broad shiny leaves and velvety red blossoms. The addition of ornaments and candles and candy canes made the whole thing look bizarre.

Edward, Veronique, and Savannah opened their gifts while the servants watched. Savannah's presents were all trousseau items, naturally. She gave Veronique an arrangement of dried mountain flowers, pressed under glass; she'd made it at the convent last summer. And to her father she gave a sketch of Arcadia drawn from the garden, with the upper and lower galleries draped in wisteria. He was deeply touched and said that nothing could have pleased him more.

Then Veronique opened a box of small packages wrapped in colored paper with bits of tinsel, one for each of the three maids, the cook, gardener, coachman, and of course Cicero. She put the butler in charge of the distribution, and the servants went off to the kitchen to have their Christmas while the St. Jameses helped themselves to the breakfast, set out buffet-style in covered silver dishes in the dining room.

While they ate, Edward talked about the fire. It was a dreadful loss, he said, the very worst time of the year for such a thing to happen, a time analogous to harvesting in agriculture. Everything they'd planned to ship out through the months of the offseason was gone, a loss of hundreds of thousands of dollars.

"But *certainement* Dom Luíz has the insurance?" asked Veronique.

"Of course. But the distressing thing appears to be the nature of the fire. If arsonists can strike in the night while good folk sleep, no one is safe."

Savannah, pushing her eggs about with a fork, looked up. "Arson?"

Edward nodded. "I understand the fire didn't break out in one area and spread. There were simultaneous explosions the whole length of the building." He put his napkin on the table. "Dom Luíz will want a detailed estimate of the damage." He kissed each of them on the forehead. "Holiday or not, I must go. I'll try to return quickly." At the foyer door he stopped and smiled at them. "I must say it warms my heart to see a family sitting at table again."

After he left, Savannah pushed herself away from the table. "Today I would like to go sightseeing. And I think it would be charitable to invite to Christmas dinner friends who are far from their homes. Dr. Haversham, if the *Esperança* is still in port, and Will Patterson."

Veronique murmured, "These persons are your husband's social inferiors. . . ."

Savannah pushed her chair in to the table. "I insist. And anyway, he isn't my husband yet, is he?" She leaned on the back of the chair. She knew now that only the demands of a huge company dinner would keep Veronique from chaperoning her everywhere. "Can you come sightseeing with me?" Veronique began to raise objections, but Savannah turned about, holding out the skirt of the white muslin dress she was wearing. "Is this too plain to wear to town? Or would the lavender peau de soie be better?"

But while she was upstairs changing into the lavender dress and planning what she'd say to Will and the doctor and Manco's "good priest," Dom Luíz arrived and asked to speak with her. Finding him alone in the drawing room and Maman nowhere in sight, Savannah turned away in the doorway. "Come into the garden," she said. "It's a beautiful day and the house is quite stuffy already."

He followed her across the back gallery and down the steps. On the gravel path he caught up with her, took her elbow firmly, and steered her to the white wrought-iron furniture on the grass. They sat in facing armchairs. He stared at her a moment, his pointed beard dark against the white linen suit he was wearing. At last he said, "No sketching today?"

She arranged the ruffled edging of her sleeves. "Not yet, although I may, when I go sightseeing."

With his thumb he began turning the heavy ring on his right hand. "Where is your sketchpad now?"

"Upstairs. I understand your warehouse caught fire last night."

He nodded. "That was not the only unfortunate event. Someone also broke into my stable and took something of considerable value to me. These persons knew precisely where to look. I have begun to wonder if there is a spy in our midst."

She concealed a small yawn behind her hand. "I'm not used to being up so late. At the convent—"

But he'd gotten up and walked to the path along the back of the house, looking up toward the second floor. "Manuela, are you there?" The maid appeared above him. "Bring your mistress her drawing materials." In a few moments Manuela came into the garden carrying the pad and pencils; he motioned for her to remain nearby. He sat down again and went through the book page by page, dwelling longest on the pictures of Manco. "Now things become clearer," he said.

Idly, Savannah drank the lemonade Cicero brought them. The air still smelled of the burning, but now the sun's warmth brought out the fragrance of the surrounding blossoms. She said, "What things?"

"For example, your extraordinary interest in the Palácio."

"Extraordinary? I don't know what you're talking about." Overhead the leaves of the mango rustled as a macaw flew about the lower branches.

The Baron's cold eyes remained fixed upon her, but he directed her attention to the page open on his lap. "You do not know this man?"

"Of course not. I simply saw him about the ship. He was the first real Indian I'd ever seen. A curiosity."

He turned the pad in Manuela's direction. "Have you seen this man hanging about here?"

Manuela looked down as she answered, as if she felt guilty about something. "No, Your Grace, only on the ship."

"To your knowledge, has your mistress ever spoken to him?" The maid shook her head. He drew a thin black cigar from his vest pocket and lit it, then he sat back, watching Savannah through the rising smoke. After a time he looked at Manuela. "Get Senhora St. James."

Veronique came out from the kitchen, wiping flour from her hands and taking off her apron as she walked. Dom Luíz stood up. "She is not to go sightseeing, is that clear? She is not to leave this house except with me or one of my people. And she is to see no one. No one!"

Veronique put a hand to her mouth. The rims of her fingernails were caked with white. "What has she done?"

"I am not certain."

Savannah got up. "I haven't the faintest idea what you're talking about, but you are not my father and you have no business telling me—"

He slapped her with such force that she was thrown to the ground. Cicero, standing nearby, bent forward, then dropped his hands to his sides. Savannah got to her feet and braced herself against the back of her chair. She gave the Baron a bright smile. "Am I to conclude this means we are no longer engaged?"

She saw the steely flash of his eyes. "On the contrary, my dear, I am more anxious than ever to give you my full attention. Unfortunately, I have urgent business matters to attend to." Maman followed him into the house and through the foyer to his carriage, apologizing at every step. He ignored her and drove away.

Savannah said, "Please have the gig brought round. I'd like to go to town now."

As Veronique's hands flew up in the air her apron fell unnoticed to the ground. "You do nothing such! You remain exactly here until Edward—Cicero! Cicero!" He stepped forward. "Go to the dock and find Senhor St. James at once. Bring him! Say it is urgent."

Watching Cicero hurry away, Savannah said, "That's absurd. I want to see the Cathedral in daylight and perhaps speak with that priest who preached the sermon last night. Quickly, before the sun becomes too hot. Manuela, please get my parasol." Manuela didn't move. "Well, then, I'll just have to go without it."

But as she moved quickly up the steps and into the foyer, Veronique began shouting "Stop her!" in three languages. By the time she got to Portuguese, the servants had come running from all over the house and Manuela got ahead of her at the front door. Savannah said, "Get out of my way." Behind her she heard Maman say she was having *paroxismo*, a fit, and the cook, the other maids, and the gardener drew nearer. Veronique cried that she was *louco*, out of her mind, and must be put back in her room before she came to harm. The servants closed in upon her.

Edward found her in her darkened room, the windows tightly shuttered, the doors to the gallery locked, and the blinds drawn. Seeing that she sat quietly on a boudoir chair, he sent away the two maids who'd been watching her. He sat down facing her and said, "Perhaps you'd better tell me what you did to incense the Baron so."

"Aren't you interested in knowing what he did to me?" Her cheek still burned and the lavender peau de soie was torn from the struggle to get her up the stairs.

His fingers trembled slightly as he passed them across his forehead. "Perhaps your maman is correct in her estimation. Perhaps your mind is . . . distracted. The sudden change of climate—"

"It's a great deal simpler than that. I despise the Baron. He is repulsive and brutal, and nothing you do or say will make me marry him."

He was silent for a time, nervously fingering the drooping ends of his moustache. "I suppose it was a mistake to expect you to adjust so quickly to this environment. This society is unique in certain respects." He took a turn about the room, trying to gather his thoughts, then drew his chair closer to her and sat down again. "Brazil is a plantation society. Until quite recently, a slave-owning society. Do you understand what I'm saying? There was only the Master. He was the law. He literally had the power of life and death over his people—including his wife and children. Like the old patriarchs in the Bible. In Brazil a father could execute his son for disobedience."

She shrugged. "I don't see what this has to do with me. I'm not his child. I am your child. How can you let him—"

He took her hand. "It has everything to do with it. Women here are chattel. Because, I suppose, the men who settled this land came alone. They intermarried, or at least interbred with the slaves, with the Indians and the Africans. It was never frowned upon, it was never hidden, yet this mixed-blooded people is far more snobbish about race than any North American. Fair skin has always been indicative of the highest rank—

of blue blood." He turned her hand over and traced his finger along a vein on her inner wrist. "If you will only understand and be patient, the Baron will cherish you as his most precious possession. And there is no limit to his generosity when he is properly disposed."

She was wet under the arms, and the petticoats and undergarments beneath the peau de soie stuck to her body. "But Father, I don't want that. Maybe you and Maman really believe you are offering me a wonderful life. But I can't be a piece of property. I hate the thought of it."

"Of course, child. But we are all chattel in one way or another. We are obliged to earn our bread somehow, men out in the world and women in the home. Man owes his allegiance to an employer, to a government or principality, and woman to her husband. Our security demands that we attach ourselves to a man of power. Obedience is the homage we pay for his protection. That's the way it's always been. Civilization is built upon it."

It was midday now. The room was stifling. He rose and opened the doors to the gallery and stood a moment, breathing the fresher air. "Indeed," he said. "Only in the protected environment of marriage does a woman flower."

There was a soft tapping at the door and Cicero looked in, appraising her anxiously as he said, "Massa Edward, lunch is ready."

Luncheon was served to them at a table in the garden. Veronique did not join them. Savannah bided her time over the breaded cutlets and parsley potatoes. At last she said, "Isn't it possible for a woman's capacities to flower in work? In teaching? Or nursing?"

St. James sliced his meat precisely. "She does all these as a mother. Motherhood is the greatest challenge any human faces." He dabbed at his chin with the linen napkin. "Your maman is a perfect example of the creative aspects of homemaking."

"I cannot imagine myself making swan boats out of pastry. Will Patterson said magazines would buy my drawings—"

"Of course you'll draw, my dear. The Baron has said you may have a studio. Artistic talent like yours is an enduring source of satisfaction. . . ."

"That's not what I mean. Can't you understand?"

After a moment she said, "I'm sorry, Father, but I can't

help the way I feel. I know my refusal to marry him will be embarrassing for you. . . ."

He threw up his hands. "Haven't you comprehended anything I've said?"

She got to her feet. "I would rather starve than be the Baron's wife."

His eyes clouded with anger and pain. "That statement means nothing to you. I wasn't yet fifteen when the war ended. In the South there were districts where nothing would grow. Thousands of acres had been burned off. Many fields were literally soaked in blood. We hadn't any seed anyway, and no field hands to do the planting. We gathered berries in the summer. In winter we ate bark." He laughed quietly. "We'd saved the family treasures, but they were no good to us. Nobody had the money to buy our silver anymore. Finally I took Madelyn to Mobile. I carried her most of the way; she was only seven. Because our father was a hero, they let me pay for our passage to Brazil with gravy ladles and cold meat forks." He threw himself back in the chair in an attitude of nonchalance, polishing a knife blade on his sleeve. "But, Miss Savannah, next time you consider throwing away a life of comfort in favor of vows of poverty and chastity, I ask you to recall that your grandmama—my lovely, fragile, exquisite mother—used knives like these to dig roots out of the ground to feed us, going without herself to put something, anything into our mouths, until she starved to death."

Savannah went to him. She put her arms around him and said, "I'm so sorry, Father. Truly. But all that was a long time ago. You can put the bad memories behind you."

He shook his head. "Have you any idea what it costs to maintain a ménage of this magnitude in a city where everything must be imported? Forgive me, child. Matters of economics are beyond you." He looked up at the sky burning beyond the branches. "Finish your lunch. It's time we went inside."

But she remained at his side. "Father, what happened to Aunt Madelyn?"

He touched the lock of hair that fell across his arm. "She died. The death certificate said lung fever, but for all I know she may have frozen on the streets of Paris. Or starved. She chose to spurn a brilliant marriage, and she was not equipped to earn her bread as a governess or even a cook. So she died. You must not throw your life away as she did."

"She was to marry the Baron, wasn't she?" He didn't answer. "Yesterday he spoke of her." St. James sighed and looked away. "And I'm just like her, aren't I, Father?"

"No. Not at all. You are a good, intelligent, and reasonable girl. You will not throw your life away."

"But I *am* just like her, don't you see?"

There were no dinner guests. The three of them ate in silence, Veronique watching Savannah all the while. Afterward, Edward offered to teach her how to play chess, but she said she was exhausted and retired early. When the house fell silent, she bundled a few things in a pillowcase and climbed down the wisteria vine.

Jaime and Ignacio were watching the house. They seized her and carried her back inside. They called for rope, and while Edward watched anxiously, they tied her arms to the bedposts. A few minutes later a strange doctor arrived and gave her an injection. The last thing she remembered was Cicero bending his worn face over her, stroking her forehead and murmuring, "There, there, missy, don't take on so. Jest rest yourself easy and don't fret. You gonna be awright. Ever'thin' gonna be awright."

22

It was several days before Will realized something had happened to Savannah. Perhaps that was because he'd failed to take her problem seriously. He'd looked upon the whole situation as a farce: rubber monopolies, Chinese-style war lords, forced marriages . . . in this day and age, on the verge of the twentieth century? Will found the fear inspired by Rio Mar ludicrous, like something out of Dr. Haversham's beloved comic operas. Consequently as they'd sailed up the Amazon toward Manáos, Will had had an increasingly vivid impression they were not traveling to a real place. The curtains would open on the "Paris of the Jungle" and this Baron would be standing on the dock in the costume of the Lord High Executioner, straight out of *The Mikado,* and he would be singing that he'd "got a little list." As for Manco, he too belonged in a comic opera—playing the mysterious Gypsy bandit.

The bizarre police action that took place when the *Esperança* anchored at Manáos was in keeping with the picture.

When Haversham told him the authorities were looking for Manco—who was, they insisted, a dangerous criminal—Will chuckled delightedly. And that whole first day in the city, with Manco's escape being talked about wherever people gathered, Will had to keep suppressing a bitter smile. When the police had finally permitted them ashore, Haversham saw to it that Will got a decent room. He took him to the Hotel Internacional, where Will found the Turkish leather chairs, rope portieres, and overwhelming potted palms of the lobby amusing; they reminded him, again, of a stage set.

The doctor helped Will stow his gear in the dreary little room he'd been assigned; then the two of them set off for a tour of the town. They walked through the business district where the profusion of saloons, barbershops, gentlemen's outfitters, and diamond merchants astonished Will. He was struck too by the pervasive odor of rubber; the open doorways of the warehouses in the dock area showed thousands of large brown balls of the stuff stacked clear to the eaves.

The streets adjacent to the wharves were narrow, hot, and malodorous, most of them unpaved and full of stagnant puddles. The small shops along these streets had no front walls, so their shelves and counters full of cheap jewelry and jungle souvenirs could be seen by passers-by. Will declined the doctor's offer to help him select a dried snakeskin or a necklace of wild pig's teeth to take home. He found this trashy clutter depressing, for it bore no relation to the exotic jungle he'd come to find. They moved on.

Past the poor residential streets where dark eyes observed them from shutters made of wood slats, they came to a broad avenue lined with mango trees. Here, and around the margins of the well-landscaped public squares, the architecture was more appealing. Some of the walls were whitewashed stucco, but others were covered with gleaming tiles. The houses were covered with elaborate woodwork, carved arches over the windows, ornate corniced doorways and fluted pilasters, all painted in pastel shades.

Coffee and orange trees grew wild, and one of the parks was edged with an avenue of majestic silk-cotton trees. In the public gardens carved bridges arched over meandering streams, brilliant tropical blossoms bordered the walks around the bandstand, and there were more exotic trees than Will had known existed, jacaranda, fig, croton, eucalyptus, and dozens of varieties of palms.

As the two of them walked along the cobbled streets, Haversham began perspiring heavily. He suggested that they stop for a cool drink, and they crossed the square to the Café Amazonas. Suddenly Will felt desperately tired. There was an oppressive weight and a disturbing electric tension in the atmosphere. Although Haversham was already breathing heavily, they quickened their steps. Still they were caught in the rain which began to fall in steaming drops on the hot pavement of the square. Far above, wind whipped the tops of the palm trees. By the time they pushed open the garish blue door of the café, thunder was rumbling from one wall of the jungle to the other.

Inside it was warm and dark. Electric fans with large black blades turned slowly overhead. The middle of the place was filled by marble-topped tables with gilded iron legs. There were no women here, and no music. The men, most of whom appeared to be German or English, were rolling dice for their drinks. Both Will and Haversham sat quietly for a few moments, savoring the comfort of sitting down, even in these straight chairs.

The waiter, a young Brazilian wearing a tie and a long white apron, came over, and Will ordered a beer for himself and a whiskey for Haversham.

Haversham, after watching him soberly, began to chide. "You should have let me hire a trap, old fellow. You're quite done in."

Will insisted he felt fine, but he was lying. Every bone and joint ached.

"Won't do to get yourself tuckered out in this climate. Have you any idea of the death rate here? Appalling. Not too many years ago down at Pará twenty-five percent of the population was wiped out in a single season. Combination of yellow fever and smallpox."

Will was vaguely aware he'd been punishing himself for the misery he'd felt each time he thought of Savannah. This love was simply the onset of another handicap, a chronic illness he had not yet learned how to live with. No one need know. He must simply keep on doing what he had to do and avoid making an ass of himself.

The beer was a disappointment; it was a dark stout from England and served sickeningly warm. He called the waiter and asked what it would take to get beer that was cold. The young man brought him two small lumps of ice, which doubled the cost of the drinks and did no good at all.

Strange how his years of dreaming of the jungle were dissolving in a miserable glass of beer. He longed to return to the hotel, to have a bath and lie down. He said to Haversham, "How long will the rain last?" Haversham said an hour, or maybe an hour and a half. Will sighed and watched the torrent beat down on the deserted square.

The sky grew brighter, and the doctor led Will out of the café and into the street. After they'd gone a block, hobbling along together under Haversham's umbrella, Will said, "What does a man like me do when he falls in love?" The doctor said nothing. He clapped Will clumsily on the back, ending with an awkward embrace. Will paused on the paving stones. "I mean it. I don't know what to do."

"There's nothing you can do, old chap. Except grin and bear it."

Of course, Will thought, *what did I expect—a prescription?* "Right you are," Will said. "Cheer up. Look on the bright side." And the two of them arm in arm labored through the spent rain grinning like a pair of skeletons.

Will resisted the temptation to call upon Savannah all the next day, but by the following evening his resistance was entirely exhausted. At Arcadia an elderly Negro in a starched white jacket answered the door and told him the St. Jameses were spending Christmas Eve at the Palácio Rio Mar.

That night Will shared a last supper with Haversham before the *Esperança*'s midnight departure for the upper Amazon. Seeing the doctor off for his twelve-day jaunt to Peru made Manáos depressing for Will; having no heart for the Mass and pageant at the cathedral, he went to bed—only to be awakened later by the sound of explosions. He dressed and hurried to the wharf area, where a fire was sweeping through the Rio Mar warehouse. The English-speaking clerks in the hotel bar said it was probably the work of anarchists. When Will questioned them further, they shrugged and explained that insurrection was the South American equivalent of the cricket match. He asked, "But why here, in the middle of the jungle?" One of them told him the border between Brazil and its neighbors was always in dispute.

No doubt that fellow Manco, who was a mountain Indian, was working to help one of the Andean countries wrest control of the Amazon from Brazil, Will thought. It was the sort of thing these crazy South Americans had been doing to each other for three or four centuries. Still, remembering Haversham's earlier disbelief in Manco's railroad, Will was puzzled.

Savannah continued to dominate his thoughts. Late on Christmas Day he called again at Arcadia, this time with a gift: He'd bought her a box of French pastel crayons. But Veronique, looking distraught, said Savannah was ill and could not receive him.

During the days that followed he did a lot of sightseeing. Pondering what he saw and heard, he began forming the outlines of several dispatches. He sensed the presence of not one city here, but several. There was the frontier town, brutally ostentatious and peopled by *banditti* in tailcoats. Away from the bars and hotels, the chance encounters at band concerts or the observatory revealed an entirely different town, one inhabited by soft-spoken Brazilians who were polite, hospitable, cultured, and great lovers of the arts.

Will found these latter far more interesting, and for several days he worked on an article about them. But in the end the first dispatch he sent off by telegraph to New York was on an entirely different topic. He headlined it: *Main Ingredient in Amazon Rubber May Be Blood.*

He'd stumbled upon the story by accident. One morning as he drank his coffee in the hotel dining room and practiced his Portuguese by reading a local paper with his dictionary beside him, he came upon an article about atrocities in the jungle. He saw the name of the Rio Mar Rubber company in the headline and, after several minutes of searching the pages of his dictionary, translated the words: *guards at Rio Mar landings accused of using Indians for target practice.*

When he brought it up at luncheon with a pair of Englishmen, they simply shrugged and changed the subject. They did not deny the story or dismiss it as a fabrication. They shrugged as if to say: Of course it's true, but what can you do about such things in a country like this?

So Will went to the office of the newspaper, *O Farol*, "The Beacon." Fortunately the editor, a man named Oliveiro, spoke English. He showed Will notarized depositions of men who'd managed to escape from Rio Mar landings. They told of the killing of forest Indians. The guards would make an example of some of them in order to inspire the others to work harder. One of the depositions described systematic mutilations imposed when a tapper's yield fell short: a finger the first time, then a toe, an ear, and so on. Will spent a couple of hours using his dictionary on the material to satisfy himself that Oliveiro was not exaggerating. When he'd finished, the editor urged him to make copies of the documents. He said there was no hope of putting an end to this cruelty by local means: The world must be informed of these horrors. Will spent another hour taking detailed notes, then he thanked Oliviero and went away to work on his dispatch.

The next morning Oliviero himself made the papers. One of the English clerks read the news item aloud for Will:

> "DISTURBANCE AT EDITORIAL OFFICE OF *O FAROL*. In a spontaneous demonstration of support for the Baron do Rio Mar, who is well known for his philanthropic and humanitarian acts, a party of public-spirited citizens last night called upon Mr. Oliveiro to remonstrate with him concerning his slanderous attacks on the Rio Mar Rubber Company."

Will rushed to the office of *O Farol*. The place had been burned out, the presses were smashed, and Oliveiro was missing. Standing in the midst of the wreckage, Will shuddered to recall that he'd thought of this place as a comic opera. And simultaneously he felt an intensifying anxiety for Savannah.

Yet his journalistic instincts would not permit him to send off a dispatch about atrocities in the rubber business without seeking some kind of "other side" to the story. He went to the downtown office of Rio Mar Rubber and asked to see the Baron. The office was austere, with whitewashed walls, clerks on high stools scraping pens in ledgers, and the smell of rubber everywhere. After a tedious wait in which Will watched the fan turn slowly on the fly-specked ceiling, a powerfully built mulatto brought his card back saying, "His Excellency never speaks to journalists."

Will stood up, trying not to lean upon his cane. "I am preparing a series of articles for publication in the United States. I should not wish to discuss the rubber business without consulting its most powerful entrepreneur. If I were to do so, would not your employer be displeased?"

After another long wait, the mulatto returned to say, "His Grace thanks you for your courtesy, but he regrets the press of business prevents him from seeing you."

Once again Will found himself alone among the bookkeepers, so he knocked on the frosted glass door that said *Col. Edward St. James, C.S.A., Treasurer.* A weak voice answered, "Yes?"

Will entered and put his hand out with his card as St.

James rose behind his desk. "Colonel St. James, I am acquainted with your wife and daughter. We sailed to Brazil together."

St. James wiped the perspiration from his forehead with a handkerchief and politely waved Will to a chair beside his cluttered work space. "Good of you to call, sir. Most kind."

"How is Mrs. St. James?"

"Well, thank you, Mr.—ah, Patterson." He had glanced at the card. "I see you are from Baltimore. Many of you folks were with us in the war, were you not, sir?"

Will nodded. "And how is Miss Savannah?"

St. James frowned and shuffled the papers in front of him. Will saw that his fingers trembled. He said, "Alas, not well. Not well at all, I regret to say."

"May I ask the nature of her illness?"

"A difficulty in adjusting to the . . . environment here."

"I'm sorry to hear it. Is there anything I might do?"

He frowned as if trying to remember something. "She is, however, fortunate in having the best medical attention that can be obtained here. The Baron has his personal physician attending her."

Although the room was stifling, Will felt chilled. He said, "We spent some delightful hours together on shipboard. Perhaps I might call and cheer her."

St. James shook his head slowly. "Out of the question, I fear. Quite out of the question. But I must say, sir, I do most sincerely appreciate your concern. It is most kind of you to inquire." He rose.

Will stood also. "Will you be good enough to convey to her my regards?"

"Indeed I shall, sir."

The last thing Will saw as he left the office was St. James staring out the window across the city, his restless hands fingering the edges of his papers. The helplessness of the gesture strengthened his suspicion that Savannah's father was powerless to help her—as powerless as Will himself. Still, he continued to call at the house each day, and each day he was rebuffed, usually by Veronique. At last the old butler whispered to him, "No use you comin' round here all the time. You can't he'p her."

Will spoke desperately. "Where is she? What's wrong?"

The black man narrowed his eyes. "Don't you go makin' trouble for her. You go away and leave her alone. Go back where you come from. Ain't nothin' you can do."

Will limped back to his hansom cab, raging at his helplessness. What could he do about these atrocities? Must he simply turn his back, go home, and write a book about the beauty of this exotic jungle city? Impossible; he could never leave until he knew Savannah was safe.

And now even the city itself repelled him. He prowled the streets, driven by the idiot hope he might see her passing in her father's gig, that she would pull off her broad-brimmed hat and wave it to him, laughing to let him know that all was well. Then he could leave this gaudy city where open cesspools reeked behind the shops of diamond sellers, where people spent money as if driven by a fever, where all night long there was the sound of drunken violence, and where the cry of the lottery ticket hawkers rang out like the moral at the end of a fable: *"Vale quem tem!"*—You are worth what you've got.

He'd had no response to his dispatch about the target practice, although he called at the telegraph office each day. He was running out of money. And still he could not leave, not until he had seen Savannah.

When a search of his pockets showed his total assets had shriveled to thirteen dollars, he started playing poker. After three nights at the tables he had enough cash to live on back home for a full year . . . or start a revolution of his own . . . or to take Savannah anywhere she wanted to go—provided he could find her.

23

The strange doctor came every night and again each morning. Although her hands were no longer tied, Savannah made no attempt to get away. She drifted in and out of consciousness, unaware of time.

Someone was always in the room: Manuela sitting in a corner watching her, or Cicero bathing her head with cool cloths. He fed her porridge and broth, whispering continually that everything would be all right. She said, "I don't want that pudding." He told her it wasn't pudding, it was broth. "Liar," she said.

St. James tried to reason with her. He told her the wedding plans were going forward. The chef who was to do the ice carvings had arrived from New York. Orphans from the convent were being taught to scatter flowers down the nave of the cathedral. Her tongue thick with thirst, her hands numb, and her vision clouded, she whispered, "I refuse to be Reconstructed."

Sometimes she dreamed of Manco. She seemed to see him standing in a corner of the room looking at her sadly and shaking his head. She did not understand him. Did he want her to marry the Baron? Or was he sad because he was not a magician and could not spirit her away from the *boiuna?*

At other times she had the nightmare, the one in which she was seized and carried away.

Once she awakened to hear Edward and Veronique quarreling at the foot of her bed. Veronique whispered angrily, "Tell her the truth, Edward!"

He said softly, "My pride does not permit it."

"Your pride!" She laughed bitterly. "Too bad this pride does not prevent you from *détournement de fonds!*" Then Veronique began to weep. "Go to jail, then," Veronique said. "But what is to become of me?"

Savannah said, "Why don't you sing to me?"

St. James knelt beside her. "Child, are you awake? You must help us. Are you listening? I have gotten into some difficulty with my bookkeeping work. A matter of the transposition of a few figures, not terribly serious. The Baron is quite willing to overlook—"

Veronique pushed him aside and took Savannah's face in her hands. "He will go to jail if you don't come to your senses!"

Savannah said, "You used to sing to me when I was small. You held me in your arms and rocked me."

Edward held her hand. "You had a nurse, an English nanny. That's who it was."

Savannah grasped his hand tightly. "Get her for me, Father. I want her to sing to me."

"She's gone, child. But maybe Dom Luíz can find her for you. Maybe he will take you to look for her. Would you like that?"

"Go away," she said, and closed her eyes.

When she opened them again, Dr. Haversham was taking her pulse. "Are you here?" she said.

"Just back from Peru. And not a minute too soon, I'd say. You appear to be a bit off the mark, missy." She put her arms around his neck and began to sob. "Hold on, now. That won't do. Won't do at all. Let's have a look at you."

"Don't let me go. Promise you won't."

"Nonsense. Have you dancing the jig in no time at all. Sit up now and let's give a listen to your chest."

She heard the rain beating on the gallery, torrents of rain down all the spouts and gutters, running down the cobbled streets, past the Cathedral Plaza and the docks. "Take me to the river. I want to touch the river." He looked into her eyes, examined her fingers, pressed the nails and watched them. She said, "I need to go there. When I touch the river, I'll be all right again."

Haversham looked at her steadily. "What have they been giving you?" He shook her shoulders. "Pay attention now, missy. What have they been giving you?"

"Pudding."

Haversham came back once more. He brought her oranges and bananas, and made her eat them while he watched her. He told her he must go to Pará now on the *Esperança*.

"He took my pearl," she said. "He threw it away somewhere when he took my clothes off."

"Now pay attention, missy. I've told them not to give you anything but good, wholesome food."

She pulled him close. "Veronique is not my mother. I was stolen on the way to school."

After that the other doctor did not return. She continued to sleep a great deal; she was weak and dizzy and her head ached, but she knew day from night. She lay in her bed with her eyes closed, thinking.

Once, in the middle of the night, she saw Manuela on a chair in the corner of the room. She whispered, "Manuela, will you help me?"

Manuela came to her side. "What you want?"

"Please help me, will you? I'll give you my pearl when I find it. I know it's somewhere on the floor, in a corner, behind the bed or under the rug. Find it and take it, you can have it."

"What you want?"

"Go to the hotel, the big one—what is it?"

"Internacional?"

"Yes, that's it. Ask for Mr. Will Patterson. You know, the American. Tell him—" She motioned Manuela closer. "Tell him I'm being held a prisoner because I refuse to marry the Baron."

"I will do it, senhorita." Manuela smiled.

The next time she saw Manuela alone she said, "Did you tell him?" Manuela nodded. She lay still, listening. The room was dark and very hot; on the gallery the rain fell. What would Will do? Bring the police? Later, while Cicero straightened her covers she whispered, "I sent Manuela to the Internacional with a message. Has Mr. Patterson come?"

"Shoot, you think she he'p you?"

She stared at the ceiling. There were dampness stains on the plaster shaped like continents, oceans, rivers. "Then he's not coming."

"He *bin* comin'. He come limpin' up them steps every day since you bin sick. Every day fo' ten days."

She raised up on her elbow. "Where is he? Is he here?"

"The Missus keep sendin' him away. She say you too sick to have company. She tell him you got the fever."

She caught the sleeve of his white coat. "Cicero, you must talk to him. Tell him I need help."

Cicero shook his head. "What he gonna do? He cain't he'p you. You wanna git outta here? You do what they say."

Shutting her eyes again, she said, "Ten days? It seems like ten years. Did I miss the wedding?"

"No'm. That's Thursday. This here is Monday. Three days yet. Come on now and drink this tea."

He held her head up while she sipped, his coat rustling with starch. "Cicero, *he* hasn't been here, has he?"

"Who?"

"The Baron."

"No'm. He on the river somewheres chasin' whoever burnt up his warehouse. I hear they doin' it to him ever'where. Santerém, Óbidos, Iquitos. Ain't hit Pará yet. Tha's the big one, the one they's worried 'bout. But he be back time fo' the weddin', you kin bet on that."

That night her father sat reading beside her bed. Veronique came in with Raoul. Savannah kept her eyes shut; when she did that, they always talked as if she were deaf. Raoul said, "Why did you let that Englishman see her?"

Veronique said, "He forced his way in—"

"What did you tell him?"

"We said she's lost her mind, but we wish not to put her away, so we must keep her quiet."

"He is a meddler. He went to see our doctor and threatened him. The Baron will be displeased."

St. James spoke up. "But since he came, she's getting better. I was afraid she'd become permanently distracted, but now—"

Veronique sniffed. "Now when she's awake she schemes and tries to bribe the servants."

"Are you sure she isn't faking?" Raoul grasped Savannah by the shoulders and shook her while her head rolled around and the whites of her eyes showed. "The Baron says that if she is not better by the time he returns from Pará tomorrow, she's to be moved to the Palácio. Our staff can give her the care she requires, and His Grace feels there are other methods of treatment that might prove effective."

They left the room together, their voices fading as they descended the stairs, and one of the kitchen maids came to sit with her. After a while Savannah said, "I'm hungry."

In the morning she asked for more food and, with Cicero's help, she sat up and ate it. Veronique, disbelieving the reports, came into the room and watched her doubtfully. Savannah said, "What day is it? Did I miss New Year's?"

Maman said, "It is the fifth of January."

"I want to go to the bathroom." Veronique helped her get up, but the room blackened before her and she slid to the floor. Veronique helped her back into bed, covered her up, and watched her. About an hour later Savannah said, "The fifth? I must have been very ill. Had I a fever?"

Edward came home and the two of them drew up chairs and kept their eyes fixed anxiously on her face. Though weak, she seemed not only rational, but uncommonly tractable. She said, "Has anyone been to call? I've missed Mr. Patterson and would like to see him, but if you don't think I ought to . . . I'm sure you know best. I hope I haven't made too much trouble for you. I can't remember anything past Christmas Day."

Edward and Veronique looked at one another, relief showing in their faces.

"Was I terribly fretful?" Savannah went on. "I do hope not. You're both so very good to me. And dear Manuela, watching by me through the nights. I must have a great deal to confess. Is it possible for a priest to call? I remember the sermon we heard on Christmas Eve. That dear old man. He looked like a saint, didn't he? I felt I could unburden my heart to him. But of course, if you think I'm not yet strong enough . . . Will he perform the ceremony?"

Veronique said slowly, "No, the bishop will officiate."

"Am I to have attendants?"

"Dona Esmeralda is being permitted to leave the convent for the day so that she can be your maid of honor."

She closed her eyes as Veronique clasped Edward's hand. He kissed Savannah's forehead and murmured, "Rest now, dear child."

That afternoon the rain stopped for a time. She asked if she might have some air. Edward hung her hammock on the gallery and carried her outside. She saw at once the absence of wisteria. It had been hacked off close to the ground. She said she felt a chill and would like to go inside again.

She was, that evening, dressed and sitting in a chair when Dom Luíz arrived. He said, "I am delighted to find you have recovered."

"Thank you, Your Grace."

"I understand you've asked to see a priest."

"I am not accustomed to missing confession. Nor Mass."

"I had no idea you were so devout."

"I hope you have no objection."

"No, certainly not. I will send my own priest to you." After a silence during which Savannah kept her eyes fixed upon her hands clasped in her lap, the Baron said, "You seem uncharacteristically subdued."

"I have been ill."

"Nevertheless, at the cathedral on Thursday you are not to appear somber. It is a wedding, not a funeral."

She lifted her eyes to him. "I have not been told about the ceremony. I don't know the order of service or the responses. I am afraid I might make mistakes. Will someone teach me what to say?"

"There will be a rehearsal tomorrow evening. After we will attend the opera."

Her hand went to her chest. "I hope I'm strong enough. I would not wish to appear unwell, Your Grace."

He studied her a moment. "I find the change in you most remarkable."

She touched her forehead. "I'm sorry, I have difficulty remembering what's happened. I dreamed so many things." Her hand moved to her cheek. "I seem . . . I seem to recall . . . did I quarrel with you?"

"Indeed. You said I had no right to tell you what to do."

She fell to her knees beside him just as she used to do when Mother Dominica was cross with her. "Please forgive me. I promise to try very hard to overcome my faults."

He drew her between his knees and pressed her body to

him. "Yes," he said, "we will overcome all your faults together." He took her face in his hands and looked deeply into her eyes. "You will be very good, I promise you." He'd begun to breathe heavily. When he kissed her his mouth was open. She felt his teeth against her lips. She pressed them tightly together, but he began to bite her mouth and when her lips parted, he ran his tongue along her teeth. With one hand he grasped her jaw, forcing her teeth apart. Then his tongue pressed deep into her mouth. It tasted strongly of black cigars. Her stomach clenched.

There was a knock at the door. He released her and called out angrily, "What is it?"

Cicero said, "Man at door say you got a telegraph message from Pará."

Dom Luíz got up. He said, "After the wedding, anyone who disturbs me will be fed to the piranha."

24

She scarcely slept all night; but in the morning she felt stronger. Whenever premonitions of defeat entered her mind, she recalled the taste of black cigars and resolved anew to get away or die trying.

At least now she had opportunities. The first would be at the rehearsal. During the practice walk down the long nave she might break and run; she remembered side entrances along the way. But perhaps the opera would be best: If she slipped away into the crowd, pursuit would be more difficult. And finally, if everything else failed, there was the wedding itself. There she might announce that this marriage was against her will and ask the dignitaries who were present for asylum. Veronique had said everyone would be there—the governor, the chief of police, the bishop of Amazonas.

But she must think through everything carefully: a means of escape through the city, concealment in a wagon or in some building until her passage on a ship could be arranged. For that she would need help. She must find a way to contact Will.

She went from one thought to the other as if they were pieces of a jigsaw puzzle, trying to find two that fit, trying to find a corner or an edge. She forced herself to walk back and forth across her room. It made her breathless, but she didn't get dizzy; her stamina was returning. During the day she ate five times. By late afternoon she felt energetic, but increasingly distraught, for she still hadn't formed her plan.

She rummaged among her memories of the Christmas pageant. What was the area like around the cathedral? She recalled wide vistas, the plaza, the surrounding avenues; but she could recollect no narrow side streets. On the other hand, the grand opening of the opera house . . . wouldn't there be scores of carriages waiting to discharge or pick up their owners? The traffic and confusion would help. And inside the building, there would be stairways, boxes, corridors, crowds. She was certain of one thing: She would get only one chance, and she must choose the best possible opportunity. It would have to be the opera. But what then? Where would she hide? How could she board a ship when she had no money?

She rocked slowly in her hammock on the gallery, the last and most difficult questions reverberating through her mind accompanied by the creak of the hammock cords. From time to time carriages passed on the side street, their horses' feet ringing on the cobbles. One vehicle, a hansom cab, drew up slowly and stopped across the street. No one got out. The driver slumped in his box and began to doze. She recalled seeing a hansom like that before, but she paid scant attention, knowing now that the Baron's men watched the house all the time. It occurred to her to lean over the railing and shout at them. *Do you expect me to fly from the gallery? Make a rope of my hair?*

Then she saw the cane hung on the rim of the cab door. An ivory handle, carved . . . carved in the shape . . . was it a dog? Yes. Will's cane.

Below her the gardener was trimming the grass along the edges of the gravel path. In the bedroom Manuela had started repacking the trousseau in its trunks.

Her drawing materials had been taken from her. She hadn't even a pen and writing paper. She knew, though, that her father was always leaving books about. Casually she went looking around the bedroom; she found a book of verse on a table. In passing she picked up the purple lace hat Manuela was about to pack. She put it on and, looking in the mirror, tugged at the violets on the crown. "This is my favorite. Do you like it too?" Manuela didn't answer. Savannah dropped the hat back into its box, picked up the book, and returned to her hammock with a large hatpin in her hand.

It took her several minutes to squeeze enough blood from

her finger to write on a blank page: *Have cab at opera.* When
it was done, she turned the corner of the page down as far as
she could and closed the book. She stood at the railing as if
watching the gardener work, holding the book in front of her
and tapping it against her chin from time to time. She saw
Will lean forward in the cab: He was watching her. The
gardener came to the end of the path, got up stiffly, and
brushed the damp earth from his knees. Then he took his
tools to the other end of the garden to begin working there.
When his back was turned she spun the book up and outward
toward the street. It caught on the top of the garden wall,
teetered, and fell on the far side. Will tapped the driver's seat.
The hansom turned slowly, stopped in the shadow of the
garden wall, and a moment later headed back toward town.

When they started out, the western sun was gilding the
treetops. There would be no time to change after the rehearsal, so they had to wear their opera clothes. Still, a gig
containing a man in a white tie and tails and two women with
bare shoulders and feathers in their hair did not seem out of
place on the streets of Manáos at sunset.

Savannah felt stuffed into her dress and couldn't imagine
how it would have fastened had she not been ill. It was pale
blue satin embroidered with seed pearls. The pointed bodice
made breathing difficult, which was just as well, because she
was certain one good breath would expose her bosom entirely.
As she'd climbed into the gig she'd clutched the top of her
bodice anxiously, and now as she pictured herself stepping
down again at the cathedral, she longed to rip off her elbow-
length gloves and stuff them down her dress for decency's
sake. But Edward and Veronique seemed to feel she was
perfectly decent; they smiled across at her approvingly, and
Maman reached over once to secure the strand of seed pearls
entwined through Savannah's hair.

She watched the streets ahead, eager to see the Cathedral
Plaza again. Did moments of happiness leave traces in the air?
Was Manco, far off in the *selva*, thinking of her as she
thought of him? It didn't matter if she had to run from the
opera to the dock; it wouldn't matter if she had to swim. But
where would she swim? He might not be in the jungle; he
might be back at Pará. The telegraph message last night said
they'd burned the warehouse there; after the Baron had gone,
Cicero told her. Sailing downstream to Pará took only half as
long as the upstream trip. She could be in Pará in three days

. . . if she could get aboard a ship . . . if that's where Manco was . . . if . . . if. . . . Better not think about any of that now. One step at a time. Get through the rehearsal. Get to the opera. Get away.

Yet the cathedral spires drew no closer. In fact, they were receding. She said, "Father, isn't it the other way?"

"What, my dear?"

"The cathedral."

"Yes, it is. I must say I've never seen you look more enchanting. Your maman's taste is unerring."

She looked wildly from one to the other. "You said we were going to the wedding rehearsal and the opera!"

Concerned, they both reached for her hand. Veronique said, "We are, *chérie*, we are."

And St. James added, "The rehearsal is in the Baron's private chapel. Please try to be calm, child. Your illness has clearly left you quite highly strung. We'll be careful not to tax your strength. It's going to be a lovely evening, and you just let us know if you become fatigued."

She tried to picture herself leaping from the carriage, sprinting between the houses with yards of blue satin streaming out behind her. If it were only dark, she might have a chance. But now? Impossible.

The coachman steered the horse through the Palacio's wrought-iron gates. Passing the main entrance, he stopped at the chapel doors. Numb with dread, she let herself be handed down from the gig by Dom Luíz. He murmured, "Exquisite, exquisite," but he was looking at her breasts, not her face.

The chapel was nearly full. The Baron led her past the house servants, the gardeners, and the stable hands, saying, "I trust you have no objection. They will be unable to attend the service at the cathedral tomorrow." At the top of the altar steps she saw an aged priest, flanked by a deacon and an acolyte. Below them the rest of the wedding party waited. The Baron's men, led by Raoul, stood on each side of Porfirio, who was to be best man; and on the other side there was a young nun. Savannah would have known Esmeralda anywhere; she had the wide, dark eyes of her mother's photograph and a deep olive complexion made richer by the stark white of her coif. She took Savannah's hand, whispering, "I'm so glad to see you at last."

The priest introduced himself as Father Ferreiro. He said, "I understand you have been ill, so I will try to be as brief as possible. Just before the *Libera nos* I will turn and say over you prayers upon the nature and solemnity of the union you are entering. Then, the Mass goes on as usual until the last blessing, where once again there are special admonitions. I will sprinkle you with holy water, and the Mass will conclude as usual. Have you questions?"

She said she understood. "Very well, then. Let us begin." Feeling Esmeralda's hand in hers gave her a twinge of regret. If she got to the opera, if she got away . . . tomorrow in the cathedral there would be nothing but the children scattering flowers. . . . Would Esmeralda understand why Savannah could not go through with it? And Porfirio, who'd never been anything but kind to her, what would he say? He'd shrug and lift his sad dark eyes. And her father—would he really go to jail? Perhaps he would, and she tried to feel remorse for that, but she couldn't. Sometimes she felt she was simply an investment to her parents: the education, the trousseau, the concern for her health, for her appearance, seemed all calculated to bring in a return.

Now the priest was praying over them. She wondered if God would ever forgive her for defying Mother Dominica's teachings, for disobeying her father, for mocking this holy sacrament by pretending to take part in it. *Bend*, Mother Dominica had said; *bend or you will be broken.* She closed her eyes, thinking: *You made me, surely You can understand how I am; will You strike me down because I cannot bend?*

She heard the last blessing; then the priest sprinkled them with holy water and lifted them to their feet. The Baron took her in his arms and kissed her, as everyone surged close to them. Esmeralda embraced her while St. James pumped the Baron's hand. Veronique said—with tears filling her eyes— "Now you are a baroness!" Then her father kissed her tenderly and said, "Dom Luíz said you had such anxiety about the ceremony, it seemed a kindness to—" As she stared at them, the Baron took her in his arms again; he whispered, "Why share the sweetness of this moment with the world? We'll go through it again in public tomorrow, but from this moment we will not part, not even for a moment."

The Palacio staff had lined up to pay their respects to the new mistress; one by one they bowed or curtsied to her; but halfway through the kitchen maids she fainted.

When she opened her eyes, she was lying on Esmeralda's bed. She saw Veronique's anxious face next to the nun's white coif. Esme said softly, "Are you feeling better?"

Savannah closed her eyes, then opened them again. "Has it been long?"

"No, just a few moments. Nero carried you here from the chapel. Soon after he'd put you down you opened your eyes."

Her mouth felt dry. "I must get up. We mustn't miss the opera."

Veronique said, "You were exhausted, no? The service was too long. I will have a tray for you prepared. When you eat, you will be better."

When she'd gone, Esmeralda drew a chair close to the bed and took Savannah's hand. "Is there anything I can get you? Is that cloth cool enough?"

She hadn't noticed the compress on her forehead. She said, "No, everything is . . . Esme, why did you decide to become a nun?"

The tawny cheeks flushed against her white headdress. After a moment she said, "I found it difficult to pray here."

"Porfirio told me you pray for the immortal soul of your mother."

Esme studied the crucifix in her hands. "I pray for my father too."

Savannah turned her face away.

"Do you understand him?"

"I think so. He believes he has a mission, a God-appointed task. He is to bring civilization to this wilderness."

Savannah raised her head from the pillow, but dizziness forced her down again. She said, "But why is he so demanding? Porfirio. Me. Everyone."

"He feels we all exist to serve his purpose. And in turn, his glory shines upon us."

"But you disagree. Don't you? And he let you go."

Esme smiled sadly. "No, he hasn't. He expects me to come back to him each day."

So not even a betrothal to the Lord was a guarantee against her father's implacable will. And no one would want to help a wife flee. There were laws about that. The despair that had overwhelmed her after the service in the chapel welled in her throat, filled her eyes, and choked her with sobbing. Esme took her in her arms. She said. "I know he can be frightening, but God will strengthen you, Savannah, He will bear you up. Trust Him. And I will pray for you every day, I promise."

Savannah clutched at Esme's garments. "Help me! Help me get away from him. Please! I must escape!"

"You can't. Wherever you hide, he will find you. He feels

God has given you to him, just as God has given him the *selva*. He would pursue you like an escaped tapper. But if you do as he wishes—"

Veronique came in with the tray. Fighting her weakness, Savannah sat up and forced down the soup and toast. Then she insisted on getting up and going downstairs. In the drawing room, where the men were having drinks, she went directly to the Baron. He rose to greet her. She said, "Your Grace, I am so sorry if my dizzy spell distressed you. I know our appearance at the opera is important, and I am quite recovered now."

She was forced to ride with him in his carriage. Esmeralda had returned to the convent for the night, and the Baron insisted that Porfirio ride with Veronique and Edward. The instant the coachman closed the door Dom Luíz pulled her roughly to him. She managed to turn her face away far enough to say, "Excellency, my coiffure!"

"Be still," he hissed, and drew her across his lap.

She forced herself to laugh good-naturedly. "Do you want me to appear disheveled?"

"You will not appear disheveled if you are still. Now, kiss me as a bride should kiss her husband." His beard rasped across her face and his mouth bore down hard upon hers. He bent her head backward until her breasts sprang free of her dress. He seized one of the nipples between his teeth, holding her free arm behind her back with one hand and running his other hand over her body, under her skirts. As he began exploring her with his fingers she struggled to get free, but each time she moved, he bit her nipple harder. Tears ran across her temples and along her ears, but she refused to cry out. At length the carriage slowed and he released her. When he spoke she saw his teeth gleam dully in the dimness of the carriage. "After tonight you will not resist me again, I promise you. Your first lesson in your marital duties will be so thorough, it may leave you marked for life. Rest assured, you will never forget this night. Not as long as you live."

25

The opera house, the Teatro Amazonas, had originally been a modest project. They'd planned to spend three or four thou-

sand pounds, less than $20,000. But by the time they'd imported the iron framework from Glasgow, the marble from Italy, the 66,000 colored tiles for the dome from Alsace-Lorraine, the one hundred crates of furniture from London, and from all over Europe the skilled artisans who could put the whole thing together, the cost had been multiplied by more than a hundred. Now, on opening night, the cost was two million dollars, and the bills were still coming in.

But the citizens of Manáos weren't worried about money tonight. Hadn't the rubber merchants of the Amazon a world monopoly on something everybody needed, the white exuding sap of the rubber trees, of which there were at least a hundred million in the jungle?

So now all Manáos society was converging on the Teatro Amazonas, some arriving on foot and others in carriages, the men in stiff shirts with diamond studs and gold watch chains, the women holding their long trains by diamond-studded loops. Outside the red stone building they lingered in the grove of trees they called the Orangerie or walked among the marble columns of the portico.

When the door of the Baron's carriage was opened, Savannah saw in the light of the Teatro colonnade that her breast was bleeding. The Baron got out first and as he stood waiting for her she pulled off her long gloves and arranged them between her body and the bodice of her dress to keep the scarlet stain from seeping through the blue satin. Then, avoiding his touch, she went quickly up the steps into the foyer.

There, against the cream and rose Carrara marble pillars, she saw massive chairs, jacaranda wood carved with jungle vines. Since her legs had begun to feel like a pair of hardwood trunks, she sank into one of the chairs, speculating about how she'd ever get through this crowd, through the opera, through the evening. She'd hoped Will would be here in the foyer, that he'd greet her formally and pass her a note with instructions on the escape plan. She'd decided not to tell him she was married. But he wasn't there.

The Baron had been intercepted by the greetings of several men; they shook hands and clapped him on the back, looking toward Savannah. He got free of them and came to take her hand. He told her that Governor Ribeiro had requested that they join him for champagne before the performance. Perhaps that's where Will was. She got to her feet.

The Salão Nobre, or Noble Reception Room, hummed with the conversation of the governor's guests. They helped them-

selves to caviar and champagne under a domed ceiling where
Venus and other nude goddesses reclined on clouds that lay
above the tops of lush jungle trees. Savannah tried to ignore
the pink bodies, but that wasn't easy; the reflections were
caught in the large mirrors around the room. The Baron
grasped her elbow and steered her toward a small, dark-
skinned man who looked young but puffy and debauched. As
they approached him, Dom Luíz murmured angrily, "Smile,
this is the governor!"

As the governor bent to kiss her hand, his eyes, level with
her bosom, seemed intrigued by the stitched white finger pro-
truding from her bodice.

Edward, Veronique, and Porfirio joined them in the foyer.
They barely had time to be ushered into their box, when the
orchestra began to play. Still, there was no sign of Will. In the
light of the gigantic chandelier—suspended from a ceiling
where, again, goddesses and cherubs floated in the sky above
the jungle—Savannah scanned the theater looking for him.
Their box was in the first tier, raised only a few feet behind
the orchestra seats, so Savannah could see most of the theater.
Will's blond hair would stand out in this gathering; running
her eyes along the rows of orchestra seats between the boxes
and the stage, she became convinced he wasn't there. As the
overture continued, she borrowed Maman's opera glasses and
scanned the curved gilt balconies. It was fruitless. He was late
or hidden in a back corner of one of the boxes, or he was
somewhere in the balconies above her. She'd have to wait for
him to show himself.

She leaned on the gilded iron balustrade watching the stage.
From time to time the Baron leaned close to her; always she
looked away. The smell of his breath and the sight of his
hands made her sick. At last the lights dimmed. There was
nothing to do but wait for the intermission. She forced herself
to pay attention to Ponchielli's *La Gioconda*. Now, whenever
Dom Luíz tried to speak to her, she pretended the jolly chorus
of Venetians singing before the Palace of the Doges on the
stage was holding her transfixed.

But her search for Will never ceased. Even though her eyes
seemed fixed upon the stage, she could detect any movement
among the boxes or along the aisles. She'd realized, too, that
the men who lounged about the corridor behind the boxes or
stood under the globe-shaped electric lights that marked the
exits were the Baron's men, dressed in white ties and tails in
place of their usual business suits. She suspected that some of

the ushers were gardeners she and Porfirio had passed in their tour of the Palácio grounds.

There would be an intermission at the end of Act II, and no doubt Will would approach her in the crowded foyer. The moment she saw him she would begin to move slowly among the guests, until she got close enough to whichever door Will seemed headed for.

On the stage the singers were appalled by the sound of the evil duke's cannons. The hero, despairing of escape, set fire to his own ship; and the curtain came down on Act II. Savannah stood as the lights grew bright, but Dom Luíz said, "Porfirio, have champagne brought. I have no desire to be buffeted by that mob."

Savannah said, "But we've barely seen the rest of the theater, the lounges and the portico—"

"Another time. Sit down, Savannah."

So again she watched the aisles, the boxes, the orchestra seats, the upper tiers of balcony. Will was not there. What would he do when she failed to appear in the foyer? He must show himself, even from across the room, if only to put her mounting fear to rest. *Please*, she thought, *please, I'll never ask for anything again, I promise.*

"Looking for someone?" He was leaning close to her.

"Everyone. I find the women's dresses enchanting."

He handed her a glass of champagne. As she sipped he put his arm around the back of her chair. "If you are seeking the crippled gringo, he has been unexpectedly detained." She turned to him. "Now smile," he said. "You must laugh as if I said something amusing. Remember we are a devoted couple, without a care in the world."

During Act III, despair descended on Savannah. It made no difference what she did. Whether she cried out or fainted or climbed over the balustrade into the orchestra seats, the end would be the same. The Baron's men would carry her away. Esme had been right. There was no escape; she'd been mad to think of it. And cruel to involve Will. She longed to cry out: *What have you done to Will? It's not his fault I hate you; let him go!*

Manco was right. She didn't belong in this exotic wilderness. That was why he'd refused to take her with him. He alone could take this opera house and sweep the Baron's guards away. But he'd denied her that deliverance because she was useless, as out of place here as Venus in her painted jungle.

Her defeat was palpable, a distinct physical sensation, a weight upon her chest, so heavy that every breath took effort. Her eyes were dry, yet she felt as if she were trudging across the ocean floor, crushed under a great sea of unshed tears. She wondered why her heart didn't stop beating, pressed down by the weight of her despair.

She would not go through this night. She would delay in the bath or in Esmeralda's dressing room. She would find a knife, a letter opener, a hatpin. Anything. If there was nothing, she would reach into the fireplace and use a burning log to set fire to her nightgown. Perhaps Esme would pray for her immortal soul.

The curtain fell on Act III. The Baron said, "We will leave now. I detest Gioconda's suicide. Edward, don't get up, stay for Act Four."

Savannah sat quietly, resisting his pressure under her arm. "I wish to see it," she said. She reached for the program she'd been handed when they arrived. She turned to the summary of the action, reading aloud from Act IV. "To a dilapidated palace on an island off Venice, Gioconda has brought her rival, Laura—" The lights dimmed, the curtain rose, and the Baron sat down. But before darkness fell on the box once more, Savannah had seen the note written in the margin of her program: *At the start of Act IV go to the ladies' lounge.*

It took her two or three minutes to stop trembling. Then she whispered, "I need to go to the ladies' lounge."

Dom Luíz shook his head. "We're going home."

"No, I've waited too long already." She got up.

He nodded to Veronique. "Take her, and get her back here quickly. I wish to leave before this crowd blocks all the exits."

As they went down the corridor, Savannah expected to see Will; he must have escaped the Baron after all. But he was nowhere in sight, and Nero followed them.

The lounge was elegant. Sky blue carpet, wallpaper of silver fleurs-de-lis on a blue background, and deep blue velvet settees all around the room. There were a half-dozen women lounging about. When Veronique saw them, she lifted her nose as if avoiding an odor. They were gaudily dressed, in multicolored gowns of chiffon, or clinging silk that seemed to be made of scarves. They wore high-heeled shoes and black stockings. Their faces were full of color—azure eyelids, vermilion cheeks—and two of them were adding more. Not one of them was white, at least not completely.

Veronique hurried her into the lavatory. After Savannah

used the water closet, she stood at the marble basin, slowly washing her hands. Her breast had stopped bleeding, but it was discolored and painful. Veronique watched her throw the bloodstained gloves away. Savannah said, "Don't pretend you care what he does to me. You have never cared, have you?"

Veronique said, "Hurry, he'll be angry."

Savannah dried her hands. She had no idea where her deliverance would come from; but she decided that if Will wasn't waiting outside the lounge, she would run as far and as fast as she could until they caught her. At least the high society of Manáos would have that to discuss over tea tomorrow.

As she and Maman walked through the lounge the gaudily dressed women rose. One, who had her spangled skirt hoisted and her foot perched on a chair, drew a slender knife from her garter. Two others pinioned Veronique's arms while the first one laid the blade against Maman's fleshy throat. "One sound, senhora, just one, and I will slice your windpipe like a stalk of celery." For emphasis she added a gurgling sound. Veronique's eyes were wide and her lips trembled, but she made no noise. The woman gagged her with scarves and tied her hands behind her back. Savannah, confused and concerned for Maman in spite of herself, said, "Don't hurt her." One of the girls winked, as if it were all a prank.

They dragged Maman into the lavatory, put her into a water closet, and tied her down on a commode. By then, finding the knife gone from her throat, she'd begun to moan. The one putting her weapon back in its place in her garter laughed. "Groan and grunt to your heart's content," she said. "They'll just think it was something you ate."

A petite black girl locked the cubicle door from the inside and climbed out over the top. Meanwhile the others had been pulling Savannah's dress and petticoats off. They opened a carpetbag and took out a scarlet Spanish dancer's dress, tightfitting to the knees before it flared into cascades of ruffles. They got her into that, then drew her to a dressing table. With three of them working on her at once, they braided her hair tightly and pinned it to her head, fitting a black wig over it. Somebody working from behind her added a high comb and a red lace mantilla. In the midst of the frantic activity, Savannah said, "Where is Will?" Nobody answered.

"Wait, Elena," the black girl said. "She's pale as a fish."

The one with the knife agreed. They painted her lips and covered her eyebrows with black pencil, while Elena gathered up the blue satin and stuffed it into the carpetbag. "Now," Elena said, "watch us, do exactly as we do, and follow wherever we go. Walk behind Egypt"—she nodded at the black girl.

But as they started out, Egypt cursed. "Not like that, you can't walk like a nun!" Savannah took two practice steps, swinging her hips seductively. The others nodded. The seven of them, laughing and gossiping, sauntered out into the corridor. Nero glanced up, then looked away, clearly disappointed. The two girls in front moved close to him. Like the Baron's footmen, Nero's black eyes stared ahead. Egypt drew a feather from her hair and tickled his nose. Savannah, moving in the midst of the other five, passed by unnoticed.

There were several ushers at the main entrance and, beyond, Savannah saw that the Baron's carriage was the first in line. The girls teased the ushers as they had Nero, saying they had to get back to be ready for business because it was going to be a busy night.

Savannah drew her lace mantilla across her face as they passed the Baron's carriage, while Elena caressed the footman standing by the door. Then they moved away from the opera house, dancing flamenco steps with shouts and laughter and hand clapping, down a street, around a corner . . . and then up the steps and into the Contessa's Palace.

26

When Savannah and Veronique failed to return from the ladies' lounge, Dom Luíz sent Raoul after them. Nero assured him they hadn't come out. Accompanied by ushers, they went in and found Veronique. When her hysterics subsided she described the streetwalkers who'd molested her, but it was not a helpful description. The ushers at the main entrance were no more specific; the ladies of the evening were voluptuous and enticing, but the color of the hair, the height, the dresses, all these details remained vague.

It seemed clear, however, that the Baron do Rio Mar's lovely bride had been kidnapped on the eve of her wedding. The entire police force of the city, along with soldiers from the small local garrison, the employees of Rio Mar Rubber, and the Palácio staff were all thrown into the search. Word spread that the Baron was offering the enormous sum of

20,000 milreis—over eleven thousand dollars—for information about his fiancée's whereabouts. The reward was the talk of the city. Mobs roamed the streets turning over carts, poking sticks into the creeks and ponds, knocking down the chairs in the bandstands of the parks, and stopping in at the bars with increasing frequency.

At the Contessa's Palace the evening's entertainment was about to begin. The building's first floor contained several salons and a small private theater. The second floor was devoted to the girls' bedrooms and the baths, one of them so large the tub was the size of a small room, and it was surrounded by couches. On the third floor there were several rooms; there the Contessa and her staff had their private quarters.

Savannah had been taken up the back stairs to the third floor. There she was turned over to the girls' masseuse, Bitte, a blond German girl built like Brunhild, five feet ten inches tall and weighing 175 pounds.

Bitte took Savannah into a rose-colored bedroom with mirrored walls. She said in limited, heavily accented English that Savannah was to remove all her clothing and get into bed.

Savannah protested, but Bitte placed her large hands on Savannah's shoulders and swiftly pulled the red dress down, saying "Ve haf lots customers tonight, must make quick!" Catching sight of Savannah's discolored breast, she moaned and embraced her briefly. "Ah, *liebschen*, be not afraid. Man try dat here, Contessa tell him take his money other place and I t'row him out quick."

Her clothes gone, Savannah got into bed and pulled the sheet to her chin. Already Bitte had gathered up the discarded dress and mantilla. As she started out the door, Savannah said, "Is Will here?"

"Vill? I do not know Vill. But you not be alone long time." She closed the door and locked it from the other side.

Savannah piled up the rose satin pillows and sat with her knees pulled up to her chin and the sheet wrapped around her. She wasn't cold, but she couldn't stop trembling.

Her escape had been so narrow she didn't want to think about it. Still, the *if*'s ran like a litany through her mind. If she hadn't insisted upon staying to see Gioconda's last-act suicide ... if she hadn't decided to pick up the program and read it ... right now, this moment, she would be at the Palácio.

What difference did it make where she was? Anything was better than that.

The room was beautiful, once you got used to the way the mirrors multiplied every image a dozen times. It had walls covered in rose tapestry, white furniture and a white chaise longue, thick strawberry-colored carpet, and an immense bed covered in deep-pink satin. Through the open windows, where sheer white curtains swelled in the light breeze, she could hear noises from the street below. Carriages drew near, stopped, and pulled away again. From time to time groups of people passed, speaking loudly. Inside the house she could hear sounds coming from the lower floors: guitars being played, someone singing in French, and raucous laughter. Savannah was exhausted, still weak from the ten days in bed, and worn out by anxiety. She'd nearly fallen asleep when she heard a key turn in the lock.

The man who entered was about three feet tall, including his silk top hat. His head seemed too big for his body and he had a large-featured, heavy face with sad eyes. He wore a meticulously tailored little dress suit with a ruffled shirt and tails that almost touched the floor. *"Boa noite, senhorita,"* he said as he locked the door from inside. He began undressing with care, draping each garment over the back of the chair.

Savannah watched fascinated as he sat on a low footstool to take off his black patent leather shoes and his black silk stockings. These last he rolled into tiny balls and placed inside each shoe; then he lined the shoes up carefully under the chair. After that he stood up and removed his pants.

He'd gotten his shirt unbuttoned by the time Savannah got her mouth to work. She said, "What in the world are you doing?"

Taking off the shirt, he came over to the bed. Savannah, horrified, demanded that he not move another step.

Finding that the high silk hat was still on his head, he apologized and hung it on one of the bed posts. Then he climbed up on the bed. He said, "Forgive, my lady. I have not introduced myself. Albert." He held out his hand and mechanically she took it. "Actually, Albert is not my real name, but the Contessa always calls me that because she says I am a prince of a fellow." He smiled.

Savannah, clutching the sheet to her throat, raised her voice another note. "I insist that you get out of this bed at once!"

"Yes! The lamps!" He slid to the floor and circled the

room, turning the lamps down low. "Much better," he said, "much more romantic, don't you agree?" Again he clambered onto the bed and slid under the covers.

She moved as far away as she could without falling off the bed. He lay on his side facing her. He said, "You'll have to lie down, though. It's no good if you don't. But whatever happens, senhorita, do not remove your wig. That's very important."

She remained propped on the pillows. "It is?"

"Yes. I don't think they'll get this far, and if they do they'll have to break down the door to get in. Then I am to leap up and down on the bed and scream, 'This is my night off, Bitte's the cashier tonight, give her your money and leave me alone with Carmencita!' Then, the Contessa says, they will all laugh at me and go away."

Savannah lay down facing him. After a moment she said, "I have all the pillows on my side. Do you want one?"

"Thank you, no. I never use a pillow."

They lay still, listening to the music. At length Savannah said, "Were you the angel on the crèche?"

She saw him grin in the dimness. "Yes. You must have recognized me by my voice. Voices are very characteristic. Most people, however, do not listen to voices. Although the voice may appear at variance from the physique, it may be much closer to the person's true nature. Take Bitte, for example. Her body is large but her voice is small and very sweet, which is entirely in keeping with her nature: gentle and compassionate. And me, although I am not large, I have a deep strong voice because I am very brave and surprisingly powerful. Although, of course, I do have faults. I am immodest, as the Contessa frequently reminds me."

Savannah shook her head seriously. "You are the soul of modesty, Albert." Then she asked, "Do you work for Manco?"

"No. I work for the Contessa. But we helped him with the crèche. It was a wonderful pageant, don't you think?"

"Did Manco get you all to rescue me?"

Albert shook his head. "Senhor Manco has been away. We haven't seen him since Christmas Eve."

"I don't understand. A friend, Will Patterson, was supposed to help me. Have you seen him?"

"I don't know him."

"Then, why did the girls rescue me, Albert?"

"Because the Contessa told them to. She is a very clever businesswoman. You will do well here."

Savannah shook her head. "I can't stay."

"Don't be afraid. It's perfectly safe. You don't ever need to go out if you don't want to. And you will make a great deal of money. I know," he chuckled, "I am the cashier!"

The steady noise from the lower floors changed; there were loud footsteps on the stairs. Savannah began to tremble, but Albert took her hand. After a time the sound faded away. They lay there listening for a long while. Soon Savannah found it impossible to keep her eyes open. With Albert still holding her hand, she fell asleep.

The search continued. Docks and warehouses were ransacked, along with all the hotels and restaurants, and every bar and every brothel. The investigation was thorough, with one exception: The squad dispatched to the Contessa's Palace, disconcerted at finding their superiors (including the governor himself) *in flagrante delicto*, backed off quickly.

Still, the investigation was not entirely fruitless. Sometime during the night (probably at the Contessa's, although the chief of police was scrupulous about protecting his sources) an informant had confided that the girls who'd tied up Senhora St. James were as mystified by the disappearance of the girl as the police were. They'd played a prank on the Frenchwoman simply to punish her for insulting them, for saying they shouldn't have been allowed in the Teatro. The red-haired girl must have slipped away then. They hadn't seen her leave and they knew nothing about her disappearance. They had, of course, felt sympathy for her: such youth being married to such age. Naturally old Rio Mar had to insist she'd been kidnapped; his pride wouldn't permit him to say anything else. But, the informant whispered, talk on the street was saying the girl simply saw her chance to get away and took it. Perhaps the chief of police ought to ask himself: Where would a well-born young lady, fleeing a loveless marriage, be apt to go? Then he might canvass the churches and convents and watch all vessels departing for Pará.

Governor Ribeiro had scarcely begun to drink his coffee the next morning when the Baron do Rio Mar, followed reluctantly by a delegation of rubber merchants, called upon him. The governor made no attempt to conceal his irritation; it had been an exhausting night. Dom Luíz began by reminding Ribeiro how much money the rubber business contributed to the State Treasury. Then he insisted upon knowing what the governor intended to do about the attacks of these anarchists, these vandals, these arsonists, these kidnappers.

Ribeiro interrupted him. "Luíz, do not attempt to turn an individual business matter into a state emergency. Your warehouse was the only one attacked. It is clearly a grudge fight. Someone has a grievance against you."

The other rubber merchants agreed readily with the governor. It was really none of their affair.

The Baron waved at them impatiently. "And what of your wives and daughters? No woman in Manáos is safe."

The governor smiled; he was on good terms with the chief of police. "Luíz, there are other possible explanations."

Rio Mar's fist slammed on the desk. "I tell you these revolutionaries have kidnapped her! No doubt there'll be a ransom note, a demand for money—"

"If that occurs," Ribeiro said, "then we will know she has been kidnapped. In the interim I feel the State of Amazonas has done all it can."

The governor rose to his feet and the other businessmen moved toward the door, but Rio Mar strode around the vast desk and grasped Ribeiro by the front of his dressing gown. His face was contorted by rage as he said, "You idiot! Don't you know they're out to destroy me?" He released his hold and the small man sank back in his chair. "If they destroy me, they will destroy you. And I will let them. But they will not destroy *me*, do you understand? I will fight this war alone, no matter how long it takes or how much it costs. When it's done, Ribeiro, you and the rest of these idiots will be gone. And good riddance."

Downstairs at the entrance, Raoul waited by the Baron's carriage. Seeing Dom Luíz striding toward him, he said, "Will he help?"

Dom Luíz didn't answer. He got into the carriage and sat staring at the floor. Raoul hesitated before closing the door. After a moment he said, "The cathedral service is only two hours away. Something must be done."

The Baron looked up. "It's not to be canceled until the last moment. Tell the driver to take us back to the Palácio. I am ready to question that cripple again."

In the darkened study at Arcadia, Edward St. James lay on his leather couch. He was shaking with fever, and Cicero wrapped a woolen shawl around him. Edward said, "I cannot understand it, Cicero. Why would those anarchists want to harm a lovely young girl? What has she ever done to them?"

Cicero held a cup to Edward's lips. "Massa Edward, you jes' stop gittin' yo'self riled up. Didn't you ever think maybe she don't want to marry ol' Rio Mar? That maybe she done run away herself?"

St. James half raised himself up in disbelief. "She's such a clever girl, she saw very clearly the advantages—"

Cicero stood looking down at his employer. "You blind. Yes, you is. She jes' like Missy Madelyn. And she hate him jes' like Madelyn did. She done run away too. And if you cares 'bout her at all, what you best start worryin' 'bout is him, that Rio Mar. He gonna track her down and hound her to death jes' like he did Madelyn. And that's God's truth."

Edward closed his eyes and turned away.

27

The day before, Will had awakened in a cell. Watching the dim light coming in from a window high in the wall, he wondered what time it was and how long he'd been unconscious. Was he fully conscious now? Yes, his senses seemed sharp enough: The floor he lay upon was stone, the walls wood, the window barred. But he could not move; the bonds that tied his hands and feet held fast. He gave some thought to shouting, but what would he shout—"Don't you realize I am a citizen of the United States of America?" An absurd thing to say here.

So although he ached from the painful position of his limbs and the damp chill of the floor, he lay quietly. He got quickly past the stage of not believing this was really happening to him, and he began thinking what a marvelous dispatch this would make. *Six Hours in a South American Prison* by William S. Patterson. That ought to bring in at least two cents a word. Six hours? Or twenty-six?

The light at that high window wasn't getting brighter. Rather, it seemed to be ebbing. Then it was twilight, not dawn. Six hours would be right then. If that was so, he hadn't missed the opera after all.

If all this went on much longer his dispatch would run to several installments. The opening paragraph would say: "Of course it was all a dreadful mistake; that was the first thought that crossed my mind when two men in dark business suits dragged me from my hansom cab." Should he tell how he'd fought? Or how indignant he'd been? It was all so hackneyed, like a scene from the penny dreadfuls he used to read as a boy.

From sheer instinct he'd clutched his cane and begun to strike with it, while his other hand had kept a death grip on his writing case. It must have been at that point they'd knocked him out. Now, as he lifted his head from the floor and turned it painfully to look behind him, he could see his possessions strewn around the room: his hat, cane, raincoat, and the writing case. The case had been opened. He saw his journal, pencils, and the book Savannah had thrown him, all looking as if they'd been examined and thrown aside.

He searched his memory to discover what the local authorities might have against him. There was the interest he'd taken in the rubber business, especially those alleged atrocities. So much time had elapsed without a response to his dispatch, he'd begun to wonder if the telegraph worked even when the operator insisted he was getting replies. Perhaps only the editor's answer had gone astray. Had the piece been published already? Had it caused a stir in diplomatic circles? Were explanations being demanded in London, Washington, and Rio de Janeiro?

Or was his offense simply his constant attempts to see Savannah? He'd had no plan until he saw her on that upper gallery and she threw him the book. Seeing her note, *Have cab at opera*, his heart had leaped: She was not ill, and she wanted him to help her get away. Now he understood why he'd been playing poker with such dedication (like Manco, he'd thought, as if this were a business). He would use his winnings to hire a launch and take Savannah down to Pará. There he'd head straight for the American consul and seek asylum until they could get aboard a ship leaving Brazil. He'd take her wherever she wanted to go.

Only they'd grabbed him moments after she'd thrown the book, and they'd chucked him into this cell. She'd be watching for him at the opera . . . and here he lay, helpless, while the afternoon waned and evening drew nearer. So much for his comic-opera vision of Manáos. This cold floor was quite real, and there was nothing stagey about these bonds.

Most of the light had ebbed from the window when he heard movement outside the cell. A padlock rattled, a bolt slid, the door opened, and a man stood before him. He had gray hair and a gray Vandyke beard; he was wearing evening clothes. The young man with him looked Chinese, but the older one was ordering him in angry Portuguese to do something. The young one knelt down and cut the bonds while the older man stood in the open doorway shouting *"Cadeiras!"* Chairs were brought. The gray-haired man sat in one of them and motioned toward the other. Will could not get up; he seemed fixed in the position he'd held all afternoon. With the help of a guard, the Chinese man lifted him into the chair. By this time the older man was apologizing effusively in English. "An unforgivable error has been made! Sheer incompetence. I cannot apologize enough for the stupidity of my employees!"

Will wondered what response the penny dreadfuls called for, but at this moment his joints required his full attention. He massaged his wrists, his ankles, his knees, wondering if blood would ever flow there again, if he'd ever get warm, and how long it would be before he could walk.

"Allow me, sir." The older man stood up and bowed. "Luíz Alvarez e Costa, Baron do Rio Mar." He sat down again, adding, "And you, sir?"

"Will Patterson." So this was the infamous Baron.

"Mr. Patterson, the journalist? I believe you sent me your card. A request for an interview, is that not correct?" Will nodded. The Baron turned to the Chinese man, who stood in front of the door. "Raoul, what ever made them think this was one of the anarchists? Does this man look like a destroyer of property? See that those responsible for this outrage are punished severely."

"Yes, Excellency."

The Baron glanced at Will's belongings scattered on the floor. "And pick up these things!" Raoul bent to collect the cane, the raincoat, the writing case. As he picked up the book the Baron stretched out his hand and took it. "A volume of English verse, I see. Thomas Moore. I am unfamiliar with his work."

Again he wondered what time it was. The Baron was already dressed for the opera. Will said, "He was an Irishman, a writer of popular songs." He watched the Baron turn the pages. It seemed important to keep talking. "Perhaps you've heard some of them. 'The Last Rose of Summer.' 'Believe Me, If All Those Endearing Young Charms.' "

But the Baron continued leafing through the book as if looking for something. He found it. "Here's a curious line.

Perhaps you can interpret it for me: *'Have cab at opera.'* "
He tilted the page toward the ebbing light. "Why, it appears
to have been written in blood! As a man of letters, what is
your opinion of this verse?"

Will took the book and turned to the front. "There's no
publication date, but I believe this may be a first edition. That
would make this volume seventy or eighty years old. Who
knows what childish games it's been a part of?"

Rio Mar studied him a moment. Will stared back at him,
making a mental note to describe the Baron's eyes as looking
like the steel rivets in the side of a battleship. At last Rio Mar
said, "I believe you were aboard the *Esperança* with my
fiancée. Be so good as to describe for me the nature of your
relationship with her." The Baron snapped his manicured fingers; Raoul produced Savannah's sketchpad and opened it to a
drawing of Will himself. She'd caught his naked look, his eyes
yearning from the page; he wondered if everyone could tell
his love for her in that look.

Will took the pad and turned the pages. "Do you intend to
question the ship's doctor? The captain? What of these, the
gulls, vultures, and butterflies?"

Rio Mar drew from his pocket a slender cigar. Raoul
stepped forward and lit it for him. Through the veil of smoke
the Baron said, "Mr. Patterson, why do you keep watch on
Arcadia?"

"I am a student of architecture. I find such things as trans-
planted antebellum plantation houses fascinating."

Rio Mar sighed and looked at his silver pocket watch.
"Come now, Mr. Patterson. You and I are both men of the
world. It should be as clear to you as it is to me that my
fiancée is a very young, inexperienced, and excitable girl. She
suffers from anxiety about her new life. She is fearful of the
pomp and importance of the cathedral ceremony. She has
misgivings about her station in life as mistress of my Palácio.
So in a fit of panic she conveys to you a distinctly melo-
dramatic message. Indeed, as you yourself said, it was a childish game, nothing more. So let us discuss this as men, not
children. What did you intend to do?"

Will tried to look nonchalant and remained silent. The
Baron stirred impatiently. "Mr. Patterson, I am trying to be
patient, but I have very little time. In a few moments I must
be in my chapel. We are being married now, before the
opera."

Will lost control of his expression. It was only a moment;

he felt the blood drain from his face and his heart clench with pain.

The Baron saw it too. "I see," he said, and smiled. "So the lovely nymph smiled upon the half-man and he was smitten!" Laughter rose in his throat. "A legless Galahad, going to rescue her. From me!" He stood. "Thank you, Mr. Patterson. You have been most amusing."

Will forced his knees to lock so that he could get to his feet and said, "Then I shall be on my way."

The Baron's teeth showed when he smiled. "Not yet. I am a cautious man. You will be free to go tomorrow, after the public ceremony. I shall do you the favor of keeping you from making a fool of yourself at the cathedral." The chuckle rose again in his throat. "After all, we can't have you riding down the nave on a commandeered ox and running your lance through the bishop."

After he'd gone, the guards came in and tied Will up again. As the night wore on, he realized that he would never be released. While those first few hours of detention could be explained by the Baron's story that his guards had mistaken him for one of the arsonists, there could be no excuse for continuing to hold him after his identity was known. But Will wasn't afraid of death. Even pain terrified him less than it might someone who hadn't spent a lifetime dealing with it.

In the morning, his captors dragged him outside, hoisted him into a cart, hauled him out of what he now saw to be a large stable, and took him toward the Baron's Palácio. But instead of propping him against a wall and shooting him, they carried him upstairs. There, to his complete surprise, he was stripped and lowered into a hot, scented bath.

As soon as the shock wore off he felt hope stirring: Had Savannah assumed her position as mistress of the Palácio? Had she begged for Will's freedom as a wedding gift? Was she nearby? He listened for her step, for the whisper of her garments as the dark-skinned woman named Juana massaged his back and legs; but he heard nothing. A maid appeared with his clothing, which had been cleaned and pressed while he was bathing. When he was dressed and leaning upon his own cane, a footman led him from the room as if he were an honored guest, and they proceeded toward one of the smaller dining rooms.

It could have seated dozens comfortably, but the Baron was alone. Placidly he rose and said, "Ah, Mr. Patterson!" as if this was a pleasant surprise. He offered him a cup of coffee and a plateful of omelet, and Will, totally disoriented, accepted the food Raoul served him. Each time the doors opened, he hoped to see her, but it was always another liveried servant bearing more platters.

The Baron was chatting amiably as if this were the interview Will had requested. He spoke of the rubber business, making it sound vexing. A great deal of work was required, but labor in this region was almost nonexistent. In addition, everything had to be imported at great cost—tools, food, medicine. By the time the government imposed its taxes, there was very little profit left.

Will might have been at a board meeting of the railroad back home. Perhaps all businessmen spoke this way. Still, there was a difference in the Baron: He behaved as if he were not so much a tycoon as a king. Watching, listening, nodding from time to time, Will waited for an opportunity to ask when he might see Savannah.

The Baron pushed aside his plate, and Raoul used a silver knife to cut the tip from his master's cigar. Studying Will through the bluish smoke the Baron said, "I believe you made some inquiries about certain accidental shootings at the rubber landings." He snapped his fingers and Raoul handed him a sheaf of papers. " 'Main Ingredient in Amazon Rubber May Be Blood.' Really, Mr. Patterson. I wouldn't have thought you capable of such sensationalism."

"Where did you get that dispatch?"

Rio Mar smiled. "It is possible to buy anything, if you have sufficient capital. In this case I was performing a public service. The price of rubber is as capricious as a headstrong woman. It is important for the economy of this region and for the markets of the world that only the proper information be disseminated. I have, once again, saved you from making a fool of yourself, because the accounts you read were gravely exaggerated, probably from some political motive."

Will sipped the brandy a servant poured for him. "Exaggeration always begins with a fact of some sort."

Rio Mar waved his cigar. "I don't deny there may have been some minor incidents. The guards we are forced to hire are, regrettably, the scum of the earth—ex-slavers, overseers from the Barbadoes—who knows what they are? But they are the best we can get, and we cannot possibly watch them all the time. But atrocities? I assure you I keep a very tight rein on all my enterprises, and I know of no atrocities." He paused a moment, caressing his brandy glass. "You have been watching for my bride, haven't you?" Rio Mar asked. Will nodded.

Rio Mar chuckled. "Satisfy my curiosity, Patterson. I hope to tell the story to my grandchildren. How did you intend to slip away with her?"

"May I see her?"

"Of course." He waved to Raoul, who left the room. "Now: what had you planned?"

"I was going to hire a launch to take us to Pará. There I would seek asylum with the American Consul until I could book passage out of Brazil."

Raoul came back carrying a pile of papers. "There," Rio Mar said. "See her?" Will saw a line drawing that had been made from her photograph. The lettering was in Portuguese but the format was familiar: It was a stack of reward posters. At first he grinned, but that was not sufficient outlet for his gladness at her escape; he threw back his head and laughed. Rio Mar watched him. "I know where you were last night. And I know now her disappearance has surprised you: You haven't the face for cunning. But I must know who else was involved in her scheming and what the plans were."

Will got to his feet, conscious of the servants behind him. The Baron, watching him, said, "She could not have eluded me on her own. No girl—no woman—is that resourceful. Tell me who else was involved. What would she have done when you failed to appear at the opera? Where would she hide in Manáos?"

"I insist that you return me to my hotel at once. I have had enough of your hospitality."

Rio Mar got up. "Surely you do not relish the thought of spending more time in the stable. If I permit my assistants to question you, I can assure you we will get our answers very quickly. But then, you will be in no condition to return to your hotel. As it stands now, my staff—in pursuit of the vandals who destroy my property—made an honest mistake when they apprehended you. I have apologized and offered you my hospitality. Any report you make beyond that will simply be the word of a foreigner against the word of the state's wealthiest citizen. If, however, it becomes necessary to question you more intensely . . . in that case you cannot possibly be permitted to leave the Amazon. Surely you understand my position." He leaned forward. "Where is she, Patterson? Tell me where to look and you will be on your way back to the United States. My launch can have you in Pará the day after tomorrow. What do you say?"

Will sank back into his chair. He opened the cigar box on the table, reached for the Baron's silver blade, cut the tip, and waved for a servant to light it. He took two thoughtful puffs before he answered, because he was searching his memory for the best possible penny-dreadful line. He found one to his liking in a half-forgotten western tale. He leaned his elbows on the table and said, "You onery polecat, whyn't you go piss up a stump?"

28

When Savannah opened her eyes, it was nearly eleven. The first thing she saw was Albert's top hat perched rakishly on the bedpost; and the second was Coco the monkey watching her from the foot of the bed. Then she saw the gray-haired woman in a silk dress the color of old pewter. She was seated at the boudoir table in the rose satin bedroom. "Hello. Who are you?" Savannah asked.

The woman turned and smiled. "Good morning, my precious. You've been asleep a long time. Are you fully rested now?" As she spoke, she moved to the bedside and, still smiling, stood looking down at Savannah. Behind her dusky lenses Savannah could see only the outline of her large eyes. Above the silver frames her eyebrows arched, darker than her hair.

"Yes, thank you," Savannah said, stretching. "This is a lovely bed." There was a lump under her head; the black wig had come off during the night. "They didn't search this far, did they?"

"No. We found sufficient distractions for them downstairs." She touched a strand of hair strewn across the pillow. "You don't remember me, do you?"

Savannah sat up and looked at her. Then recognition made her throw herself into the Contessa's arms. "Of course! You're Mr. Estyn's friend! Jocelyn's father! How could I forget that day at the Botanic Gardens and Claridges? But what are you doing in Manáos? I don't understand." She pulled away to look at her. Although she couldn't see the expression of the Contessa's eyes, the rose-tinted lips were smiling.

She caressed Savannah's cheek. "Of course you don't, my golden dove. But it's too long a story to tell you on an empty stomach." She pulled a tassel on the wall, then helped Savannah put on a wrapper. Soon after, the door was flung open and Albert came in carrying a large coffee pot. Bitte, laden down with a breakfast tray, followed. Two chairs were drawn up to a small table set with a linen cloth and rose buds in a vase. "Bless you, my treasures," the Contessa said. Then the two of them were left alone.

Savannah, famished, almost fell upon her food. After a time the Contessa said, "I'm delighted to see you appear none the worse for wear, in spite of your ordeal." Savannah grinned above another forkful of omelet. The Contessa pointed toward the bruised breast. "Did he do that to you?" Savannah pulled the wrapper closer. Softly the Contessa said, "How are you otherwise?"

"All right, I suppose, except that the touch of his hands made me feel like retching. He's tricked me, you know. The wedding rehearsal last evening was the real marriage, and if your ladies hadn't gotten me out of the opera house, I'd be dead now. I'd made up my mind, and I would have gone through with it."

The Contessa got up and knelt at Savannah's side, taking the girl's face in her hands. "I'm so sorry, dear, I simply couldn't get to you any sooner." She looked away, shaking her head. "How you must have suffered these last weeks!" She looked back to Savannah's face. "Well, you're safe now. We'll put all that behind us, won't we? This is the start of a new life."

Savannah had cleaned her plate. Seeing her glance around the table, the Contessa got up and put her own untouched dish in front of the girl. Grinning sheepishly, Savannah began to eat again. Between mouthfuls she said, "You haven't told me what you're doing in Manáos."

The Contessa's uplifted hands indicated the walls. "My business is here. Of course, I travel a great deal. There's a turnover, so recruitment is a constant necessity."

"Did Mr. Estyn ask you to watch over me?"

The Contessa's expression remained unreadable behind her glasses. She said, "Do you know what this place is?"

Savannah nodded. "My father says these are women of easy virtue."

The laughter cascaded. "Virtue is never easy, only vice is easy. And even vice becomes difficult at times. Do you object to being here?"

Savannah got up and began examining the lamps and vases

around the room. "You want me to work for you, don't you?"

"Would you?"

"No, I wouldn't." Savannah didn't look up from the bowl of camellias on the dresser. "You've gone to a lot of trouble, you saved my life, and I'll be eternally grateful for that . . . but I'm sorry, I don't think I approve of people selling their bodies."

After a pause the Contessa said, "But then, my precious, what will you do?"

"I don't know what I want to do . . . only what I don't want to do."

"Sometimes, child, we find it necessary to do things we don't want, simply because we have no choice."

Savannah turned. She sensed a great disappointment in this pretty woman; but that couldn't be helped. She said, "I believe there is always a choice."

The tinted lips smiled sadly. "Only if you are willing to die. But self-destruction, like virtue, doesn't come easily." She rose and came to Savannah's side. "Well, first we must get you some clothes. You'll be quite safe here, but you must never leave this apartment without your wig, Carmencita. And never leave these rooms at all between the hours of two in the afternoon and two in the morning."

"Will you help me find my friends?"

"Of course. The Estyns are where they always were."

"Do they know what you do?"

"Europe is five thousand miles away. On my letterhead, this is a school. Do you want to go to London? Or Paris?"

"Neither. I want to find Will Patterson."

The Contessa paused at the wardrobe. "Who is that?" Savannah explained about the book she'd thrown. The Contessa looked troubled. "You may have cost that young man his life, Savannah. Well, I'll look into it."

"And," Savannah said, "I want to find Manco."

The Contessa, kneeling to take underclothing from the bottom drawer, seemed to be giving her full attention to the pink satin bow on a tucked chemise. "And what do you want with Manco?"

"I love him and I want to follow him wherever he has gone."

"And does he love you?"

"Yes, but he wouldn't take me away with him because I don't know anything about the jungle."

The Contessa stood up and came to put her arms around Savannah, laughing as she took her in her embrace. "Well, my dear, I think we ought to be able to do something about that."

"Can you? Can you make him come back and take me with him?"

The Contessa kissed her cheek and smoothed her hair. "I cannot make him take you away with him, love. But I can make him come back here to see you."

Savannah hugged her and began to dance around the room with Albert's small silk hat on the side of her head.

When the Contessa, shrouded in gray chiffon, entered the cathedral that afternoon, the rose petals from the canceled wedding were still being swept from the floor. She found the priest kneeling off to one side, in an alcove called the Lady Chapel. He said, "Father, will you hear my confession?"

Father Antonio got up. She followed him to the dark confessional booth. He seated himself on the other side of the screen and said, "Well, my child?"

She said, "I have taken Savannah from Rio Mar."

He sighed. "I see. Did she come away willingly?"

"Yes. He'd already mistreated her."

"Is she at your place?"

"Temporarily. She's safe there."

"Then to Europe?"

"That's not what she wants. She's fallen in love with Esteban and wants to go upriver with him." She saw the dim outline through the screen; he was shaking his head. She said, "I know it's out of the question. He's told her that himself, but she won't believe it. And that's not all: The Baron tricked her. The wedding rehearsal was an actual nuptial Mass. She is already married to him."

"Consummated?"

"No. They were alone only a few minutes, in his carriage. He put his hands on her, but nothing more."

"Then it can be annulled. But not here. She's not safe anywhere in Brazil. You know that." She nodded. After a moment he said, "Have you told her?"

"I started to, but . . . I suppose I thought she'd remember me. But why should she? There's no reason, is there?"

"Madelyn, you must tell her."

"Tell her what? My name? Then she will be ashamed because her father's sister runs a bordello."

"Tell her you are her mother."

"Is that any better? It is worse. She already believes I am trying to recruit her into service for the house."

"Do you want her to continue believing her real parents will force her to marry Rio Mar?"

"Then how do I answer her next question? If I am her mother, who is her father? My brother? If not my brother, then who? Is that what you really want me to do?"

He bowed his head. "I think she has a right to know how you tried repeatedly to get her back, and how much you suffered. And how you wept and prayed for her every day. I think she has a right to know all that; I think you have a right to tell her. You are entitled to her love, Madelyn. Claim it now."

"No. I will only make her unhappy. All I want is for her to be safe. In Paris, perhaps, in an apartment with her friend Jocelyn. Perhaps she'll go to the Sorbonne. Cicero says she's a wonderful artist. That dear old soul; I'd have lost my mind these last two weeks if he hadn't come to see me every day."

"So Savannah and her friend will live in Paris. And you? Do you retire and rent a flat across the way so you can look at them through opera glasses?"

"I am a family friend of the Estyns. So it would be natural for us to see one another in Paris. Then one day she'll marry someone she loves; I want that for her more than anything."

"Will they wish you to visit them? Will they let you see the children? Will they ask you to stand as godmother? Tell her the truth, Madelyn. If you don't, she will break your heart and never know she's done it. You have no right to jeopardize her conscience that way. What you suffer from is not her shame, but yours. When you are no longer ashamed of your life, she will not be ashamed of it."

She put her hand against the screen as if to touch him. "Dear Antonio. You have been telling me the truth ever since I was a little girl, haven't you?"

She heard him laugh quietly. "Isn't it time you began listening?" She sighed, but didn't answer. He said, "She is so like you. Does she also have your willful heart?"

Madelyn nodded. "I'm afraid so."

"Then I shall pray for both of you."

"And Esteban, too, Father. When I mentioned her name to him, he seemed angry. I think he may care for her, but he won't permit himself to."

"Then it's imperative, for his sake as well as hers, that you get her out of Brazil. Nothing must interfere with Esteban's work, Madelyn."

"And nothing must interfere with Savannah's happiness. You must understand—that is first with me. . . . Will you come to see her?"

"Only if she wants me to."

Madelyn again lay the palm of her hand upon the screen. "You will. And you will love her, no matter what she says or does, just as you have loved me. You know everything I've done, and even my darkest thoughts; yet never once have I had the feeling that you ceased to love me. I want Savannah to know you."

"Very well. I'll come to see her."

Savannah spent an hour in the Contessa's private bath. At last she dried herself and went back into the bedroom, where clothing lay on the bed. She was a little taller than the Contessa, but the pale pink dress fit well. She liked its simplicity; it was soft and free of the bones and flounces Veronique was so fond of.

As she sat at the boudoir table brushing her hair and tying it back with a pink ribbon, she began to listen to the Contessa's voice in the next room. Quietly Savannah opened the door into the sitting room. The Contessa was walking back and forth, dictating a letter to Elena, who sat writing at a cream-colored Louis XIV desk. Elena no longer looked like a streetwalker; now she seemed prim and businesslike enough to be a governess. She wrote swiftly on the rose-colored letter paper, stopping at the end of every line to dip the pen in the inkwell. The Contessa walked to the window and stared out at the city. "Read me that last again."

Elena read the line, "I am writing to inform you that . . ."

The Contessa nodded. "That I have obtained some very special merchandise. A virgin, a natural redhead with eyes of an unusual violet color, and young, not yet seventeen. I am certain to be offered a great deal for her, but since you are a particular friend, I will give you an opportunity to enter the bidding, which unfortunately must be closed in ten days time. . . . That's all. I'll sign it." As she turned from the window she saw Savannah in the doorway.

Savannah's chin lifted and her eyes burned angrily. She said, "Thank you for your hospitality. I will leave now."

The Contessa went to her. "My precious—"

But Savannah pulled away from her embrace. "I will return

the clothing later. And I shall pay you for the night's lodging. But I will not stay in this place another moment."

The Contessa dropped her hands and looked at Elena. "Tell her whom the letter is for."

"Esteban Manco," Elena said.

Savannah gasped. "You would sell me to him?" Tears had begun to run down her cheeks and her hands clenched at the sides of her skirt. "You are an evil woman. I never dreamed there was such evil in the world as I have seen in this town." She turned back into the bedroom and crossed toward the door.

The Contessa followed her. "Savannah, listen to me!"

The door was locked. Savannah faced her. "I insist that you open this door at once." Vaguely she was aware that the Contessa was weeping too. Still, when the other woman's hands reached for hers, she said, "Don't touch me!"

The Contessa clasped her hands and looked down at them a moment. Her lips were trembling. She drew a ragged breath and said, "You know Manco. You know he denies himself everything. It is difficult to manipulate a man who has no vices. He will not come here simply because you want him to, or I want him to, or even if he himself wants to."

Savannah shouted, "He loves me! I know it!"

The Contessa shook her head. "It doesn't make any difference whether he loves you or not. He won't permit it."

Savannah turned and leaned her forehead against the door. "He was afraid something might happen to me in the jungle. That's the only reason he left me behind."

She felt the Contessa's arm around her shoulders, but she didn't pull away. The Contessa said softly, "If he wanted you with him, my dearest, you would be there. Believe me. If Esteban wished the Andes moved, I think it would be done."

Savannah began to sob. "He said . . . he had no time for me."

The Contessa stroked Savannah's hair. "That's right, love. He has time only for the oppressed." Savannah grew still. "Let's see if he will rescue an innocent virgin from the clutches of a wicked bordello keeper."

The Contessa's pink lips were smiling now, but Savannah remained troubled. "He wouldn't save me from the Baron."

"Because he's a man, and men think it's better for a woman to be married to a man she despises than for her to tramp the world, unmarried, with a man she adores."

The Contessa had drawn Savannah away from the door.

They sat on the chaise, the girl still locked in the older woman's arms. Savannah said, "Manco isn't like other people."

"No, he isn't. But when it comes to the institution of marriage, all men are the same. Esteban's cause, he believes, demands his entire dedication; so even if he loves you, he could not offer you marriage himself. Now let's see if he loves you enough to be concerned about your virtue."

Savannah shook her head despondently. "I don't think he cares about me at all."

The Contessa embraced her again. "Dearest, we will know in ten days. He may descend upon me with an army."

"And if he doesn't?"

"Then we'll know you must forget him."

Savannah shook her head. "I'll never be able to do that. I'd rather work for him the way other people do, even if he pays no attention to me."

The Contessa stroked Savannah's hand. "If he's going to love you, he must love you as you are. That is what love is. Only here, where passion is bought and paid for, can roles be played.

"Well, we must get that message off to him. Then we've got to get busy. In the next six days we must treat you like a new recruit." She pulled Savannah to her feet and looked at her fondly. "Welcome to the Contessa's Palace, Carmencita."

29

Savannah found living at the Contessa's was much like being at school. It seemed like a girl's dormitory, except that here everyone slept late, had coffee in bed, and spent a full hour in the bath before breakfast.

Still, there were lessons. Elena, who had been a dancer, taught the others flamenco steps. Egypt played the drum, Artemise and Francesca played guitars, and Maxine sang. Music, however, was only part of the curriculum. The Contessa, who frequently reminded them that youth wouldn't last forever, insisted that they learn to keep accounts and study letter writing, polite deportment, and fine needlework. They were required to attend to these pursuits whenever business was slow. Then, when it came time to leave, they took with them an official-looking diploma which announced that this individual had completed a course of study at L'Ecole Normale De Manáos, Rue Epaminondas, Manáos, Brazil—*Directrice*: Luciana, Contessa della Mirandola.

There were at present sixteen girls, each with a small room of her own on the second floor. Special customers, the ones who paid extra or made arrangements to spend the night, were taken to the large rooms on the third floor. Albert called these the bridal suites. Savannah looked in at them, but wouldn't enter; she liked the girls' little bedrooms better. Each was the size of a nun's cell, but filled with ornaments and souvenirs. She felt she could see into each girl's mind by looking at her room.

Morgan, for example, was English and she kept a framed photograph of Queen Victoria over her bed. During the evening she turned its face to the wall. She kept a parrot, too, and taught him to talk. When Morgan had company the bird, whose name was Charlie, had to be covered up. Not, Morgan said, because she didn't want him to see, but because he made rude remarks.

On her dresser Liliane kept a picture of an earnest little boy with short pants, a stiff collar, and slicked-down hair. His name was Marcel and he was with Liliane's mother in a little village outside Rouen. She'd been working twelve hours a day as a seamstress in Paris, but she'd never been able to send home more than two or three francs a week. Things were different now. She showed Savannah her bankbook: she had 12,000 Swiss francs to her credit. In one more year she was going home to buy a little house and open a dressmaking shop. Marcel would walk to school each day, and when he came home she'd always have something hot for him in the oven.

"I will wear black, only black," Liliane said. "I'll say I am mourning my husband, a sailor from Marseilles, lost at sea. I will live across the square from the church, and every time the bells ring I will throw a shawl over my head and run to prayers. Everyone will say: 'She is a saint!' "

Egypt, the petite black girl who'd locked Veronique's cubicle from inside, resisted self-improvement and asserted that she'd never grow old. She looked about fifteen, but confided to Savannah that she was really twenty-one, and added that she'd found the secret of eternal youth. It was: Never worry. The Contessa, unconvinced, scolded Egypt often about her refusal to plan ahead, and also about her cigars, dainty little cheroots. The Contessa told Savannah that Egypt had no family at all.

When she was a few days old, she'd been placed in the bin at the foundling home in Pará.

The best part of the day was the time spent in the bath. The tub was so large that several of them could fit into it at once. The others lay around the edge on the tiled floor or on the heaped cushions. Maids carried steaming buckets of hot water, and soon the air was moist and warm. Charlie chuckled in his cage in a corner, and Coco scampered about stealing combs and small jars of scented cream. The girls reclined naked. Sometimes they ate fruit: mangoes, pomegranates, or oranges.

At the convent the girls were never permitted to show their bodies. They bathed once a week wearing an old petticoat, reaching up under it with a sponge to wash. They were not to touch themselves or each other. One girl who was suspected of touching herself in bed at night was made to sleep with her hands tied.

So Savannah was fascinated by the sight of the Contessa's girls so at ease in their bath. Gaya, a beautiful Polish Jew with breasts like veined alabaster pears, tipped with nipples the color of wine, used a soft hairbrush on the hair between her legs, making it shine like silk. In the water Maxine was scrubbing Liliane's back, and Francesca was rubbing a fragrant oil into Egypt's brown skin, stroking it into the dimples on Egypt's lower back and down the length of her legs. As the others reclined on the blue and green tiles, waiting their turns for Bitte's massage, the sunlight falling through the steamy window panes lay like an eclipse rimming the curves of their bodies.

The bruise on Savannah's breast provoked questions and advice. Several of them told her where to kick the next man who tried that. Gaya put her brush aside and gazed at Savannah, her luminous dark eyes seeming to search for a language in which to communicate, since Gaya spoke no English and Savannah no Polish. At last Gaya spoke the word in Portuguese. She said, *"Virgem?"*

Bitte answered, *"Ja,* she iss virgin."

Savannah found them all looking at her. Egypt jumped to her feet and snapped her fingers like castanets. "When it's gone, it's gone forever. Permanent. Like a tattoo."

Watching them, listening to them, Savannah thought, *Am I really here? Or have I somehow fallen into a reverse image of school where night becomes day and the uniforms are wrong and everyone discusses all the things you're told never to talk about?* Yet she felt perfectly at ease, as if she'd always belonged.

Bitte had finished massaging Maxine and said, "Elena, you now?"

But Elena said, "Isn't it tonight, Bitte?" Bitte nodded, her ruddy German face blushing. Elena said, "Then we'll do you."

Several of them pulled Bitte into the water and washed her hair. Afterward they buffed her nails and twined ribbon into her braids. As they worked, Elena explained to Savannah that Bitte had a steady customer who wanted only her. He was a clerk who could afford to come only once a month, but he always spent the night because he loved going to sleep in Bitte's arms. Bitte's body, Savannah saw now, was beautiful; it reminded her of the voluptuous pink goddesses on the opera house ceiling. She tried to picture Bitte's little clerk asleep, and ended thinking of Manco, wondering what it would be like to sleep in his arms, to have the last thing she saw when she closed her eyes be his face, and to see it again in the morning when she awakened. She said to Bitte, "Do you love him?"

Egypt and Maxine laughed, but Bitte looked down and said, "*Ja*, I luf him."

"Are you going to marry him?"

"*Ja*, ven ve both save enough. Next year, maybe."

Albert pounded on the door to tell them it was breakfast time; they dressed quickly and went to the dining room on the main floor. The Contessa sat at the head of the table. When everyone was in place, she said grace. As the food was being handed around, she told them solemnly, "As you know, Margarida is leaving today." They all looked at a slim girl dressed in a high-necked white muslin dress; her hair was done in a tight bun. The Contessa said, "I'm not going to talk about how much we'll miss you, dearest, or we'll all begin to cry. But I have spoken to the chief of police, and you will have no trouble on the dock or at Pará."

Francesca said, "Why are they searching everybody?"

"That brings me to the next topic—Carmencita. The search for her isn't dying down, it's intensifying. And the reward has been doubled. The Baron has raised it to fifty thousand milreis. Almost twenty-five thousand dollars."

Bitte, who was bringing another platter to the table, murmured *"Gott im Himmel!"*

"Five years' work," somebody else said.

Egypt turned to Savannah. "If you went back, would he give you the money? I mean—"

The Contessa said, "She's not going back to him. It is very important that no one finds out that she is here. If word gets out, Rio Mar will tear this place apart and you will all be out of jobs."

Savannah said, "I don't want to endanger anybody—"

Morgan said, "Listen, we've been in danger before, the lot of us," and the others agreed.

"At any rate," the Contessa said, "it's only for ten days or so, but let's all be very careful. Now it's time to go into the salon. Margarida, dear, you'd better finish packing."

The large salon was a lavender room with immense purple ottomans and sofas. At the far end there was a small raised stage with curtains of purple velvet. The Contessa made the girls cross the stage one at a time, then walk down the steps and sit down somewhere in the room. As they moved she corrected their posture and carriage, the placement of their feet and hands, and the way they seated themselves. Clapping her hands impatiently, she said, "Elegance! Our guests pay for elegance! If they wanted a slut, they could find one on any street!"

When the walking lesson grew tiresome, Savannah roamed into the carpeted foyer, where Albert sat on a high stool, putting money away in the drawer of a tall desk. "See," he said, "they pay me eighteen milreis or ten American dollars or two English pounds or whatever the currency is, and I make change. Then I give them one of these." He showed her a brass token. "They give it in turn to whichever girl they like."

Savannah said, "And what are these gold medals?"

"They cost five times as much. For one of these they can spend the night. At closing time or in the morning the girls give the checks back to me and I write it down in my book."

"And then you give them the money?"

"No. Half of it goes to run the house, and the other half goes to the girls, but the Contessa makes them put two-thirds of their share in the bank."

"Do they make a lot of money?"

He rolled his eyes and spoke confidentially. "Gaya makes the most. I've seen her turn in seven gold tokens in a week, so after paying the house and putting her savings away, she still has almost sixty dollars a week for perfume and feather boas!"

Margarida, all packed now, came downstairs. The coach-man, Raimundo, who acted as the doorman during business hours, was carrying her trunk. The Contessa came in from the salon and embraced Margarida; the others gathered around, looking tearful. The Contessa said, "Remember, if you ever fall in love, never tell him you have been here. You will only unburden your own heart at the expense of your lover's happiness. If you must confess, find a good priest." She kissed Margarida, then unwound a long string of pearls from her neck and put them on Margarida, saying, "Don't forget—if you ever need me, just send word."

Margarida nodded, blinking, and whispered, "Thank you, for everything." They embraced and one after another the others kissed Margarida good-bye. Then she went quickly out to the coach.

As the carriage bearing Margarida to the dock passed the Hotel Internacional, Raoul was driving away in the Baron's coach. He'd been to get Will Patterson's luggage. Bribing the desk clerk generously, he explained that the American was eager to learn about the rubber business, so he was going upriver and would not be coming back this way but, rather, would return to the United States by way of Peru. The desk clerk had grinned "How many crazy gringos have gone off into the *selva* and never returned?" And Raoul had grinned back, "Well, sometimes their heads turn up." The clerk had chuckled, "Yes, that's right—heads the size of oranges, courtesy of some friendly tribe like the Jívaro!"

30

Savannah found the business hours in the Contessa's Palace long and dreary. She was required to remain in the private apartment on the third floor from two in the afternoon until her bedtime. She could watch the carriages arriving at the front door, and she could listen to the sound of the music, the singing, and the laughter; but she could not leave.

She tried not to count the days since the Contessa's letter had been sent off to Manco, off somewhere deep in the *selva*. Nevertheless, she knew at any given moment how many days had passed, how many hours, how many minutes.

She tried, too, not to speak of him, although the day Egypt

and Francesca had taught her to play poker, his name had come up. Savannah had said, as casually as she could, that he'd been on the *Esperança*, playing poker every night. Egypt stretched out her arms and said, "When I am rich I'm going to keep a man." Ignoring their laughter and the derisive comments, she went on, "And he's going to look just like Esteban Manco. Tall, dark, and slender as a sword!"

After the whistling and catcalls had died down, Savannah said, "Is he ever . . . a customer?"

"No," Egypt said, and sighed. "Whenever he comes here he stays upstairs, in the Contessa's apartment." So at night Savannah wandered through the rooms of the Contessa's apartment, touching the arms of chairs, the mantelpiece, doorknobs, clocks, wondering if his hand had rested on each. There was a small chamber on the other side of the sitting room, a plain little bedroom where the Contessa slept now that she'd given the rose satin room to Savannah. Standing in the little chamber, Savannah thought, *Does his head rest on this pillow?*

She thought the waiting was going to drive her mad. She'd drawn sketches on the rose writing paper and played with Coco for hours. She'd wound up the Contessa's Swiss music box and danced around the rooms to the sound of the chimes, gongs, banjos, and snare drums hidden inside the machine. She poked around in the Contessa's vanity, trying on powders and perfumes, arranging her hair in various styles, and painting her face with rouge from a pot. She'd explored the closets, trying on all the Contessa's dresses one after another.

One evening she grew so bored she thought about leaping from a window or sliding all the way down to the main floor on the bannister or setting fire to the drapes so that firemen would arrive, or anything, anything, but this dreadful empty waiting . . . and she decided to go downstairs. She put on one of the Contessa's evening dresses and the Carmencita wig. She painted her lips and her cheeks, put a black lace mantilla around her face and long gloves on her arms, and carried a carved ivory fan.

She encountered no one on the second floor. Keeping the fan open before her face she went down to the foyer. Albert, busy making change for a fat man in a tuxedo, did not look up. Savannah stepped into the small gold parlor.

Keeping close to the wall in order to pass through the room unnoticed, she moved on into the large salon. The room was so dimly lighted the lavender walls seemed dark purple. Standing close to the closed draperies, she watched the stage, where to the gentle chords of a guitar Maxine was singing a love song. As the song ended, she saw the accompanist strike the final chord on his guitar and look up. Now that her eyes had adjusted to the darkness she saw him clearly. It was Porfirio. For a moment they looked at each other, then Savannah turned away, into the arms of the Contessa. Without a word the Contessa gripped her elbow and began steering her back upstairs. Once inside the apartment, the older woman faced her angrily. "What is the matter with you? Have you lost your mind?"

"I was bored, that's all. I can't stand being cooped up like this."

The Contessa lifted her hands in despair. "Would you rather be cooped up in the Palácio? Don't you know Porfirio is here tonight? Right on the stage playing his guitar!"

"I know. He looked at me—"

"Oh, Lord." She sank into a chair and covered her face, but only for a moment. She raised her eyes to Savannah's gaudy face. "He probably couldn't see you in that light."

"No. He knew me. But he won't . . . he was glad. I know it. He was relieved. I suppose he thought I'd drowned myself or something."

"Well, it's true he has no reason to love his father. . . . Poor Porfirio. He buys gold tokens so he can sit all evening playing his guitar. I suppose because we are kind to him and make no demands. But he could never hold out if the Baron questioned him." She went to the window. "And there is João waiting with the carriage. You dare not even go near a window tonight!" She drew the shade.

Seeing the Contessa trembling, Savannah took her hands. "I'm sorry I have upset you. I promise not to do that again."

The Contessa bit her lip, shaking her head anxiously. "I don't think you realize the danger you are in. If just one person gets a glimpse of you, they'll turn you in for the reward. Don't you understand that? It's a temptation, that much money, even for people in this house, for the servants, for anyone. And if the Baron gets word that you are here, how can I keep him from taking you back? The police can do nothing; you are his wife." She paced the length of the room, but seeing the effect her words were having, she took Savannah in her arms. "Well, we'll have to trust Porfirio, that's all. I am sure you are right. He has a good heart. Did anyone else see you?"

"No. Everyone was watching Maxine."

"Then come. Sit down. It's all over now."

The Contessa drew her to the sofa and sat holding her in her arms and Savannah found that she had an almost irresistible urge to weep. "I don't know what's the matter with me," she said. "So much has happened to me since I left the convent. I've changed so. I never used to cry. But then, I never felt any of the things I've felt since I came away from there. I mean, I used to feel warm or cold, hungry or frightened—"

"Frightened?"

Savannah frowned. "I think I was afraid of . . . love, I suppose." She twisted her hands together. "When men I don't like touch me—like the Baron and like that sailor on the ship—I feel very angry. I'm afraid of—it's as if I'm a bubble and what they want to do will break me. I'll vanish; I won't be myself anymore."

"And Esteban?"

"When he touches me, it's just the opposite. I feel safe." She looked up, embarrassed; she hadn't intended to talk about her feelings for Manco. But she added, "I can't believe that's wrong. Do you think it is?"

The Contessa kissed her cheek. "Of course not."

After a moment Savannah said, "Do you . . . receive guests?"

The Contessa laughed. "No, my angel."

"Never?"

"Never. It isn't done." Seeing how puzzled Savannah looked, she said, "Some women who run houses like this have a man of their own, perhaps someone who works there. But the madam never takes customers herself."

"Then you are always alone."

"Yes, child."

"And are you . . . lonely?"

The Contessa smiled. "Some women are fated to love only one man for the whole of their lives. When he is gone, no one else seems worthy to be in his place." She was quiet a moment, then she said, "Do you understand, dearest, that Esteban is a man with a mission? Such men cannot love us as we need to be loved. They are forever going away, leaving us with empty arms."

"Yes, I understand," Savannah said.

The Contessa sighed. "People who love each other ought to be together all of their lives, and when they are old. . . ." She closed her eyes briefly. "But you are not going downstairs any more, are you?"

"No. I really do promise. Only I wish—"

"What, love?"

"I wish I could have talked with Porfirio, to ask him if he's seen Will Patterson. I can't stop thinking about him. Will's so—" She fingered the lace edging on a sofa pillow. "He's so open to every hurt. When you look in his eyes, you feel as if you could see all the way down to his toes. You know he's been hurt again and again, but he's never gotten used to it, or grown a shell. When you've said something careless, his eyes just get very still. Then he looks away and doesn't say anything."

"And does this Will love you, dear?"

"Love me? I don't know. But if I've cost him his life, I should have stayed at the opera and gone to the Palácio and died there. Who am I that I deserve to claim somebody's life for my freedom?"

The Contessa took her hands, as if by squeezing them she could cut off this train of thought. "Getting yourself caught won't help your friend."

"But what if I told Porfirio to take a message? I could give myself up if the Baron lets Will go."

Shaking her head, the Contessa said, "Rio Mar would beat your whereabouts out of Porfirio, then he would come here with a force of men and tear the house apart until he found you."

Savannah got to her feet and paced the sitting room. "I hate feeling so helpless! I hate not being free to do what seems right. I hate not having any choices!"

The Contessa smiled. "Did you not tell me there is always a choice? And you were right."

She got up and took Coco from her writing desk, where he'd begun taking things out of the drawers. She put him behind a sofa cushion, where he curled himself up and went to sleep. Savannah sighed and sat on the sofa again, idly stroking Coco's head. The Contessa watched her a moment, then sat close to her and took one of her hands. "Dearest love, don't you think you have a right to be happy?"

Savannah looked up startled. "No. Do I?"

"That's what they taught you at the convent, didn't they?"

"Yes. Mother Dominica said earthly life is a series of tests. You must pass them all, and then you'll go to heaven."

The Contessa laughed. Then she put her arm around Savannah. "And they never told you that you are good and dear and lovable, did they?" She pulled the black wig away and loosened the auburn hair, stroking it tenderly. She said, "No wonder you are afraid of feeling anything."

She looked deep in Savannah's eyes as if she was searching for something. At last she said, "Did no one ever hold you in their arms?"

"Only Manco, on the ship."

"But before that? Not one of the nuns?"

Savannah's eyes took on a faraway look. "When I was very small someone held me. She rocked me in her arms and sang me a lullaby. My father said it was an English nanny. She was very beautiful, I think, but I can't really remember her face." She sighed, "Anyway, something terrible happened. I have a nightmare about it. Someone comes out from a doorway and grabs me, and I am always so terrified. But it's just a bad dream."

The Contessa held Savannah's head against her breast, murmuring in a choked whisper, "Oh, my dearest child, I am so sorry. If only I can make you understand—"

The door opened and Albert came in breathlessly. "Better come down, Lady Contessa. The governor is plenty mad. He wants Gaya and she's already got a gold one."

The Contessa leaned her head back against the sofa. "Let him have two others. On the house."

"I already said that. He demands to see you. Says he's coming up—"

So the Contessa went downstairs to mollify the governor. When she was free to come back up again, Savannah was already asleep.

31

"Wake up, my dear, Father Antonio is here!" The Contessa pulled the covers from the rose satin bed. "He is my dearest friend. When I was very young he was my teacher, and he's been my confessor ever since my first communion. Come, wash your face and put on your dress."

When Savannah entered the sitting room, she saw the man who'd preached about the City of God on Christmas Eve. He was middle-aged; his dark hair was gray at the temples and he had the soulful Portuguese eyes that were becoming so familiar to her. He was clean-shaven, thin, and ascetic-looking; he reminded her of the pictures of saints. But more than that, his face as he smiled at her seemed radiant with love and compassion; she felt blessed by his gaze.

Instinctively, Savannah went to him and knelt. His hand rested a moment on her head. The Contessa was saying, "I hope you don't mind, dearest. I asked him to come and talk with you."

"It's been more than two months since I left the convent. I have a great deal to confess," Savannah said.

The Contessa quietly left the room. Father Antonio lifted Savannah to her feet, and they sat down together on the sofa. As she talked he watched her, nodding in encouragement. When she began twisting the lace handkerchief in her fingers, he gently took her hand. He said nothing until she'd finished telling him everything—how much she'd hated Maman during the long shopping trip in Paris and on the ship; how little respect she had for her father, and how bitter she was about the arranged marriage. Then how she'd run away after being married in a solemn nuptial Mass. Finally, she told him of her two great sins: She'd put her dear friend Will in danger, and she'd planned to destroy herself. And now, of course, she was in a place of evil.

She found him smiling at her. "I'm here too," he said. "I come here often. Isn't it wonderful to know God's mercy is greater than all our sins, yours and mine and everyone's?" Seeing her frown, he leaned a little closer. "Are you disappointed? Do you want me to be shocked? To say you are the world's greatest sinner? That you deserve a long penance? What would our Lord say to you?" After a pause he said softly, " 'Go, and sin no more.' "

"You are saying I'm to go back."

"No, that's not what I am saying. In the eyes of the Church you are not married. The nuptial Mass must be celebrated by the man and woman freely; the priest is simply a witness to the rite they themselves perform. If one of the parties is under duress, there has been no Mass. In addition, I understand the marriage was not consummated. So there is not a valid marriage."

Her hands were still now. She'd dropped the handkerchief and was staring at him, her eyes wide and her lips parted. "I'm not married . . . ?"

"Not in the eyes of the Church. Civil law, however, presents other problems, especially when there is sufficient money for bribery. You must leave Brazil quickly, Savannah. You must go to Rome and get an annulment. I will write a letter explaining everything. These things take time; you may be in Rome several months. But then you will be free." He raised his eyes beyond her. "And in the meantime, child, pray earnestly to be delivered from evil. For the sake of your immortal soul, do not hate those who have wronged you. Protect yourself from evil; fight it every step of the way, but return blessing for cursing. God knows how hard it is for us, but He rejoices in earnest struggle to be good."

Savannah felt as if a tightly coiled spring in her middle had begun to unwind slowly. "I'm not married," she repeated. "And it's not wrong to go away. . . ." She smiled uncertainly. "I had to do it anyway, but I thought—"

"You thought God had washed His hands of you."

"Yes!"

He looked into her eyes. "From time to time God chooses certain individuals to do some great task for Him. During these periods Satan uses every weapon to pull the person down, even innocence and beauty. Even the dearest wish of our hearts."

"Do you mean love?"

"Not love. Love seeks the good of the beloved above its own. I mean passion, Savannah. Passion can exact a terrible price."

After he'd left, she found herself picturing Satan on a stool behind a high desk passing out gold tokens.

It was still early when she went to the bath; most of the girls weren't out of bed. Savannah hugged Bitte and, suddenly rid of much of her anxiety, she asked Bitte to teach her how to give massages. "Then," she said, "I can help, and you won't have nearly so many to do."

Bitte agreed. After Savannah bathed, Bitte massaged her, explaining as well as she could with her limited English what the different movements were supposed to do. Savannah lay face down, relaxed and happy, trying to feel each set of muscles soften under Bitte's warm hands.

When Liliane came in, Bitte and Savannah massaged her together, with Savannah watching Bitte's hands moving on one of Liliane's legs as she moved her own along the other. Savannah tried, but Liliane began to giggle. She said, "Your hands are so light, they tickle," and Bitte told Savannah she must press with all her weight.

Elena, watching from the tub, spoke up. "Don't wear her out, Bitte. She may not sleep tonight." Savannah blushed. Ten days had passed. She wasn't embarrassed, but she felt confused. Would he come? Did he care? Would he hold her in his arms all night? And should he? Was it wrong?

The others began exclaiming over her, asking questions, offering their best dresses and jewelry. They drew her into the tub and washed her hair with scented soap. Seeing that the sun now shone fully on the windows, they opened them outward to let air into the room and made Savannah sit in the sunshine while Egypt brushed her hair dry and Francesca polished her toenails. As Egypt's hand followed the brush down the waist-length copper hair, she said, "If I were as beautiful as you are, I would be the mistress of a king."

Savannah sighed. "I don't feel beautiful. I never have. And anyway, what good does it do when the one you love doesn't have time for you?"

Francesca shook her head emphatically. "You can make him forget all about time; all you need to know is how to make him happy."

Gaya had gone to her room and now came back with a small vial of perfume. She said, *"Um minuto . . . antes. . . ."* Her dark eyes searched the corners of the room for the words she needed. One of the others said, "She means put it on just before you see him." Gaya nodded, then pantomimed opening the vial and placing a drop of scent at the wrists, the inner elbow, the throat, the two dimples on the lower back, behind the knees, and at the top of the inner thighs.

Savannah said, "Thank you. Thank you all very much." As she spoke, she pulled free of their hands. She felt an urge to flee, but her wrapper was on a peg across the room.

Elena slipped an arm around her and said, "Don't be afraid." Over her shoulder to the others she explained, "Savannah doesn't know anything. That's it, isn't it?"

They gathered around her. Morgan studied her seriously, eyes close to Savannah's face. "Is that the truth, luv? Ye don't know a bloody thing about it?"

Savannah lifted her shoulders a little. "Maman said my husband was to teach me."

Several of them laughed at that, and said that's why business was so good. Francesca said, "One of my steadies is coming this afternoon. Do you want to watch? He wouldn't mind."

"The Contessa would," Elena said. "She's not to be downstairs during business hours."

Savannah said, "I don't think I'd care to watch anyway. But thank you for offering."

"Then we'll show you," Egypt said. "Bitte, come here. You're the man." Bitte protested, but soon she was laughing as several of the girls pulled her out of her wrapper and drew her over to the heap of cushions along the wall. Then the others moved back to watch. Egypt sat beside Bitte, close enough to whisper, "What's your name, love?" Egypt caressed her cheek and nibbled at her ear. "João. I love the name João. It sounds like a tiger's roar. Are you a tiger, João?" The others groaned and told her to get on with it. Egypt moved hands gently over Bitte's body saying, "Don't be shy, my tiger." She pushed Bitte down and nuzzled up to her like a brown kitten, all the while caressing her thighs, her buttocks, and the mound of curling flaxen hair between her legs. Savannah watched fascinated as Egypt nibbled, kissed, gently bit, and even licked Bitte's body. There was, to her astonishment, nothing violent or painful in this playful tenderness, nor anything furtive or guilty. It was nothing like the Baron's harsh embrace. But soon Albert beat upon the door announcing breakfast. Laughing, the audience fell upon the lovers and threw them in the tub to cool off.

Savannah was relieved to find the Contessa absent from the breakfast table. The girls laughed more than usual, but Bitte as she went back and forth from the kitchen seemed subdued. At last, after another of her disappearances through the swinging door, Egypt proposed that they take up a collection and send Bitte's little clerk a gold token for tonight.

Savannah couldn't eat. Seeing the girls' tenderness with each other had brought it all back, the way Manco held her face like a chalice in his hands, the warmth of his lips on hers, the strength of his arms around her. She was no longer afraid of anything but the thought that he might not love her.

Asking to be excused, she left her plate untouched and went up to the special rooms at the other end of the third floor, those "bridal suites" she wouldn't enter before. Now she wandered through them, touching the pillows and the lamps and imagining being here with him. She liked the last one best. It was done in shades of green, with the color of moss, new grass, spring leaves. She thought that in the darkness of night the room must seem like a jungle.

She closed the door and lay on the bed, trying to imagine him there with her. Would he let her touch him the way Egypt had touched Bitte? Could she kiss the hollow at the base of his throat, the ridge of his spine, the curve of his firm belly? Might she place her hand on his outer thigh and feel the muscles tensing there as he moved? Remembering those moans of pleasure she closed her eyes like Bitte and thought how wonderful it would be to show her love for him by bringing him such sweet ecstasy.

32

The sun had faded, and from the massed gray clouds rain was falling when Manco, wearing the long cassock and broad black hat of a priest, slipped into the side door of the Contessa's Palace. He went directly to the private sitting room, where the Contessa was working at her desk. She'd been expecting him and looked up without surprise. His dark face looked more implacable than ever; his lips, bracketed by the narrow black moustache, were tense with anger and barely moved when he said, "How much?"

She put down her pen, her head tilted. "I can't reveal the other bids. Surely you understand. It would not be ethical."

He stood just inside the closed door, his eyes narrowed and his head turned slightly away from her in distaste. "I am astounded to find you are such an evil woman."

"It is an evil world, my friend."

"How much?"

She moved her account books aside. "She is an extremely valuable property. I have gone to considerable expense and trouble to prepare her."

He took three long steps and stood in front of her. "Open the safe." Moving without haste, she went to the wall and turned the dial. He looked at the neat bundles stacked inside and said, "Which are mine?"

"The pouch of diamonds and this cash." She drew out five packets of currency and began to read the labels aloud. "Three thousand pounds, five thousand dollars—"

"Take it all."

Her eyebrows lifted above the frame of her spectacles. "An extremely generous bid."

"Then it's done."

"Not quite so fast." She put the money back and closed the safe. While he watched impatiently she looked into the empty bedroom and surveyed the third-floor hallway. Behind closed doors once again she said, "Breakfast will be over soon and it is important that we are not disturbed. Please sit down." He refused. Seating herself in one of the gray brocade arm chairs she said, "I am not without some interest in the child's future. I want to know what you intend to do with her."

"Such solicitude."

She lifted her shoulders slightly. "I guarantee my transactions, at least for a short period of time, and a girl who is happy is a far better risk."

"Surely you know I intend to free her."

"Indeed. I thought you only liberated Indians."

He crossed to the window and scowled out at the downpour. "I have no time for clever conversation. Rio Mar himself has been dynamiting warehouses, vandalizing stores, sinking people's launches, apparently in an effort to gather support in his fight against us. It's working. Now every policeman and soldier in Brazil is after us. Getting in was difficult; getting out may be impossible." He turned his heavy-lidded eyes back to the Contessa. "Listen carefully. You are going to do exactly as I say. You will take her out yourself. Both of you will dress as nuns. Say you are making a pilgrimage to Lourdes. Do not remove your disguises until you reach Europe."

"And then?"

"See to her education. Enroll her in a good school. If you need more money I will get it." He walked over to her and leaned his hands on the arms of her chair. "I will want a full account of your actions and I will have you watched. If you betray her again—"

"When her education is complete, she'll be able to look after herself." He went back to the window. Rain pounded on the cobbled streets, and thunder cracked from one rim of the jungle to the other.

The Contessa said, "I'll send for her."

He crossed the room so swiftly he caught her hand before it touched the bell pull. "No! I will not see her. Not now, nor at any time." He released her hand.

"Esteban," she murmured, "you do love her."

He drew away from her. "I must go. Remember: Do not attempt to betray her again."

She ran to the door and barred his way. "Stay! I had to find out. When you made no move to stop the marriage—" He took her by the shoulders and moved her aside. "Esteban! There were no bids! She wouldn't. And neither would I." As his hand grasped the doorknob the Contessa threw herself upon him. "She will not go unless you force her to. She's determined to be with you." He paused. She continued, more quietly. "She won't come away with me because she loves you. She wants to follow you through the jungle."

He went to the mantel and leaned upon it. The ormolu clock ticked harshly in the silence. "All right. I'll tell her to go."

She'd begun to pace the room, her hands clasping and unclasping in front of her. "No, wait. That won't do." Her silver shoes made no sound on the dove-gray carpet. "Breakfast must be over. She'll be coming upstairs any moment. I've got to think." She opened the sitting room door and stood listening in the hall. "I hear the girls. Come with me." He followed her past the stairwell and the servants' bedrooms. "In here," she said, drawing him into an empty room and closing the door. It was the first of the bridal suites, the Red Room. The scarlet draperies were closed; the room was dark. She lit one of the lamps, her image glowing in a dozen reflections, and she sat down on the red silk loveseat. Manco sank into a high-backed chair nearby.

"Are you certain you don't want her to wait for you?" she asked.

He shut his eyes. "No. I do not want her to wait."

"Then you must break her heart. You must free her to love someone else, some clean-faced English boy with a big house in the country where she can raise horses and dogs and babies." He sighed heavily, but said nothing. "You must spend the night here, Esteban. In this room—with another girl." His eyes opened. "Believe me, my friend," she said, "it is the only way."

She got up and began to move about the room, staging the scene for him. "I'll be evasive. I will attempt to conceal your presence from her. Then I'll see that she finds out by accident. She'll say she doesn't believe it. She'll want to see for herself. I'll try to stop her. She'll force her way in and find you in bed with . . . it had better be Elena, she's the most dependable. You must be indignant at the intrusion and say to Elena, 'What's happened to this place? Is there no privacy left? Get packed, I'm taking you upriver with me.'" The Contessa paused, satisfied. "Yes. That should do it. Savannah will run from the room into my arms. I'll hold her until she cries herself to sleep. Then in the morning she'll let me take her away. She will grieve. A long time, perhaps. But then—" She realized Manco's eyes were fixed upon her.

"You are a strange woman," he said.

She laughed. "I told you my girls are actresses. I enjoy staging performances."

He got up and joined her in the middle of the room. Gently he took the dark glasses from her face. For a long moment he looked into her dark lavender eyes. "How blind I've been," Manco said. Then: "Forgive me. I should have helped you from the start. If you had told me—"

She touched the shoulder of his cassock briefly, comforting him, and sat down on the loveseat as if she were suddenly exhausted. "They took me by surprise," she said. "I'd planned to take her from the convent myself in the spring, at the end of her last year. I was going to retire. I'd present myself as her Aunt Madelyn. She doesn't know me, you see, and there was always the chance she might refuse to come away. But I never dreamed they'd interrupt her education. I got a letter saying Veronique had been to Lausanne to get her. I'd no idea what for, until the marriage banns were announced four weeks ago at the cathedral. By then, she was aboard the *Esperança*. . . . But at least now she knows what they are—Edward, Veronique, Rio Mar."

He sat beside her and took her hand. "And you still haven't told her?"

She shook her head. "No one knows but Antonio. That's been the hardest part—not being able to talk about her." Her smile trembled. "But Esteban, is she not lovely?"

He put his arm around her shoulders and held her close. "Yes. She is more beautiful than any bird of paradise, or any passion flower, or any sunset."

They smiled at each other while the tears fell from Madelyn's eyes. She said, "And she's good, isn't she?"

"Yes. And very brave. She laughs at storms. Did you know that?"

"And she's intelligent." He nodded. "Not bookish, like my brother Edward, but quick." She looked away. "I know there's nothing more boring than a doting parent."

He shook his head in denial of boredom. "I never told you how we found Tomás—"

But Madelyn's outpouring could not be stopped. "She's so warm-hearted, worrying herself sick over that crippled American who's disappeared. And she's kind. Not effusive, because it's hard for her to show affection—she's not used to it. She told me you were the first person she could remember who'd held her close—" Madelyn stopped and put a hand to her mouth. "Oh my dear, forgive me!" She touched his face tenderly, as she might a son. "Tonight you're going to send her away, and I'm babbling while. . . ." And gently she kissed his burning eyes.

It was at that moment that Savannah saw them. She'd gotten up from the bed in the last of the bridal suites, wondering if this Green Room was the best after all. Perhaps he'd prefer to forget the jungle for one night. Bitte would be in the Blue Room. That left the Red. Were the mirrors everywhere, or had she imagined it? From the bed would you see yourself? She hoped not.

They hadn't heard the knob turning or the soft sliding of the door across the scarlet carpet. In the loveseat before the fireplace, their backs were to the door. The Contessa herself was in the arms of a lover, the man she said she'd always loved, a man whose black hair in the soft red lamplight was iridescent as a blackbird's wing and whose dark face was carved like the mask of some ancient god.

Savannah fled down the stairs, around the landings, down to the door and through it into the street and the blinding rain.

33

Albert had seen her go. He slid from his high stool and began shouting. "Carmencita! Carmencita!" But she was gone, out the side door. Raimundo, standing ready to unlock the front entrance for the customers, watched speechless as Albert scampered back and forth in the foyer. "Girls! You there, Morgan! Egypt! Carmencita's gone outside!" They grabbed their shawls and ran into the rain, and Albert, with all but his short legs hidden by a great black umbrella, lagged behind them.

There was little traffic. Vendors had found shelter under awnings or in the arcades in front of shops. Those who could afford to were drinking in the bars until the storm would let up. Savannah ran heedlessly, stumbling over the rough cobbles in her thin slippers. She was heading toward the cathedral because she wanted to die and she had a feeling only Father Antonio could stop her.

Egypt, running freely like a boy, overtook her at the edge of the Cathedral Plaza. She caught Savannah by the arm, was shaken loose, and caught her again. "Stop! You want to get sent back to that one who hurt you? Is that what you want?" Savannah stood still but looked at Egypt as though she didn't recognize her. "At least let one of us collect the money if that's what you're going to do." Savannah let herself be led out of the open and into a sheltered doorway.

By then Morgan had caught up with them. She said, "What's the matter wi' ye, luv? 'Ave ye gone daft?"

Savannah looked across the square where the tops of the palm trees thrashed in ragged unison. Egypt said, "Maybe she's sick."

Morgan felt her face. "No, I don't think so. 'Ey, maybe it's that man of 'ers. Maybe 'e ain't coming. Is that it, luv?"

Egypt reached up and hugged Savannah. "You want me to get him for you? I'll find him."

Savannah began to tremble. Morgan and Egypt held her until Albert came along, looking like an umbrella with feet. Francesca and Maxine were behind him. Egypt said, "She's crazy in love and her man stood her up."

"No," Savannah said. "He loves *her*."

Morgan took the cape Maxine had brought and wrapped it around Savannah's shoulders. "Don't you worry, luv, we'll take care of 'im. And 'er too, if you want." Then, with Albert's umbrella held over their heads, the girls took Savannah back to the Contessa's, ignoring her protests.

Once inside the house they began to whisper. When Bitte met them at the door, Albert said, "Does she know?"

"*Nein*. She is upstairs mit somebody."

"Then," Albert said, "don't let her find out. She be plenty mad. Get everybody dried off quick."

Egypt went first to make sure the way was clear, and soon they had Savannah in the bath. She let them pull the wet clothes from her body and dry her off; then she waited quietly while they got themselves changed. She was numb now; she no longer cared what happened. She'd allowed herself to feel. Now she knew that led only to betrayal and anguish.

Elena came in. She said, "Where have you all been? I'm supposed to run the class today—" Seeing Savannah's bereft look, she said, "What's happened to you?"

But in the hallway Bitte was calling, saying the Contessa

wanted to see Elena upstairs. They continued drying their hair with towels and soon Elena returned. She stood inside the door, leaning against the wall and looking troubled. "I don't understand. What's going on? Savannah, what's happened?"

"Manco doesn't love me. I thought he did, but he's loved her all the time. All the time."

"Her? Who?" asked Egypt.

"Me," Elena answered. "The Contessa wants me to spend the night with him in the Red Room. I'm to be there at nine."

They all looked at each other for a moment, and finally Savannah said, "But I saw them together. In the Red Room. The Contessa was kissing him."

"Is that all?" Morgan said.

Egypt added, "She kisses everybody! Albert. Raimundo. Everybody."

Savannah's mouth felt dry as an oven. "But you said he stays in her apartment when he comes here—"

"But not in her bed," Elena said.

Egypt said distinctly, "He never stays with any of us."

Savannah sank to a pile of cushions, shaking her head. "I was going to make him take me away."

Egypt turned to Elena. "Why not? It would work. The Red Room is dark."

Morgan said, "If she wore her wig—"

Elena, shaking her head, backed away. "But we don't know what this is all about. There must be a good reason—"

Morgan laughed. "Sure, there's a bloody good reason. 'E wants somebody for the night and she's sending in 'er best!"

"And Carmencita will be very good," Egypt insisted. "Her heart will be in her work. And look at her!" They appraised her body, the unblemished whiteness of her skin, the rosebud nipples, the copper-gold hair.

Elena shuddered. "She'll kill me. She'll throw me out for good."

Morgan took her arm reassuringly. "We'll say we put you up to it—"

"Like the Frenchwoman," Egypt added. "We'll tie you up and lock you in the water closet."

But Elena continued shaking her head. Morgan said, "Come on, it's only a lark. Be a sport!"

Egypt said, "Look at her, Elena. She loves him. Let her have him tonight."

Elena leaned closer to Savannah. "Is this what you want?"

Savannah, fully aware for the first time since she'd run outside, took Elena's hands. "Yes. I want to find out for myself how he feels about me. I want to see if he will let me make him happy. Yes, I want to spend the night with him."

Elena touched Savannah's cheek, pulling a strand of hair away. "You know he'll just leave you again in the morning. They always do—"

"He's always leaving me anyway."

"No. This time it will hurt much more."

"All right. But they come back too, don't they? Maybe he'll come back."

Elena stood up. "I think we ought to tell the Contessa first."

Savannah rose and faced her. "No. Please. It's important." She glanced from one to the other of them, trying to conceal her lingering distrust of the Contessa. "You see," she said, "they say he reads minds."

Egypt nodded solemnly. "That is true. Men who play cards with him swear it."

Savannah finished with assurance. "So even if she promised not to let him know, she might not be able to keep our secret."

After a pause Elena nodded and Egypt, unable to contain a delicious shiver, hugged Savannah.

At eight o'clock the Contessa and Savannah had supper in the sitting room. Savannah tried to behave normally, but she couldn't. Her thoughts raced ahead, making her fork tremble on its way to her mouth and the wine in her goblet ripple as if a wind had touched it.

The Contessa seemed uneasy also, and when the meal was over she remained in her chair, tapping her polished nails on the edge of the table. At last Savannah said she was exhausted and would like to retire early.

She listened while the Contessa paced back and forth in the sitting room. After a while Savannah heard her go downstairs. She waited another two or three minutes, then went to the stairwell and whistled. Elena came up and got into the rose satin bed. Savannah covered her up and turned the lights out before she went off toward the bridal suites.

A few minutes later the Contessa was back upstairs, standing in the doorway of the darkened rose bedroom. She nodded to Albert. He said loudly, "Message for Senhor Manco!"

The Contessa crossed the bedroom and confronted him at

the hall door. "What do you mean, bursting in when some-one's asleep? Of course Senhor Manco isn't here!" Then, in a whisper she added, "The Red Room!"

But there was no movement from the bed.

The Contessa raised her voice. "Albert, Senhor Manco isn't here!"

Still the humped-up covers remained motionless.

The Contessa went to the bed and drew back the comforter. "Elena Rodriquez!" she cried. "What are you doing here? Where is Savannah?"

Elena sat up. Even in the dim light from the hallway she looked sheepish. "She's in the Red Room."

"The Red Room?"

"It was her wish. I . . . we . . . arranged for her to be with him."

The Contessa began wringing her hands. "How dare you? How dare you? That child—" She stopped. "I should have known she'd be up to something." She'd begun to laugh, stopped herself, and laughed again. "He's going to think I tricked him."

Albert came to her side and tugged at her dress. "Hey, Lady Contessa—maybe he won't care."

She hugged them both. "Maybe he won't. Poor Esteban! He would have to be made of stone—like the Andes. . . ."

Morgan and Egypt had dressed her in the Spanish dancer's costume, with the black wig and the lace mantilla. Outside the door to the Red Room they whispered last-minute instruc-tions. Egypt said, "Whirl into the room so your skirt flares out. Then turn your back and close the door. Bend over and lift your skirt all the way and pretend to adjust your garter. Then he'll look at your legs and not your face."

Savannah, unsteady in the high-heeled shoes, put her hand on the doorknob and took a deep breath. She was quaking. "I can't," she whispered.

Egypt said, " Of course you can."

Savannah took another breath, crossed herself, and went inside.

Manco was sitting in the high-backed chair near the hearth. A burning log in the fireplace threw a fitful light upon the stark planes of his face; the rest of the room was dark. A few minutes earlier one of the other girls had stuck her head into the room to tell him there had been a change of plans: The

Contessa's newest girl, Carmencita, would be the one to act out this charade with him.

So now as Carmencita closed the door, he barely glanced at her. He got to his feet, walked over to the scarlet bed, and began undressing, paying no attention to the way she lifted her skirt and adjusted her garter. Keeping her back to him she went to the other side of the bed and began undressing. She heard him say, "You are Carmencita?"

Softly she murmured, *"Sim, senhor."*

Carefully she removed the lace mantilla and dropped it to the floor without disturbing her black wig. Then the red dress slipped down over her shoulders and fell. Her one-piece undergarment, opened down the front, fell also. Still she kept her nude back to the bed. She was trembling, but he hadn't noticed. He'd gotten into bed and sat up with the sheet pulled over his body; he was staring moodily into the fire. She pulled her wig off. As her hair fell over her shoulders and down her back he turned his head. She faced him. His eyes flared briefly, then she saw his jawline harden. He said, "What are you doing here?" He sat up, swinging his legs out of the bed.

She ran around to him, cutting off his escape. As she knelt before him, her hair framing her like a wreath of fire, her hands grasped his thighs.

He looked away. "What is this? What has she done to you?"

"She doesn't know. She sent Elena, but I got Elena to let me come to you instead."

He placed his hands on the sides of her head, smoothing her hair and looking at her sadly. "Then it's off, you see. It was all a scheme to make you go away to Europe where you'll be safe. Get dressed now. I want you to leave with the Contessa in the morning."

"Kiss me, Manco. Kiss me the way you did on the ship. Hold me in your arms again."

He took her hands from his neck and pulled himself free of the bedcovers. He stood, reaching for his clothes. She got to her feet and put her arms around his neck once more, pressing her breasts against his chest and her belly against his. "Hold me," she whispered. "Take me in your arms, then I will go." Slowly he put his arms around her. She kissed his neck, the hollow of his shoulder, the shadow beneath his ear.

Slowly, indistinctly, she heard the sound growing deep in his throat, a low rumbling groan that swelled until it burst from him like a volcano. He bent to her, kissed her mouth fiercely, while his hands moved over her body until he'd cradled her in his arms, lifted her into the air, and carried her to the bed, all the while whispering her name again and again as if it were an incantation.

She awakened to find the chill Amazon dawn filling the room with gray light and Manco lying beside her sleeping. Far away in the jungle a bird called. She thought: *He will leave me now*. And then: *I am not a virgin anymore*.

She did not move, but lay on her side gazing at his closed eyes, the high bones of his face, the long limbs where beneath the bronze skin sinuous fibers twisted. The life beating in his body seemed perilously frail; the tip of an arrow or the fangs of a serpent could pierce his flesh. And Savannah herself would sicken; her life would ebb away with his, now that they were one.

She grew dizzy remembering the night. He had wrought miracles upon her body, cleft her to him with such force that he left her racked and spent. *At last*, she thought, *his mark is on me: all of me*.

She longed to touch him now, but dared not, for, awakened, he would hear that bird cry and lift his eyes beyond her to the *selva*. She understood now what Elena meant: After this night it would hurt more when he went. Already she found herself cherishing her memories as if he were already gone.

He had laughed during the night, his teeth gleaming in the darkness. There was in his loving a relentless tenderness; he was preemptive and demanding, his dark face bent over her intently.

So this was love: to know and be known, in parts of herself she'd been unaware of. All those parts of her had come to life at his touch. In an astonishment of devotion she'd kissed his hands and all the hollows and depressions of his body, the fine black hairs of his moustache, the ridge of his cheekbone, the hollow of his temples, the faint cleft of his spine. Now she felt exhausted and sore, but utterly alive and not yet satisfied.

She'd taken Elena's place to find out whether Manco loved her; what she'd learned was the depth of her love for him. She knew that she was doomed to love this man forever. For the rest of her life happiness would depend, not on comfort or peace or safety, but on his presence.

She lay listening to his breathing. Those hands, so strong yet so delicately made, had caused her to tremble with a strange ecstatic fear. The hands were soft now, upturned like chalices which, even as he slept, seemed to hold her heart.

No longer able to resist the need to touch him, she lay a finger on his throat where the pulse throbbed. He opened his eyes; her heart faltered. He turned toward her smiling and they lay face to face gazing at each other.

He raised his hand and touched her cheek. His eyes were no longer the impenetrable black she'd known before. Now they were touched with gold, as though the volcano that erupted last night glowed now in banked and smoldering fire. But his eyes were as black as ever; what she saw was herself reflected in them: her hair flaring on the pillow, lighting his dark eyes with gold. He said, "What is it?"

"I don't want this to end." His eyes closed slowly, a withdrawal. She said, "Lock the door. Let's not leave this room ever."

He drew her close to him. When he spoke, she heard the murmur in his chest, the pulse in his throat, and felt his breath upon her ear. He said, "What am I to do with you now?"

34

Esteban Manco had been born high in the Peruvian Andes. He did not know the location of his village or the name of his mother; his earliest recollection was of the priests at the crumbling monastery where he'd been left a foundling. That had occurred on St. Stephen's Day and prompted the choice of his Christian name.

Almost at once the fathers had been struck by Esteban's intelligence. Even if (as one or two of them insisted) his age exceeded the three years or so he appeared to be, his quickness of mind was remarkable. As the years passed, they began also to remark about his height; he overheard frequent references to his Spanish blood. Later he understood this meant that one or perhaps many of his female ancestors had been raped; but at the time, he enjoyed the favor his heritage won him.

Although he learned everything he could get the priests to teach him, his hunger for knowledge remained insatiable. He read every book in the small library of the monastery and then went back to read them all again. The brothers, who had come to Peru from all over Europe, taught him languages to keep him occupied—Spanish, Latin, Greek, English, French, German—and set him to work making translations. When that palled, they devised mathematical problems to keep him out of mischief. On the whole, however, his education remained spotty, old-fashioned, and narrowed by theological limitations.

The priests worked earnestly to channel his enthusiasm into proper courses, stressing that his primary function in life was to be good. Esteban was warned that his inordinate love of learning might be a snare to draw him away from the lowly station God had assigned him.

For a time, when he was twelve or thirteen, this thought deeply tormented him. At last he confessed his anguish to Father Cristoforo, who tended the kitchen garden. The old man, who never in his five decades in the Andes had ceased to grieve for the little Spanish seaport that had been his home, looked kindly at Esteban and then lifted his eyes to the mountains rimming the horizon. "Who know God's intention?" he said. "Perhaps it is His will that the talents He gives us not be buried, no matter who we are. If you become learned, might you not be the first of your race to rise in the Church?" His lined face creased in gentle amusement as he looked down at his earth-grimed fingers. "Then my mission in God's design would be to fill you with nourishing vegetables."

Later Esteban understood that Father Cristoforo was unique. Homesick as he was, the priest truly loved the Indians. The other men of God, however, looked upon them with distaste and saw their ministry as a penance they did not deserve. Esteban began to think about his race.

I am, he explained to himself as he dug the small mountain potatoes out of the ground in Father Cristoforo's garden, *an Indian. I am one of the Quechua, the people of the Inca. My ancestors built forts, palaces, roads, and farming terraces of enormous stones so cunningly fitted that even now you cannot insert a knife blade between them, and which continue standing through many earthquakes while newer buildings fall around them. Everywhere in these mountains are monuments of the Inca builders. And I am their descendant.*

He hoped these thoughts would comfort him; he hoped they would still the growing unease that interfered with his struggle to be meek, obedient, and self-effacing. But they did not, for it was clear to Esteban that the Quechua had fallen out of favor with the Lord. Although they crowded into the chapel on all the holy days (wrapped in their colorful ponchos, the men wearing pointed wool caps with ear flaps, the women in their brimmed felt hats), this devotion did not soften the harshness with which the priests treated them. Watching covertly, he saw that the men of God were careful not to touch the Quechua when giving them communion.

The boys at the monastery school were sent back to their homes when they neared manhood. Orphans like Esteban were kept on a few years longer to work as servants. Because he had a gift for teaching he was permitted to become a brother. He also learned the rudiments of medicine and was useful in the dispensary. Nevertheless, in response to his inquiries it was made clear to him that he could never be a priest.

When young white men fresh from Spain became his superiors, he suppressed his dismay. Some of them meant well, some did not; but none was well qualified for the work, and all of them believed the Quechua were inferior, filthy, and stupid. Esteban prayed more earnestly than ever for the grace to accept his place in life. And all the while his heart ached at the sight of those devout Indians kneeling at Mass, ragged, starving, debased, and subservient, like beaten dogs. Remembering the wealth the Spaniards found when they arrived in this land three and a half centuries before, he asked himself what had happened. How could this be God's will, that the Spaniards be fat and warmly dressed while the Quechua shiver and go hungry? Had it been His purpose that the Indians be converted and simultaneously enslaved?

When he was about sixteen he was chosen to be a bearer for the bishop of Lima, a man who weighed 300 pounds and had to be borne on a litter up and down the narrow mountain trails to visit all the missions. For centuries, perhaps for millennia, the ancestors of these youths had traversed on foot the high passes. It was arduous work, work that only mountain people could do; in the thin, chilled air lowlanders sickened and lost their footing. Yet it was painful even for Andeans. The limbs ached and the breath seared the lungs. Esteban's companions dulled the pain by chewing coca leaves mixed with lime, but Esteban denied himself the solace of the drug, for he valued his mental clarity above his physical comfort. As a result he felt acutely his own and his companions' degradation, especially when at hostels along the way the bishop took from his mouth and threw to his bearers the bits of meat he found too tough to chew with his decaying teeth. The others fought over these scraps; Esteban in his pride and anger went hungry.

He asked the priests to send him to a remote mission, anywhere the labor was hard, so that he might exhaust his fury in good works. He was sent to the transmontane jungle, to the misty cloud forest on the east slope of the Andes. There he helped clear ground beside a river and build a mission, a chapel, a dispensary, a school. The forest Indians, distrustful, came slowly to the priests. In a year, however, they lost their fear of these men in long white robes, and two hundred of them came to live at the jungle mission. Esteban and the others treated their diseases and taught them; they gave them clothing and Christian names. Esteban enjoyed the work, for he felt affection for the shy, childlike people of the forest.

He had nearly forgotten his rage when white men came to gather laborers for their rubber trails. The priests held up their crosses and cried out the name of God, but the white men laughed at them and fired their rifles, killing the children and old people and driving the rest of the Indians aboard their launches. Esteban, standing by the river, never forgot the look of utter betrayal on the faces of the captives.

He found the only surviving child hiding in the dispensary cupboard. It was the small boy Tomás. Without speaking to the other brothers or the priests, Esteban took Tomás in a canoe and left that place. Driven by his rage, he paddled upstream many days. At last his canoe came to rest on a strip of beach above the rapids. He and the boy paused there two days and then went on. After four months of traveling, they reached the old monastery. Esteban left Tomás in the care of Father Cristoforo and began to wander.

Everywhere he went it was the same: A handful of men, the descendants of Europeans, owned the land, the houses, the fields, the mines; and everywhere the Indians, those to whom the land truly belonged, were in subjection.

He worked beside the Quechua in the fields their ancestors had terraced and irrigated for the Inca. Like them he knelt beside the *huacas*, piles of stones raised in reverence to Pacha Mama, Lady Earth. And like them he slept with the Quechua women who lived in smoky huts pegged to the mountainsides. Watching their high-boned tranquil faces, hewn like the rock surrounding them, he sought traces of his people's ancient greatness, but found none. They were patient. And they were drugged by the coca leaves their ancient master, the Inca, had forbidden them to chew, but whose use their Spanish masters encouraged.

Wandering in the high passes, Esteban came upon a rope bridge swinging across a thousand-foot chasm. A child told him the bridge was safe. Each spring the people of his village built it anew because their ancestors had been ordered to keep it in repair in case the Inca himself should one day pass this way. Knowing that the last Inca ruler had been executed more than three centuries ago, Esteban marveled at the obedience of these people, and asked the boy if he knew who the Inca was, whereupon the child recited in order the name of every Inca ruler from the mythic first of them, Manco Capac, Son of the Sun, to the last one the Spaniards executed. Esteban gave the boy his loaf of bread and crossed the bridge. From that day he had a family name.

He traveled south across Lake Titicaca to Bolivia and the mines where Indians labored without seeing the light of day. It was there Esteban understood his true mission. He found that he had become a revolutionary.

He gained entrance to the mines dressed as a priest. He led only thirty men to freedom. Four guards were killed and Esteban himself was caught; he escaped and fled northeast down the Madeira River into the Amazon jungle. There he lived among the forest tribes, skirting settlements and avoiding the rubber landings. In a year he came out of the jungle with his plans made.

When Alexander von Humboldt explored South America a century before, he discovered, in the dense wilderness along the border between Venezuela and Brazil, the Casiquiare, a natural canal linking the Orinoco River with the Amazon. Using it Humboldt was able to travel from the Caribbean to the Rio Negro and Manáos, which at that time was a cluster of thatched huts. The Amazon had long been known as an east-west waterway linking the Atlantic with the Andes' Pacific slope; now Esteban saw it as the key as well to north-south traffic in the interior of the continent. He believed it would be possible to traverse virtually the whole of South America without going near the coastal strongholds of the Europeans. He thought it feasible to follow the inland waterways southward through central Brazil to Argentina—perhaps as far as Patagonia and even all the way to the Horn—provided your craft was strong enough to skim the downward cataracts without being crushed and light enough to be carried around the rapids where the ground was rising. But heavy-laden, armor-bearing Europeans were not fit for this travel. Only the Indians could do it, an alliance of Andean endurance and jungle lore.

In the past the mountain Indians and the jungle Indians, though racially linked, had split, and had never rejoined. There was between them mutual suspicion and dread. Esteban longed to free all the Indians: his own passive and demoralized mountain people; the forest peoples in bondage to the rubber estradas and those dying of the whites' diseases and in danger of forgetting how to live without matches and guns; and the impoverished cattlemen of the central pampas and the arid backlands of the northeast. He planned to make the interior of South America once again a safe and well-protected haven for the native peoples.

In the years since his failure in the mines he'd learned how to get what he needed. In Europe he'd spent his days in the great libraries of the major cities, studying military tactics, Napoleon's strategic use of rivers, and the engineering of dams, canals, and man-made lakes. At night he gambled, made deals, and found backers for his "rubber railroad." The financiers of the world knew nothing of the *selva* except their greed for its fabled wealth. Manco was mysterious but persuasive. He spoke of riches, of hidden cities in the depths of the forest, of lost Inca gold. The financiers' eyes narrowed; they licked their lips, pressed money upon him, and begged for controlling interest. Buying arms was also easy. There was a shortage of wars; the gun merchants were hungry.

Meanwhile the work in the jungle went forward. A series of canals and artificial lakes was nearly ready for the rising of the water when the rainy season reached its peak. The last link was a river called the Rio dos Maranhas. But this was Rio Mar Rubber territory. The Manconistas—an army now, most of them freed from the rubber estradas, the mines, and the enormous sugar, coffee, and cattle estates—had systematically destroyed every rubber landing on the Maranhas. Rio Mar, however, unlike the smaller entrepreneurs, would not simply move his operations to another river: he would fight back. This was welcomed: Esteban longed to drive out of Amazonia this man who was responsible for the deaths of thousands of laborers. Certainly, too, the Manconistas' scheme of jungle waterways could not become functional so long as the Baron's launches patrolled the region as if it were his personal fief.

Nevertheless, Esteban wanted to choose the time and place for this inevitable confrontation, and he was not yet ready. He had no intention of playing hide-and-seek with Rio Mar on the Maranhas, whose name meant "River of Entanglements." It coiled, circled, and doubled back upon itself.

Individual lives had no significance to the Indians. All that mattered was the village, the tribe, the race—the peoples of the forest, the mountains, the pampas, the desert. And this was the reason Esteban, whose heart ached with affection for thousands of people, had never loved a woman. He had been forced to suppress all feeling, to harden himself. In the *selva*, no man was sentimental about a woman; a man's leadership depended upon his strength of mind as well as body.

So at first, aboard the *Esperança*, Esteban's contemplation of Savannah had been disinterested, detached. She was the most beautiful woman he had ever seen. After he learned her name she ceased to interest him until he saw her in the storm at sea and witnessed her exultation in the violence of nature. Then he saw her as an unspoiled wild creature. He would have liked to free her, to take her from Rio Mar's gilded cage and turn her loose, but he had no time for her. The fact that he found her haunting he interpreted as a weakness in himself; he'd been too much among Europeans.

Yet as time went on his torment increased. His return to the *selva* and the labor of the operations there brought him no relief.

When the Contessa's letter reached him, he was ashamed of the joy he felt at learning Savannah was not with Rio Mar, yet his motive in attempting to buy her was to send her away in the hope he could forget her. But then, when he held her in his arms in the Red Room, he knew he could not put her out of his life any more than he'd been able to put her out of his mind. Now his cause had a rival in his heart, and he knew that for the first time since his ill-prepared attack on the Bolivian mines he had done something on impulse.

Still, as he gazed at her now, smiling at him, her hair strewn across the pillow and soft as silk in his fingers, he felt, not regret, but an unaccustomed lightness of heart, an unfamiliar impulse to laugh aloud. For the first time in his life he was happy. And it seemed to him quite natural that he should be happy.

Once more he took Savannah in his arms.

35

There was a knock at the door. Savannah thought: *Now it is ending.* There was a pause and then another knock. Manco said, "What is it?"

Albert opened the door and, standing on tiptoe so his eyes were level with the doorknob, he said, "It's O.K., Lady Contessa, they're awake!" The Contessa came into the room, followed by Bitte with a breakfast tray.

Savannah, filled with dread at the intrusion which marked the end of their time together, turned away; but Manco was glad to see them. He said to the Contessa, "Send someone to get Father Antonio. Have you a wedding dress?"

The Contessa laughed. "Listen to him. He's gone mad with love." She pulled a table close to the bed and poured coffee.

Manco sat up and caught her hand. "I must leave quickly. Send for him at once."

Again she laughed. "What? Spoil a perfectly delightful romance with marriage? You need not make an honest woman of Carmencita. I give you my permission to love her and leave her."

He did not release her hand. "What I want is your permission to marry her."

She worked free of his grasp and waved Albert and Bitte from the room. Then, moving around to Savannah's side of the bed, she said, "Good morning, my precious." Behind her dark glasses she was staring intently into Savannah's eyes. "I am glad you are so happy, dearest." She kissed her and said quietly, "Tell Esteban why Father Antonio is not going to marry you this morning."

The bitterness rose again in Savannah's heart, this time against the Baron. Hadn't she suffered enough at his hands? Must his trickery deprive her of everything? What had the Contessa said? *Esteban is a man, and men believe marriage is a sacred institution. . . .* She turned to him. "Because he thinks Satan will use me to interfere with your work." She touched his hand. "Anyway, a wedding is only words in a prayer book. I am married to you in the only way that matters. Nothing a priest could say would make me more married to you than I am now."

She saw the Contessa's small teeth indent a rose-colored lip, but she refused to meet her eyes. After a pause the Contessa turned to the armoire and took out a satin peignoir."Here, child, you must bathe and dress."

Savannah put the garment on, but made no move to follow the Contessa from the room. She took a cup of coffee from the breakfast tray and sat down on the loveseat near the fireplace. Manco, accepting the dressing gown the Contessa offered him, joined her there. With the older woman standing indecisively in the background, Savannah and Manco looked at each other over their coffee cups.

Savannah said, "In the jungle, far from chapels, how do the Indians get married?"

"I would go hunting and kill something for you, a tapir, or a peccary fat enough to feed a village. I would bring it to your hut and say, Here, woman, cook this for me. And that would mean I want you. If you don't like me, you'll just leave it there on the ground, and I'll give it to my mother or my sister to cook for me. But if you want me too, you will take the game and the women of your family will help you cook it. The next time I walk off into the forest you will follow me and we will make love there, on the ground."

The Contessa clucked impatiently. "There's a steamer leaving for Pará at three this afternoon," she said. "We've a great deal to do before we're ready to leave." She took their cups away. "God forgive me, I had the nuns' habits stolen from the convent laundry this morning. Bitte's ironing them now."

Savannah turned to look at her. "Whatever are you talking about?"

"We're going disguised as nuns. Esteban thought of it."

When she looked at him inquiringly, he said, "But first we're going to be married."

The Contessa circled the loveseat to face him. "That's nonsense, Esteban. There's simply no time. If you insist on marrying her, do it properly. Finish your war and join us."

He began kissing Savannah's ears, her throat, the back of her neck. "You must go away. Now more than ever."

Hurt, she studied the molding at the rim of the mantelpiece. "I thought you, at least, would understand how sick I am of having decisions made for me. I'm not a child anymore." Even as she said it, she knew she was acting like one. Still, she persisted. "Not once has anybody said to me: Savannah, what would *you* like to do with your life?"

He released her and stood watching, not smiling, yet with a

faint loving appreciation playing around his eyes. "Savannah, what would you like to do with your life?"

"I want to go with you into the *selva*. I want to help you do whatever it is you are doing, until it is finished. Then I will be glad to go anywhere you want me to go. Only I want us to go together." She placed her hands on his chest. "Please, Manco, let us be together."

The Contessa paced distractedly about the room, but she said nothing. Manco kissed Savannah gently and stroked her hair. "It won't be long. A few months, with luck. Without it, a year at most. And the sooner you go, the better it will be. When I know you are safe—"

She backed away from him. "I won't go," she said. "At least I can stay here and wait for you. You can come to see me from time to time."

The Contessa shook her head. "We've pressed our luck too far already. Any day, any moment. Dom Luíz will learn that you are here."

Ignoring her, Savannah said to Manco, "He can't touch me if I am with you in the *selva*."

The Contessa stepped closer. "That's nonsense, my precious. In Europe the time will pass quickly—" But seeing this was useless, she said, "White women cannot live in the *selva*; they sicken and die."

Savannah's eyes held to Manco's face. When he said nothing, she lifted her chin and said firmly, "I won't leave here. If you force me aboard a ship, I will jump overboard."

He drew her close to him. His hands lay heavy on her shoulders and a frown of impatience and fatigue drew his dark brows closer together. "You leave with the Contessa at three."

She had never been as frightened as she was at this moment, yet her fear of his anger was nothing compared with her fear of being parted from him. With a steadiness that surprised her she said, "No, I will not."

The Contessa intervened to break the tension of their locked gaze. "Esteban, she is not one of your Manconistas. She will not obey simply because you order it. She must be made to understand the reasons. Tell her what it is like upriver."

He sighed and moved to the window, clearly restless to be gone. "On the river the sun will blister your skin to running sores. In the forest the trails are under water, but we must traverse them at a run in spite of that. If you wear stout shoes, your feet will break out in a form of rot, but if you go barefoot like the rest of us, you will step on thorns."

The Contessa urged him on. "Tell her of the pium."

He turned back toward them and Savannah was struck by an impression of deep exhaustion. She sensed that, rather than longing for the *selva*, as she had imagined, he dreaded it. Her resolve to go with him grew firmer. "The pium are clouds of gnats so small no netting can keep them out. They are almost invisible, but when you slap your flesh to stop their itching, you find you've smeared yourself with the blood they've gorged."

"And tell her of the fire ants," the Contessa said. "And the chigoes that lay eggs under your toenails."

Savannah went to him and touched the deep line where the moustache framed his mouth. She said, "Then how do you live there?"

"I am used to it. But even then, it is a continual misery."

"Then we will be in misery together. Isn't that better than being miserable apart?"

He sighed, shaking his head. "Don't you understand that your being there will make it harder for me?"

She spoke softly, without the rebelliousness she'd shown before; but her decision was firmer than ever. "You don't know that. You are judging me by others. You have never given me a chance to show you what I could do—or be."

For an instant he saw the face of Father Cristoforo, lifting his eyes from the earth at his feet to the mountains, and saying that perhaps it is God's will that our talents not be buried, no matter who we are. Yet that was a different thing entirely. Still, he understood what it was to be prejudged, and he hesitated.

The Contessa said, "How often are you sending downriver for supplies?"

"Every fortnight. I can't keep enough quinine on hand. Or antiseptic. And canned goods are always running out."

"Then take her for two weeks. Let her see for herself—"

His head jerked back impatiently. "I can't spare two weeks! The rains came early this year."

The Contessa stepped between them. "Do you want her jumping off steamers and wandering through the jungle to find you? Take her. Let her get her fill of it. Then send her back to me. I'll treat her sores and insect bites and fever, and then we'll go to Rome."

"No, it's out of the question." He began gathering his

clothes. "You will leave for Pará this afternoon, and that is final. Get ready."

There was a knock at the door and Elena entered. She said, "There is a man to see you, that Tristão who is a waiter on the Booth Line steamer. He says to tell you the Baron do Rio Mar has closed the Amazon."

Manco was very quiet. He said, "Where?"

"The narrows at Óbidos. He's gotten naval vessels sent up from Rio. Every boat is being searched and every passenger is being questioned."

Savannah said, "Then I can't get out of Brazil?"

Manco crossed the room and studied the harbor. The Booth Line steamer was anchored off shore. There were a dozen riverboats and one police launch. "There are two ways," he said. "Through the jungle to the Caribbean, or over the Andes to the Pacific. Either way takes months." He turned. "And there is no time."

Savannah went to him. "Then let me go with you and help. Surely I can do something."

He seemed unmoved, lost in thought. "Perhaps you can," he said.

It took the Contessa and her girls nearly three hours to get Savannah ready, but at last she stood before the long mirror in the pink bedroom—disguised as an African woman, because they said she was too tall to be a forest Indian. Her skin was stained dark brown; she was barefoot and wore a mission dress of flowered chintz. Her hair was bound up in a head cloth, flattened on top to support the basket she would carry on her head. She found her transformation oddly appropriate, somehow in keeping with her changed feelings.

He stood behind her, dressed as a riverman. His striped cotton pants were held at the waist by a rope. He wore no shirt, but bracelets of woven fiber were pushed high up on his muscular arms. Around his neck hung animal teeth threaded on a strip of tanned hide. His shoulder-length hair hung loose; and pulled low over his eyes there was a large hat of palm straw.

He vetoed most of the items the Contessa wanted to place in Savannah's basket. She ended with a compact bundle: a towel and soap, comb and toothbrush, one other dress, a warm wrap for the rain, and some drawing materials, which Morgan insisted were needed to keep her from going berserk.

"Walk several steps behind him," Egypt said.

"And," Morgan added, "whatever you do, keep yer blinkin' eyes down."

"What if someone speaks to me? Should I learn a few words of African?"

Elena shook her head. "On the street women don't answer. Let him do all the talking."

Egypt added to the advice. "If anybody speaks to you, act shy. Cover your mouth with your hand and look away."

Savannah grinned. "All that with a basket on my head?"

They said their good-byes downstairs at the side door. The Contessa stood in the midst of her girls, holding Savannah close. "Don't cry, my precious," she said, "your complexion will run." But she was unable to stanch her own tears.

Savannah said, "Forgive me for mistrusting you—for thinking that you . . . I mean, I do so thank you for everything. You have been very good to me."

The Contessa studied Savannah's face a moment. At last she said, "Do you still disapprove of this establishment?"

"No. Not anymore. It is a splendid school. I don't know why you are so good to me. But then, you are good to everyone. Isn't she?" The others murmured assent.

The Contessa said, "My concern for you is special, my treasure." She cleared her throat, paused, and began anew, her voice a bare whisper. "When we meet again we will have a long talk. I have many things to tell you." She stopped and distractedly touched Savannah's shoulder, then looked away.

Manco opened the side door and surveyed the street. Softly Savannah said, "I won't be coming back. No matter how dreadful it is, I won't complain. Not once. I will make him let me stay."

Manco opened the door for Savannah. The nearest girls hugged her while the Contessa swiftly embraced Manco, saying, "Take care of her."

"With my life," he answered. Savannah followed him into the street. Turning back for a final look, she saw the Contessa's face stiff with anguish. They waved to each other, and Savannah turned away.

The midday sun was dimmed by haze, but heat rose from the cobbled street. They must, without attracting attention, make their way through the business district, past the market and the warehouses, to the wharves. There, under a dock, a canoe waited. They would paddle it out of the harbor to a cove where a river steamer had been waiting since yesterday, under the pretext of having engine trouble.

Watching her bare brown-stained feet, she noted how much hotter the stones were when she moved away from the shadow of buildings. The basket on her head was no more difficult to manage than the lexicon she'd been forced to balance during convent deportment lessons. What she did find difficult was staying several steps behind him, not speaking to him, not touching him, not overtaking him and making him take her in his arms. She tried to concentrate on the surroundings, on these pastel-colored buildings with their top-hinged shutters propped open, or on the dark river gleaming beyond the warehouses, on this city of Manáos where so much had happened to her and which she might be seeing for the last time.

Tomorrow and the day after that these smells would still rise from the hot street, the sweet stench of rotting fruit, roasting coffee, spices, Brazil nuts, stale fish, and the choking reek of rubber . . . but she would be far away and Manco would be holding her in his arms.

36

Nero had seen them leave the city.

He was a big mulatto, mute since the age of twelve, when Dom Luíz had found him watching nine-year-old Esmeralda bathing. The Master, overtaken by one of his rages, allowed the boy to return to his duty of guarding Esme only after he'd made him a eunuch. Nero appeared to recover from his punishment, except for his inability to speak.

Now that his mistress had entered the convent Nero had no formal assignment at the Palácio, but Dom Luíz found him useful for standing about the city's bars, markets, and docks collecting information, which he was able to communicate to Raoul by signs and drawings. People spoke freely in his presence. Because he was mute, they assumed he was deaf as well—and stupid. He was neither.

He recognized Manco immediately as the man who'd been his captor, who'd kept him on a launch in the river, but who had not harmed him. That fact made the experience more than memorable; it made it incomprehensible. Familiar with the Baron's treatment of prisoners, Nero had expected to die horribly. Yet he had not even been questioned. Nevertheless,

he would have reported Manco's presence in the city had he
not, a moment later, recognized Savannah.

The last time he had seen Esmeralda was the night of the
opera. Seen her, that is, close at hand; for he spent some part
of every day outside the convent, watching for a light in
Esme's cell or waiting to see her cross the cloister to the
chapel when the bell rang for prayers. That night he'd observed the concern in Esme's face when Savannah fainted
after the wedding ceremony. After he carried the girl to
Esme's room, he watched the way Esme bent over her,
trying to revive her. Then later, as he escorted Esme back to
the convent, he saw tears fall upon the stiff white collar of her
habit. Seeing him watching, she smiled and told him what
troubled her. (She always spoke to him as if he were a dear
lifelong friend, which he was, having loved her for as long as
he had memories.) She said she was weeping for Savannah,
who did not want to marry the Master. She told him that she
was afraid something would happen to Savannah, just as it
had to her own mother and Porfirio's mother.

If Nero could have spoken he would have said: *I will guard
her for you, if that is what you wish.* But since he could not
speak, he simply looked at her. She understood, and touched
his hand. And he would keep his wordless promise. He was no
longer afraid of the Master. What more could be done to
him? Not even his life seemed of value now that Esmeralda
was safe inside the convent and had no need of him.

So although Nero followed Manco and Savannah at a distance and saw them take a canoe and paddle out of the
harbor, he did not report this to Raoul. When the convent bell
rang for midday prayers, Nero was atop the wall, hidden by
the branches of a jacaranda tree. When he saw the nuns
hurrying along the cloister to the chapel, moving quickly, one
at a time and close to the building with their heads bent, he
timed his throw so that the stone wrapped in paper bounced
once and rolled to a stop in front of Esme's feet. He'd drawn
a canoe on a black river, and in it a brown-skinned girl whose
hair he had colored red.

Savannah had followed Manco through the city quietly
enough, although, looking at her covertly under the brim of
his straw hat, Esteban had seen the amusement in her brown-
stained face. When they climbed down the ladder into the
canoe moored under the dock and he began to paddle them
away from the town, she sat stiff in the bow, her hands

clenched on the thwarts and her head, under its African wrapping, turning eagerly from side to side as if she longed to devour the view with her eyes.

She'd been disconcerted by the sight of the riverboat waiting for them in a cove beyond the city. It was a battered-looking paddlewheel steamer with every inch of deck space covered with cargo—stacked wood, caged chickens, piles of boxes and sacks, containers of rice, beans, cloth, pots, pans, salt, sugar, and a tethered pig that looked so sad Savannah wondered if it knew its fate. The vessel, which was called *La Paloma*, had once been white but now was streaked with rust; it looked barely seaworthy. But in fact *La Paloma* was a ruse. Its captain, Gonçalves Fulgencio, was one of the Manconistas, and his river trade gave him opportunities to ferry goods, people, and information for the Liberator. There was, however, no time for Esteban to reassure Savannah, for no sooner had they gotten aboard and made the canoe fast by a line to the stern, when a river patrol bore down upon them. Esteban ordered her into the galley with the cook Filomena, who put Savannah to work scouring pots in a tub of brackish river water the color of strong tea. The galley, no bigger than a broom closet, was hot as perdition. Filomena was a *cabocla*, half white and half Indian, and so old she hadn't a tooth left in her head. She was very dirty, and the reek of her pungent dinner made Savannah's stomach turn. She kept scouring, however, for the tramp of shoes and the scraping of cargo across the deck outside the galley made it clear the boat was being searched. Catching a word of Portuguese here and there, she heard Gonçalves protesting that he must be on his way before the pig and chickens died of the heat.

Hearing the footsteps come nearer, she began to tremble. Without a word Filomena poured Savannah a tin cup of the sugar cane rum called *cachaça*. Tasting like a mixture of molasses and kerosene, it seared her throat, brought tears to her eyes, deprived her of speech, warmed her belly, and stopped the shakes dead in their tracks. Placidly working her empty old jaws, Filomena downed a pickle-jarful of the stuff and bent over her work. It didn't even make her blink.

Soon, after a scurry of steps and the snarl of the patrol's engine, Manco appeared in the galley entrance. He was dripping, having spent the time over the side and underwater, but otherwise he seemed well. He told Savannah it was merely a routine search. Then in Portuguese he said, "Filomena, this is Senhorita Savannah."

Filomena put down her knife and the onion she'd been peeling, wiped her hands on her grimy apron, and took Savannah in her arms. Savannah, to her own surprise, found herself returning the embrace heartily. Filomena said, "*Sim, senhorita*—you, me, we cook!" Already the concoction had begun to bubble on the black iron stove. It seemed to be made of dried salt codfish in a sauce of hot red peppers, onions, and garlic cast adrift in yellow grease. Savannah was glad to get out on deck.

The men, Gonçalves and his crew of three mestizos, drew near to look at this tall girl in her mission dress, squinting at her lavender eyes. Filomena drew close too and peered nearsightedly, while Savannah herself could not decide where to look. After a moment the cook spit on her finger and rubbed the stain on Savannah's arm, showing her bare gums when she cackled at the sight of the white skin beneath the dye.

Esteban spoke to them, telling Gonçalves to get up steam. The others set to work hauling the anchor aboard and throwing cut logs from the deck into the boiler. At the sight of the broad black river and its coffee-colored foam slipping past the *Paloma*'s side, the exultation Savannah had felt on leaving Manáos returned. Moment by moment this churning wake was widening her separation from that city where so many dreadful things had happened to her; it was taking her farther from Veronique and Edward and, most of all, from Rio Mar. The realization that Manco was indeed taking her upriver with him made her want to join in Filomena's delighted crowing. Although the *Paloma* was surely not the Red Room, still they were together, and each day now, whether ashore or afloat, she would waken in his arms.

That thought aroused in her a craving for his embrace. She looked toward the bow where he had stationed himself, but when he turned to meet her gaze, she felt suddenly disheveled and unkempt. She went inside, this time to the tiny cabin Filomena said was to be hers. It was little more than a linen cupboard with a bunk and a small porthole where she could watch the tree-lined shore slip by. But at least it was private.

She found that most of the items Manco had vetoed had been slipped back into the basket the Contessa packed for her. There was a white muslin dress, scented soap, an embroidered cotton gown, cologne and a towel, a toothbrush, hairbrush and comb, stout shoes, a warm wrap, and a small package. She tore open the paper and found a wooden box with more than five dozen soft French pastel crayons in a rainbow of colors. Inside there was a note.

> My dearest child, this was a gift to you from your friend Mr. Patterson. He took it to Arcadia when you were being kept in your room. Cicero thought you ought to have it. I did not wish to darken your farewell with sad news, but the girls learned Mr. Patterson was checked out of the Internacional by Raoul, so apparently your friend is dead or worse. I am so sorry, my treasure, but there is nothing we can do. It is such a very big jungle. Take care and come back to us as soon as ever you can. Love, and more love—C.

Manco found her sitting on her bunk with tears falling into the crayon box. He read the letter and took her in his arms. She said, "The Contessa told me I had probably cost him his life. How is it I am living?" she cried. "How dare I?"

His hand was warm on her cheek. He said, "Do not underestimate Will Patterson. Strength of mind is more useful than strength of body, even in the *selva*."

She sighed raggedly. "Forgive me for crying." He touched her head, kissed her lips and her eyes. Then he said, "We will be on this river two days more. There will be other patrols." And with that he left her quickly and went back on deck.

The Baron do Rio Mar used his field glasses to scrutinize the river. Upstream, ahead of his yacht *Primavera*, a battered old paddle steamer labored against the current. It was *La Paloma*.

In the weeks since the kidnapping of his bride (Dom Luíz still insisted her disappearance was a kidnapping), his search for her continued unabated. When he got no worthwhile response from the hundreds of reward posters picturing her, he'd doubled and then tripled the reward.

He'd sent trusted men to all the river towns, especially to Óbidos, the point halfway between Manáos and Pará. There, the Amazon narrows to a deep channel between high banks a mere bow shot apart. It is the one truly defensible point on the river. But they had not caught her, or her captors, at Óbidos. All his measures, in fact, had proved fruitless, and Dom Luíz had taken to prowling the streets of Manáos in his carriage.

Every day he badgered his sons for information—all but the useless Porfirio, who was more distracted, more ineffectual, and more drunk than ever. The Baron drove his employees out into the streets day after day in search of bits of gossip. Yet even though his men had been ordered to pay generously for any lead, it reached a point where each new circuit of the bars and casinos turned up less and less. Eventually there was not even a wild rumor. Not even the most blatant lie for a Rio Mar banknote.

Then a lead turned up at a café near the Cathedral Plaza; a bartender had seen something. He could not remember exactly which day it had been; it was raining, and all rainy days were alike. But there'd been a fracas in the square, some quarrel among prostitutes, the sort of thing you pay no heed to. But these weren't common street whores; they were girls from the Contessa's Palace. It appeared that a new one had tried to run away. Albert, that dwarf cashier, and a few of the girls dragged the new recruit back inside. She looked like a nice little piece. A redhead.

Dom Luíz had sent Raoul at once. The Contessa herself was not available, but he talked with her assistant, Elena, in a sitting room on the main floor. Raoul said, "We understand you have a redhead. My employer is partial to them. Money, of course, is no object. I would like to see the girl."

"I regret to tell you that you have been misinformed," Elena said, "We have, alas, no redheads. Although one of our girls does love to play at dressing up. Would you like to see her?"

Raoul nodded, his calm Oriental eyes watchful.

Elena moved to the doorway. "Raimundo, would you please call Egypt? Tell her the gentleman is interested in a redhead."

There was no delay, for the Contessa had seen Raoul arrive. Egypt's entrance was intriguing. First between the velvet portieres her hand appeared, covered with rings. Then the arm, tinkling with silver bracelets. Next, her small foot crept coyly over the threshold. Raoul got up and strode impatiently to the entrance. He found a small black girl grinning impishly at him beneath a magnificent carrot-colored wig she'd marcelled with hot irons until every curl was rampant as a lion's mane.

Next came the report of the seller of lottery tickets, who said he saw a riverman pass through town, followed by tall Negress, a Watusi woman. The police launch was alerted, but found nothing. The *cachaça* of Gonçalves Fulgencio was, however, very good; they'd confiscated a dozen bottles. But women? Only the toothless old cook and her helper, a skinny African girl.

But then there was the crude drawing of a red-haired creature in a canoe. Dom Luíz was paying one of the convent servants to keep watch on Esmeralda, and his daughter had been observed throwing it away. When the Baron saw it, he took to the river himself.

Now from the foredeck of his yacht he watched the rusty paddle steamer, knowing he could overtake it whenever he chose. He'd instructed his captain, Eustacio Moraes, to keep the *Primavera* hidden in the narrow channel between a string of islands and the riverbank. Moraes joined his master and held the match for his cigar. The Baron said, "You remember my bride, do you not?"

"Of course, Excellency. Did I not follow the ocean liner bearing her from Pará to Manáos?"

Dom Luíz handed over his field glasses. "Tell me what you think of that nigger on the deck."

Moraes peered into the eyepieces and turned back to his employer. "She seems to be conversing with a pig."

"But does she look familiar?" The Baron adjusted the glasses for increased magnification. "Look at her eyes."

Moraes squinted through the lenses a moment. Then he turned to the Baron a face slack with astonishment. "Her eyes are light!"

"So they are, Eustacio."

"Shall I overtake the *Paloma*, Excellency?"

The Baron smoked his cigar. "There is no hurry."

Moraes looked from his master to the *Paloma* and back again. "If I may say so, Your Grace—"

"Yes, Eustacio?"

"Who could have imagined the young lady would seek employment on a filthy riverboat?"

The Baron smiled. "She is a prisoner. That one, the tall Indian who acts as lookout on the bow—I have encountered him before. He is the anarchist who dynamites my warehouses."

Moraes glanced around at the *Primavera*'s weapons, shrouded in canvas to protect them from the humidity. "Whenever you give the word, Excellency—"

"I know. But we can take them whenever we choose. Perhaps when they tie up for the night."

"But here the river is broad, Excellency. They may run all night, if there is a moon."

"Then we will wait until they tie up to cut wood for their boiler. In the meantime, if we are patient we may learn something."

"What, Your Grace?"

"Where he goes, this Manco."

37

The Rio Negro above Manáos is wide. Although the water is dark, it is translucent, and Savannah could see the flick of fins and the sinuous undulation of strange shapes in its depths. Filomena, horrified by Savannah's declaration that if she could not have a bath soon she'd jump overboard, had whispered darkly of the bottomless river depths where lived the *cobra grande*, a snake larger than the biggest steamship. Its eyes, she said, glowed in the dark like ovens. When Savannah spoke of this to Esteban on the evening of their second night on the river, he laughed.

"Is it true?" she asked.

"Of course. And it swallows riverboats for breakfast and ocean liners for lunch."

Uncertainly she watched his face. "But there are snakes in the river, aren't there?"

He smiled. "Not here. Here there are only electric eels and stingrays."

Savannah's thirst for knowledge of the *selva* was an expression of her love for him, because he seemed part of it, as mysterious and incomprehensible.

"How big is the *selva?*" she asked, looking out into the green jungle.

He lifted one shoulder as if words failed him. At last he said, "It is ten times the size of France."

The *Paloma* made its way around another bend in the river, revealing yet more measureless forest, a choked mass of stifling vegetation. "Here, near the middle, it stretches at least a thousand miles in every direction." He put his arm around her. "There are vast areas no outsider has ever seen. Villages, even whole tribes we know nothing of and will never be able to find. Men walk into the *selva* and vanish. Did they die? Or are they still living somewhere in there? We will never know."

She shuddered and leaned closer to him, imagining that he had refused to bring her with him and she'd been forced to travel here alone in search of him.

Watching his profile, she sensed how different he was here, on the river. He was even more alert, more alive. He watched everything keenly all the time. He sniffed the air, studied the debris floating downstream, watched the trees along the shore, listened to the bird calls. Earlier that day he'd known exactly when the rain would begin, as if he'd heard it in the distance the way one hears a freight train before it appears on the horizon.

Gone, too, was the deep sadness she'd seen in his eyes on board the *Esperança*. He no longer spoke of the blood and tears in the river. Indeed, she had made him forget the rage that had burned in him since childhood. Each day she seemed more wonderful to him. Her radiance was remarkable. She was luminous, like some rare natural element. Her response to the river and the *selva* was like her delight in their loving. Not cool, experienced, and matter-of-fact like other women, but with moist eyes and dewy lips, like a greedy child. How he longed to have her to himself in some room an ocean and a continent away, where he might forget the eyes of the betrayed.

At night she stood watch beside him. Suddenly he was still. She said, "What is it?"

"I hear something. Go into the cabin."

She went, and heard the sudden ceasing of the steam engine. The paddlewheels slowed and stopped; the water coursing over them dripped softly into stillness.

Aboard the *Primavera* Dom Luíz saw the *Paloma*'s wheel halt. He barked to Moraes, "Cut the engine!" The yacht, running without lights against the riverbank where the current was not strong and where the foliage shrouded in darkness even the *Primavera*'s white flanks, paused. In midstream the *Paloma* began to drift in the strong current of the swollen Rio Negro.

Gonçalves said, "I hear nothing. Do you hear it now?"

"No," Esteban answered. "But something has awakened the monkeys over there." He lifted his chin toward the shore.

"Perhaps it is a jaguar. I have seen claw marks on the trees along this stretch of river."

The *Paloma* began to turn slowly. The monkeys chattered

angrily, then were still. From the banks of the nearest island came the sound of a sharp crunching, and the grind of jaws at work as a sea cow fed on the grasses in the shallow water. Savannah heard it too and wondered if the *cobra grande* had surfaced for a midnight snack. Manco told Gonçalves to start the engine up again. But he prowled the deck all night.

When the *Paloma* got under way again, the *Primavera* followed at a distance of a mile or more. Mario paced the deck of the yacht restlessly. He was the youngest of the Baron's "palace guard" and had always been impetuous. He was eighteen and had remained close to his sister, Manuela, who was only a year older. They were the children of Juana, who was still Dom Luíz's body servant even though he now took younger women to his bed. Mario said now, "Let's attack and kill him while it is still dark. We can sink the *Paloma* and no one will ever know."

The Baron said, "I wish to see where he goes."

Eustacio came on deck. "Excellency, they hug the shore as if seeking a particular destination."

Together the three of them stood on the foredeck, the Baron using his field glasses in the darkness. "They are turning from the main channel, Eustacio. What is there?"

"A tributary, Excellency. One of your own rivers. The Maranhas."

"Is not this where all of my landings have been attacked? Then perhaps he leads us to his headquarters."

"Excellency," Moraes said, "the *Primavera* is fast and well armed, but she is not a battleship. Perhaps it would be wise to dispatch a messenger in one of the small boats. Twenty-four hours' hard paddling with the current and he will make Manáos."

"I'll go, Your Grace," Mario said.

Dom Luíz shook his head. "No need. We shall simply pinpoint the location of his headquarters and take him alive, along with my property. Then, Mario, you may sink the *Paloma* if you wish." He turned to Eustacio. "I wish to see your chart for the Maranhas."

The sight of the river on the map, a twisting line that coiled like a snake, made the Baron smile. "Do you see that, Mario? He will never run all night in this maze; he will tie up to shore when darkness falls again. Then I will pounce upon him like a cat."

* * *

She watched the sun rise. In the night they'd left the Rio Negro and turned into a tributary not much smaller than the main river; it seemed to her more like a bay than a stream. Manco had pointed out the effect of the rising water. The trees were drowning in it. Soon even the tallest of them would be immersed to their crowns. The Amazon would become an ocean, the tributaries would be seas, and the swamps would turn into lakes.

She watched the great trees, shrouded in soft skeins of mist, draw nearer as the river narrowed. The forest wall was unbroken but for an occasional opening where animals came to drink along the shore, wild dogs and swamp deer. Even at this early hour it was hard to tell where fog ended and water began.

The sun burned through the clouds, poured through the openings, and spilled onto the surface of the river in flakes of gold. As the light brightened she saw the forest rising from the mist like the battlements of a great prison, a Bastille of vegetation, and it seemed impossible that man could ever enter there except as an intruder.

When Manco took his turn at the wheel, she sat on deck with Will's pastels and tried to sketch the shoreline. Yet the foliage really did not interest her and soon she began drawing Manco.

Now the *Paloma* slowed. They approached the riverbank and tied hausers to the trees. Esteban, Gonçalves, and the three crewmen went into the forest to cut wood for the boiler. Savannah sat on a box in the stern drawing the foliage and watching the parrots, the toucans, the macaws.

Watching the forest now, she felt a yearning to enter it, as if a siren song were luring her to death and destruction, following Manco into that green gloom.

And as she watched, unaware of anything but her love, Dom Luíz drew near.

38

The *Paloma*'s hausers were tied to trees on the riverbank. Savannah, sitting on a crate on deck, looked up from her sketchpad to see, some fifty yards away, the Rio Mar launch and Dom Luíz on its foredeck, dressed in a white linen suit. He threw his cigar away and bowed ironically to her. She screamed.

Filomena came out of the galley and, walking quickly across the deck, hauled on the boat whistle three times. The men were on their way back along a forest trail. Manco reached the bank first, leaped aboard the *Paloma*, and ran to the helm. Behind him Gonçalves and the three crewmen dropped the logs they were carrying and raced onto the steamer, casting off the lines and poling against the bank as Manco maneuvered the *Paloma* away from shore. Aboard the *Primavera* Dom Luíz smiled, calmly watching the unmoving paddle wheel as the distance between the boats narrowed.

But a new sound arose. Under the *Paloma*'s rust-stained sides there throbbed a secret heart, a powerful engine. Manco had bought it as salvage from a wrecked cruiser. Now the two screws beneath the water line began to turn, and to the Baron's astonishment he saw a turbulent wake spewing from the *Paloma*'s stern. The *Paloma* moved out into the Maranhas and got under way, first doing two knots, then three, and by midriver she'd reached ten.

The Baron roared at Eustacio to get up more speed, and in the open the yacht slowly gained. Manco took shortcuts across wide loops that were becoming oxbow lakes, using the steamer's shallow draft to plow through channels that were little more than flooded ditches. The *Primavera*'s owner raged at the necks of land he could not cross and bellowed for more speed.

The stack of logs on the *Paloma*'s deck was diminishing swiftly, for the wood they'd gone ashore to get had been left behind. Esteban watched for a moment while the *Primavera* gained in the race. He looked at Savannah sitting on the deck with the frightened pig in her arms, and took an ax to the railings. The dining table and benches went next. Still the *Primavera* overtook them.

Gonçalves shouted, "Shall I make for shore?"

"No," Esteban said.

"We can't make it to the Semnome!"

"We must!"

The *Primavera*'s gun covers were off. Mario eagerly prepared to man the big machine gun on the prow. On the Baron's signal he sprayed the Maranhas with warning shots; the bullets pocked the surface ten yards off the steamer's stern.

Esteban scanned the shoreline, where the trees stood in water high up their trunks, and turned back to Gonçalves at the helm. "The swamp is flooded," he said. "Up ahead there's an *igarapé*. Remember?" Gonçalves nodded. "We can do it," Manco said.

Suddenly Gonçalves grinned. "Get me some more furniture." They took their axes to the paddlewheel, and kept just out of range for another mile.

At the *igarapé* Gonçalves veered into the narrow opening in the forest. Overhead, the branches of trees splintered the *Paloma*'s superstructure and tore the awning off the deck. Once they were through the wall, however, the forest opened out into a dark sheet of brackish water with shimmering reflections of the patches of sunlight high above, in the dense canopy of vegetation held up a hundred feet above them by the gray columnar trunks.

Still, this was no place for a steamer. Manco, hanging on the bow, called warnings of fallen trees and shallows. The *Primavera* followed, but only after Dom Luíz threatened to shoot Eustacio if he held back.

Mario tried to hold the *Paloma* in his sights. It was visible beyond the intervening trees, veering among them and making turns by pushing against nearby trees with poles and slinging bolos around the ones in front and hauling in on the lines. Mario fired repeatedly, but succeeded only in gunning down a few saplings.

But the *Primavera* was sleek and moved steadily through the narrow flooded galleries. The Baron urged Eustacio on while the crewmen stood stupefied in their starched white uniforms watching trees drag their limbs across the yacht, knocking deck chairs into the green-scummed mire.

Up ahead the *Paloma* slowed. Away from the river the ground rose and the swamp grew shallower. Manco gave Savannah a pole marked for the steamer's draft of five feet and showed her how to take soundings. She learned quickly not to roil the water, for the mud darkened it so that she couldn't see the bottom and the pole sank uselessly into the muck.

The depth was decreasing rapidly. Manco told the crew to lighten the vessel. They heaved the pig onto a hummock of dry ground just off the side, where it stood uncertainly a moment and then began rolling in the cool mud. They hauled Filomena's iron stove out of the galley and shoved it overboard, where it gave off a violent hiss of steam before it sank slowly into the mire. Filomena blew her nose fiercely on her apron, but then she began chucking away her pots and pans as if this were the carnival at Rio.

It was, after all, the stove that saved them. It had sunk

below the surface in the *Primavera*'s path. The sharp keel scraped along the iron obstruction and her rudder, with a clangorous wrench, was ripped off, leaving the yacht helpless. Dom Luíz, lighting cigars and throwing them overboard, cursed the universe that had spawned this stinking water-logged forest and vowed to return to this river with a flotilla of battleships. His burning eyes followed the *Paloma* until it was lost to view among the trees.

Even after everything but the medicines had been thrown overboard, the steamer scraped bottom continually. All of them, including Filomena and Savannah, poled the vessel laboriously through the marsh. The men slipped over the side again and again to hack away at obstructions with axes and machetes, chipping a course over a fallen hardwood trunk or using ropes to haul large branches out of the way.

At times they seemed to be sailing over the land as the thick mat of floating grasses parted before them, slipped along their sides, and closed over the wake. The forest was dark and silent, but alive with reflections and ripples, as if they were traversing the floor of a primeval ocean.

Gradually Savannah found the soundings showed the water deepening, and Manco said they were coming out of the swamp onto the Rio Semnome, the Nameless River. His smile was wry. "We found a short-cut today." The others laughed.

The men were exhausted and fell to the deck to rest while Filomena built a fire on the planking to heat the dinner. Savannah looked around at what was left of the *Paloma*. "This is all because of me," she said softly to Manco.

He touched her cheek, his hands blistered from the ax handle. "Only the timing is because of you. He would have come after the rest of us sooner or later."

"Will he come back?"

"Yes. But by then we should be ready for him."

After they'd eaten, they felled a tree and cut up its dry, higher branches for fuel. With her steam up, the *Paloma* limped out of the swamp and moved up the Semnome on the one screw that still worked.

Although it was raining, the river seemed bright after the gloom of the drowned forest. After an hour they tied up at a small clearing where three men were waiting. These were not mestizos, not *caboclos* like Filomena and the others: They were real forest Indians, short, stocky, powerfully built, and—but for a sort of wrapping wound around their loins and a lot of red paint with black lines on it—they were naked. They carried bows and arrows that were taller by far than the men themselves.

The condition of the steamer struck them as hilarious. They leaned against each other, helpless with laughter, before they helped load the boxes of medicine, bandages, and antiseptic into their large canoe. It was a montaria, a native vessel more than twenty feet long, about five feet wide, and it had across its midsection a palm-thatch shelter. Savannah got into it as Manco instructed her and waved ruefully at Filomena as the *Paloma* drifted forlornly downriver out of view.

The montaria moved up the narrow Semnome, riding so low in the water the splash of a paddle sent drops over the thwarts. Manco paddled with the Indians, two men working in front of the shelter and two behind. They worked rhythmically, never stopping even to eat. Coarse bread and bananas were washed down with river water, the food and drink thrown into their mouths with one hand at the end of the downstroke.

Esteban, working directly in front of the shelter where Savannah lay on a pile of rolled hammocks, told her again to stay covered. He said over his shoulder, "Even in this haze you will get badly sunburned."

But she couldn't see anything under the low-hanging covering of braided palm leaves, and there was so much to look at.

By evening there were clouds of insects. Filomena had warned her not to scratch the bites of the few insects they'd encountered when the *Paloma* had put in to shore. Filomena had laughed when Savannah complained about them; she'd said, "These insects nothing! This good river! Black water!" Here on the Semnome the water was a muddy olive brown —and the insects were vicious. White mosquitoes smaller than fleas; gnats so small they were invisible until you felt their myriad pinprick stings and saw their tiny bodies fill with your blood; larger black bugs whose bites left dozens of raised blisters; and a fly whose poisonous bite was cumulative: the second bite hurt more than the first and the third more than the second and so on until by the tenth or fifteenth you could hardly keep from crying out. She wrapped herself in netting, but the tiny insects got through it and clustered on her wrists, her ankles, in her ears and hair, and around her neck inside her dress. She at last lost control and started swatting so violently she rocked the montaria. While the Indians frowned at her, Manco told her to keep still.

By the time they climbed ashore to make camp for the

night, her misery exceeded all the descriptions of jungle travel. She was badly sunburned, she ached from the long hours cramped in the canoe on piles of luggage, and her face and hands were swollen from the hundreds of insect bites and stings.

She sat on a log while the montaria was unloaded. Esteban kept talking to her, as if she could, like a child, have her attention distracted. He said they must stop for the night because the overhanging branches made this river treacherous after dark. They'd chosen the largest clearing they could find, but still it was so small they had to cut away the underbrush before they could haul the canoe out of the water. He said it wouldn't do to tie it up because the water level might rise or fall several feet during the night. If it rose, the montaria could be dragged under by its mooring; if it fell, they might find the canoe hanging from a tree by morning, its contents spilled out and washed away downriver.

Savannah eyed the tangled thicket that surrounded them. There were swarms of insects here, too, but she no longer bothered to wave them away; she just sat still, trying not to breathe and wanting very much to die.

The montaria was unloaded and hauled ashore now. The Indians paused to rest. Their skin seemed thicker than hers. While they slapped at themselves from time to time, the creatures seemed a mere annoyance. She marveled at their nonchalance.

They talked to each other and to Manco in a strange tongue full of consonants and grunting. At last she said, "Are they talking about me?"

Esteban nodded. "They say the enemy I stole you from must have been glad to see you go."

"Why?"

He smiled. "Because you complain and do no work."

She raged at the convent education which had taught her no obscenities for use on such occasions.

The Indians, hearing something, got to their feet. In the trees overhead there was a rushing of leaves: Monkeys were passing above them. They took their bows and arrows and ran into the forest, but Manco stayed with her. She tried to help him gather wood for fire, but when she bent over her head throbbed with pain. She watched him make a tripod of green saplings and hang a pot of water over the flames.

When the Indians came back, they had killed three monkeys, two of them large and black, the other small and gray like an old man. She turned away while they singed the hair off over the fire, gutted the animals, and cut them up for the pot. The monkeys' stomachs were filled with fruit, which the men indicated by their expressions was a great delicacy. Manco said it was simply food the monkeys digested first, and that food in the *selva* is too scarce to waste. She tasted the drink they made by adding water to the mixture; it was very sweet, but she didn't care for more. Still, as the main course boiled, the cooking odors made her long for dinner.

While they waited, Esteban bathed her stings and bites with boiled water and antiseptic, then applied ointment to them. By the time the stew was ready, she was feeling better and ravenously hungry. Although she was forced to admit the meat was delicious, when she found in her spoon a tiny hand like Coco's, she could eat no more.

As the swift night fell upon the jungle, they hung hammocks among the trees at the edge of the clearing. She was exhausted, and even as Esteban was wrapping her snugly in mosquito netting, her eyes were closing. Yet she could not sleep. The insects whined loudly about her all night, along with huge fireflies and immense moths. She slept at last near dawn, only to awaken a short time later shivering in the chill of dawn on the river.

The men caught fish for breakfast, drying a few over the fire to take aboard the montaria. Savannah forced herself to eat a bowl of farinha, which reminded her of library paste and sawdust. They loaded the canoe and pushed off again.

Shortly after the sun rose above the trees, the penetrating damp of morning gave way to a searing heat. Nothing moved, not a leaf, not a palm frond, no smallest spray of the ferns. The silent forest seemed a bas relief done in green stone.

Only the tawny water of the Semnome was cool, but Esteban warned her not to trail her fingers over the side. Then, knowing she needed reason and not rules, he threw a fish into the river, which immediately boiled with the flailing of piranha. The Indians began to spear them without even rocking the boat. She shuddered at the sight of the fish, black and fat as little pillows. Their snapping jaws sounded like scissors and their teeth looked like rows of razor points. Even as they died, the jaws clicked loudly in the bottom of the boat. Esteban said they must be handled with care, for even when dead they could bite off a finger or a toe. They had them for dinner, grilled on a rack over the campfire.

That night she was feverish and even more miserable than

she'd been the night before. She wanted only to sleep, but again the choking cloud of insects gave her no peace. Esteban built a smoky fire under her hammock to drive them away, but it did little good and the smoke burned her eyes and made it hard to breathe.

At last she began to fuss, to mutter angrily, tossing about in her hammock, getting out of it to wrap her netting more tightly around her, then getting in again only to climb out and stamp around the clearing, flailing at the mosquitoes. The Indians, awakened, watched her through the smoky haze, looking from Manco to Savannah and back to Manco again. She realized they were waiting for him to make her be quiet, to shut her up, perhaps violently. At last he said, "We warned you of the discomforts."

Stamping back to her hammock she said, "You exaggerated!" But even as she spoke, she gritted her teeth so hard her jaws ached. At last she fell into a deep, tormented sleep in which she dreamed that piranhas with clicking jaws leaped from her soup to attack her.

39

When she awakened the canoe was loaded and they were ready to leave. She rolled out of her hammock so that Manco could bundle it up, but when she stood, she grew dizzy and the morning blackened before her eyes. Manco examined her hands and feet. On her right big toe he found a small wound, a clean and bloodless puncture an eighth of an inch in diameter.

"You've lost blood to a bat. Rest today." He got her a tin cup of coffee and gave her bread and bananas to eat. Then they pushed off.

She slept all day under the palm-thatch shelter. Late in the afternoon she awakened as the canoe bumped the shore. They climbed out of the montaria and one of the Indians ran a little way down a trail into the forest and stopped by an immense tree. The Indian took a club and struck the tree with great force, and the hollow reverberation sounded through the forest like a drum. By the time they'd hauled the canoe ashore and unloaded it, six more Indians had walked into their midst, materializing out of the forest.

Like the others, these men were almost completely naked.

Their black hair was cut short, as if a bowl had been placed over their heads. Their small eyes had a fold at the outer corners that made them look Oriental.

They emptied the montaria and carried it off to be hidden in the forest. Although they seemed to make a point of not acknowledging her presence, she got the impression they were making remarks about her, and that the remarks were not compliments.

Esteban took a moment to ask her if she was feeling better. "Yes," she said, "only I'm so hot. You said I could get this stain off. May I bathe somewhere?"

He shook his head. "These men say the trail up ahead is under water. Soon you will have more of a bath than you will want." The Indians took up the heavy boxes of medicine and hung them on their backs in woven slings like hammocks. Then they took off at a smooth trot. "Take off your shoes or your feet will give you trouble," Esteban said.

She tied her shoes together and draped them over her shoulder, wondering if she could force herself to walk barefoot in the jungle. Esteban put her belongings into a bark cloth bag coated with rubber and fitted it into a sling; then he put the band across her forehead so the bag hung down her back. She said, "Why can't I just carry it?"

He took up a load even larger than the other men were carrying and said, "You'll see."

She did. It took both her hands to keep from slipping on the muddy trail. Although the path was clear, it was narrow, and she kept tripping over vines thin as thread and strong as wire. Yet when she lost her footing, she dared not clutch for support without great care, for the trees had rings of spike-shaped thorns. The load on her back took getting used to, for it thumped about from side to side awkwardly. At last, she thought wearily, I am an Indian woman.

From time to time they crossed bridges made of a single tree felled over a stream. The men, burdens and all, ran across, but Savannah, unable to keep from looking down into the opaque water that was the haunt of five-foot electric eels, clung to the slippery trunks and went ignominiously across on all fours. Steadily she fell behind.

Esteban kept looking back at her and at last came to help her. He did not say: *Now are you willing to return to Manáos?* But she was afraid that was his thought, so she smiled grittily and began to trot like the Indians. Still, he stayed behind to watch her.

Soon the trail was under water. They waded, knee deep at first, then thigh deep, and at last waist deep. She had to cling to the hanging vines and pull herself along. Twice she stepped on a thorn. Cold mud squeezed through her toes until she was chilled and sickened. She fell into holes, slipped down steep banks into water-logged ditches, and climbed out only to lose her footing once again. Each time she laughed grimly.

But then the rain began to fall, torrents of rain pouring from the invisible sky beyond the high matted treetops. The Indians cut palm fronds and tied them into bundles to make umbrellas, but she kept dropping hers and soon left it behind. Almost blinded by the deluge, she slogged on, sliding, falling, and mindlessly getting up again, willing herself not to give in.

At last Manco halted them. Swiftly they built shelters of palm leaves on frames of branches. They carried with them embers, dried grasses, and small sticks wrapped in moss and bark cloth, and with these they made fires under the roofs of the shelters. Savannah sank to the wet ground, drenched, cold, miserable, and too tired to shiver any more.

Manco hung her hammock from the branches of the shelter, helped her climb in, and wrapped her in his poncho. She was too tired to eat, but he fed her spoonfuls of warmed farinha gruel. Then he got into the hammock with her and, rocking gently in his arms, she slept like a child.

When she awakened the shelter was empty. She thought it was still raining, but when she stepped outside she found she'd heard only the steady dripping from the trees. That sound, and the laughter and splashing of the men bathing in a stream a short distance away, somehow failed to break the immense quiet of the *selva*. The forest gallery had drained during the night, so the trail was moist but no longer flooded. She looked about her, feeling as though she'd come back from the dead with all her senses intensified. It was dim and cool as the convent cellar, but there was a smell of ripeness, of fertile soil. Far above, points of sunlight pierced the high unbroken roof of dense verdure, striking the wet leaves into an iridescent shimmering.

The tree trunks rose farther than she could see, farther than she could guess. Out of sight in the branches a stampede of monkeys shook the leaves, and there fell a shower of raindrops, then the plop of nuts and fruits, and finally a silent wafting of flower petals from unseen blossoms. Their faint fragrance settled on the trail.

There was another fragrance . . . coffee. She returned to the shelter to find that Esteban had made breakfast. She was starving. Even the bananas and farinha tasted good to her today. She and Esteban smiled at each other over their tin cups; he was glad to see her feeling well.

They broke camp and ran along the trail for what seemed a very long time. There was no way to tell the time of day, for they never saw the sky. At length they came out on the edge of another river and she saw that the sun was at high noon. Looking at the swift mustard-colored torrent, she wondered how they would cross, but the men reached down into the river's shallows and hauled out two canoes, filled with rocks and sunk there. They turned them over, dumped them out, and cleaned them in the water. Then they loaded the supplies into them and pushed off, down this river to a fork and up another one, a clear stream of deep blue. Manco told her this was the Rio Escondido, the Hidden River.

The current of the blue river was powerful, and even though they hugged the shore, the men were forced to paddle mightily. Then, when the sun was halfway to the tops of the trees to the west, Savannah heard a sound like a dozen freight trains . . . the roaring of rapids. Soon the river was filled with black rocks where the water foamed white and boiled up in clouds of spray.

They beached the canoes and unloaded them. Then they carried the supplies by hand over the treacherous rocks of the riverbank, Savannah scrambling along behind them with her bag. On a beach above the rapids they put down the supplies, and Manco told her to wait here for them; then the men ran back the way they'd come.

She sat among the boxes, trying to blot out the river's deafening roar and watching the way the water sluiced between the largest rocks. Much later she saw them coming upstream, hauling the unloaded canoes on long lines of ropy vines, tying the vines from tree to tree along the bank as they pulled the boats one after another over the obstructions in the river. As the spray blew away she saw one man in each canoe, paddling furiously to keep clear of the rocks, while the others on the bank hauled on the ropes tied to the bows. The man in the first canoe was Manco.

She ran helplessly along the bank, wild to reach him somehow, lest he slip away from her and be lost forever in the boiling river. Among the trees of the rock-strewn bank the others strained, slipped, fell, and rose to brace themselves and pull the ropes once more. Beside herself with terror and not knowing what else to do, she got in line with the Indians and hauled on the rope when they did. Twice she lost her footing and fell among the rocks, but she climbed out and pulled again. When they'd finished, when the last canoe was safely on the beach above the rapids and Manco stood beside her on the sand, she touched his back because she needed to, whether or not it was seemly, and was surprised to find her hands were bleeding. At the sight of those abrasions his brows contracted. It was almost as if he felt the pain in his own body. The Indians had shed what little they wore and had flung themselves into the quiet shallows for a swim. She followed Esteban away from the beach, upstream along the bank a short distance. She said, "What is it? Are you angry with me?"

He shook his head but did not look at her. He paused on an overhanging rock and stared into the clear blue water where the sand of the bottom lay in faint ridges. He said, "I should never have brought you here. I knew it was wrong." She reached out her hand to touch him again, but withdrew it and instead looked at the rope burns on her palm. He turned around to her and said, "I must have been mad. I must have lost my mind there in the Red Room." Then he said gently, "Do you want to bathe now?"

She nodded and then paused, embarrassed at the idea of swimming with ten naked men. He took her arm and led her farther upstream along the bank. When she made no move toward the water he said, "It is safe here. The current is too swift for predators."

Holding her cotton dress above her knees, she waded into the river. But then, hearing him laughing behind her, she turned. He said, "I thought you wished to be an Indian woman." When she nodded he said, "Women of the forest are not ashamed of their bodies."

"I am not ashamed. It's called modesty."

Once more he laughed. "Carrying modesty about with you in the *selva* is harder work than hauling canoes up the rapids." Smiling and shaking his head, he went away beyond the rocks. She undressed and slid nude into the cold water. Although shocked at first, soon she found it invigorating. She came up from a dive to see him standing on the rocks again. Her sling with her belongings was in his hand. He dug among her things until he found the cake of scented soap and threw it to her. Then he threw aside his clothing and dove into the water, swimming into the river far beyond her. She watched the rhythmic movement of his arms until he was lost to her sight, moving so smoothly he made no ripple on the surface of the water.

She scrubbed herself clean of the last vestiges of brown stain. Then she washed her hair until her scalp ached. When at last she got out of the water and lay on a flat rock to warm and dry herself she felt new, the way a snake must feel when it has shed its skin.

A splatter of water made her open her eyes. He was standing over her, dripping from the river. "You are so beautiful," he said.

She sat up and hugged her knees to hide her nakedness, but she did not leave the warmth of the rock. She said, "What clothing do women of the forest wear?"

"A little paint and some jewelry made of seeds and shells. That's all."

"And what about the men? Are they like the Indians with us?"

"Yes. They wear a penis sheath and on special days a headdress made of toucan feathers."

Penis. She'd never heard that word before. Embarrassed, she reached for her dress, but he took her in his arms. "The others," she said.

"They are making camp." His skin was cool and his mouth tasted of the clean river, but she drew away and looked around furtively. "I can't," she said.

Smiling, he said, "Follow me." He led her into the *selva* and on a bed of soft mosses and dry grass they made love like a man and woman of the forest.

When they returned to the high bluff a few feet above the river, where the others had made camp, she averted her eyes from those of the Indians. But they seemed unaware that anything had happened. They were fishing in the shallows with their bows and arrows, and soon the catch was broiling on a rack of green branches over the fire, and in the embers they were roasting turtle eggs found on a sand bank.

That night they slept on the beach without stringing up their hammocks, Savannah and Manco wrapped in the same blanket. There were few insects on this river and she should have slept well, but she could not. She lay awake long after the others slept, listening to the distant roar of the rapids and thinking about the changes taking place in her.

When she'd asked Manco to let her prove herself, she'd had no idea what she was getting into. Yet she had not collapsed, had she? She'd even seen a change in the Indians' attitude toward her, since she'd ripped open her palms on the tow rope. Before, only one of them ever communicated with her, making signs and telling her the names of things. The others had treated her like the village idiot. She didn't even know what to call them. Esteban said a man's name was rarely spoken until after he was dead because they believed if an enemy knew your name, it gave him power over you. So these Indians were called "Grandson of Ruratano" and "the One Who Wears a Boar's Tooth"; the man with the scarred chest was known as "Him the Puma Clawed." She'd given up trying to make friends with them.

Nevertheless, tonight at dinner they insisted she get a whole fish of her own. After that they watched her eat a roasted turtle egg. When she smiled and nodded emphatically, they were delighted. Esteban murmured, "Do you really like it?" She clasped her hands ecstatically and said, "It's disgusting!" But to please the men she ate another.

Perhaps in time she could, like Manco, move easily in both these worlds, the cities and the *selva*. Perhaps in time she'd be of some use to him and not a burden.

Now she lay with her head upon his shoulder, feeling his chest rise and fall. What had Veronique said? A virtuous woman does not enjoy the bed of marriage. Savannah was not, she supposed, a virtuous woman—nor was she married to the man whose bed she shared.

Her delight in their loving astonished her. It was not the way Morgan and Egypt had described it. She felt no impulse to cry aloud in joy. Rather, she felt a quiet happiness because she was sharing this intimacy with him. She loved the touch of his body on hers, the weight of it full length upon her. She loved the closeness, the feeling that they were one body. She loved to hear his sharp intake of breath and then his soft sighing at the end. She loved the knowledge that she alone was able to give him this happiness; it was something none of those others who called him Liberator could do for him.

She fell asleep at last. In the morning she awakened hungry again for his love. When their eyes met, he read her desire and his eyes smiled. He got up and went into the forest. Shyly she followed him, watching the slender print of his bare feet in the moist earth and shivering to contain her happiness.

40

The Baron's last remark to Will had been made as he threw the confiscated dispatch about atrocities at the rubber landings into the fireplace in his study. He'd said, "You wish to learn about the gathering of latex? I'll see you get a thorough education."

This had taken place about a week after his bride's disappearance from the opera; it had taken several days for Dom Luíz to satisfy himself that Will knew nothing of Savannah's whereabouts; he was, as he'd said, a cautious man. But then, since there'd been a certain amount of violence involved in the questioning, the Baron was faced with the problem of what to do with Will. Sending him upriver to be educated seemed, in Rio Mar's view, an expedient solution. Then, as if in answer to Will's unspoken question, he'd said, "Of course it would be simpler to kill you."

Will's sarcasm had remained intact. "But you are too humane for that."

"Hardly. The fact is, it would be wasteful. Tappers are becoming increasingly scarce, and—" he smiled down at Will's legs—"half a tapper is better than none."

So Will, after a six-day journey up one river after another until he lost count of them, found himself disembarking from a small river steamer onto the desolate clearing of a Rio Mar Rubber Company landing. It was a depressing sight, a half-dozen miserable huts raised on stilts in preparation for the rising of the river, which already threatened to spill its mustard-colored flood over the warped dock.

Although the rain had stopped earlier in the day, the sun was hidden by a haze, and the bare clay of the clearing remained a slippery muck. When Will lost his footing and fell, none of the emaciated men standing on the veranda of the largest building moved to help him. He badly needed his cane, but it had been taken from him; he'd been using it as a weapon every chance he got. Still, he reminded himself that at least they'd flung the rest of his belongings on board the steamer with him to make it look as though he'd gone off of his own free will. These belongings he was now trying to carry up the steep steps to the veranda under the impassive scrutiny of that line of dark-skinned men, their bony arms and legs exposed by the rags that must once have been shirts and pants.

By the time he'd dragged his leather traveling bag, writing case, overcoat, and umbrella to the floor of the veranda, he was aware how bizarre he must look. He suppressed the impulse to explain that since he'd left Baltimore he'd gotten to Amazonia by way of Europe in the dead of winter and that at this moment he'd be delighted to give them all his possessions, except for the writing case. He'd need that for documenting the beastliness of their employer so that the world would come to their rescue. But the men—Negroes, mulattoes, Indians, Portuguese, and a ruddy Caucasian whose eyes burned with fever—had lost interest in him when the door they'd been queued up to was thrown open. Will followed them into a dim room he saw was a company store. Behind a long counter a swarthy fellow, the first well-fed man Will had seen here, stood ready to fill the workers' orders from the shelves that lined the walls. Other men stood among the sacks of flour, rice, and beans; they had pistols jammed into their belts and Winchesters slung across their backs.

Each time a worker stepped to the counter and mumbled the list of his needs, the counter man, who was respectfully called Senhor Carlos, turned toward the small room visible through an open door at the back of the store. There a pale, handsome man with kinky red hair and Negroid features worked at a ledger. He was neatly dressed in a white linen suit and spoke in soft, cultured tones. As the counterman said each worker's name, the keeper of the ledger turned a page, traced his finger down the figures, and delivered the judgment. "Yes, Felipe may have beans and flour this week, but no sugar or salt until his bill comes down."

He'd seen Will, but said nothing; and Will, who was better at deciphering spoken Portuguese than speaking it himself, waited in line trying to recall the words for his situation. But in the end he needed no phrases. When his turn came, the supervisor, ledger in hand, came out of the office and spoke to him in elegant English, with the accent of the British West Indies. "Mr. Patterson, is it not?" Will nodded. The man's long nails were beautifully manicured and he wore a ruby ring. He raised his hand gracefully. "Jesuino!" One of the tappers who'd had his turn at the counter and was collecting his rice, turned obediently. The supervisor said to Will, "Jesuino speaks a little English. You will share his hut and learn from him how to be a *seringueiro*." Will recognized that the word for rubber tapper came from the word for syringe, because that was one of the first things white men had made from rubber.

Meanwhile Senhor Carlos had been gathering Will's supplies: coffee, flour, sugar, beans, rice, dried meat, and a packet of salt, along with a hammock, fish hooks, a small ax, tin pans and a pail, a basin, a pottery jar, several small cups, and a lantern. The supervisor checked these over and copied the list into his ledger, adding the sum neatly in the right-hand column. Will said, "What is that you are writing down?"

The man's forehead creased as he raised his eyebrows. "Your indebtedness, of course. You owe the Rio Mar Rubber Company five hundred and fifty milreis. And in the future you will address me as *Capataz Baptiste, sir*."

The tapper called Jesuino plucked at Will's sleeve. "Please come now, senhor."

It took a moment to do the figuring, but then Will raised his voice. "That's ridiculous. Over three hundred dollars for some black beans and a couple of tin pans?"

The tappers who had been shuffling out onto the veranda with their supplies stopped moving. In the sudden quiet Will sensed that the men with guns had stepped closer. The overseer's voice was as patient as ever. "Of course not, Mr. Patterson. The principal item is the cost of your passage upriver."

"Well, Capataz Baptiste, *sir*, since I came not of my own accord, but as the guest of the Baron do Rio Mar, I will not pay it. Be so good as to erase that entry from your book."

Baptiste's pale yellow-brown eyes widened in a calm, untroubled surprise, the way he might have looked if his chair had murmured a p otest against being sat upon. At the same time Will felt a heavy hand on his shoulder and found one of the armed men directly behind him. Coiled in the guard's other hand was a bul whi . The man addressed the overse r in a voice like a frog's croak. He said, "*Quantos*, Capataz?" How many?

Baptiste shook his head and spoke in English. "Can you not see this is a gent'eman, Macedo? If you whip him he might die of fright, and we nee a *seringueiro* on that estrada. So instead of twenty lashes, we will fine Mr. Patterson for his insolence." He moistene his pencil point and made another entry on Will s ac nt. "Disciplinary fine, five hundred d fifty milreis." He t e ledger, smiling with sat tion, although his eyes remained menacingly cold. "Each time Mr.

Patterson is troublesome, we will double the amount of his debt. On the other hand, if he behaves himself, works very hard, and eats very little, his bill may be paid in ten years or so—if he lives."

Jesuino picked up Will's valise and his bundle of supplies and led him from the store. Will grabbed his writing case and followed, too angry to speak. They crossed the muddy clearing and made their way toward a canoe beached several feet above the water line. Rounding a rough shed, Will was stunned by the sight of several men tied to trees at the edge of the forest. They were unconscious, or perhaps dead, their heads fallen forward, knees slack, the bonds holding their arms high. Will's legs buckled and, fighting the urge to vomit, he tried not to look, to keep on going, since there was nothing he could do. Yet he could not keep his eyes from them. He decided to memorize this scene, to be the correspondent he'd set out to be.

The men had been mutilated: fingers gone, bloody swelling where toes had been. One of them had no ears, just dark holes in the sides of his head. A line of ants, each one an inch and a half long, formed a busy two-way stream between the victims and the jungle.

Jesuino came back and, freeing one of his hands from the load he carried, crossed himself and gripped Will's arm. As he helped him toward the river, he spoke quietly, as if they might be overheard. "*Borracha* no big enough." Will gazed at him dully. Jesuino said, "*Borracha*. Ball of latex. First time too small, one toe." Will waved him away and limped frantically toward the water, where he retched for several minutes before he was able to climb into the canoe.

After Jesuino had maneuvered the low craft into midstream, Will, sitting in the bow, took up the spare paddle and began to work. He'd learned to canoe one summer while under the care of an unorthodox doctor and reveled in a form of motion in which legs were secondary. Now he found that the work against the strong current helped him to manage his rage. Soon he was matching Jesuino stroke for stroke. In midafternoon Jesuino steered into a side channel and threw a line around a branch as if he were using a lasso. While they ate dried fish, washed down with river water, they talked— Jesuino with his few dozen words of English and Will with the Portuguese phrase book from his writing case.

Jesuino told him he'd been a *vaqueiro*, a cowboy, from the drought-blanched country called the *sertão*. Will had read about Brazil's Wild West, which was in the Northeast, where the land bulged out into the Atlantic. It was a grim and desolate place, a region of sand, cactus, thorns, shale, rock, and petrified forests. Every few years the country's normal aridity intensified into a drought so extreme that even the rattlesnakes were driven from the desert into the towns in search of water. At the height of the *secca* those who could still walk came into the coastal cities, just as the snakes had come into their villages; and like the snakes the people of the *sertão* reeked with death, with the cholera, smallpox, plague, and yellow fever of their unburied dead. Yet when the *secca* abated, those *sertanejos* who were still alive returned to their violent land with its killing sun and thorny vegetation; it suited them.

Jesuino told him that when all the cattle died and there was no ox to pull a cart, he'd carried his wife in his arms all the way to the port city of Fortaleza, to the hospital run by nuns. But by the time he got her there she was dead, and when they took her from his arms he fell down too. It was the only time he ever slept in a bed; the sheets were cool against his skin and he thought he had awakened in heaven. After he was well, he stayed to help them; he carried water, ground corn, scoured the stone courtyard on his knees, scrubbed and wrung out those beautiful bedsheets. That was where he learned a little English.

But then he grew homesick for the *sertão* and he began to roam the streets of Fortaleza asking other *sertanejos* if the drought had ended. One day he met a man who wore a linen suit as white as bedsheets; he had a diamond ring on each hand and one of his teeth was gold. The man said the *secca* had not ended, but in the forests of the Amazon, latex gatherers were needed. Working there a single season earned a man enough money to return home and live like a king the rest of his life, with land of his own and great herds of cattle. Most wonderful of all, it cost nothing to go there: Everything would be taken care of by the rubber company.

That was eight years ago, and not only was Jesuino not getting rich, but also his indebtedness on the ledger page had grown no smaller. The Capataz told him he ate too much.

Looking at Jesuino's slender body, where bone and long muscles were thinly covered with skin that seemed, even after eight years in the dim haze of the Amazon, still burned by the harsh desert sun, Will laughed. Jesuino joined him, but his merriment ended quickly. Casting a furtive look along the trees of the riverbank, he yanked the rope free of the branch and pushed off toward midstream. Will wondered if the very vegetation spied for Rio Mar.

It was evening when they hauled the canoe onto higher ground at the rim of a swamp, an apparently endless sheet of dark water filled with standing trees. The hut was a ragged thatch of palm fronds, with its floor of hardwood planks set on the stumps of four felled trees. Steps made of halved logs led to the single room, some ten feet square. The only furniture was a rough-hewn bench and a couple of upended logs. There were hooks in the roof supports to hang hammocks. Jesuino's few possessions—a ragged blanket, a couple of torn shirts, and a holy picture of a Byzantine Virgin—had been hung from the ceiling on cords treated to repel the ants.

While Will tried to stow his belongings away, Jesuino built a fire on the clay platform that served as a stove. Although there was a kerosene lamp and a couple of candles, Jesuino said they would attract insects, so they ate their meal of beans and coffee by the light of the small fire. After that there was nothing to do but go to bed.

Will lay in his hammock listening to the jungle, feeling as if he'd dreamed all this. He heard Jesuino softly saying his prayers. It seemed indecent to listen, yet how could he not? He caught a word here and there, but understood only the first and the last of them: Mother of God and *inferno verde*—green hell.

When the prayer ended Will said, "Don't you want to escape?"

"I pray for this, senhor."

Will had wondered if for the *sertanejo* this water-logged prison might seem bearable, or perhaps acceptable as the will of a bloodthirsty god. He said, "Then why don't you go?" He heard the gentle creaking cease as Jesuino's hammock stopped swaying.

"Go? Where is to go?"

"Anywhere away from here."

"Senhor, you know nothing of this place."

"You have a canoe."

Jesuino's voice dropped to the low tone he used in fear of being overheard. "The guards, senhor. All day, all night, they watch the river with their Winchester guns."

"Couldn't we slip past them in the dark?"

Jesuino sighed. "There are more landings on this river than the senhor have fingers, and at the *boca*, the mouth, where this river join the one they call Solimões, is a steamboat. Is not possible to pass all these places in dark."

Will sat up and leaned toward him. "We could hide in the side channels by day and travel only at night. When we get to Manáos—"

"We be dead. The river is much danger at nighttime. And even if we get to Manáos, still we be dead. One hundred lash with tapir-hide whip, senhor. No man live from that."

"Then into the forest. They could never track us through this jungle."

Jesuino was silent a moment, as if pondering the magnitude of Will's ignorance. "Senhor, there is a snake in this forest. When this snake bite a man, he fall down on the trail *paralitico*. He not can move anything. All he do is scream while the ants they eat him alive."

Will drew closer. "Jesuino, I know the *selva* is dangerous. But it is possible to travel through it. Other men have done it. We would carry nothing but our weapons and live off the land."

"Or die off the land, senhor, while we walk in circle."

"No, listen." He began explaining about the map of South America, how if you travel to the north of the Amazon you will come to another river, the Orinoco, which will take you to the sea. He spoke of the explorers, the men of science who had gone through the *selva*, and how they lived along the way with friendly Indians.

Jesuino said, "Men of science, perhaps, senhor. But *seringueiros*, no. The men of rubber have made slaves of Indians, killed them, raped their women. And even if the senhor say he is no *seringueiro*, he is North American man of science, they cannot help him. In the time of high water even Indians starve in the *selva*. The game runs away and the fish sleep in the bottom of the river. Go to sleep, senhor. The *seringueiro*'s day begins two hours before the sun."

41

Will awakened shivering. It was dark as a mine and no sound came from the surrounding forest but the steady drumming of the rain. Jesuino was sitting on a stump near the fire, working with his *machadinho*, the tapper's small ax. He moved it deftly up and down, stripping a sturdy branch of its twigs. Nodding toward the pan of coffee on the stove, he said, "Drink, senhor, and warm yourself. I finish very quick."

By the time Will swallowed the harsh coffee, Jesuino was done and proudly showed his handiwork. It was a forked stick of hardwood, fashioned to serve as a crutch. Will tried it out, stumping about the hut with agility, to Jesuino's delight. Touched and at a loss to express his gratitude, Will clapped his friend on the shoulder.

"Come now," Jesuino said, "we make you a *seringueiro*." But before they lit their lanterns and stepped out of the hut into the downpour, Will insisted on sharing his wardrobe. The contents of the leather valise astonished Jesuino: linen shirts, one-piece underwear, a blue velvet smoking jacket with satin lapels, monogrammed handkerchiefs, a tuxedo; but he could not be persuaded to accept any of it until Will drew his attention to the thick line of ants already preparing to carry off his garments into the forest piece by piece. After an anguish of indecision, Jesuino set off for his day's work wearing striped pajamas and an evening cape topped off by a jaunty plaid deer stalker's cap.

Even after dawn the forest remained dark. Gradually, however, Will's eyes adjusted to the gloom and he was able to discern the almost invisible trail, no wider than a man's foot, that led from one rubber tree to the next in a five-mile circle which turned back at last into the little clearing and the hut. The rubber trees, a hundred of them on Will's estrada, or avenue, were two or three hundred feet from one another and separated by other kinds of vegetation. They were easy to recognize by their scars. They were smooth, tall, and straight, averaging about eighteen inches in diameter. Beside each one there was a stick driven into the ground to hold the latex cups for that tree, seven of them if the tree was young and strong, four or five if it was weaker. Jesuino showed him how to reach up with his *machadinho* and make the cuts vertically at the same height around the trunk. "Do not pull off the bark," he said, "and do not cut into the wood, for that hurts the tree and the Capataz will grow very angry." At the base of every cut a cup was fastened with fresh clay. By the time each tree was prepared, the white latex had already begun to drip into the cups. When all the trees had been cut, they found themselves back at the hut. They stopped long enough for a breakfast of cold porridge and set out again. This time they carefully scraped with their fingers the two or three spoonfuls of latex from each cup into a tin pail. Long before the end of this round Will's clothes were wet, his shoes were full of mud, and he was exhausted; but Jesuino said the day's work was less than half finished, with the hardest job ahead.

While Jesuino heated up a midday meal of boiled rice and coffee, Will lay in his hammock, cold and aching. Fretfully he said, "This is absurd. There must be a better way to do this. Why can't we divide the estrada so there's no need for us both to slog ten miles a day along that muddy trail?"

Jesuino looked puzzled. After a moment he said quietly, "No, Senhor Will. All these trees we do this morning are your estrada. I have my own to do still." Abashed, Will got up from his hammock. "Then this afternoon I will help you do your avenue."

But Jesuino assured him there was much to be done here at the clearing. When they'd eaten he led the way to a low shed that served as a smokehouse and showed Will how to coagulate the latex by dipping a paddle into the sap to pick up a thin coating, then turning the paddle slowly so the latex cured in the smoke of a fire made of nuts from the uricuri palm tree. A cone fastened above the fire directed the smoke onto the paddle, but much of it escaped and drifted around the shed. Will found that the gas given off by these nuts, which were about the size and shape of pigeon's eggs, smelled like creosote. It caused him to choke painfully, and after a time he realized the fumes were carbonic acid, the gas that fouls the air of mines. It turned the latex brown and dried it out so the next dip into the pail put another thin coat on the paddle. After four hours' work he had pains in his chest, inflamed eyes, a violent headache, and a ball of rubber the size of a very small loaf of bread. His watch showed that it was not yet four o'clock, but he went to his hammock and slept fitfully until the next morning.

The days that followed varied little from the first, except that Will did his estrada alone. This freed Jesuino to work at his own faster pace, so he finished smoking his latex by the time Will came in with his pail; and Jesuino always helped Will in the shed, giving him a chance to get out and breathe from time to time. Still, Will grew more tired every day, for he slept badly. The thorns along the trail were like metal spikes; several had gone clear through the soles of his shoes and his feet had become badly infected.

The insects were a ceaseless torment too. He was covered

with raised black blisters from their bites. The ants, which came in several colors and ranged in size from almost invisible to monsters of an inch and a half, were the worst. It was bad enough that they bit into your flesh and ate the clothes off your back; but they were devouring his books as well. He'd come to loathe this jungle that had been the haunt of his dreams for so many years.

He hated the rain which, even when it ceased in the atmosphere above the forest, continued to fall from the trees. He was always cold, except at midday, when the hot, moist air condensed on his flesh so that he was drenched in sweat and the insect bites all over his body stung in the salt of his perspiration. And he hated the perpetual darkness, that endless twilight the sun never dispelled.

He tried hard to remain civilized, to keep up appearances. He washed his clothing often, although it would not dry unless he hung it over the fire. His valise was covered with a mold like thick gray fur. After the first week his watch refused to run and his razor was encrusted with rust so he could not shave; but he learned to trim his beard with his *machadinho*.

And he tried hard to keep to his plan, which was to get what his countrymen called "the goods" on Rio Mar—and then get out. To this end he kept his journal faithfully. He carried it with him in a rubber-coated bag slung from his shoulder and worked whenever he stopped to rest his legs, writing down all the things Jesuino was telling him during their long talks. He wrote in shorthand, which he'd taught himself during his early days as a reporter. The Baron had of course amused himself by reading here and there in Will's journal; but Savannah's name appeared nowhere, so the Baron had found the material of little interest. Now it was Will's intention to put these pages in the hands of the nearest American consul and demand a full official inquiry. Even if he had to walk on his lacerated feet all the way to Venezuela to do it.

Yet he knew he had no chance without Jesuino, who wouldn't even talk about it, except to say, "It's no use, Senhor Will. And anyway, it is not necessary to go. Is only necessary to wait." So now the words of Jesuino's prayer irritated Will. *Mother of God, let the Liberator find me before I die in this green hell.* He was waiting for a messiah! What nonsense, Will thought. Crazy fanatic *sertanejo*.

42

In the time since Tomás had been rescued from the Baron's stable, his wounds had healed. Still, the Liberator had refused to let him work, to conduct raids on the rubber landings or to join the force at the canal. So Tomás had spent his time hunting to put meat on the cooking fires. Alone in the *selva* he forced himself to run until his chest ached, and when the hunt was over he swam upstream against the strong current of the Escondido. Now that Manco was returning from Manáos he would see that Tomás had regained his health.

And it is true that when the Liberator stepped from the canoe onto the dock at the first landing above the Escondido rapids, he embraced Tomás and said, "Are you well?" But then the others crowded around him, the men to greet Esteban and the women to look at the tall white girl he'd brought with him, and in the midst of the crowding the Liberator was asking for reports on the progress of the canal. All the way across the clearing and up the steps of the main building the chatter continued; the people were always overjoyed when he returned, for even though they kept on working in his absence, following the orders he left them, still there was a persistent anxiety that only the Liberator's presence could dispel.

So it was almost an hour before Tomás was alone with Esteban in the old company store the Liberator used for an office when he was at this landing. Esteban said to him, "You owe the senhorita your life. You will guard her when I am at the canal." He pointed at the tall white girl outside.

Tomás knew then that this woman was important to the Liberator, that he had some plan in which she played a part; and he said, "Yes, Esteban, I will."

Through the rain the Escondido looked like a gigantic gray snake twisting along the edge of the jungle and past the deserted clearing. Nearly everyone went off to work on the canal each day, in spite of the rain. They said the water was higher this year than they had ever seen it and they had to work fast. They never told Savannah why.

Every day she paced the length of the veranda, watching the rain drum on the steps, the outbuildings, the dock. It seemed to her that she'd been miserable ever since they'd arrived here. She felt completely cut off from Esteban, as if this mob of people, the Indians and part-Indians and the handful of Negroes and the strange cowboys they called *sertanejos*, all these people who were his followers stood between them, separating them, just as they had that first day. As their canoe neared the dock at the clearing upriver she'd said to Esteban, "Will we stay here now?" He answered, "You will stay here." You. Not we.

They'd climbed onto the dock and stood in the midst of a crowd which included Indian women and children. Esteban stood tall among them, moving through the crowd toward the main building. As he passed, the people grinned. He spoke to them, touching some, smiling at others. Again there was the wordless communication she'd seen on the trip, the meaningful nod, the lifting of the chin, the shrug, the eloquent hand movement. She wished she understood.

The women averted their eyes from her, smiling behind their hands. Their eyes were dark and very bright. She paused to admire a child being carried on his mother's hip. His black hair gleamed in the faint hazy sunlight. When she touched him, the young mother smiled and shyly fingered a strand of Savannah's hair. Soon all the women and children clustered around her, feeling her hair, her skin, her long fingernails, even her toes. She controlled her discomfort, continuing to smile and nod as she drew away from them to follow Manco.

The women took her hands and led her up the stairs at the other end of the building and into a large room at the corner. It was airy, with windows on two sides, and it had a few pieces of furniture. The women drew her attention to the hammock hooks on the wall and pantomimed that she would sleep in this place.

She slipped the sling from her shoulder and set it down on a bench. Immediately the younger girls began going through her things. She managed to grab her crayon box and put it out of reach under a rafter. Undeterred, they sniffed her soap, her nightgown, her underwear. They took turns using her comb and brush and were on the verge of tasting her cologne when she stopped them and showed them what it was for. After that she had to place a drop on every wrist in the room.

At last she lost patience. She gathered her things and stowed them all out of reach. Still they remained, lining the walls of the room, crowding the window sills, looking in from the veranda. She was so unnerved she wanted to scream: Leave me alone! They would not have understood. Later she saw that. All their lives they lived together, in communal huts in the native villages. They bathed together, ate together, worked together, and slept with their hammocks slung in tiers around a central hearth. Every facet of their lives was public. And now Savannah's was too.

So every day she paced the length of the veranda while the cold gusty wind blew rain in her face. Even here she knew she was being watched; Tomás always watched her. He spoke both Spanish and Portuguese well, so with her six years of convent Latin and the Portuguese she'd learned (or perhaps remembered) at the Contessa's, they were able to converse. She asked him to teach her to speak Indian, but Tomás shook his head. He told her that there were at least 150 Indian languages in the *selva*. She said, "Isn't there a main one that will help me understand the others?"

"There are several. The Jesuits used the one called Tupi, so now in many places people understand that one."

"Then teach me Tupi." Tomás took her from room to room telling her the names of things. Then he took her into the forest and told her what to call the various trees and plants. He taught her how to see things—a green parrot screened by green leaves, or the line of sauba ants, which looked like bits of leaf that had grown legs because each of them walked carrying a piece like a sail over its head. He warned her never to enter the forest alone. "The *selva* here is very heavy. If you get just a dozen steps off the trail you will become confused and begin to wander in circles. That is how people become lost."

She asked Tomás about the canal. She wanted to know why Esteban was always busy there. Tomás said they were joining the Escondido to the Semnome in order to avoid the rapids. Farther up the Manconistas had a hospital. "But," he said, "the ground rises toward the upper Escondido, so we must build something called locks that open and close."

She said, "It sounds impossible."

He smiled. "If the Liberator tells us to do it, that means it can be done."

She liked Tomás, but while his cheerful instruction helped to pass the time, it could not make up for Esteban's absence. And Esteban was absent all the time.

She'd waited for him that first night. She'd put on her embroidered nightgown and lain awake in her hammock listening for his quiet step; but he had not come to her. At dawn she threw her wrap over her shoulders and went looking for him. He was in the room he used for an office, drinking coffee and studying a pile of maps. He had worked all night.

He looked up, his face clouded with worry. "Is it morning? I must leave for the canal." He left the room, went across the clearing, and got into a canoe.

Savannah spent most of that day angrily trying to sketch the children who followed her about, but found she'd distractedly drawn the geometric designs of the Indians' garments. Once when Manco came back drenched, muddy, and exhausted, she railed at him. "I never see you. I have nothing to do. I don't understand these people."

Weariness softened his voice to a whisper. "I told you how it would be," he said, and turned away. That night he slept on a rush mat on the floor of her room, but he did not take her in his arms, and when she awakened in the morning he was gone.

At least at the Contessa's she'd had somebody to talk to, instead of this awful loneliness, this feeling there was no one who could understand how she felt. At times she went to the kitchen and sat with Içu, who was the wife of Caetano, one of those sunburned cowboys from the Northeast. She and Içu couldn't talk much; Içu could speak Tupi, but very little Portuguese. Yet whenever Savannah appeared in her kitchen, Içu poured her a tin cup of coffee and forced upon her a plate of whatever she happened to be cooking at the time—small sweet bananas, sliced and fried; or toucan meat. That was considered a great treat, but Savannah had a terrible time eating it because it was blue.

She wished she could talk to Içu, but she could only accept the coffee Içu gave her, and nod or smile. Whenever Caetano appeared, Savannah left the kitchen. He was thin and wiry and his eyes seemed to smolder with hatred. Savannah couldn't shake off the feeling that she was the object of his rage.

Once she'd asked Tomás about it. He was distressed by her question, yet he was too honest not to answer. He said, "Caetano believes you are bad luck. He says you are going to get us all killed." Tomás smiled. "He's a *sertanejo*." The way he said it, she understood he meant that Caetano was a little crazy. But she was reminded of what the Contessa had said about Will, and she wondered if she was fated to bring harm to everyone she cared for.

Sometimes when she couldn't bear the loneliness any longer

she would stop her restless pacing on the veranda and go into Manco's office. The door was never locked; not even the Liberator had any privacy. The room always looked as if it had been abandoned in haste, the maps still open on the table; the book he'd been reading left open, face down; his tin cup of coffee not quite finished. She sat in his wicker chair, a leftover from the former rubber landing manager. Closing her eyes, she tried to feel his arms around her. It was impossible: These days he was so very far from her.

She'd followed this man hundreds of miles into the jungle, scarcely knowing him. Did anyone know him? Did he speak his deepest thoughts to anybody, to Tomás or Caetano? Was Savannah the only one completely shut out of his mind, or were all of them? In order to enjoy his approval, was it necessary to make no demands, to accept his presence or his absence with equal grace? Could she ever conceal her hurt over his neglect?

She leafed the book he had been reading, looking at a line here and there. An envelope fell out. She recognized the Contessa's writing by the word *Esteban*. She took out the letter.

Something is afoot. Ships are being outfitted in the harbor and there's a rumor naval vessels are on their way from Rio. If the Baron is going to pursue you there, hadn't you better send my darling back to me? Liliane is retiring, going home to Rouen and her little Marcel. Savannah's French is excellent. I could send her out with Liliane on the *Esperança* under Haversham's care. He can report that Mademoiselle is ill and keep her in her cabin. Then I could remain here long enough to find out what Rio Mar is up to before I join her in Rouen. But we must act quickly. The *Esperança* is due to sail in a week when it returns from Iquitos.—C.

She folded the letter and put it back. Maybe she ought to go. At least she'd have Liliane to talk to. But when she raised her eyes to find him standing in the doorway, mud to the thighs and wet clear to the roots of his hair, her hurt changed to fear for his well-being and anger that he should so expend himself. Before she could censor her reaction she cried out, "Look at you! You're going to get sick! Why must you always be running off to that canal?"

He glanced at her, sighed, and crossed the room to a cupboard, where he began looking for something.

She went to him to make amends. "I'm sorry. It's just that

I'm alone so much, I'm getting all muddled. I don't know what to do, and I wanted to help you."

"You are. Simply by being here." He selected a packet of diagrams and leafed through them, picking out several sheets to carry with him. He would be gone in a moment.

She touched his arm. "That's not what I wanted. Why can't you take me to the canal with you?"

"That's out of the question."

"I know it's hard work, and I'm not good for much, but I ought to be able to do something to help you try to get it finished."

He looked at her. "Try? We *must* finish. If we don't, all the work we've done will be for nothing. The whole plan will fail." He took a step past her, toward the door, but then paused and touched her face. "I'm sorry if I've been abrupt. We are having serious trouble. A hostile tribe is in the vicinity. Headhunters. There have been warning signs along the trails, arrows driven into trees, dead snakes draped over the branches at eye level. They want us out of here."

"Can't you scare them off, fire warning shots at them?"

He shook his head. "I didn't come into the *selva* to make war on the forest peoples. We will not fire at them even if they kill us all. That's the only way to prove we mean them no harm." He slipped the diagrams into a rubber bag.

"Shouldn't you change into dry clothing?"

He paused, as if fatigue had slowed his thought processes. "Yes, I suppose I should."

"And I'll get you some coffee from Içu." She moved quickly to the door, glad to be doing something for him at last, besides just being there. But at that moment an Indian woman came in carrying dry clothing for Esteban in one hand and in the other a tin cup of hot coffee. Savannah could not stifle her pain. She turned away, her eyes filled with tears.

Tomás saw the senhorita come out of the office and run the length of the veranda to her room. He knew that sometimes women sat alone and wept for reasons no man could understand; he would approach her later and offer her another language lesson.

As it turned out, he never did. Caetano sent word the hostile tribesmen had struck; they'd ambushed six Manconistas and killed them.

When Caetano's messenger led them to the place, Esteban stood silent for a long time. Tomás looked from one body to the other, recognizing the men slowly by their clothing, and thinking that even now the killers had made camp not far from here, on the bank of a river so they could use hot sand to fill the heads and shrink them, because for the trophies to be good, they must begin work on them quickly. At last Esteban said, "They obeyed the orders. They did not draw their guns." He did not speak again. When they got back to the landing he went into the office and sat silent in the wicker chair, sunk into himself, the way Tomás had often seen him when he had decisions to make.

Tomás left him alone and slowly walked the length of the veranda thinking of the men who'd died. It was then he discovered that Senhorita Savannah was gone.

43

Caetano's face was lean, the lips thin, the nostrils flared like an animal's. Leaning both hands on Manco's map table, he said, "They won't be far during the next twenty-four hours. Let us find them and attack now."

Esteban raised his eyes. "Attack? Will that restore our friends?"

"It will stop them from killing any more of us. We must do as they have done, an eye for an eye. We must show them that we also can take heads. There are some Jívaro among us; we know how to do it."

Esteban said, "Caetano—" He spread his hand on the map where the canal ran between the Escondido and the Semnome. "No doubt this is part of what they feel is their territory. That makes us invaders. Perhaps our operations have driven away the game and back in the village their children are eating ants, grubs, and the white worms they find inside the ingá nuts."

"Does that justify the taking of six lives?"

"No, it doesn't. But they warned us. I should have stopped the work and gone in search of them. I should have prevented this."

"So now you are going to let them get away."

"No. I am going to give them presents."

In a movement almost too swift to be seen, Caetano impaled map and table with his knife. The blade stuck between Esteban's thumb and forefinger. Esteban did not move, but continued looking intently at Caetano's face. After a moment Caetano grasped the knife and pulled it out. He said, "You are my Liberator. I owe you my life, and I would gladly die for you. But since you went away to Europe this last time, you have come back crazy. You bring that woman here, and now you talk of presents for the savages."

Esteban got to his feet and moved to Caetano. "Yes, they are savages. Almost as savage as the white men who come here. But at least they are not savage for profit." He put his arm around Caetano's shoulders in a brotherly embrace. "And who knows, perhaps the savagery of these headhunters, their constant warring with its gruesome rituals, is a way of keeping their numbers within bounds. If we can help them increase their food supply, perhaps their savagery will no longer be necessary. Is that so crazy, Caetano?"

Tomás waited until Esteban saw him standing inside the door; then he said, "I cannot find the senhorita." Esteban looked beyond him, out the open doorway. It was midafternoon; the rain had stopped. "None of the women or children saw her leave. It must have been when we were looking at the dead men. I'm sorry."

"We will have to search for her," Esteban said. "Call everyone together."

Caetano smirked in disgust. "You refuse to search for the headhunters, but for this white girl, for her you—" He spat over the railing into the clearing.

Esteban said, "We may find the headhunters now whether we mean to or not."

"Liberator," Tomás said, "shall we issue the British rifles?"

Manco shook his head. "You know we are not here to kill Indians. Not even the ones who are living in the Stone Age."

Caetano watched him carefully. "Not even if they have the senhorita?"

Esteban blinked slowly. "Not even then."

At first when Savannah had run in tears from Manco's office, she'd sat miserably in her hammock thinking: *He doesn't love me at all.* She didn't want to stay where she wasn't wanted, where Caetano hated her and Esteban had no need of her. She was just a lot of trouble for him. Father Antonio was right: He said God had chosen Esteban to free the Indians and nothing must be permitted to interfere. Tears filled her eyes when she thought how she'd railed at Manco, telling him how miserable she was. She'd been thinking only of herself. She'd behaved like a child. What must he think of her? What must they all think of her? She blew her nose and washed her face at the bowl and pitcher on her table.

How could she have been so childish when she loved him so? Even if his work kept him away, even if all she could do was sit in his empty chair holding a book he'd been reading . . . that would be enough until his task here was done and he could take her away to New Orleans or London.

She went along the veranda toward his office. She was going to tell him how sorry she was for behaving badly. If he'd already gone, she would wait.

The clearing seemed unusually quiet. All the canoes were gone from the dock. Even Içu's kitchen was deserted; meat broiling on a rack above the flames had burned black. On the veranda an old Indian woman rocked slowly in a hammock. She knew this woman understood none of the languages Savannah could speak, but she said to her, "Where is everyone?" and gestured around at the empty clearing. "Where is Içu? Where is Tomás?" She used one hand to indicate small people and said, "Where are the children?"

The woman broke into animated gibberish, pointing upriver and making violent gestures that seemed to pantomime arrows being shot and machetes chopping. Esteban had spoken of trouble, of warning signs, of headhunters. And now this old woman was miming throats being cut. Esteban . . . was he in danger? She shrieked, "Where is Esteban? Where is the Liberator?" Again the woman pointed in the direction of the canal.

When the weather was too stormy for canoes, the Manconistas used a trail; it left the clearing and went through the *selva* parallel with the river. The sky had cleared; there was a momentary blindness when she stepped from the sunlight into the deep shade of the forest. Still, the trees were dripping from the day's rain and she felt clammy. She began to run along the trail, her shoes making her stumble clumsily on the tree roots and vines. Soon she was forced to pause for breath.

She stood there, silent. It was a hungry quiet; she felt watched by all the leaves. And she was no longer sure of the trail. It seemed to have disappeared in the tangle of growth. Still, she must hurry; she must find Esteban and make certain he was all right, that whatever had happened at the canal, whatever the old woman was babbling about, had brought no harm to him. She must simply keep on in the same direction; inevitably she must come upon the canal.

The sound of the river was muted now. Which direction was it coming from? She didn't know. She decided to climb a tree to look for the river, but she'd rested her hand on the trunk without looking first, and she cried out in pain. The bark was covered with caterpillars eight inches long and black, with hideous coral heads. Fine hairs imbedded in her palm burned like hot needles. Rubbing her hand fiercely on her dress, she looked for water to wash off the burning hairs; but the pain blurred her vision and she stumbled into a spider web stretched like a sticky veil between the trees.

Frightened now, she began to run, only to fall over a log and once again cry out in pain. The fallen log was a mass of biting ants, which now swarmed up her legs. Flailing her skirt violently, she managed to brush the ants away, but she was bitten many times and for several minutes afterward imagined she felt them crawling between the clothing and her skin.

Remembering what Tomás had said about wandering in circles, she forced herself to stop. She found another fallen log and checked it carefully for insects before she sat down. It took effort to stop trembling, to be still, to think quietly. She must pull herself together and walk calmly in a straight line, keeping her eyes watchful so nothing would startle her and make her run again. She must refuse to imagine that the vines were alive, that the tendrils she passed were reaching for her, and she must walk calmly until she came to the river, or a stream that would lead to the river. Or one of those big hollow trees that stood up on their roots like pulled taffy and that made a booming drum sound when you struck them with a club. That's what she'd do; she'd find one of those trees and bang on it with a big stick until someone found her. . . .

Through the underbrush they ran. There were seven of them. Their hair, jet black and glossy, hung below their waists and flowed like manes behind them. Their skin was the color of chocolate and their bodies were tattooed with the pricks of thorns dipped in dye. Some of them bore the scars of spear wounds. Their teeth were stained black and filed to sharp points like the piranha's.

They had made camp on the bank of an *igarapé* a short distance from the river so their position would not be seen. The dripping heads had been carried strung on lengths of bark passed through the mouth and out the neck. They laid them face up on the sand while they gathered wood for the fire. Then, hearing the drumming, they'd left three men to guard the heads and set out to investigate. Now, seeing it was only a woman by the sapopema tree, they stepped from the forest cover.

Savannah, not having been to the canal or the hospital Tomás had spoken of, did not know all the Manconistas; yet she knew there were many kinds of Indians among the Liberator's followers. She laughed and said, "I'm certainly glad to see you!"

At first they watched her warily. Everyone knows the forest is filled with evil spirits, like the *curupira*, a red-headed dwarf. Sexless and devoid of the physical equipment needed for bodily secretions, it wears its feet turned backward to confuse those who would follow it. But this creature in the white dress was no dwarf: She towered over them. Was she Kumareme, daughter of the Thunder God who smashes rocks in the sky when he is angry? Watching her uncertainly, they whispered to one another; when she spoke loudly to them, not softly like a woman, they backed away in fear. She followed, talking loudly all the while; then, tripped up by the clumsy feet which had no toes and looked like the hide of a tapir, she fell. They paused. Would the daughter of the Thunder God fall down on the forest trail?

Their leader turned to face her, brandishing his spear. They saw fear in her face. The leader poked her with his spear point, and she cried out in pain. The others jabbed at her also, her cries reassuring them that they need have no fear; this was no spirit, just an ugly woman with sick-looking skin. One of them stepped up on a log to peer into her eyes, which were more like the eyes of a sea cow than a person. Another yanked at her flowing red headdress because he wanted it for himself. Meanwhile the leader, wondering if she had the body of a woman, ripped her dress away. She began to fight them, and the leader struck her down with his war club. Standing over her they spoke of the other things they might do to assure themselves this was indeed a woman like any other; but there was no time now, they had much work before them. They tied her arms behind her with bark thongs, got her to her feet, and dragged her to their camp, where they threw her down a few yards from the fire and set to work.

They had taken six heads. Although others could help, preparing them was the responsibility of the killer. Each man knelt before his trophy and parted the hair straight down the back from crown to neck; then he cut along the line and carefully peeled the flesh from the bone. Some additional cutting was needed at the ears, eyes, and nose. But then the skin and muscles came away, leaving the skull clean and bare except for the teeth and eyes. They laid the skulls aside. Using a bamboo needle and the chambira palm fiber that makes good hammocks, they carefully stitched up the incision and sewed around the neck edge to strengthen it for handling. Three bamboo splinters skewered the lips shut. The eyes were closed by setting small pegs against the eyebrows. They plugged the nose and ears with wads of cotton.

By now the fire was roaring, They unwrapped the red clay pots they'd carried packed in leaves, and filled them with water. Into each pot they placed a boneless head. Then the pots were set in the fire. While the flames heated them, the men rested for a time. Laughing, they set the skulls on spears driven into the sand and danced around them shouting, *"Hai io, hai iorama!"*

Savannah had not been fully conscious when they'd thrown her down. Now she lay on her side, astonished at the intensity of the pain in her head. She watched the men dancing foolishly in the sand. Their feet were broad, the toes splayed out. There were ugly things on the ends of their spears, reminding her of the aftermath of a monkey hunt. She smelled the meat cooking now and felt sick, perhaps because of the pain in her head.

The men watched the clay pots carefully; the heads must be removed just before the water reached the boiling point, otherwise the flesh would soften, the hair might fall out, and the trophy would be spoiled. At the proper moment they poured the simmering water out and threw the pots away; none was ever used twice, for the shaman with his magic had made them sacred.

Now the heads had shrunk to a third of their original size, but the work was far from finished. Using gourds, they scooped hot sand from around the fire and filled the heads with it. As soon as the sand cooled, they poured it out and added more from beneath the flames. In between, they used handfuls of palm leaves to pluck hot stones from the fire. With these they ironed the faces, gently smoothing out the wrinkles and squeezing all the oil from the skin.

Meanwhile Savannah, who had worked herself up to a sitting position, began to understand what was happening. When she vomited on the ground they ignored her, but when she got to her feet and began to stumble out of the clearing, they knocked her down and tied her to a tree. That was when she started screaming Manco's name mindlessly again and again. After a while they stuffed her mouth with palm leaves and tied hemp around her jaws to keep them shut.

Yet, as the hours passed, her fear ebbed. The savages were still too busy to bother killing her, and surely any moment now the Manconistas would find her. She hoped they would kill every last one of these monsters. But then the thought came: What if these were the remains of Tomás and Caetano and even . . . ? She was afraid to look, afraid of what she'd see. Yet she had to know.

It took her an eternity to satisfy herself that none of those . . . *things* they were dumping out and filling with sand over and over again was . . . anyone she knew.

At last, after hours of work, the heads were finished— smooth and hard as leather, and each of them the size of a large orange. They were not distorted, but perfectly proportioned. With the long hair hanging down, they looked like gruesome dolls.

It was deep night now. The men ate the food they carried and lay down around the fire. Surely, if she were going to be rescued, someone would have come by now. She hadn't wandered very far from the landing; she was certain of that. Then why had no one come? Were they all dead? Had these savages killed everyone? If that was true, she no longer cared what happened to her. If she could not live with Esteban, she didn't want to live at all.

She began to pray. She begged forgiveness for every wrong she'd ever done and pleaded to be taken at her death to wherever Manco was. Heaven or Hell. It made no difference.

While Tomás and Caetano were gathering the Manconistas into the clearing at the landing, Esteban marked on his map every stream within a half-day's march of the spot where the six men had been killed, for he knew the warriors would need sand, water, and firewood. He split his force into groups, assigning one to every stream. Darkness had fallen when the report came back to him. One of the groups, running through the forest with torches, had found footprints. Several persons had been walking there, and one of them wore shoes. Tomás saw pain film Esteban's eyes.

By the time the Liberator had reached the footprints by the sapopema tree, the search party had seen the banked campfire across a stream not far away. Esteban stood looking at the scene from the forest, Savannah lying in a heap at the foot of the tree they'd bound her to, the finished heads on a log near the fire, the warriors sleeping. Caetano whispered, "I'll cross downstream so we can attack from all sides."

Esteban said, "Yes, we will surround them. But we will not attack. I will go in alone." He turned to Tomás. "What are they?"

"They look like Namawateri."

"Can we speak their language?"

"Close enough. It's related to Ahawe."

Caetano said, "If they attack you, we will fire on them."

Esteban said, "No."

Caetano lifted his chin toward the Manconistas standing like shadows in the surrounding foliage. Their eyes were fixed on the six skulls impaled on spears in the clearing. He said, "I will not be able to stop them."

Esteban said, "Then remember, if any of those warriors is struck down, you will have to kill them all and leave no trace. Are you willing to do that? For if you do not, in a matter of days you will have to face the entire tribe."

Half an hour later, after completing his preparations, Esteban crossed upstream, circled the camp, and leaped from the forest into the midst of the savages. The watchman they'd assigned was nodding by the fire and, taken by surprise, they stumbled to their feet with startled cries. Esteban saw, at the corner of his field of vision, Savannah lift her head. He gestured toward the skulls. "You have killed my brothers. My other brothers surround you in the forest because they want your heads." The warriors peered anxiously into the darkness. Esteban went on. "I will not let them kill you because I want the brave men of the Namawateri for my friends."

They murmured among themselves. The leader struck the lazy watchman a blow on the side of the head and told him to serve their guest. Together the leader and Esteban sat on the ground, Esteban facing the water with his back to Savannah. The other warriors formed a circle around the two. Esteban drank from the gourd of fermented drink called *masato*. He said, "The men you killed were of my tribe. They were helping me move a river from one place to another place." In the background he heard murmurs of disbelief. He looked across the stream at the opposite bank. "I do not like those trees over there. I will make a clearing." He pointed in that direction. At the signal Tomás detonated the charge of TNT. The explosion ripped away a chunk of *selva* ten yards wide. Several of the warriors fled into the forest, but were forced back by the ring of Manconistas. Their leader, though he trembled with fear, had not moved. Esteban said, "I want you to leave my men and my new river alone. Otherwise you will anger the River Spirit who is my father."

The leader moistened his lips and looked around at his confederates, who'd crept back into their places. They spoke among themselves. After a few moments the leader said, "We will be friends of the son of the River Spirit."

Esteban said, "That is good. My friends receive presents from me." Two of the Manconistas came into the clearing carrying a basket. Esteban took from it mirrors, fish hooks, a pound of colored glass beads, and some clothing. He put a bright red shirt on the leader and fastened the front with a large safety pin. Each of the warriors insisted upon opening and closing the pin. Esteban watched them closely. Then he turned to the leader. Pointing toward the Escondido he said, "My big *malocca* is up that blue river one sleep, two sleeps. You are welcome to visit my *malocca* as long as you come in peace. There is food there for you, for your children, for your wives, along with strong magic to drive out the spirits that make you sick. But leave your weapons in the forest. I do not allow weapons in my *malocca*. As for these—" He began gathering the skulls. "We need these for our rituals. I will take the heads as well."

He collected the heads from the log beside the fire and gave the basket to two Manconistas, who carried it away. Then, as if it was a chance discovery, he saw Savannah and laughed. "I see you found my worthless Second Woman. She does no work, complains in a loud voice, and runs away whenever I do not watch her. I had hoped an enemy would steal her. Since you are my friends, I do not wish that trouble upon you." He cut her bonds and pushed her toward the forest. "I will take her home and beat her with a club."

But when he got her home he shut the door of her room upon them and made love to her with an anguished grieving intensity, saying again and again, "I almost lost you."

44

The next morning she awakened in his arms, wrapped with him in his blanket on the rush mat in her room. He opened his eyes and smiled at her. "Are you well?"

She stretched, then nestled close to him again. The recollection of their passion filled her with wonder. She said, "I am well." Would their happiness always be like this? Quarrels, separations, anguish, and terror broken by an hour or two of inexpressible ecstasy snatched here and there on some riverbank? When he was away from her she was always seized by panic for fear she might never see him again. And at those times she could not remember how he looked, not the details. She wondered now if this was her damnation, to have her happiness in perpetual jeopardy so that even the sweetest moments had always the flavor of sadness. She ran her fingers lightly over his face, over the dark brows and the narrow moustache, memorizing his features as if she were blind, and wondering for which of her sins she was being punished with this sorrow.

After a time he said, "It is no longer safe here for you."

She turned in surprise. "But you made friends of those savages."

"Rio Mar is coming after us. I am going to take you to the hospital up the Escondido. But first we must go over to the Semnome."

He'd translated the things he'd said about her to the head-hunters. Had he meant any part of them? She said, "Why do you never tell me you love me?"

"It seems unnecessary."

She turned away, looking out the window.

He took her face in his hands and looked deeply into her eyes. "I love you so much that my mind clouds and my heart aches at the thought of you."

He gathered his clothing and crossed the room. At the door he said, "We are leaving for the Semnome in half an hour."

She watched the muscles move along his shoulders. He knelt in the prow, paddling three strokes on one side, then three on the other, and with each stroke she felt the thrust of forward pressure he transmitted to the canoe.

They'd come away alone. The others stood at the dock, helping Esteban load the craft with canned goods and boxes of medicine. She watched his shoulders, the bend and straightening of his back, the grip of his hands on the paddle. She felt sick with love. She longed to be grafted onto him like an orchid growing high on a trunk.

Pointing toward a tree on the riverbank, one drenched with foliage, she said, "Are those vines a part of the tree?"

Between strokes he glanced over his shoulder. "No, that is a parasite. By the time the vine is strong enough to stand alone, it will have killed the tree."

He told her the names of the palm trees. Some of them looked like lace fans against the sky; others, like giant feather dusters. She said, "I never dreamed palm trees could be so beautiful." He told her they were more than beautiful; they made life possible.

"They are shelter, clothing, fuel, rope, tools, wax, oil, dishes, bread, meat, drink." Smiling, he glanced back at her. "One day I will show you. I will make a meal for you: palm fruit stew, bread made of coconut flour, milk, nuts, and the greatest delicacy of all, heart-of-palm salad."

Discerning an opening in the forest wall, he plunged his paddle deeply on one side and turned from the river. It was the canal. The digging had been completed. Only the system of pulleys to operate the locks remained unfinished; but soon they too would be done. She helped him unload the canoe and carry it around each lock. The forest deepened.

In late afternoon he drew the canoe up on a bank and together they built a shelter of palm fronds laced to woven saplings. While their dinner of dried fish warmed over the fire, they bathed together. Afterward she massaged him with the fragrant palm oil he carried for treating wounds.

How wonderful his body was, bronzed and firm like burnished wood, a golden brown beside her pale flesh. He always smelled and tasted like the forest, like clear water and aromatic wood. Her heart ached with gladness. She thought: I don't deserve this happiness.

Whenever he took her in his arms his hands were heavy, warm, and gentle. His touch was deliberate, but deft and familiar; reverent, yet confident. Still each time was a miracle, an event of unparalleled import. He approached her the way a priest approaches the altar. And in the sacrament of love, ecstasy overtook them.

Late in the afternoon of the next day they put into a settlement on the bank of the Semnome. There was a large clearing area, with a garden and a long thatched Indian house where a dozen natives wearing mission clothes sat on the steps. At the back of the clearing there was a white chapel and a house not much bigger than a packing box, also painted white and very neat. Such tidiness seemed unnatural here. There was no sound, not even the barking of a dog, although a chicken stepped carefully in the shadow of a shed. By the time Esteban had tied the canoe to the dock, a priest came out to greet them, his white cassock glaring in the sunlight. Esteban gave him boxes of salt and quinine. The two men, speaking rapid French, went inside the white house together. Savannah waited on the dock, growing restless. About a foot above the ground a layer of gnats droned, thick as a blanket.

Manco appeared outside the chapel and beckoned to her. She walked across the clearing to the small tin-roofed church. Esteban said, "Savannah, this is Father Pierre. He is going to marry us."

She looked around the clearing at the silent Indians in their flowered shirts and dresses. Manáos seemed so very far away, thousands of miles and hundreds of years away from this place, where time had stopped so long ago. All that was another life. *I was,* she thought, *another person then; nothing that happened in that life happened to* me.

She nodded and followed him into the chapel. They knelt together at the altar before a plain wood cross on the back wall. She barely heard the words, the priest's mouth moving soundlessly as in a dream.

Esteban lifted her to her feet and kissed her softly.

Father Pierre insisted they dine with him. Esteban got tins of food from the canoe and the priest jovially prepared a supper of tinned meat, wine, and salad from his garden. He seemed lonely and throughout the meal talked volubly, asking about Europe, about Pará and Manáos. By the time they'd finished eating, a violent storm was whipping the surface of the river into frothy waves; the wind tore branches from the trees along the bank and threw them into the water. Esteban accepted the priest's offer of shelter for the night and hung their two hammocks in the little parlor.

Savannah lay awake, shivering with fear. What had she done? Was it a terrible sin? Had she endangered Manco's immortal soul as well as her own? She practiced ways of telling him. *Esteban, he tricked me: They told me it was a rehearsal, but when it was over they said it was a real nuptial Mass; but Father Antonio said there was no marriage.*

Yet in her mind's eye she saw a wall thick as the edge of the *selva* spring up between them. She saw his eyes heavy with accusation, the eyes of a man with reverence for the institution of marriage. She'd not only made him commit adultery, but bigamy as well. Perhaps they would both be sent to prison now.

What if they were right about his poker playing? What if he could read minds? What if he knew already and was waiting for her to confess? What if all this were a test of some sort and each day she failed to tell him the truth, he loved her less, until he ended hating her, sending her back to the Contessa?

In the morning she was burning with fever. Father Pierre put clean sheets on the bed he kept for the sick and Manco moved her there. He sat beside her, giving her things to drink and covering her each time she threw the bedclothes off. She said to him, "When did you know you loved me?"

"I always knew."

"Then why didn't you save me? Why did you leave me to the Baron? You wouldn't leave Manáos until you'd freed Tomás, but you wouldn't save me."

He wiped her face with a cold cloth. "Tomás was a prisoner. You know what they did to him."

"He was going to do the same to me."

"You are free of him now."

"Because of the Contessa. Not because of you. What happened isn't my fault."

Soothingly he told her nothing was her fault, nothing was wrong. It grew dark. She awakened to find him watching her sadly. He said, "Savannah, are you unhappy? Don't you want to stay here with me?"

"Does it matter?"

"Yes, of course."

"It didn't matter when I wanted to get away from the Baron."

Toward dawn she opened her eyes again. He looked desperate with worry. She said, "You must leave here. Carry me to the canoe. Your work must not be interrupted."

He made her drink water and take more pills. He held her still. "Savannah, it is all right. I have sent word to Tomás. He will bring a doctor here."

"Good. They will care for me and you can go on."

She went from shattering chills to raging fever, then back to the racking shivers again. Her head throbbed. There was a taste in her mouth of rotting fish and she was drenched with a malodorous sweat like pungent mold. She watched his shadow thrown on the wall by the priest's oil lamp. Two shadows now. They spoke French. She heard him say, "I cannot bring her fever down. She is afraid."

Father Pierre said, "Afraid?"

"Yes. She is terrified of something. I feel it."

She tried to confess to him, babbling phrases in Latin from the nuptial Mass, trying to explain what had happened, but he didn't seem to understand her. At last she clutched his hand. She said, "Don't let me die. If you tell me to live, I cannot die."

He grasped her shoulders fiercely, "I forbid you to die. Do you hear, Savannah? I forbid it!"

She slept. When she awakened her headache was gone. It was dark, but for the small shaded oil lamp. Outside, the jungle was still; it must be the dead of night. Esteban, who'd sat beside her bed for days and nights, she knew not how many, slept in his hammock between her bed and the wall. In the nearby chair Father Pierre slept, his head sunk on his chest. She was not going to die.

Then there were sounds, swift footsteps, the door bursting open. A nightmare, surely: Mario, the youngest of the Baron's men, the one who looked so much like Manuela—why would she dream of him raising his long knife over Esteban's hammock? And Father Pierre getting to his feet and another man pushing him down, saying: "Padre, this is another man's wife, we are taking her back where she belongs." Then the shadows on the wall, the long knife lifting and plunging, lifting and plunging. And Esteban rising from the hammock, on his feet and turning to her, taking a step toward her bed, his face pale and his lips forming her name, and the blood spurting from his chest as he fell to his knees, his hands clutching her mosquito netting and Mario still behind him, striking at his back with the knife. She went to the floor, trying to gather him into her arms, screaming his name, his eyes closing, her gown drenched where he lay against her. Then they dragged her from him, carried her out through the night to the dock, and when she fought them, they struck her down and lay her in the canoe. She opened her eyes as they lifted her aboard a small steamer like the *Paloma*. Mario's knife was in his belt, still bloody. She clutched it and moved to drive it in her breast, but he struck her down again and she was still.

Later, but still the dark of night. The steamer overrun with Manconistas. Caetano was screaming, *"Manco!"* All of them were screaming his name with tears in their eyes and killing Mario and the men with him, while the steamer careened sideways in the river and crashed into the bank. Then the explosion, a pale orange ball of flame bursting the boiler plates and pieces of the vessel falling from the sky like rain.

The deck tilted slowly and the river rose over it, washing Savannah clean of all the bleeding and the tears.

It was the unhappy duty of Eustacio Moraes, the yacht captain, to inform the Baron of the disaster. Dom Luíz looked up from the papers on his desk, the color rising to his cheeks. "What was that idiot Mario doing up the Semnome? I told him to keep the other end of that swamp under surveillance."

"Excellency, he was doing that, while I installed the new rudder on the *Primavera*. But then that *matteiro*, Bartolomeu—"

"I know who he is!" the Baron muttered impatiently.

"Bartolomeu was marking virgin rubber trees to lay out new estradas along the Maranhas and the Semnome, when he heard there was a white woman dying of fever up at that French priest's mission. So Mario went up to have a look."

"And?"

"He saw nothing for two days; then that anarchist stepped out of the priest's house for a breath of air. So Mario took the steamer that had brought me parts for the yacht—" Eustacio watched Rio Mar angrily throw down the matches he found too damp to light his cigar. He said, "Mario was very loyal, Your Grace. He wanted only to please you by killing that anarchist and bringing the young lady back to you."

Dom Luíz rose and walked to one of the long windows overlooking the formal gardens. "And now I do not even have her body to bury." He turned back. "You are certain she's dead?"

"Yes, Excellency. The Semnome is a very bad river."

"Piranha?"

Eustacio nodded. "I went looking for them when they had not returned by midmorning of the next day, so it was a matter of a few hours. We found parts of the vessel, but no bodies. Neither our people, nor any of the anarchists. Your Grace, allow me to express—"

The Baron interrupted him. "And what of the *Primavera?*"

"I brought her down with no trouble, but the repairs were temporary. Another two weeks of work here will be required."

Dom Luíz waved him away and gazed thoughtfully at the glittering water of the fountains. The peacocks strutted slowly along the pathways. She had been a very beautiful woman. A Botticelli woman. He had not loved her, but he'd had great hopes for her, and the new heir she would give him.

And now the indictment against these anarchists had

lengthened. They must be made to pay for the destruction of his property, for the kidnapping and death of his bride, and for the heir he did not even have the pleasure of conceiving.

45

The swamp had risen to within a few feet of the hut; Will and Jesuino used the canoe on parts of their estradas. The rubber trees, however, were yielding less and less each day. Jesuino said they went to sleep in the time of high water; tappers then must lie in their hammocks and try not to starve until the rivers went down again.

Still, Jesuino remained cheerful, and his good nature inspired Will to keep up a good front also. One night they celebrated the eel Jesuino had managed to catch for their supper by dining dressed raggedly in Will's opera clothes. Afterward they smoked dried hemp in Will's meerschaum pipe.

One day Will awakened so feverish that Jesuino told him to stay in his hammock, saying, "I will tap your trees today." Will tried to get up, but was racked by a fit of such violent shivering he marveled that his teeth weren't rattled loose. Later he awakened to find Macedo standing over him, shaking his hammock and calling him *indolente*. Baptiste stood behind him. He said, "So, Mr. Patterson, this is why you bring no rubber to the landing. In that case, I can extend you no more credit." When they left they took the *borrachas* stored under the hut, ignoring Will's demand for a receipt.

Not long after that the food ran out. Will remained beset by chills and fever, so Jesuino took the small *borracha* he had gathered since the visit of the Capataz and went to the landing to beg for a sack of flour and some beans. He was gone three days. At last Will heard the canoe scrape against the bottom step where the swamp now lapped against the hut. Leaning on his crutch, he worked his way to the door and found Jesuino unconscious in the bow. His back had been laid open to the bone by a lash and one of his toes was gone.

He succeeded in dragging him into the hut, where he nursed him as well as he could. But nothing did any good. His body was burning, his lips cracked, his eyes red with fever. In his delirium he talked constantly.

"Senhor Will," he hissed, "are they coming? Do you hear them on the trail? They come in the night."

Will said, "It's all right, don't be afraid."

"They say, do you want to come with us? And they take you away with them, not downriver past the landings, but up, up, where only Indians can go." Will rung out a cloth in a pail of water and placed it on Jesuino's burning forehead. He pushed the cloth away and grasped Will's hand. "I have heard there is a hospital there with clean white beds, but that may be a dream."

Will lifted his head and held a cup to his mouth.

"Sometimes they run through the forest carrying torches and crying '*Manco! Manco!*' They call you to become one of his chosen people."

"Manco?" Will echoed.

"And sometimes he comes himself, the Liberator himself touches you with his hand, saying, 'Come with me, I will take you from this *inferno verde*.'"

That strange scene aboard the *Esperança* came back to Will, the silence that fell, the vendors pulling off their hats and bowing their heads as he passed. This, then, was the lunatic dream he'd seen burning in that dark El Greco face. Will said, "Upriver which way? Up which river, Jesuino?" But Jesuino was unconscious. Rain beat relentlessly on the thatched roof and slammed against the makeshift door of woven branches.

He died just before morning. Will held his hand and watched him for a long time, continuing to wipe his face now and then with the cool cloth. He looked peaceful, quite free of pain.

Will knew he need not stay here now. He would take the canoe and go, not down past the landing but up where only the Indians could travel. But first he must rest.

He fell into his hammock and awakened shivering. The hut was awash with water. The fire was out and the last of the matches floated in the faint tide across the floor. His mouth was dry and his tongue felt swollen. The fever still burned in his body and it was some time before he had the strength to get up and wade to the doorway.

The interminable sheet of water was pocked by rain; there was no ground left, only water and half-drowned trees. On a branch a dozen feet from the hut three urubus sat watching him, their beaks hooked and their heads bald for rooting in carcasses.

The canoe was no longer there at the step. The rope remained tied to the hut, but the other end was frayed where the violence of the storm had ripped the craft free and floated it away.

He could not bury Jesuino. There was no ground left, and he hadn't the strength to dig anyway. At last he managed a crude sea burial from the steps of the hut. He dressed his friend in an assortment of decent clothing, wrapped him in his hammock, and slid the body into the water, weighted down with his valise, packed with every heavy object they had left—their lanterns, pails, cups, basins, and cooking pots.

He turned the pages of his books looking for a still-legible passage to read aloud, but most of them had little left but the stitching.

It no longer rained incessantly. The waters had reached a standstill; as far as Will could see, there was standing water, stagnant, a vast pool crammed full of rotting trees, rotting vegetation, rotting animals, rotting men. Most of his time was spent searching for something to eat. He fished from the steps, but most days caught nothing. He tried to lasso the urubus, but always failed. He swam short distances among the trees, hacking at the bark with his *machadinho*; then he ate the bark. He chewed his leather belt like a cud and held his pants up with a piece of rope. When his pants fell apart, he ate what was left of them. Now he was naked; the rubber-coated bag which held his journal hung from his neck like an albatross.

He kept smelling food: oyster stew, Maryland fried chicken, hot cocoa, toast with apple butter. Sometimes he awakened believing he was home and had been having a very bad dream. Gazing out at his vegetal prison he cried: "Yes, you are right, I don't belong here. Let me go!" But there was no reply.

Sometimes he saw Savannah. She looked as she had aboard the *Esperança*, like a Gibson Girl, all in white and carrying a ruffled parasol. She was walking on top of the water, appearing, disappearing, and reappearing among the distant trees. He watched hungrily, but secretly, out of the corner of his eye, not letting on he saw her. He knew it was a trick. The *selva* was trying to lure him into its depths.

One day he awakened and stepped from his hammock to find that the water in the hut had receded. Kneeling on the doorsill, he pondered the flood. A leaf floated past his bearded reflection. A veined green leaf with a central rib and smaller branching lines, like the map of the Amazon.

As he watched, the leaf turned slowly and drifted on. He raised his eyes and saw a fleet of leaves, a flotilla of them, an armada, all drifting slowly in the same direction. He said, "Going to the ocean, are you? I want to go too." But they were not floating downriver; they were drifting in the opposite direction, into the swamp.

What would make leaves drift upstream? Wind? There was no wind. Jesuino had been here eight years and he said he'd never seen such high water. If the swamp at its other end was spilling over into another river, he could get across it by canoe. Now, before the water fell any lower. Quickly, quickly.

From time to time great trees, their foundations undermined by the flooding, crashed into the water; but they were hardwood and sank. The few floating logs he found foundered under his weight. Still he kept dragging logs about, hacking off their branches.

At last he had four logs that would float. He lashed them together with lianas. Then he pried the floor of the hut loose from its stump foundations and fastened it on top of the logs. When the raft moved out from the bank, floating evenly and shipping very little water, he wept with gladness.

46

Savannah had been dreaming she was a child. A woman bent over her, rocking her in her arms and singing softly. The lullaby made her feel safe and contented. As she awakened the song ceased, but the rocking continued. Although the hammock of interlaced palm fiber was smooth and free of knots, it hurt her back. She'd grown thin; too little flesh covered her bones and it hurt to sit or lie for long in one position.

The song began once more, a murmured chanting; but it was not the woman in Savannah's dream. Rather, it was the small daughter of Tukara, playing with a nearly featherless macaw. The tame bird was kept for plucking arrow feathers; the child played with it as if it were a doll, rocking it in her arms and singing it a lullaby.

When Savannah's hammock swung, the clearing in the center of the village rose and fell beneath the low-hanging roof of thatch. The midafternoon sun glared on the earth, beaten bare by footsteps. There was no sound but the child crooning.

Beyond the other women's houses and the large men's house at the edge of the clearing, dense forest circled closely. Even the path connecting the village to the river was cloaked with vegetation, and no canoes were ever left where they might be seen, for the people of this tribe avoided contact with others.

They'd been on a fishing expedition when they found her. They had dammed a stream and squeezed into the water the juice of barbasco, the fish-poison root. Then they'd used nets to haul in the stunned catch. One of the children, chasing a stray fish downstream toward the junction of their river with the Semnome, came upon Savannah. After the steamer sank she'd clung to a piece of wreckage as a reflex, not an act of will. She was waiting only to die. In the darkness, when the debris hit a snag of fallen tree trunks, she'd climbed out of the water to escape the painful cold. Feverish and delirious she lay there, losing and regaining consciousness and opening her eyes at last to find the villagers standing around her. They did not look like the headhunters: Their teeth were not filed, their hair was cut, and they had women and children with them. She said, "Please cover me; I am so cold." After they talked among themselves for a time, she was placed in a hammock slung from a pole. They carried her many hours.

She was cared for in the house of Inamona, who lived with her daughters and her sons' wives and all their children, except the boys of more than twelve years, who were allowed to hang their hammocks in the men's house that guarded the entrance to the village. Inamona had fed her tea made of bitter leaves until her fever ended. When Savannah cried out in the night, sobbing Manco's name, Inamona pushed the logs farther into the spoke-shaped fire on the dirt floor near Savannah's hammock and rocked her gently, singing in the strange vowel-filled language of these people.

Savannah was almost well now; yet she remained weak. The walk to the river to bathe with the other women exhausted her, and she spent most of her time sitting quietly in the sunshine or rocking in her hammock. Often while the women worked, Savannah watched the children; and they watched her. They pointed to things and told her the words for them, laughing at her pronunciation. The children never quarreled, nor had she ever seen an adult strike a child. And the children never lost patience with Savannah, teaching her again and again the words she needed to speak with them.

Now, the women hurried out of the cookhouse. They had heard the men returning from hunting and they hoped there would be meat for dinner. Shiriana, the wife of Inamona's second son, handed Savannah her baby to rock while the women gathered firewood and set the clay cook pots to boil. The child, a boy of about two, was named Kushawe. He loved her hair; he lay it across his face, looked through the glinting strands, and laughed.

She could not stop herself from thinking about Esteban. They hadn't even let her hold him when he was dying. Over and over before her closed eyes she saw him reach out to her, his face the color of ashes, his pale lips forming her name; then he fell slowly to his knees, dragging the netting of her bed in his clutched hands.

The baby, curious, touched the tears on her cheeks. His mother, Shiriana, smiling and speaking excitedly, took Kushawe from Savannah and pointed toward the doorway. Outside she saw below the low-hanging palm leaves of the roof, the lower part of the men's bodies, bare but for their penis sheaths. She was so used to nakedness now she never thought of it; her white nightgown hung from her shoulders in shreds. At the entrance of Inamona's house the headman's first son was speaking to her. He pointed to the peccary, the wild jungle pig that his brothers had set on the ground behind him; then he pointed to Savannah, and to the cooking pot at the center of the log fire near her hammock. The women grinned behind their hands. Even Inamona looked pleased.

Savannah stared at him. He was about five and a half feet tall and wore rodent's teeth pierced through his ear lobes. He had bathed in the river on his way to the village and then carefully painted his body with wavy lines, black from soot mixed with animal fat and red from the seeds of the urucu bush. His body was muscular and tense. He strutted back and forth before the doorway, trying to await her answer with a show of bravado, while the rest of the villagers stood in the clearing, watching. The women of Inamona's house were pulling her from the hammock and leading her toward the door. Inamona handed her the sharp bamboo knife, saying, "You cut it, then we help."

She went out the door. The headman's son was speaking gruffly, showing her with his spear how he had killed the peccary. It was the first time—the very first time since she'd been carried into this place unnumbered days ago—that she felt like laughing. But gravely she arranged the words she needed and said, "No. I cannot be wife to first son of headman. I thank the headman's first son. I have husband." He scowled, shouted, shook his spear at her, while his brothers murmured angrily. She said, "My husband is son of River Spirit. Very angry if I go with other man. Bad luck for this village of my friends."

The headman's son strutted away enraged. She had shamed him in front of everyone. His brothers took the peccary to his mother's house across the clearing. That night in the secret chamber at the back of the men's house, the sacred flutes no woman was ever allowed to see were played for a long time.

Gradually her strength returned. She learned to make bark cloth by taking strips from a tree, peeling off the outer bark, and pounding the inner bark until it got thin and became several times its original size. She developed strong muscles helping the other women; their work was hard. Like them she carried water twice a day from the river to the village. She learned how to get up from the ground with a heavy basket of manioc tubers on her back, to skin and cut up meat, to shred food on a grater made of piranha teeth, to fell a tree to get nuts and palm fruits, to smoke out bees and take their honey, to sharpen a bamboo knife on rocks, to carve wood by using a rock hammer and a spike from the chonta palm.

The reminders of Esteban did not diminish. The taste of nuts and fruit brought back his praise of palm trees; in the evening the sight of large fireflies moving at the edges of the clearing reminded her of how the Manconistas ran through the forest bearing torches in the night. But these memories no longer made her weep. Her grief still made her heart ache, but it was becoming an old ache, familiar as a garment she never removed and no longer had to think about.

Among these people the word for "world" was the same as the word for "trees." If she had the words to tell them of the world beyond these trees, would they believe her? Esteban had said: *There are whole tribes we will never be able to find.* And looking toward the forests of the upper Semnome, he'd said: *Perhaps there, time has stopped.* She would spend the rest of her life among these people, in a Garden of Eden where there were serpents, but no apples. Nothing mattered anymore; she was at peace with her grief.

Shiriana's little sister was the wife of Inamona's third son. Although she was only about thirteen years old, she was going to have a baby. One day the child went into the forest alone and an hour later came back carrying an infant son. She'd already bathed both herself and the child. Savannah said to

Inamona, "What if something had gone wrong? What if she died alone in the forest?"

"Then we would let her baby die, too." Savannah was appalled by such heartlessness, but Inamona explained that it was out of their concern for the baby that they would let it die, because every living thing should have a mother. Among these people the word for orphan meant "one who is cold."

That night as Savannah fell asleep she tried to recall the voice of the woman who sang to her when she was small. "Mother," she whispered, "hold me. My heart is broken." But the only face she could remember was the Contessa's.

She grew very tired of their admiration of her hair. Red was considered strong magic for warding off evil. That was why at crucial times they painted their bodies with urucu.

Someone was always admiring her hair; and in the forest you were supposed to give away what was admired, for envy was very dangerous. That was what put a snake in your path or made you fall ill with fever. So one day when Shiriana was fondling her hair, Savannah cut off a lock and gave it to her. Shiriana was overjoyed; she braided it with great care and made a bracelet, which she wore high up on her arm with a wooden band carved out of a Brazil nut pod and an ivorylike circlet made from an armadillo's tail. But then Tukara was hurt and angry, so Savannah gave her a lock too. Soon she was besieged by begging, tears, and threats until she began to feel like the tame macaw kept for arrow feathers. At last in a fit of irritation she used a bamboo knife and cut off all her hair so that every girl in the village could have a bracelet. In the night she could hear the young men visiting their wives in the women's houses, and often the next day she saw a copper-colored armband pushed high on a hunter's muscular arm.

Once she'd done it, she was glad. She felt freer, and certainly much cooler.

Still, there were other annoyances. The women of her house were terrified when she said she wanted to see the sacred flutes. After long, persistent questioning, Inamona told her that the flutes, which must be given the proper care because the ancestral spirits of the tribe lived in them, had once belonged to the women. "Then," Inamona said, "the men carried water and made farinha while we went hunting, and they couldn't pierce us unless we wanted them to." The men, she said, had gotten the sacred flutes away from the women, but guarded their power with extreme care lest the women get the upper hand again. And for this reason there were rigid rules about the objects men and women were forbidden to handle. For men, the water pots were taboo; for women, it was the weapons.

Watching the headman's first son shoot arrows in the clearing, she'd drawn close in fascination. He was so strong he bent the man-tall bow as if it were a twig and, shooting straight up into the air, he hit the center of a mark a few feet in front of him. But when she asked him to let her try, he grew so angry he aimed in her direction. She stood a few feet from him, smiling. He watched her, his dark eyes narrowing. Then he loosed the arrow. The taut string of twisted palm fiber sang. He caught the arrow with his bow hand, its point less than a foot from her heart.

When he'd stalked out of the clearing, the women of her household clustered around her. "Were you not afraid?" they said. No, she hadn't been. She could not explain to them her feeling that she was already dead.

It was this sense of death-in-life, rather than contempt for their customs, that made her disregard the warnings about walking alone. The men's rules said they had the right to attack any woman found alone in the forest except one who was giving birth. But Savannah, once she'd gotten well, found the constant companionship unbearable. The continual pressure of the others' presence filled her with despair because now when she closed her eyes she could no longer remember Esteban. She'd lost not only her love, but even the memory of it. So on days when the men went hunting, she sometimes slipped away alone to sit on the riverbank.

Listening to the birds, looking at the sky, watching the sunlight on the water, she remembered the way he swam that day on the Escondido. She saw again his hands gripping the handle of his paddle, tying a canoe rope, touching her body. She had almost regained the memory of his face when she heard the men.

There were six of them: the headman's first son, his brothers, and two of his brothers-in-law. Grinning, they encircled her completely, cutting off escape. Already they were unfastening their penis sheaths. Turning slowly in their midst, she stood as tall as she could and said, "I am the woman of the River Spirit's son. He watches over me. If you touch me he will take the breath from your bodies."

First Son laughed and grasped her arm. She kicked him ineffectually. He struck her a heavy blow on the side of the head. Reeling, she backed away and lost her footing on the sandy riverbank. She was frightened—not of death, but of defilement. She cried, "I am Esteban Manco's woman. You must not touch me!" Their hands gripped her shoulders, forcing her down. Two of them held her legs spread wide. She smelled their breath; she felt the grit of earth under her hands. First Son knelt between her knees. Straining to turn away, she saw the sunlight glint at the water's edge, and in the branches above she saw distinctly a small green parrot, watching the scene with its head cocked. She remembered Charlie. And she remembered Morgan, who lived for a time with a magician and had helped Savannah pass the time by teaching her simple tricks. She said, "If you do not leave me alone, the son of the River Spirit will fill your head with stones and you will die. Already he has begun. Look!"

First Son was startled by the pebble she drew from his ear. He looked at it askance and drew back, his eyes wide. She sat up and drew from his other ear a stone the size of a small bird's egg. Muttering, he scrambled backward on his haunches. She rolled over onto all fours, clutching more pebbles, then stood up in the puzzled circle. One after another she drew stones from their ears. Stiff with fear they drew back from her, their mouths moving as if they were thirsty. Once away from the riverbank, they began to run among the trees. She sat down, shaking, and did not leave that place again until the other women came to bathe.

47

Jesuino was right, Will thought, it was no dream. He stood on the hospital's second-floor veranda, looking around at the Manconista installation on the upper Escondido. The hospital beds did indeed have clean white sheets.

The place was built not on the riverbank, but two miles inland, on an island in the middle of a lake joined to the Escondido by a stream which could be closed so that it was concealed by foliage. The island was large, but the installation covered it completely. The place was insect-free and fully defensible.

The buildings of the compound reminded Will of sketches he'd seen of military outposts in the American West. They were made of timber from the surrounding forest and enclosed by a stockade of trimmed logs, sharpened to points. Inside the wall there were, in addition to the hospital, several dormitories—long, communal houses. Besides the many outbuildings, the cookhouses, the tannery, the armory, the offices, there was a dairy and pens for chickens and turkeys. As near as Will could tell, some five hundred people lived here, and many more came from the river and the forest to visit, trade, and be given medical attention. The residents shared everything, including the work.

They'd found him with his raft lashed to the riverbank where, with the last of his strength, he'd tied it. He couldn't paddle upstream because he was too weak, so he lay down in the hope that they would find him. Later Tomás told him that he'd looked like a skeleton and had ranted at them in English. At last he said, "Manco." They laughed and said, *"Sim, sim— nós estamos Manconistas!"* Then they helped him into a canoe, where he lay down with his ragged journal still in its bag around his neck and his arms holding close the rude crutch Jesuino had made.

Here at the hospital he was cared for by a sandy-haired young Scottish doctor named Murray MacNair. Manco had recruited him in Edinburgh by arousing his interest in medicinal plants of the *selva*. Upon his arrival on the Escondido a year and a half ago, he'd been provided with facilities not only for practicing medicine but for gathering data on the remedies used by the forest peoples: leaves, roots, bark, and juices. Quinine, he told Will, was only one of a whole constellation of antimalarial drugs. He was particularly excited about a plant juice that stopped bleeding, even massive internal hemorrhaging; used externally, it speeded healing and minimized scarring. Another substance healed burns with astonishing rapidity, relieving pain immediately; he pointed out to Will a child who had fallen into a cooking fire and was badly burned on both legs, but now had scarcely a scar to show where the injury had occurred.

He asked Will if he experienced pain in his legs, and Will admitted that he did, almost continually. MacNair told him that some of the substances the natives used for hunting and fishing were, he believed, relaxants that might be used to counteract muscle spasms. He said that if his theory was correct, such medication might relieve Will's pain and permit him to exercise his legs and strengthen them. His course of treatment for Will called for a tea made of tree bark three times a day, and increasingly long periods of swimming fol-

lowed by massages with warm palm oil. In time Will had no
further need for his crutch, yet he carried it as if that would
make up for the fact that Jesuino had not lived to see the
Liberator.

Will almost didn't get to see Manco himself. When Will arrived at the hospital, he'd been told the Liberator lay near
death. When Will asked about him, MacNair explained that
some time ago he'd been called to travel to the Semnome to
treat a woman suffering from fever—possibly black water
fever, which was always fatal. But they arrived at the mission
to find Esteban had been the victim of a vicious attack. He'd
been stabbed repeatedly and was bleeding to death. He could
not possibly be moved.

The gravest injury was a two-inch-wide stab wound in the
left atrium of the heart. Immediately MacNair employed the
jungle specific for hemorrhaging. Opening the chest, he was
encouraged at finding minimal bleeding inside the chest cav-
ity; but aside from cleaning up, there was nothing more he
could do but watch and wait. When Esteban sank deeper into
unconsciousness, MacNair decided to risk a transfusion.

He asked if there were any known relatives of the Liberator
among the Manconistas. There were none. Were there any of
his tribe? Any mountain Indians of any sort? There weren't.
Tomás said, "But he has told me I am as a brother to him."

MacNair said, "You'll have to do." Using small tubes made
of rubber, he connected Tomás's radial artery to Esteban's
median vein, watching closely for signs of adverse reaction.
And almost immediately, the color returned to Esteban's face.
Father Pierre, who'd been praying at the bedside, murmured,
"Dieu merci."

Still, MacNair could not repair the heart. His only hope
was that it would repair itself. After two weeks they risked
moving him through the canal and up the Escondido to the
hospital, where MacNair insisted upon complete bedrest for
his patient. But, he told Will, it was almost impossible to keep
Esteban Manco quiet. He demanded hourly reports. How
were the locked doors working on the canal? Were the medical supplies sufficient? What of the fields—would there be a
good harvest? Had the headhunters come in friendship?

In the late afternoon he would talk with Will on the hospital veranda. Will showed Esteban his tattered journal, which
he was recopying and improving upon each day. He told him
of the book he meant to write when he got back home. Esteban answered Will's questions readily; their conversations

were stimulating to both men. The fact that Will took notes on Esteban's explanations forced him to verbalize his theories, his conclusions, and his plans with greater precision.

Even so, there were certain things Will found it very difficult to understand. He said, "Do you have the right to deny the world something it needs as badly as it needs rubber?"

"If the rubber business is to continue, it must be changed drastically. Further, rubber must not be the only activity pursued in this region, because the rubber business builds nothing of value to the native peoples, it puts nothing back into the selva; all it does is take something away. Even then I would not object to shipping rubber out of the selva. What I object to is the killing of the Indians and the immigrants brought here to tap the trees."

An Indian woman brought them drinks made of pineapple juice and palm fruits. MacNair's prescription for both of them called for as much nourishment as they could get down. Will was feeling marvelous, better than he had in years. But Esteban had not regained his strength. It seemed only an act of will that kept him going.

MacNair came along to chide Will for staying too long. He was fearful Esteban would be getting tired. Yet he was pleased with the Liberator's pulse rate and after listening to his heart he said, "Starting tomorrow you may walk a short distance on the veranda every afternoon."

Yet the next day as Will watched Manco walk slowly along the veranda, leaning on Tomás, he was dismayed by his friend's condition. The grace, the lightness of step, the resilient strength was gone. He looked like a walking dead man. Aside from the times he lost himself in their conversations, he seemed diminished—in some strange way, muted. The quality that had drawn Will to him on the Esperança had deepened into a profound sadness.

One afternoon Esteban seemed more reflective than ever. All Will's efforts to engage him in talk of his mission among these people failed. Will felt uneasy; he couldn't have said why. Perhaps it was because, now that he was well, he was going home to write his book. He had more questions he wanted answered, and mixed feelings about leaving. Yet he must go; surely his family had given him up for dead. And he must expose Rio Mar and the dreadful cruelty of the rubber business. He would leave tomorrow for Manáos, take the first available vessel to Pará, and then get aboard a ship for the nearest North American port.

After a long silence Manco said, "I tire so easily now. I wonder if you would write a letter for me and deliver it in person when you reach Manáos? It's long overdue. I just couldn't seem to do it." He gazed off across the lake to where a flock of large white birds had settled in the trees. Of course Will said he'd be glad to do it, and got pen and paper. Esteban gave him the address—Luciana, Contessa della Mirandola, Rue Epaminondas, Manáos—and then began to dictate. "I have lost her. I swore to guard her with my life, but she is gone and I am still alive." The silence that followed lasted so long Will cleared his throat. Esteban's gaze moved from the lake to Will's face as if he'd forgotten his presence. He said, "She will want to know how it happened. Ask Tomás to tell you the details and add them to the letter. You are a writer. If there is anything that can be said to comfort her. . . ."

Will found Tomás in the room he used on the ground floor of the hospital, and Tomás told him the story he'd been able to piece together of the attack. Caetano and the other Manconistas had been lost when the steamer blew up; there was nothing left but wreckage. The first word Esteban said when he regained consciousness after the transfusion was "Savannah." When Tomás told him she was gone, he didn't speak again for many days. Tomás told Will, "There are piranha in the Semnome. They are drawn to blood, and there must have been a feast for them that night. If she was not wounded—"

Will stared at him. "What are you saying?"

Tomás lifted his shoulders. "I don't know, Senhor Will." Then he took something from a box in the rafters above his hammock. "What do you think this is?"

Will saw a circle of braided copper-colored hair. When he caught his breath and could speak, he said, "Where did you get it?"

"It came from the *selva* around the upper Semnome. A man came in with a canoe-load of nuts and palm fruits and honey to trade for salt. He said he'd gotten it from a band of hunters. He gave one of them his best knife for it. He had no idea where their village is, only that it's up there somewhere."

Will touched the silken hair. He remembered the day they sat on the deck of the ship talking about her coming marriage, and saw again the strand of hair that had escaped from the netting around her straw hat. How fragile she looked to him that day! As if he'd read his thoughts, Tomás said, "Even if she escaped the sinking of the steamer, she may be dead now.

They could have killed her for her hair. We know nothing of that region."

Will sank to a bench, suddenly weak. When the Baron had shown him the reward poster, he'd assumed she had escaped to Pará and gone off to Europe. He never dreamed she had come into the *selva* with Manco. Now, holding her hair, he felt the anguish of his love wash over him in waves. Lost. Found. Lost again.

Tomás said, "I am afraid to tell him. The doctor says only rest can save his life."

Will raised his eyes. "Don't you understand he's dying anyway?" He saw again that faltering step, the melancholy eyes gazing off across the lake, forgetting the letter he meant to write and even Will's presence beside him. "He has no hope, Tomás. He is trying to keep on with his plans for your sake and for the sake of all the others, but his heart isn't in it. I have been a patient all my life. I know you cannot live without hope."

He postponed his departure. In the morning he went with Tomás and MacNair to Manco's room. When Tomás handed him the bracelet, Esteban stared at it for a long moment. Then he closed his hand upon it and shut his eyes, seeing her fling her hair high as she brushed it in the sunlight. His heart faltered, then it began to beat harder. He said, "Outfit six canoes. And bring me maps of the Semnome with all the side streams marked."

The feast to celebrate the end of rising waters was the greatest festival of the year, for now the game was coming back into the forests and the streams were filling with fish. The people of the village spent a week preparing for it. The central clearing was swept clean with brooms made of leaves and on some of the houses the thatch roofs were renewed. The last day before the feast the men hid themselves, making masks the women must not see until the ceremonial dancing began.

When night fell Savannah was sitting on a log at the edge of the clearing, refusing to take part in the festivities. She cared for the children while their parents danced. When the little ones grew tired she settled them in their small hammocks and climbed into her own. She fell asleep at last to the sound of drums and chanting. But later she was awakened and found First Son and his brothers crowding close by her. Their masks were gone and the paint on their bodies was streaked with sweat; they carried their heavy clubs. Helpless, she was drawn into the circle of dancers, which grew smaller every few moments as couple after couple slipped into the darkness pressing in upon the firelight. Finding First Son drawing ever closer to her, she slipped into the forest, moving casually, as if in answer to a call of nature. When she was beyond the clearing she began to sprint. By the time First Son and his brothers came looking for her she had run almost a half mile along the path that led to the manioc garden. Their steps made no sound, but she heard in the stillness of the deepest jungle night the faint clicking of the jewelry they'd worn for the feast: the ropes of seeds from the Necklace Tree, the small animal teeth strung on thongs, and the bracelets carved from the armadillo. She left the trail and burrowed into the underbrush, covering herself with fallen leaves and praying the ants would not find her before the men passed by.

When silence fell and she was certain they'd gone ahead to search the garden, she got up and followed them at a distance. The small garden gleamed in the moonlight. She stood very still among the trees and watched them search the ragged manioc patches. After a time they gave up, murmuring among themselves that they must have missed her. Surely she had returned to the village, and if she had not, she would soon. No one remained alone in the forest at night.

After they'd gone she used the hanging vines to climb a tall tree at the edge of the garden. High in its upper branches she wrapped lianas back and forth to make a sling to rest in, tying herself in securely so if she slept she would not fall. But she did not sleep. She wondered what to do. She had learned enough to live alone in the forest. She knew which berries could be eaten, and which grubs. She could fold a palm leaf into a drinking cup and detect the biting, stinging ants along the trail. She could make a paste of urucu to keep gnats and mosquitoes from her skin. She knew how to make a snare for birds and traps for small animals, and could fashion a spear from palm spikes and use it to catch fish. But despite all this knowledge she could not live long in the forest. The long nights would leave her quaking with cold and she might not be able to eat the food she caught because it would be raw: she had no fire, no hardy embers wrapped in moss and dry grasses to carry along the trail.

When the last of the dancers fell into a drunken sleep she must creep back into the village and steal fire.

With the ending of the rainy season, work began again on the rubber estradas. Although the rivers remained flooded, new trees were found and marked to replace those that had been destroyed in the attacks on the landings. Capataz Baptiste began to round up and count his *seringueiros*. The work force had diminished badly. Even Jesuino and that crippled gringo were gone, no doubt to make a meal for the piranha or the urubu. Something must be done.

Baptiste was tired of trying to cope with immigrants. They didn't survive well enough in this climate. The forest Indians were best. Of course you had to keep killing a good portion of them to terrify the others into working; but there were always more, countless settlements of them hidden up and down the smaller rivers. The trouble was finding the villages. But an old jungle hand, one of the *matteiros* whose job it was to find and mark the virgin rubber trees, had made an interesting observation. The man was part Indian himself, which explained his skill at tracking. He'd told Baptiste to watch the margins of the streams for manioc tubers soaking in the quiet pools.

And that is how Macedo found the village. The Capataz had ordered the guards to patrol the smaller rivers, two in each canoe, to look for the manioc. When they found it they were to do nothing but report back to the launch where Baptiste waited on the Semnome. Then all the guards were gathered and went back to the area near the village in force, twenty-four guards, all well armed.

They attacked at dawn on the morning after the feast. The men lay sleeping heavily, some in their hammocks in the men's house, others on the ground where they'd fallen, drunk.

Savannah had climbed down from her tree and was heading back toward the village when she heard the crack of rifle shots. As she ran between the last trees she saw the armed men, rifles at their shoulders, machetes and pistols in their belts. One after another the village men were rising and running into the men's house to take their bows and arrows from the rafters. The attackers followed and dragged the old Headman into the clearing, his arms pinioned and a knife at his throat. Leaderless, the men of the village paused. Quickly they were surrounded and disarmed. When their hands had been securely tied behind them and they'd been trussed into a line for marching, the guard who held the knife cut the Headman's throat.

Now the guards began to search the other houses. Savannah, standing shocked within the shadow of the forest, heard more gunshots. When the women and girls were driven into the clearing she saw no old ones among them. Shiriana's little sister carried the newborn baby at her breast; as the guards forced the women into marching order one of them tore the child from her arms and, holding it by the feet, dashed its head against a log. Savannah screamed and ran toward the clearing. She saw little Kushawe sprint across the clearing, his naked belly outthrust as he ran. A guard looked down the barrel of his gun, moving the muzzle carefully to keep up with the child. Then he squeezed the trigger and Kushawe fell. Tukara's daughter, clutching close about her the shawl trimmed with monkey bones, darted toward the forest, but just short of her goal she was hit. A glistening stain spread through the shawl in the middle of her back. She fell, lying still, looking like a heap of rags half in sunshine and half in shadow. Now Inamona broke free and ran straight toward the armed men, shouting that they must not do these things. She faltered when the bullets hit her, but kept on until they cut her down with their machetes.

Savannah fell to the ground beside Inamona's body, clutching the woman's hand to her lips and sobbing. The men pulled her to her feet and dragged her down the trail with the others to the river. There they were put aboard canoes. All the way to the rubber landing the women wept aloud, all but Savannah, who stared ahead of her like someone just awakened from a nightmare.

By the time the Manconistas got there, it was too late. They saw the marks along the riverbank where the men and girls had been dragged aboard the launches. The trail back to the village was similarly marked by violence, the foliage torn and blood spattered on the tree trunks. In the settlement they found dozens of bodies not yet obliterated by the scavengers. Old people, children, and the warriors who'd been killed in the unequal battle. Only one of the attackers had died; there was an arrow through his heart.

Esteban, still not well enough to walk more than a few steps, waited anxiously on the riverbank. When Will and the others got back to the canoes, Tomás told Manco, "It was done with Winchesters."

Esteban turned to Will. "I ask you, who are the savages here?"

Will, sickened by what he'd seen, said, "Are all the landing managers beasts?"

Esteban nodded. "So are the owners in Manáos. The only difference between them is their tailor-made clothing."

Will and Tomás exchanged a glance, uncertainly. At last Tomás said, "One of the dead children and several of the warriors' bodies had the bracelets."

Will added quickly, "But Savannah was not there, we saw no sign of her." Will hesitated a moment, then asked to see the maps. They spread them on the riverbank. He said, "Is this where you found me?" Tomás said it was. Will said, "Then I came out of this swamp." He traced a route across the swamp to the headwaters of another river. He tapped the place he imagined Jesuino's hut had been and moved his finger down the thin line of a stream. "Then the rubber landing would be here."

Esteban, who seemed exhausted, had gotten back into one of the canoes and lay under the palm-thatch shelter in its midsection. Now he leaned forward to look at Will. "We will have to make a sweep through all the landings to find the people captured in this village."

"No. It's been months, so I am not certain, but I think I recognized that dead guard back there. I believe he works for Capataz Baptiste."

They found the swamp still flooded and were able to take the shortcut to the landing. Upriver they distributed the English rifles, beached the canoes, and attacked through the forest, leaving no guard alive. But again they were too late. More of the villagers had been killed, or lay badly hurt. And Savannah was not there.

Among the captive Indians they saw several of the bracelets. While the Manconistas gave the Indians first aid and prepared them for the journey to the hospital, Esteban questioned them. Yes, he was told, the armbands were made of the hair of the white woman who said she was daughter-in-law to the River Spirit. When asked what had happened to her, they said she fought them and was put in chains; then the headman took her away.

Will came back from a search of the landing. He said, "I can find no trace of Capataz Baptiste."

Manco turned back to the Indians. "Where did they take her?"

The natives pointed downriver and said they went away in a loud canoe. Manco asked when they left and was told, "One sleep ago."

There was no way their canoes could overtake a launch going with the downstream current and with a twenty-four-hour head start, yet Esteban was determined to try. He ordered the canoes brought down to the landing and waited with the wounded. But when he rose to walk to the riverbank he collapsed, his lips white, and had to be carried aboard unconscious. They took him back up to the fort.

48

At first Baptiste did not believe her. She was scrawny, blistered, scarred, freckled, dressed in rags, and had her auburn hair hacked off at the earlobes, Indian fashion. Macedo and the others who'd attacked the village said she'd fought like a tigress. Nevertheless, it was a good sortie. They brought in two dozen males in good condition and almost a dozen girls. Usually you had to use up some of the men to make the others work, but Baptiste was so short-handed he elected to use the girls for that purpose. He chained the men to trees and made them watch the raping of their wives and sisters. The guards hadn't had a woman in a long time. Those girls who got damaged beyond repair were used for target practice. He forced the white girl to watch, too. He was saving her for himself, and figured the scene would render her more tractable. He was, however, mistaken. When he got around to approaching her himself she sank her teeth into his neck; he was fortunate she failed to sever the jugular vein. She seemed to have lost her mind. He could have her bound and gagged, except that he was loath to call in guards for help in subduing a woman. That would be embarrassing.

While he pondered this, she screamed it again: "I am the Baroness do Rio Mar! You will be made to pay for these atrocities!"

Baptiste wondered. There was that story about the steamer that blew up on the Semnome some time ago. The men on board were close associates of the Baron, and it was rumored they were seeking a woman at the French priest's mission.

In the end he left her alone, and in the morning had her carried aboard his launch for the trip to Manáos. At the very least he should be acclaimed a hero for rescuing a white woman from the savages of the forest and bringing her downriver so that the madness brought on by her harrowing experiences could be treated in an institution. And in addition, there was the remote possibility his employer did have some interest in her, in which case Baptiste might find himself the recipient of a generous reward.

The trip downriver took three days. The madwoman was kept bound and gagged under the wooden shelter on the launch's deck. Whenever they removed the gag to feed her, she cursed them, inviting them to kill her as they had the old people and children. Even when she was not screaming at them, her eyes flamed with hatred. She spat on the food they gave her.

Savannah herself thought she had perhaps lost her mind. The scenes she had witnessed could not be true; they must be the visions of a maniac. The early-morning peace of the village broken by rifle fire. The children, Tukara's daughter and little Kushawe shot down on the run like quarry. Inamona running straight at one of the attackers, faltering when bullets hit her, but keeping on, shouting at them to stop what they were doing, and finally being cut down with a machete.

She would live no longer in a world that had such horrors in it, or with a mind that contained such demented visions. She would force them to kill her. Or she would not eat again until she died of starvation. Whichever death would come most quickly was the one she would pray for.

The work on the mausoleum had already begun. The marble was on its way from Italy, and the foundation had been laid. Dom Luíz had decided on a dome with minarets which would rise above the garden, tall and slender, as Savannah had been.

At all times now Dom Luíz wore a black armband and even acquaintances like the governor noted his air of resignation and philosophical melancholy. Perhaps it was because of this he'd been able to prevail upon Esme to leave the convent and attend him. Now perhaps his child would consent to marry someone of his choosing, the scion of another wealthy family whose property would enhance the Rio Mar holdings, and also provide heirs for Dom Luíz. Meanwhile, she eased his loneliness. They dined together every night and afterward she played the piano, often bringing tears to his eyes. The rest of her time was spent in prayer. She was—and this thought

amused him—his spiritual insurance. In the event God did not
agree that rubber tappers were less than human, having a
saint in the family would be advantageous. She reverenced
him as a daughter should, and he was certain her pure intercessions would gain him entrance into the heavenly kingdom.
And, in his grief at least, he was quite sincere. He fully
believed in it himself.

From the moment Eustacio Moraes reported her death to
him, Savannah had begun to alter in his mind. He no longer
blamed her for her defection; that anarchist had somehow
used her innocence for his own purposes. The Baron saw her
now, not as she was, but as he imagined she would have
become: graceful, complaisant, an ornament of extraordinary
value. He grieved for her the way the people of Renaissance
Florence grieved for Botticelli's model, Simonetta Vespucci.
Now, during the early mornings, Dom Luíz read Dante.

So when the landing manager Baptiste appeared before him
to announce that Savannah had been found in the jungle and
was, even now, confined aboard a launch in the harbor, the
Baron scarcely knew how to respond. His eyes strayed back to
the page he had been reading, and a rage he could scarcely
stem rose in him. He looked up. "Bring her at once! Why
have you delayed?"

This was Baptiste's first face-to-face encounter with his employer. He was awed by the Palácio, by the half-dozen assistants in dark business suits; he scarcely knew how to proceed.
"Excellency—"

"What? Has she been maimed? Is she scarred in some way?"

"No, Your Excellency. But—she fought us with club and
knife—before, of course, we knew her identity. We fear she is
. . . unbalanced. We found it necessary to keep her in bonds."

A smile played around the Baron's mouth. Savannah
sounded unchanged. He said, "Perhaps she was guarding her
virtue?"

"Assuredly, Your Grace. But she was untouched by us. We
are not animals."

The Baron tapped his polished fingertips thoughtfully on
his desk. "In that case, perhaps it would be best to deliver her
to my stable under cover of night. No need to cause talk in
the city. Raoul will superintend the operation."

Baptiste waited a moment longer, but he was dismissed.
There was no mention of a reward.

* * *

For Dom Luíz, it was the longest day in memory. At last Raoul reported to him the transfer had been made, and he went to the stable to see her. He was appalled. She was little better than a savage. Worst of all, her skin was no longer white. The rage he'd felt when Baptiste told him she was not dead rose in him again.

Aware now of the lamplight in the cell, she stirred on the straw pallet on the floor, squinted up at him, and slowly got to her feet. She braced herself against the wall; it had been days since she'd eaten.

Indeed, his Botticelli woman was dead. He began sorting through the possibilities. Commit her to an institution under another name? Arrange to include in her case history that her delusion involved using the name of his dead bride? But on the other hand, it would be so much less troublesome to have her dead.

She'd recognized him now. She said, "Are you going to try to rape me too? You will not succeed. I will kill you first."

Until that moment he could have convinced himself she was an imposter, but the sound of her voice raised in defiance stirred him. He began to think of the newspaper accounts that could be written, how the anarchists had kidnapped her, used her horribly, and how she was at last found near death and brought home to breathe her last. There would be an ostentatious funeral. Yes, she must die. But not right away.

He said to Raoul, "Put the lamp down and leave us." She watched Raoul withdraw and heard the bolt slide on the door. It was just like the riverbank, the unstrapping of the penis sheaths.

He said, "Our wedding night is long overdue."

She drew back, pushing him away, struggling against him. The more she fought, the more ardent he became. He threw her to the floor and began ripping off his clothing.

That was when she began to laugh. Mad giggles rose and rang against the high walls of the cell. Abashed, he paused. He said, "You are insane."

Helplessly she chuckled. "It's only that—" Her hilarity could not be contained. She threw back her head. "It's only that tiny penis! Like a little boy's. Or a very old man's." He bellowed with rage and struck her with all his force. She lay on her side, her wild eyes still jeering. She rolled herself into a ball, trying to hold the laughter in, but she could not.

He quickly pulled on his clothes and pounded on the door,

and when Raoul opened it he said, "She is filthy. I cannot stomach the stench. Have them clean her up tomorrow."

The next day a bucket of water and a bar of soap were brought to the cell, along with a plain gray cotton dress. Later they brought in a bed. She said, "I sleep in a hammock. Bring me a hammock." But they ignored her. At midday a tin plate of stewed chicken with red peppers was pushed through the door. The smell nauseated her, but she decided to eat. She wanted to regain her strength and strangle him.

While she was eating, she heard a guard outside the door talking loudly, as if to someone who was hard of hearing. "What, Nero? Who wants me? Is it Raoul? Does Raoul want me? Are you to stay here until I get back? All right. You stay—you hear, Nero?"

A few moments later the door opened and Esme came in. She stood in the doorway while her eyes adjusted to the dimness of the cell. Then she said to Nero, "Yes, it is Savannah." Nero closed the door from the outside. Esme embraced her, saying, "I haven't much time. Are you all right?"

Savannah blinked slowly and shook her head as if fighting against tears, but her eyes were dry. She said, "I don't know. I may have lost my mind."

"We must get you out of here. I will come back tonight." Esme hugged her quickly. A moment after she tapped on the door, she was gone. Savannah squatted on her haunches like a forest native and slowly ate all the food on the plate.

When that was done she sat down, her hands limp in her lap, and looked at the floor, the high window, the walls. In the corner by the straw pallet there was a mark. She looked, and turned away, and blinked to clear her eyes, and looked again. In childish capitals someone had printed: *Manco*. The letters were dark brown. The color of an old bloodstain.

When supper was brought she forced herself to eat again. Fish with red peppers. Where was Filomena? And what of the *Paloma*—had it been repaired? She got up and began to pace the cell. Five steps one way. Four the other.

She traced with a fingertip the letters of his name. He knew there must be more than love. In the beginning he'd said he had no time for her. She hadn't known what he meant until she saw that guard from the rubber landing look down the barrel of his gun at Kushawe, moving the point of the gun to keep up with the small running boy, and then squeezing the trigger as if it were a lemon in his hand. How many other little ones were hidden away in the forest, waiting to be found by men with rifles?

She barely felt the tears falling upon the hands in her lap as she spoke to him aloud. "Esteban, I have no more time to grieve for you. And I cannot die now, can I? Not unless I die like Inamona, running against the guns. If Esme comes to try to set me free, shall I go? Or shall I stay and endure this until I am strong enough to kill Rio Mar?"

She looked at her fingers in the failing light. They remained scarred by the manioc grater made of piranha teeth. Would her hands be strong enough to clutch his throat and squeeze until the breath left his body? And would his death save the children of the forest? No: There would still be Raoul. Ignacio. João. Jaime. And how many others? Landing managers. Guards. Murderers without number.

Where was Tomás? At the hospital he spoke of? She had looked at the maps on Esteban's work table. Even now she could draw them from memory. Up the Rio Negro to the northwest of Manáos. Then west on the winding Maranhas and north again on the Semnome. Then through the forest two days to the Escondido. No, one day—now that the canal was finished. Still, it would take forever if she had to paddle a canoe all that way against the current. But if the *Paloma* was in operation again, and if she could find it. . . .

Esme came back after dark. Nero held the door open, but then, as the three of them moved along the passage outside the cell, they heard someone coming in past the horse stalls. Esme panicked and ran back into the cell, but Savannah slipped into the storeroom across the way, shut the door, and stacked feed sacks against it. She heard the Baron's voice. He was speaking to Nero. "Don't stand there like a fool. Open the door!" She heard the bolt on the cell door. Dom Luíz said, "Hurry, you idiot!"

Just as she had done the other time, months ago, she pried the storeroom window open, climbed through, and dropped to the ground. But now she ran, not toward the Palácio, but away from it, up over the iron palings that enclosed the grounds, and into the *selva*.

But the Baron did not pursue her. He did not know she was gone. He had pushed Nero aside and opened the door to the cell. The room was dark, but in the slab of light from the doorway he saw that the bed was occupied. He slammed the door in Nero's face, saying, "Lock it and go away!"

This time he would not risk her jeering at his manhood. He

covered her mouth first, then with his other hand ripped the garment from her body. He wished he'd brought a light; he wanted at last to see fear in her eyes. Still, he could feel her struggling like a snared bird under him. He sensed her terror and he was aroused. Quickly his convulsive thrusts were finished. He slackened his hold upon her and fell spent across her body. And in that instant Esme's cry burst from her throat, a single piercing scream of horror and revulsion. The door slammed open and Dom Luíz was seized from behind. He was dragged away from her, his head locked in the powerful arms of Nero. A glance at Esme in the shaft of light from the passage was enough to make him set about breaking the Baron's neck. But Esme began to sob. She threw her arms around Nero, saying, "No—no—do not risk your immortal soul! Take me away from here!" So Nero loosed his hold on Dom Luíz, who fell to the floor dazed, and locked him in the cell. Then he took Esme back to the convent and lay down, himself, in the courtyard outside the cloister.

49

She made a circuit of the city and got to the Contessa's Palace just as Raimundo was locking the doors for the night. The Contessa held her close while the girls laughed and chattered around them. Albert hissed at them to be quiet, saying, "Gaya has a gold one up in the Blue Room!" Still holding her arm around Savannah, the Contessa led her upstairs to the apartment. There Bitte brought her a tray of food, determined to start putting some flesh on her bones without delay. After she had eaten, the Contessa helped her put on a gown and robe. The two of them sat together on the brocade love seat in the apartment parlor, the older woman touching her face, her scarred hands, the cropped hair, as if trying to assure herself that Savannah had truly come back to her. "I thought I had lost you forever," she said. "I haven't heard from Esteban in so long. I was sure something had happened and he couldn't bring himself to tell me."

Savannah told her everything that had happened and the Contessa kissed the tears from her cheeks. "I know your heart is breaking, my dearest treasure. I know."

But Savannah shook her head. "I'm not going to grieve for him anymore. When I lived in the village I was only waiting to die too." She sighed. "Time seems to stop in the forest. It's hard to know, sometimes, what really happened and what was a dream." She turned to gaze intently into the Contessa's face. "You cared for me when I was small, didn't you?"

The Contessa nodded and drew her close again. They talked until dawn. The Contessa told her that her name was Madelyn St. James. Savannah remembered Edward's telling her how he carried his little sister to Mobile after the war and paid for their passage to Brazil with the silver they'd buried in the orchard when Sherman came through Georgia. Madelyn said at first they lived at Pará, where Edward found work as a bookkeeper. But then, as the rubber business grew, they moved upriver to Manáos. She grew up under the surveillance of her brother's employer, Dom Luíz. Madelyn scarcely thought of him; she didn't know Edward had promised her to him and was waiting impatiently for her to mature.

There was no school in town then, so Edward had her tutored, and she fell in love with her young teacher, a lay brother. When Edward told her at last of the plans that had been made, she threw herself into her tutor's arms. Because he loved her too, he was unable to resist. When Dom Luíz found out, he punished him the way he always punished men who enraged him: He deprived him of his manhood. Her lover then took holy orders. "You know him, my precious," Madelyn said. "He is Father Antonio."

"And you love him still."

"Oh, yes. There has never been, there will never be, anyone else for me."

When it was learned that Madelyn was pregnant, the Baron —who was already a widower with a small son, Porfirio— took as his wife a well-born girl from Bahia. But it was his intention to keep Madelyn too. He made Edward marry Veronique, who was the St. James housekeeper. Then, as Madelyn's pregnancy advanced, the two women went to Pará and rented a house. They stayed indoors all the time with only Cicero to look after them. When Savannah was born, they returned to Manáos and Veronique said the child was hers. Madelyn was allowed to care for the baby as Savannah's devoted aunt, and in return for that privilege she was to accept the attentions of Dom Luíz.

Madelyn hugged herself as if suddenly chilled. She closed her eyes, and when she opened them again she said, "But, my dearest, even though I loved you with all my heart, I couldn't bear it. I had to run away. The first time, I took you with me and didn't even get as far as Óbidos. So the next time I went alone. I know it was a dreadful thing to do—to abandon you. But I would have died if I had remained. I hated him so. I would have killed myself, like Esme's mother—or gone insane like Porfirio's."

Savannah took her hands, looking earnestly at Madelyn with a rueful smile. "I know. I do understand. We were neither one of us made for surrender, were we?"

Madelyn nodded. "That was my mother."

"How did you live after you got away?"

Madelyn sighed. "I am ashamed to tell you. At one time I was a beggar. But then I got work with a theatrical company. At first I was an understudy and sewed costumes, but then I began playing parts. It was that—the playing of roles, the use of disguises, the creation of changing identities—it was only that that kept me from being caught and brought back here. He had agents searching for me all the time. I got so I could sense when they were getting close, and I would flee again and turn up in another country with a new name and a different accent."

"And did you . . . kidnap me?"

"Yes. I couldn't stay away from Manáos. Sometimes I came back just long enough to see you from afar. I wanted more than anything in the world to have you with me, but I couldn't subject you to the life I was forced to lead, always in danger, always fleeing to another place. But then I began to enjoy some success as an actress. I was known as Mrs. Lavinia Weston, of Richmond, Virginia. I played in towns all over the United States. Little towns, mostly, with no theaters, so we did our plays in barrooms and bars and sometimes on a hay wagon. Out there men wore guns in holsters wherever they went. I could hire bodyguards, and for the first time I felt safe. So I came back to get you. You were seven years old."

Savannah remembered. "I was going to school, wasn't I? And there was a servant who walked behind me."

"Yes. She was giggling with her young man. I had watched for several days and I knew they always met along the way. So I waited in a doorway and as you came by, I took you." Madelyn got up and leaned on the mantelpiece, trembling. "I don't know what they'd told you, but you were terrified. In the room I'd rented, you wouldn't let me near you. You became hysterical. You wouldn't eat, you grew feverish, and in another day you were out of your head. I sat beside you by the hour, but whenever you opened your eyes and saw me you began to sob. I couldn't bear to see you suffer so. I bundled you up and carried you to Antonio, and he took you back to Edward and Veronique."

Savannah got up and went to her mother and embraced her, holding her close for a long moment. Then she said, "And then where did you go?"

Madelyn had removed her smoked spectacles and laid them on the mantel. She rubbed her eyes and shook her head. "I almost didn't get away that time. His agents caught me at Pará, where I had to wait at the hotel for the next ship back to the States. I got out of there by changing clothes with a chambermaid and blackening my skin with soot. I got on board an empty coal ship on its way back to Wales." Madelyn shuddered at the memories, but she drew herself up and smiled. "I think I'd like a glass of wine. Would you?"

After they'd begun to sip the Port she poured, Savannah said, "How was it you were reported dead?"

Madelyn laughed. "Sheer good fortune. For me, at least, though not for my understudy. We looked somewhat alike, but she had lung fever, and no family to mourn her. In order to be safe, I had to remain dead: I couldn't risk being seen. Yet I had to be near you, to watch over you and find a way to make myself known to you some day. And so—" She raised her hand toward the walls of the room. "I opened the Contessa's Palace. As a modiste, a restaurateur, a hotelkeeper, I would have had to meet the public. Only in this business is it possible never to see the light of day. I became, quite literally, a lady of the evening . . . only to find they'd spirited you away."

Savannah shook her head in disbelief. "They put me in that convent and left me there all those years, just to keep you from kidnapping me again."

Madelyn refilled their glasses. "But why did they leave you there after they believed I was dead? I kept expecting them to bring you back home—"

Savannah said, "I know why. Veronique never felt anything for me. I was just an investment. The convent spared her the trouble of looking after me herself." She put her wineglass down, suddenly very tired.

Madelyn drew her to her feet. "We've talked enough for one night. Into bed with you now, my precious."

But as Madelyn drew back the covers on the pink satin bed and helped her to get in, Savannah said, "But how did you get to know Jocelyn and her family?"

"When the coal ship landed me in England, her father befriended me." Madelyn covered her up and sat on the edge of the bed. "You see, all Cicero could tell me was that you were somewhere in Switzerland. Slaves were never taught to read, you know. Poor old soul. I couldn't have gotten through all this without him." She laughed. "Have you any idea how many convents there are in Switzerland? I had to make several trips, presenting myself at each of them as a woman seeking the right school for her niece, Jocelyn Estyn, and insisting upon a complete tour of the place. I found you, finally, and rented a villa on the hillside overlooking the convent, so whenever I could get away from the business here I could sit on the balcony with my opera glass trained on the courtyard, hoping for a glimpse of you. It was a marvel you and Jocelyn became such good friends. It was the only way I had of getting news of you."

"Yes. I see." But already Savannah, nestled into the warm bed, was falling fast asleep. Madelyn kissed her and turned down the lamp. As she moved toward the door Savannah stirred.

"Mother—" Madelyn caught her breath. Savannah murmured sleepily, "Can't you stay and hold me?" So Madelyn, at last, took her child into her arms and held her while she slept.

But the next day she had to say farewell to her again. Over breakfast Savannah told her she had no time to stay in Manáos now, or anywhere but in the *selva* helping Tomás and the other Manconistas carry out Esteban's plan for saving the victims of the rubber landings.

After a circuit of the docks, Raimundo, the coachman, found the *Paloma*. It had been rebuilt piece by piece, using parts Gonçalves salvaged from other vessels—some obtained by trade and bargaining, and others by theft in the night. But now at last the steamer was in working order and ready to go back upriver. Savannah could go along, provided she was willing to leave at once. She was, especially after she'd seen the armada Rio Mar was preparing to send against the Manconistas.

The Rio Negro was at flood level, its broad expanse lapping the treetops along its banks. At Manáos the docks were under water in many places, and the harbor itself was filled with vessels. In addition to the usual native canoes, the cargo lighters, the paddle steamers that traded on the rivers, and the oceangoing vessels from distant ports, there was a flotilla of naval ships. Their objective was no secret. They were going after the Manconistas.

50

After his collapse at the rubber landing, Manco regained consciousness to find himself back in his bed at the fort, with Savannah slipping ever farther away from him. He was overwhelmed by despair. It was an anguish even deeper than his first loss of her had been, because a few intoxicating days of hope had reawakened his grief-dulled craving for her. Worse, now she was not dead, but alive and suffering. He lay helplessly chafing at Rio Mar's failure to pursue him, to turn and face him so he could fight for her.

Finding that it was more difficult than ever to make the Liberator rest, MacNair spoke of the possibility of sedating him, perhaps by force. Both Tomás and Will were convinced that sort of treatment would kill him. In the end, Will again postponed his departure, and while Tomás attended to the business of the Manconistas, Will stayed at Esteban's side.

One day as Will came to the end of a passage he was reading aloud from Sir Thomas Browne's *Religion of a Physician*, Manco got to his feet and leaned on the railing of the veranda. Will said, "MacNair doesn't want you walking."

"I can't bear not knowing what's happening to her," Esteban said. "I want to go to Manáos myself and find her."

"You know that's out of the question. What good are you going to do?"

"None, I suppose. But still, I can't bear this waiting."

Will leaned forward. "I could go. I know his place well."

Esteban shook his head. "You forget, you are an escaped *seringueiro* now. He can kill you with impunity."

"Not if I get to the governor first."

"All Ribeiro cares about is building himself absurd monuments like the opera house. To him, rubber means revenue. He isn't interested in justice. No, your only security would be in the hands of the nearest American consul, and he's all the way down at Pará. Once you get that far, you might as well go on home."

Will stared across the lake, remembering the way Savannah

appeared to him in his delirium at the estrada, walking on the water with a parasol. He said, "What about that Contessa you wanted me to write? Is there anything she could do?"

Esteban sighed. "She has no one inside the Palácio." He clenched his fists and opened them again, as if to test his strength. "I must go myself. The moment we are finished here I'll gather every man I've got."

Uneasy, Will shifted the conversation. "Well, at least your canal will be in operation soon." Esteban continued gazing off over the distant treetops in the direction of Manáos, as though willing his eyes to divine what was occurring there. Will went on. "This morning while you rested, Tomás showed me how the locks work. You should have been an engineer." Still Manco's gaze burned into the distance. Will made his tone hearty. "It's a marvelous idea. It'll make supplying this installation much easier."

Esteban released his grip on the railing and sank back into his chair. "That's not why we built it," he said. "We hope to be almost completely self-sufficient here and at the other installations we've planned throughout the *selva*. No, the canal will serve another purpose." He unrolled a map of South America on the table and swept his hand across the Amazon region. "You see, this is—in a way—a maritime country. It's a shallow, three-thousand-mile-long inland sea which—almost incidentally—happens to have a lot of trees standing in it.

"All the roads are water. And it is surrounded on three sides by country that is almost impossible to traverse with a force of any size. And on the fourth side, the east—" He placed his index finger on Óbidos, halfway between Manáos and Pará. "Here the river narrows to a deep channel about a mile and a half wide, flanked by bluffs which are easily fortified." He raised his eyes from the map and Will saw, as he had months ago aboard the *Esperança*, the burning of that wild dream. Esteban said, "We intend to take control of the river—and the whole region—by taking Óbidos."

Will laughed in disbelief. "You'd need a navy!"

Manco nodded. "Yes. That is what we're waiting for." When Will stared at him open-mouthed, he smiled. "One is, we believe, going to be delivered to us." Will laughed aloud, but Manco went on seriously. "I can't understand what's taking him so long."

"Rio Mar?"

"Yes. The rainy season is over. Soon the rivers will begin to fall. Why hasn't he made his move?"

Will tapped thoughtfully on the deck of cards they always kept nearby. "My encounters with him were not exactly social, so I can't say what kind of a poker player he would be . . . yet I would guess he's very cautious, a man who likes to bet on sure things."

Esteban leaned forward, intent. "Of course. I should have known." He smiled, gripping Will's forearm in gratitude, then reached for a sheet of paper. He drew a crude map of the canal, showing how it linked the upper reaches of the Escondido and the Semnome.

Within minutes he'd sent the drawing off downriver. The messenger took, along with the sketch of the canal, two messages, not written, but memorized in English to be spoken to the Contessa herself and no other: *The Liberator says: See that this map is found by Rio Mar.* And: *The one you love has fallen into his hands. Do what you can until I come.*

The latter message was already out of date, for Tomás arrived three days after Savannah had left on the *Paloma* for the second time. After questioning him and arranging for him to be fed, Madelyn stood at one of the windows in her sitting room for a long time. In the street below, garlands were being hung from the lampposts and the cobbled pavement was being swept clean for the parade that evening in honor of Saint John. Beyond, Rio Mar's armada rode at anchor in the Rio Negro. She longed to be with Savannah, to see that no further harm befell her.

After a time Madelyn shook herself free of her reverie and sent for Egypt.

51

When repeated telegraph messages failed to badger the government at Rio into cooperation, the Baron had sent Raoul to the capital in person. He found the administration there in turmoil. Although the two-year revolution in the south of Brazil had been brought to an end, the plotting and bitter discontents persisted. And now the young republic had another uprising on its hands, this time in the arid backlands of the Northeast—the *sertão*. There a bearded, emaciated, barefoot fanatic who called himself Antonio Conselheiro—

Anthony the Counselor—had led a ragged mob of *sertanejos* to build a stronghold in the mountains. They believed Conselheiro to be the reincarnation of John the Baptist, or perhaps another Christ.

Eager to die in a holy war, they fought like madmen. Six thousand well-equipped government troops had been besieging the rocky crossroads village held by Conselheiro, but in three months they had managed to advance only a hundred yards. Enormous bribes were required to get a dozen naval vessels sent up the Amazon, and these were manned by skeleton crews; there were almost no troops left to send. So Dom Luíz had been forced to hire mercenaries and arm them himself. It had taken months to gather a sufficient force, but now he was ready. Now that the high-water mark had been reached, soon the rivers would begin to fall and once again they would become navigable only by canoe or flat-bottomed paddle steamers.

The Baron's study had become a war room, with river maps spread out on tables. He used small counters to represent the ships and moved them about with what seemed to Raoul a kind of madness.

Ever since the morning Raoul had found his father locked in the cell, with Savannah missing and Esme at the convent in total seclusion, Dom Luíz had been a changed man. Now he scarcely slept, as if vengeance fueled him so completely he had no need of rest or nourishment.

So far, however, Raoul had succeeded in keeping him from sending the flotilla of ships upriver. Repeatedly he reminded him that they had not yet located the Manconista headquarters. Chasing the anarchists blindly through the jungle swamps and canoe paths would lead only to failure. They must first pinpoint the target, move toward it swiftly, and take it by surprise. Otherwise they would face a disaster as absurd as the 6,000 federal troops helpless before the rocks and slings of the fanatic *sertanejos*.

The Baron's innate caution responded to the wisdom of Raoul's arguments. They waited. The mercenaries were, however, costing them a fortune and formed a restless rabble prone to wander the streets of Manáos getting into fights and smashing up saloons. That, combined with the Baron's state of mind, worried Raoul. His father's frenetic activity, the pacing, the actions begun and left unfinished, the forgetfulness, the burning cigars left to fall upon the carpet, all these made Raoul anxious.

Then one day there was a stroke of luck. Raoul was work-ing at his desk in the Palácio offices when one of the footmen told him a girl had come to call. The footman leaned closer. "She says she is from the Contessa's Palace." Raoul followed him to the small anteroom where she was waiting. It was the small black girl they called Egypt, the one who'd worn that bizarre red wig the day he'd gone in search of Savannah. Today she was dressed conservatively in a ruffled white dress with a high neck, long gloves, and a parasol. Had not her bodice been a tangle of rope pearls in poor taste for daytime, she might have passed for a lady.

She grinned at him impishly. "Why didn't you come back to visit us? I looked for you every night." She'd been examin-ing with admiration the tapestry-hung walls, the marble floor, the carved English furniture. She turned to Raoul, smiling. "How come you never come to see us? Have you got your own girls here?"

He felt the color rising in his cheeks. She was, to say the least, disconcerting. He said, "What do you want?"

She winked at him. "The real question is, what do *you* want?" He moved toward the door. She said, "Do you want the Manconistas?" He stopped, watching her guardedly. She said, "And the next question is: How much will you pay for a map that will lead you to them?"

He scoffed. "You are too late. Haven't you heard? Their leader is dead. Nobody is worried about that rabble any more."

"That's not what I hear. I hear he left them so well or-ganized they can carry out all his plans whether he is there or not."

Raoul continued to conceal his interest. "Even so, what good is a map of the jungle?"

"Not the jungle, my friend. A canal. Of course, if you really aren't interested. . . ." She began smoothing her gloves, pressing them farther up toward her elbows.

"What sort of a canal?"

"One that's hidden away among that maze of rivers up there. It leads to his headquarters."

He sank into a chair, careful to make his pose seem bored and inattentive, but he was watching her narrowly. "How did you come by such a map?"

Egypt giggled. "I got it from an Indian. He liked me a lot. And me, I want cash. Or diamonds. I want passage to France and enough money to get me through one season at Biarritz or Monte Carlo, in style. After that I'll be able to manage very well on my own."

While she talked, he thought about the way Manco had been pursued up the Maranhas to the vicinity of the Semnome —and then had simply vanished. And the way all the burned-out rubber landings were within overland striking distance of that impassable river, the one with all the rapids—the Escondido. Who would have dreamed that madman would dig a canal to link the rivers? Yet it was the only explanation. He said, "We might be willing to pay for such a map. Come back tomorrow."

She tapped him with the handle of her parasol. "No, that will not do." But she said it playfully, as if he had been a naughty boy. "What do you take me for? An ignorant jungle Indian who can speak no more than three words of Portuguese? You will not get the information unless you pay me. And I want the money now. I've been waiting a long time to get out of this country. Do you think I will let you play tricks with me?" She touched his shoulder lightly. "Although I must admit I find you"—her voice grew throaty—"very exciting."

He moved a step away. "Where is this map?"

Smiling, she said, "Where is the money?"

He got from the safe in his office the equivalent of $5,000 in small bills of mixed nationalities. After he had examined the crude map she had hidden in her parasol and compared it with the chart of the Semnome-Escondido region, he gave her the money. While he watched, she tucked the bills into her stocking top. Then she drew him close and whispered in his ear, "Maybe we could go away together, you and me. What do you say?" He flushed and shook his head. She sighed, "Pity. What a time we could have in Biarritz."

The Baron, however, was incensed. Not about the map; with that, he was delighted. But he was furious because Raoul had paid for it instead of taking it by force and throwing the girl out. "Well, at any rate," he said at last, rubbing his hands as he paced about among his map tables, "now we can advance." He stared at the counters representing ships, all clustered now in the lower Rio Negro. "Send word to all the captains. We will leave at sunrise tomorrow. I will lead in the *Primavera*, but I want one of our own people—you, João, Ignacio, Jaime, men from the office in town, workers from the warehouses, even gardeners and stable hands—but men of our own on every vessel. Is that clear?"

Raoul nodded, but did not leave to carry out the orders. The Baron had stopped in the middle of the room, looking puzzled as if his train of thought had been derailed. After a moment his eyes came back into focus.

After a moment Dom Luíz said, "Two weeks, Raoul. Two weeks elapsed between the time she was kidnapped from the opera and that day I saw her aboard that riverboat, that—"

"*Paloma.*"

"Yes. Where was she all that time?"

"Perhaps right here in town. The steamer was leaving Manáos."

The Baron closed his eyes, and Raoul wondered if he'd fallen asleep at last. But he had not. "And during that time a bartender saw a red-haired girl run out of that Contessa's place, did he not?" Raoul agreed. "Now you are offered a map by a whore from the very same brothel. Does that not seem, to say the least, thought provoking?"

He got to his feet and began to pace the length of the room. "What if you needed a headquarters in the state capital? A place with privacy—"

Raoul leaned on a map table. "But where many local officials relax—and drink—and talk—"

"Even the governor himself!" Dom Luíz turned suddenly in midstride, his eyes wild. "Even my own son, my drunken idiot of an heir—used against me." Raoul watched as his father began to quiver with agitation. "They spy on me, kidnap my bride, and corrupt her in a whorehouse. And even Esme— now they've turned her against me, too. It's all part of the plot—don't you see?"

Uneasily, Raoul tried to lead him back to the matter at hand. "Are you saying this map is a trick?"

The Baron smiled cunningly. "Perhaps. Perhaps not. Women of that sort will do anything for money. Now that this anarchist is dead, maybe dealing with us is more profitable. But I am too clever for them. If they think they can outwit me—"

"Excellency—before we commit our flotilla of ships to this expedition, hadn't we better send Eustacio Moraes upriver alone to find out if the map is genuine?"

But the Baron had turned his back and was leaning on the mantel, gazing into the dead ashes of the fireplace. He said, "Who is this woman? This Contessa?"

Raoul shrugged. "I have no idea. I have never seen her.

When I went to investigate that bartender's report, she was unavailable. . . ."

Dom Luíz waved his hand, no longer interested. "Carnival. Isn't tonight the Eve of Saint John?"

"I believe so. The end of the rainy season."

The Baron smiled. "If we are leaving at sunrise, perhaps the mercenaries are entitled to a last night on the town. If they get carried away and break into a brothel while all those fireworks are going off . . . we really could not stop them, could we? . . . Not even if I myself went in person among them and tried to save the place from destruction. . . ." He leaned against the mantel, chuckling.

52

Since Governor Ribeiro was to preside over the fireworks, he and his party were not due at the Contessa's Palace until after midnight. Nevertheless, by ten o'clock everything was ready.

The girls were all costumed identically as Marie Antoinette —white satin gowns with panniers, high white wigs, black beauty marks, and jeweled masks to conceal the eyes. The governor's tastes were jaded, and Madelyn, who also had put on the evening's disguise, thought Ribeiro would enjoy the game.

While they waited, the girls drew the draperies back from the windows and watched the parade on its way to the park. The Eve of Saint John was a catch-all festival, part Christian holiday, part African magic, part Indian feast for the End of Rising Waters. Where the masses live in hopeless poverty, Carnival is the leveler. The undernourished, the deformed, the outcast, and the powerless vanish, transformed by a length of gaudy fabric, a mask, and a paper crown or a pair of horns into monarchs, fearsome beasts, even angels. Of course the parade ends, but even as the confetti and tinsel are swept from the streets, preparations begin anew for next year.

Now revelers carried fifteen-foot crucifixes and images of saints on litters covered with flowers, and the crowd surged forward to kiss the holy relics. Amid the religious veneration, there were dancers in African masks derived from Dahomey, along with Indian shamans wearing tall feathered headdresses, monkey fur, and animal teeth. Throbbing to the pulse of drums and maracas, the marchers undulated down the street like a serpent.

The Rio Mar mercenaries did not knock at the door; they battered it with clubs. Raimundo, behind the wrought-iron grille, refused to let them enter. Using crowbars, they pried the grille from its frame and burst into the foyer. There were about fifty men, with the Baron and his sons masked among them.

Hearing the noise, Madelyn, with the other sixteen Marie Antoinettes close behind her, moved into the passage outside the Lavender Salon. She saw at once the iron-gray beard beneath the mask. "Flee, my treasures!" she whispered. "Down through the kitchen, out the cellar. Use the windows if you must!"

Seeing the girls, the mob pushed forward, spreading out in pursuit along the back passages of the house. Raimundo, Elena, and Bitte joined hands to hold them back as the Contessa and Albert retreated up the main stairway.

In the sitting room, Elena gathered Madelyn's jewels and pinned them in a bag under Bitte's dress while Madelyn opened the safe. She put all the money into Albert's top hat, which he jammed onto his head. "Take Coco!" she cried, and the monkey perched atop the hat. Then she and Elena watched from the third-floor landing as Bitte carried Albert on her shoulders down against the upward tide of men.

By the time Dom Luíz—moving behind a wedge formed by Raoul, Ignacio, and Jaime—reached the top floor, the sitting room door was closed and barred by Elena. The Baron said, "Is this the one?"

Raoul answered, "No, this is her assistant."

She addressed the Baron. "The Contessa will be glad to see Your Excellency, provided you are not afraid to visit her alone." Dom Luíz blinked behind his mask and waved the men away, saying, "Search the rest of this floor."

Elena pushed the door open and stood aside, revealing a tall woman, another Marie Antoinette, standing at the window with her back to him. She was straining toward the street below, trying to count the white wigs losing themselves among the throng lit by a sky full of fireworks. Hearing the door close, Madelyn turned, her smoked glasses in her hand.

"Now, Luíz," she said, "what is it you want?" Under the gray moustache his lips went white. "No," she said, "as you can see, I am not dead." From the lower floors came the sound of furniture crashing and mirrors shattering. She went on, "I trust you are still wealthy enough to pay for these damages? Even so, hadn't you better make them stop before the cost of this revel becomes excessive?"

He wet his lips and pulled the mask away. The puffy crescents under his eyes were pale. He barely nodded, still unable to speak.

"Then call off your rabble. After that we will talk." He forced himself to move back toward the door. Raoul, patrolling the upper hallway, turned, alert for trouble. "Make them stop that racket. And get them out of here!"

Madelyn raised her voice. "And begin to assess the damage!"

Luíz closed the door and turned back to her. He had forgotten her effect upon him. It had always been like this. From the very first time he saw her. She was a child then, her auburn hair waist-long, the same lavender eyes gazing at him coolly, as they were now. She had moved to the mantel and stood very straight, waiting. His voice broke. "Why? Why did you let me grieve when you were so near?"

She laughed. "Grieve? You?"

He stepped toward her, but faltered and sank into a chair. It was suddenly difficult to recall what had happened back then. He'd made her angry and she'd left him. "But why?" he said aloud.

She spoke in a low, almost strangled voice. "Did you think I would let you have my child? Even if I were dead, I would have come back from the grave to keep you from her!"

He blinked as if in reaction to a sudden light. "Then it was. . . ." He'd always known she loved him; he should have been more patient with her. How much she must love him, to be driven to this fury by jealousy—and of her own daughter! He slipped from the chair to kneel before her. "Forgive me, my dearest—let me make it up to you—"

"Don't touch me," she cried. "Don't come near me!"

Bracing himself against the chair, he got to his feet and tried to take her in his arms. Pushing him back, she struck his face with all her force.

"I despise you!" she said. "I have always despised you. When I was a child you put your hands on me—remember? I've been sick from your touch ever since."

He blinked, shocked by her vehemence. If it was true, if indeed she hated him and had been hiding here in Manáos all along . . . then was she the one behind it all? The attacks on his property . . . turning his bride against him? Suddenly he clenched his fists and bellowed with rage. He lifted his fists above his head, shouting, "I will punish you for this!"

She ran toward her bedroom, but as she turned to lock the sitting room door behind her, he burst through. His hands slipped down the satin of her dress as she spun free and ran toward the other door. Again he overtook her and cut her off, grasping her throat as she tried to turn back. His fingers tightened, unmoved by the fists pummeling his head, his chest, his shoulders. She felt herself weakening and reached behind her blindly for something to strike him with. Her fingers brushed against the lamp base and, straining every muscle against the pressure at her throat, she clutched the neck of the lamp, turning it with her wrist, and raising it above his head. A light blow was all she managed, but the paraffin oil spilled, momentarily blinding him. He loosed his hold on her, flinging his arms upward to ward off the oil and knocking the lamp against the sheer drapes.

Flame sped up the curtains. Charred pieces broke free and fell on the bed. His shirtfront became a smoking circle, its black edges spreading swiftly across his chest. "Raoul!" he screamed. Madelyn heard running footsteps mount the stairs. She paused until she heard the sitting room door flung open; then she slipped out the bedroom entrance to the upper hallway and fled downward, crying "Fire!" to the half-dozen men she met coming up.

Already the stairwell was filling with smoke. She sped to the side entrance and out into the masked throng, another Marie Antoinette losing herself in the Carnival that never ends.

53

Savannah, sitting on the crates on the *Paloma*'s crowded deck, grew silent and withdrawn as they entered the Semnome. When first she came aboard she'd clung to the old cook Filomena, saying to her in Portuguese, "He's gone."

"*Sim, senhorita,*" Filomena murmured, pouring her a tumblerful of *cachaça*, "but they say his spirit guides the Manconistas. That is why we go back upriver to help them."

Now, moving upstream in a haze of memories, Savannah longed for Filomena's faith. But her grief denied it. Yet even

as she shut her eyes in pain, she heard his voice speaking of
the river and the *selva*.

When the steamer turned from the river into the canal, she
could not bring herself to look north toward Father Pierre's
mission, where Esteban had fallen under the blows of Mario's
long knife. Instead she kept her eyes upon the narrow channel
through the forest, built by the Manconistas from drawings
Manco had made at that table in the old landing manager's
office on the Escondido, where she used to wait for him.

Grief welled in her again and she wondered if she had not
been mistaken to return here. Could she bear the pain of her
loss where he was continually recollected? Yet she knew this
was where she belonged. She must spend the rest of her life
working as he had worked. As the steamer moved closer to
the Manconista headquarters, at last, even without closing her
eyes, she saw him clearly. Perhaps Filomena was right. Perhaps his spirit was truly here. *I will never leave you now*, she
thought. *I will always stay here where you are close to me.*

The drums warning of the *Paloma*'s passage through the
canal had caused a stir among the Manconistas. By the time
the steamer made its way up the Escondido and through the
two-mile stretch to the lake, the fields had been abandoned and
all the workers gathered at the island's dock.

From the veranda Will and Esteban watched through the
open gates of the stockade. Savannah stood looking around
her for a moment before she stepped onto the plank. This,
then, was the place he'd planned to bring her to after the
priest had married them . . . to this fort built on an island so
that it looked like a wooden castle surrounded by its moat.

Gonçalves leaped ashore, sought out Tomás, and spoke to
him urgently. They'd had engine trouble throughout the trip
and they'd lost time. So although they'd left Manáos three
days before the Feast of St. John, hoping to give them sufficient warning, now he feared the armada was less than a day
behind him.

Tomás ran across the courtyard to the hospital and vaulted
up the steps to the second-floor veranda, calling the Liberator.
Esteban did not hear him. He was standing motionless at the
railing, watching Savannah walk uncertainly into the stockade. She paused in the middle of the courtyard holding the
basket of things Madelyn had packed for her and trying to
decide which of the long buildings was the women's house.
The stockade was filled with people, hundreds of them. It was
clear they'd been hard at work: pottery, baskets, and manioc

flour were being made, while over the fires fish and game were drying. It was the first time she'd seen the Manconistas en masse. They had a distinctive look about them, and an air of purpose. Although she saw every kind of forest Indian, the tanned ex-cowboys of the *sertão*, Brazilian Portuguese, and Europeans, still they looked enough alike to be recognized as an army. Both the men and women wore their hair tied back the way Manco had worn his; and many of the men wore the moustache that was a narrow line framing the mouth. The garments, too, were like the one Esteban had worn in the *selva*—the loose shirt of a rubber tapper, cinched at the waist with a length of homemade rope. As she surveyed the scene she felt drawn toward the two-story building at the back of the courtyard, and slowly she raised her eyes to the veranda. And at once the fort, the *selva*, the world itself fell away, lost in a long heart-stilled moment of entranced regard.

Esteban, scarcely aware of his movements, cleared the railing and dropped to the ground, landing as she ran into his arms. He crushed her to him and they held each other wordlessly, drawing apart only to look, tear-blind, and to kiss; then they held one another tightly again.

At last Tomás said, "Esteban, Rio Mar is on the Maranhas." Slowly Manco blinked and raised his eyes. "Then go. You know what to do." He drew her toward the veranda stairs. On the way up he gripped the rail with his free hand and leaned heavily upon her. They crossed the veranda to Esteban's room, oblivious to everything, even to Will Patterson, who stood watching them.

Behind the closed door Esteban clung to her, saying nothing but her name, clasping her shorn head against his chest. At last he drew her to the bed and made love to her. It was a wild, sad loving, aching with the anguish of their separation and the feeling that it would take an eternity of love to make up for it.

Later he pored over her, looking intently at her cropped hair, the scarred fingers, the soles of her feet callused from her stay among the Indians. She in turn wept over the changes in him, his weakness and the scars on his chest and back. She kissed the jagged weals and begged him to let her care for him until he was completely well. "My strength will return now," he said, and kissed her as if he drew life from her mouth.

Throughout the long afternoon they talked, closing the gaps in their life together. Then he called for supper. During the meal the big fair-haired Scotsman came by, looking worried.

Esteban introduced her to MacNair. The doctor was polite, but lost no time in taking Manco's pulse. Dissatisfied, he placed his ear against the Liberator's chest. When he straightened, he was shaking his head. Manco smiled, "Better, isn't it?" MacNair nodded skeptically, looking askance at Savannah.

He held her close while they watched the moon rising over the forest. They felt a need to touch constantly, as if they were afraid this was another dream, some feverish vision that would vanish and leave them grief-stricken again. At the same time they continued talking, for that, too, helped winnow away the fear. She asked him about the rubber landings, about men like Baptiste and those guards who shot children. Esteban told her of the Manconista plan for driving that kind of rubber business out of the *selva*.

In the morning she awakened alone in his bed and felt an instant of terror. She leaped to her feet, dressed quickly, and went to look for him. She heard the conversation as she rounded the veranda's shady side. Tomás was saying, "Then they should reach the canal by midmorning." He looked the same as he had when he had given her language lessons, but now he wore a rifle slung across his back. And there, seated behind the table, was Esteban, looking well and rested, even though they'd talked and loved far into the night. And next to Esteban another man got to his feet to welcome her—Will —thinner, his fair beard fuller, his hair long and tied back, and taller, or at least standing taller than he used to. Tears filled her eyes; she gripped his hand and raised it to her lips.

Quickly, though, the group's attention turned back to the map in front of Esteban. She said, "Rio Mar?" Will nodded.

Tomás said, "The last things are being done now."

Esteban rolled up the map and got to his feet. "We should leave at once."

She didn't wait. She ran back to the bedroom and looked through the town clothes Madelyn had put into her basket. Useless here. She kicked off her shoes, wiggled free of her petticoat, and ripped half the length off her muslin skirt. She looked up to find Esteban standing in the doorway. "I'm ready," she said. "Is there room in your canoe, or must I ride with someone else?" Again, that laughter. He took her in his arms and, cupping her face in his hands, kissed her.

The command post was a railed platform high in an ironwood tree, so well screened by foliage as to be almost invisible. Yet from it the whole center section of the canal could be seen.

Esteban stood motionless, gazing into the forest. Savannah sat down, leaning her back against the ironwood trunk. In that leafy gloom parrots darted in pairs; their fluttering shook the branches just enough to let a shaft of sunshine through from time to time. Occasionally a handful of white petals wafted downward from invisible blossoms.

It seemed incredible that this could be the scene of a battle. Yet already Tomás and Esteban had lifted their heads, listening to a shrill whistle nearly lost among the forest's many bird calls. Esteban nodded almost imperceptibly. Tomás stepped to the platform's edge and repeated the sound, but with a different sequence of notes. Immediately his signal echoed across the forest, each repetition sounding more distant. The Manconistas were ready.

54

The winding Maranhas was tranquil, another whole forest mirrored in its waters; the fleet steaming upriver behind the Baron's yacht scarcely cleft the reflection. There were eight ships: the *Primavera*, a coal tender, and an assorted half-dozen gunboats and patrol vessels, one of them a heavily armored frigate. The vessels were manned by a small crew of naval personnel, along with one company of soldiers in blue uniforms with vermilion stripes; they carried lances and colorful flags. The rest of the men lining the rails were Rio Mar employees and the mercenaries recruited by the Baron all over South America.

For most of them the voyage into the jungle was a new experience. Aboard one of the gunboats a lieutenant scanned the shores with his field glasses, murmuring, "Strange country. Like a green mirage."

When the armada reached the upper Maranhas, the river quietly closed behind them. Lianas holding a dozen cut but unfelled forest giants were severed, and the great trees fell into the water. Then the Manconistas hauled a floating island into place against the dam made by the trees. With the river blocked, the route the armada would need to take to get back to Manáos was closed.

In addition to cannons, there were Gatling guns and Nordenfeldt machine guns; and on the deck of the frigate were two Krupp field pieces designed for use on land. Rio Mar had insisted on the added firepower. He intended to demolish the Manconistas' headquarters so completely that no trace of it would remain. Now to the long list of offenses against him must be added the fact that he'd nearly been trapped in the Contessa's Palace; by the time Raoul, Jaime, João, and Ignacio had managed to get him down the smoke-filled stairway, his hands were burned and his hair had been singed to the scalp. The awkward bandages on his hands infuriated him as much as the pain.

While the weapons were being checked, he ordered Eustacio Moraes to increase the yacht's speed so he could reconnoiter. Looking from the map to the overgrown shore and back again, he searched for the canal. He saw nothing. Almost beside himself with impatience, he sent out two launches to examine the banks closely. At last the canal opening, concealed by foliage, was found. The Manconistas watching from the forest were relieved; they'd begun to fear Rio Mar would never find them.

Still cautious, however, the armada sent one patrol boat in to have a look. Its captain, after an hour, reported that either the locks were left untended or the appearance of the ships had caused the natives to flee in terror, for the canal was deserted. He said they would need to operate the locks themselves, but the mechanism seemed childishly simple.

The doors of the locks were made of several thicknesses of hardwood, cross-grained and pegged, the layers running in different directions to counteract warping. Varnished and waxed with forest products, they slid up and down in wooden tracks treated with wax. A system of weights and pulleys operated the doors, which permitted the water to flow from the higher-level Escondido into one lock at a time, raising vessels in stages from the lower-level Semnome. It appeared that the flow from the Escondido was very strong; the locks should fill up quickly and, in effect, the rivers themselves would do most of the work.

The reconnoitering patrol boat led the way, its crew leaping down the gangway at each lock to hoist the massive wooden doors. Nothing untoward happened until they prepared to open the last lock: Access to the pulley mechanism was blocked by an anaconda. The snake's size was impossible to guess, for it was coiled on the canal bank in a conical shape higher than a man, its huge head waving languidly down at them from the apex. The sailors, immobilized by horror, began only belatedly to back away, stumbling over one another while their captain shouted, "Shoot! Shoot, you fools!"

Fumbling for their sidearms, they took aim and began peppering the splotched brown skin with bullets. The attack irritated the snake and made it hiss like a bellows. That hissing, loud as a train engine letting off steam, terrified the men lining the rails of the patrol boat and almost paralyzed those on the bank, where now the serpent was uncoiling, its body as broad as a man's and the immense mouth open and undulating toward them. Screaming, they fought for access to the gangplank, while the captain himself began firing a machine gun at the creature. He continued drilling the carcass with bullets long after its full length, some thirty feet, lay lifeless and coursing blood over the bank.

It was some time before another detail could be coerced into stepping ashore to operate the lock. Meanwhile the whole flotilla was penned into the middle sections of the canal. Then an eerie sound rose around them, like the wailing of lost souls. It was the voice of Tomás, speaking from the command post through one of the long bamboo tubes called sacred flutes. He said: "You may surrender now."

For answer, the Baron ordered Moraes to open fire with the *Primavera*'s forward gun. At once a cascade of arrows from the surrounding forest struck the men lining the rails. After long moments of confusion in which officers shouted frantic orders, gradually the soldiers and the sailors, rallying, prepared to fire back, aiming their Comblain rifles at the enemy beyond the foliage. The mercenaries, despite the cursing of the Rio Mar employees, stood stupidly about, unable to decide what to do. The cannons, too, were mute; before their gunners could get them firing, terror fell upon the vessels from the branches arching overhead.

It had taken the Manconistas weeks to collect enough snakes —deadly coral snakes, the ill-tempered nine-foot fer-de-lance, and the big bushmasters, twelve feet long. They'd gone far upriver into the dry grasslands to find the cascabel, a tropical rattler whose poison is especially lethal. Hanging in heavy close-meshed nets in the trees, the snakes had grown hungry and irritable. When the cords holding the bags were loosed, a rain of furious reptiles fell upon the ships. Most of the men jumped overboard.

The canal, however, had been stocked with electric eels. Those who managed to climb out of the water lay helpless on the bank, too stunned by the jolting to walk; they submitted quietly to being trussed up with ropes. The few who had succeeded in scrambling over their companions in the water without encountering the eels fled into the forest at a run, only to be caught in nets strung among the trees.

Rio Mar himself kept fighting, but with his yacht blocked by the patrol boat in front of him, he could do little. Ripping the bandages from his burned hands, he fired *Primavera*'s guns, one after another, until they were empty. At last a net was dropped upon him and he was carried off slung from a pole like the catch taken in a hunt.

By sundown the work was finished. The prisoners who'd been bitten or struck by arrows were given first aid and taken to the hospital for further treatment. Those who'd been unharmed were placed in stout twenty-five-foot montarias stocked with three days' supply of food and shoved off down the Escondido. Only Rio Mar was placed in a prison cell.

That night there was a council in the courtyard at the fort. Everyone who had suffered from the operations of Rio Mar Rubber was permitted to voice an opinion on the disposal of the Baron. Will proposed taking him to Rio so he could be tried for the murders of the thousands who had died. Some of the other freed tappers said Dom Luíz should be forced to breathe the smoke of burning uricuri nuts until he choked to death. Still others urged that he be mutilated, a toe or a finger at a time. An Indian woman said, "I know the swamp where the Mother of Anacondas is sleeping. She is longer than two montarias and has not eaten since the rains begun. Let us watch her swallow him."

Esteban and Savannah sat together on the veranda, listening to the meeting taking place in the courtyard below. At length the council, failing to reach an agreement, turned to Manco. "You decide for us," a spokesman said. "We will abide by what the Liberator chooses."

Esteban stood, looking over them, and beyond them to where the dark moonlit forest rimmed the fields on the edge of the lake. He said, "We will give him to the *selva*. We will let the *selva* cleanse itself of this corruption."

The group dispersed to the long houses, most of the people murmuring agreement. But when Esteban rejoined her in the wicker chair they had been sharing, Savannah hissed with a fierceness that surprised him, "He must be killed!"

He studied her intently in the moonlight. "An eye for an

eye? Savagery to recompense savagery? Is that what you want? Is it truly?" She nodded.

He picked up a Colt revolver that had been left nearby. "Here," he said, "take the key to his cell and kill him. The gun is loaded. Stand close and aim for his heart." She did not touch the gun. He went on, "No? Then perhaps you want to flog him. We have no whips here, but we have tapir hide—one can be made. This prisoner is yours. You may do whatever you wish with him. But you must do it. You, yourself—by your own hand." She was still a moment, then she shuddered and turned away. He put his arm around her. "Revenge, you see, is not sweet. It is very bitter. And the taste never goes away."

"I understand," she said, but she moved away from him.

The meeting had broken up and the Manconistas trailed off, the men still talking as they entered their long house and the women whispering as they led the young children toward the women's house. Savannah followed them. A baby whose mother was busy with another child whimpered on the ground, reaching his arms to be picked up. Savannah knelt beside him, murmuring. He stopped crying and arched toward her. She took him in her arms and climbed into a hammock with him, rocking gently and stroking his back as he lay upon her breast. She knew she was comforting herself, not the child; she was reminding herself what mattered, what there was the most of in the world.

The women, ill at ease in her presence, bent to their tasks, building the fires for the night, stowing bowls and implements, urging the children to their hammocks, breast-feeding their babies. But then she saw the women stiffen and draw back into the shadows: Manco had entered. After a moment in which his eyes adjusted to the dimness, he walked to the hammock and stood looking at her.

She held the baby closer, pressing her lips against his gleaming hair. "I want us to have a child," she said.

His eyes narrowed with that amused love she aroused in him. He said, "Do you know why?"

Was it simply what women like these and their mothers before them had known wordlessly since the dawn of time, that the only remedy for death is life? Or was it because she was afraid of losing him again? He bent toward her and gently took the sleeping child. Savannah got to her feet and Esteban laid the baby in her place. When he straightened, she clung to him. "I want to be one with you, to melt into you. I want . . . I want our lives to blend—"

"That will happen in our children."

"Yes. I'll search for the plant to make me conceive."

He closed his eyes. "No. It is not the time."

"Then when?"

"Afterward. After we have secured the river."

A party set out at dawn the next morning: one canoe, with Tomás and Will among the men who paddled, and the Baron, his hands tied behind him, seated under the thatched shelter. At noon on the third day they beached the craft and trekked through the forest until evening, with Will blessing MacNair and his unorthodox treatments, for he had no trouble keeping up with the others.

In a clearing they removed the Baron's bonds, his shoes, and all his clothing. He stood, pot-bellied and bandy-legged, the aging flesh hanging limp along his thighs. Will found himself empty of compassion.

Tomás found a sapopema tree and began to drum on it. He told Will the message would be heard and repeated across many kilometers throughout the surrounding forest. It said a Jurupari—a vicious and very dangerous devil who takes the form of a man—was wandering in the *selva*. No matter how many Indians heard his cries in the forest, no one would go near him. As the drumming ended, the Baron turned. His hands trembled at his sides and his mouth worked pointlessly, like a very old man's. Ignoring the others, he said, "Patterson! You are a civilized man. Make them stop this madness. Tell them I have learned whatever lesson they are trying to teach me. Tell them I will make reparations."

Will turned away, but Rio Mar sank to his knees behind him. "It isn't just my life. Can't you see? It's my immortal soul!" Night had fallen now, and the Manconistas prepared to leave him. Dom Luíz clutched at Will's legs, speaking rapidly. "Please! I must make peace with my daughter so that her intercessions will save me."

Will shook free of his hands and followed the others out of the clearing. The Baron got to his feet, but made no attempt to pursue them. He stood like a child accepting his punishment, yet not without protest. Long after the trees blocked him from sight Will could hear him howling. "Patterson! Beg her to forgive me! Make her pray for my salvation!"

55

By the time Will got back to the fort, the Manconistas had cleared out the armada by loosing many small rodents on the ships. Once the snakes had their fill they grew sluggish and easier to handle. When the last reptile had been accounted for and freed in distant forests, they'd gone aboard and gathered up the ships' manuals. Now Esteban wanted Will to help him study them.

It took them many hours, but one by one they got the vessels under way and brought them up to the fort. After that, a part of each day was spent training the Manconistas to maneuver the ships around the lake. Most of them had grown up in canoes and were adept at navigating around snags and shallows, but they were unprepared for the mechanics. They were helped, though, by the wounded sailors, who were impressed by the care they'd received.

During the hottest part of the day all work ceased. At MacNair's insistence Esteban spent the time in his hammock, reading. So every afternoon Will and Savannah sat together on the veranda. At Will's urging she was working steadily with her sketchpad; he'd convinced her his book would help Esteban's cause, and that her pictures would make more people read the story. He let her read the manuscript; she liked best those parts recording Esteban's thoughts, his explanations of the Indian view of nature, of property, of responsibility; his plan for an Amazonian Confederation bastioned by the Andes and the highlands called the Brazilian and Guiana Shields; his comments on history and politics. Although she'd heard Manco say many of these things herself, she told Will she understood them better in his orderly presentation of them.

So during this quiet time of day she refined the sketches she'd been making around the fort, showing for Will's readers the lake, the hospital, the Manconistas at work in the courtyard and the fields. She worked intently, almost unaware that Will questioned her relentlessly in his quiet way, asking her about her childhood, her education, what happened to her in the Indian village, at the Contessa's, at the Baron's Palácio.

He loved watching her. Her hair, still very short, was curly at the nape of her neck. He thought she was more beautiful now than ever.

But one afternoon as she worked, she refused to answer his questions. At length, her frown deepening, she gave up and put her drawing aside. "I can't concentrate now. Perhaps after we get back from Óbidos—"

Will picked up the drawing and looked at it. She'd sketched Esteban on the veranda, looking down at the Manconistas in the courtyard below. Will said, "I won't be here after Óbidos. I'll have to make do with the ones you've finished."

Surprised, she turned to him. "You can't leave us—he needs you." Will stared at his hands. She said, "Maybe you need a rest. You put in such long days—"

That was true, and deliberate. He wanted to be too tired to lie awake at night thinking of the two of them behind the closed door of Esteban's room. He said, "I can't stay. I've got to start attending to my own life again. Make amends to my family for staying away so long. Get the poker winnings I left in Manáos. Go home and finish this book properly."

"In your good brick house on a quiet square in Baltimore?" She was observing him thoughtfully, as if preparing to do his portrait. "You've changed, haven't you? You're no longer so . . . vulnerable."

He wished that were true. But he said, "I survived something that should have killed me. I'm over it now, that oppressive terror you feel alone in the *selva*. But I'll never get over having been there. And sometimes I think I can never again feel at home among people who have no idea what it was like."

She put her pen and ink away. "I wish you'd stay."

But Will could not. The love he'd been trying to suppress since the first day they'd met burned in him more fiercely than ever; and now, he loved them both. Their happiness was for him a deeper agony than his body had ever given him. Seeing the unvoiced communication of their eyes, their need to touch all the time, and most of all seeing them close the door of Esteban's room behind them every night . . . all of that gave Will such anguished longing that he knew he must separate himself from them. Perhaps even then the pain would linger; but one day it would be gone.

The next morning Will and Esteban heard Savannah scream. Running from the veranda into the bedroom, they

found her on the floor in the corner on her haunches like a
native woman. The basket opened in the center of the room
contained a head, shrunken to a gnarled fist. It looked bestial,
like an ancient monkey with steel-gray hair and a harsh
pointed beard, and seemed less like Rio Mar than a malicious
caricature of him.

Will took the thing away and Esteban held her in his arms
until she stopped shuddering. She said, "I heard a sound outside our door. I opened it and . . . what does it mean?"

"It means that someone among us believes I was unwise to
let him go, that my love for you has made me weak."

Tears filled her eyes. "Is it true? Have I weakened you? Am
I like a parasitic vine? By the time I'm strong enough to
stand alone, will you be dead?"

He kissed her eyes, her lips, her throat. "No," he murmured, "no." After a moment he said, "I must see that Patterson doesn't destroy it. We can be properly married now."

She blinked slowly. "You knew."

"Only after I'd lost you. Then I understood what you were
saying in your fever, there at Father Pierre's." He cradled her
in his arms. "I am so sorry. I never meant to make you suffer.
I wanted you to be happy, to stop being afraid."

"You knew, and still you wouldn't let your people kill
him—"

"How could I let their revenge profit me? Or even you?"

She almost laughed. "And I was afraid loving me had made
you weak."

The Manconistas were working now with an air of urgency
uncommon in the tropics. Hundreds of men and women
poured into the stockade, having come long distances by
canoe. Savannah guessed their number had doubled to perhaps a thousand, and she felt the pace around her quicken the
way distant drumbeats are felt rather than heard.

The armada was fully operational. Fortunately the trip
downriver would be helped by the current; but at Manáos
they would need to resupply the vessels and the tender, for
there'd be no time to stop and cut wood along the way.

Esteban himself seemed increasingly withdrawn, watching
from the veranda as if his thoughts were elsewhere. And
indeed, for the time being his work was done; he'd delegated
responsibility.

Tomás was supervising the clearing of the route. Will's

unspoken title seemed to be Chief of Tactics. He gathered data on the patrol boats they might encounter, crew numbers, armament, and fire power. His information showed the Brazilian navy no threat; although not badly equipped, it was prey to politics and even, in the country's recent history, widescale mutiny. He began to believe Esteban was right; nothing could stop the Manconistas.

MacNair was outfitting the Baron's swift and roomy yacht as a first-aid station. A dozen Indian women, trained in the hospital here, would go along as nurses. Savannah continued recording the operation with sketches for Will's book.

At dawn on the day of departure from the fort the Manconistas jammed into the courtyard. Esteban, flanked on the veranda by Tomás, Will, MacNair, and Savannah, scanned the mass of faces. He spoke in both Tupi and Portuguese, a sentence at a time in each language. "This is a war party. The mothers and the children will remain here, along with the old ones. Continue working every day. Tend the fields. Herd the manatee. Dry many fish. Make as much manioc flour as you can. When we return there will be need for food. And make *masato* for the victory feast." Laughter rippled across the crowd.

He reached into the basket on the table nearby and held high the shrunken head of Rio Mar. Hundreds of swiftly indrawn breaths rose like a sigh. "Who questions my leadership? Now is the time to choose another headman. Now, before we set out." He paused; the upturned faces were still. "If you do not want to speak out, you are free to leave. No one will harm you." He scanned the rows of people, the ex-tappers of every nationality, Indians of many tribes. No one spoke. No one moved. At last he threw the head back into its basket. "We are a new tribe. A new nation. We no longer need savage rituals. We go now to secure our territory from invasion. We seek not prizes, not bloodshed, but only the right to govern ourselves . . . to say who shall harvest the resources of our homeland . . . and how they shall conduct themselves while in our territory. We go to war to keep our tribes, our villages, our *maloccas* safe. To guard our way of life. To guard our liberty."

A cheer burst from the crowd, then the rhythmic shouting of "Liberator!" To those standing at his side it seemed a great stillness had fallen upon him, here at the epicenter of this tumult.

He lifted the basket once more into their view. "This man called himself a name which means Baron of the River Sea. He meant the great river some of you have never seen, but which all the rivers that you know at length become: the Amazon. But it was never his, nor anyone's but ours. Let us go now and liberate the River Sea from the hands of men who have no right to it!"

The Manconistas surged out of the stockade and boarded the ships of the armada. The walls of the jungle echoed with their shouting—his name, and their own.

56

Governor Ribeiro always awoke with a hangover. This morning, however, his waking was even more painful than usual. He opened his eyes to find Esteban Manco standing over him, not decently dressed in the evening clothes of a gambler, but wearing the loose shirt and broad straw hat of a rubber tapper. Further, the tall Indian had a superb British rifle slung over his shoulder and a bandolero of shells across his chest. The governor's eyes moved painfully around the spacious bedroom of the gubernatorial palace and saw in the dim light of this appallingly early hour a dozen other intruders, including a fair-haired one like that gringo journalist who disappeared some months ago and—Mother of God, a woman! Fair, too, but with her hair cut short like a man's. The governor moistened his dry mouth. Manco said, "Save your breath. No one will come to your aid."

Ribeiro closed his eyes; he must be having a dreadful dream. Silently, he began to pray: *I'll never drink again. Not one drop, Holy Mother, I swear it. . . .* He heard Manco move around the bed and open the shutters. He said, "Governor, I suggest you take a look." *If this is not a dream,* Ribeiro thought, *when I get up they are going to kill me. In my pajamas. How degrading.* The insurgent nodded toward the Rio Negro. "Your elegant White City has been blockaded." Ribeiro sat up and blinked to clear his vision, bringing into focus a line of naval vessels ringing the harbor.

Ribeiro's voice cracked with anxiety. "You're bluffing. Those are Brazilian Navy ships, sent to—" His head ached dreadfully; he simply couldn't think. The harbor blurred. He blinked and looked again. There wasn't a single native canoe in sight. Even the city's streets were silent and utterly empty. He shut his eyes and opened them again: no change. He cleared his throat, making an effort at a more authoritative tone. "Where is the Baron do Rio Mar?"

Tomás stepped forward and, reaching across the bed, dangled the shrunken head by its hair. The sight of it sent the Governor scrabbling backward among the pillows to the head of the bed.

"There will be no relief from Pará," Esteban said. "It has been, unfortunately, necessary to cut the telegraph line in a great many places." He nodded to Will, who handed Ribeiro a pair of field glasses. Manco said, "Look carefully at that frigate in the middle of the line."

Obediently, Ribeiro looked. "Are those the Krupp field guns?"

"Yes. They are aimed at the city."

"Whatever for?"

"The tender is moving in. It is to be filled with coal. Then one by one our other ships will leave their places in the line for refueling. All this must be accomplished swiftly and without a hitch. Otherwise by noon today Manáos will no longer have an opera house."

Ribeiro sighed. He'd wanted to build a new one anyway, one with a gold dome instead of colored tiles. But if these revolutionaries interfered with trade, especially with the rubber trade, where would the money come from? He said, "I'll order the coal."

"Thank you." The Manconistas moved toward the doors. Ribeiro raised his voice to ask, "Have you left any of my servants alive?" He grew plaintive. "I need my coffee desperately." He lay back down and closed his eyes. Perhaps it wasn't all bad. At least Rio Mar was out of the way. The man had always been a dreadful nuisance. And while the sight of the shrunken head had given him quite a turn, he reflected that it couldn't have happened to a more deserving subject. The British, though . . . they weren't going to like this. In spite of his headache, Ribeiro grinned. It will serve them right, the bloody bastards, acting as if they let us run our country only because we need the practice.

57

While the ships were refueling Savannah went to see Madelyn, only to stop short on Rue Epaminondas, looking at what was left of the Contessa's Palace. All the glass was gone from the windows and the walls above the openings had been blackened by smoke. Terrified, she began to run and didn't stop until she'd reached the cathedral, bursting in upon a penitent in the confessional to cry out at Father Antonio, "Where is my mother?" He calmed her fear and, when he was free, answered her questions. Madelyn could be found in her new temporary quarters at the Hotel Internacional.

The streets remained deserted, the bars closed and the shops shuttered tight. The usual vendors, sellers of lottery tickets, and street whores were in hiding; everyone was afraid there would be fighting in the streets, or worse, that those guns aboard the frigate would be fired at the city. As Savannah ran toward the hotel, she was aware of being watched by eyes behind the slatted shutters.

She pushed open the door of the hotel and heard the sound of Porfirio's guitar. There in the lobby, among the eight-foot potted palms and upholstered settees, were the Contessa and her girls. Savannah was thoroughly hugged and kissed, and then scrutinized approvingly.

Porfirio stood quietly on the edge of the group. When Savannah came to him at last, she embraced him and said, "I'm sorry about your father." He nodded in appreciation. He told her he'd known the Baron had been captured; his half brother Raoul had survived the trip down the Escondido and had gone on down to Pará to attend to business there. Egypt grinned. "I bet he's going to clean out the till and head for Monte Carlo," he said. Porfirio's eyes clouded. "Not Raoul. He will have a new *esquema* . . . scheme? . . . for to defeat those who keep him from making money in the rubber business."

Porfirio went on to say that this morning, after the Manconistas had left the governor's palace, word of his father's death had spread through the city. After about five minutes of reflection Porfirio concluded that he had no interest in the rubber business, so now he proposed turning the Rio Mar

Palacio into "the most marvelous bordello the world have ever seen."

The girls, especially Egypt, were enchanted, but Madelyn shook her head. She said it had been her intention for some time to retire from the business, and now that she might one day become a grandmother, she felt it was time to make the break.

Immediately Elena and Porfirio agreed upon a partnership. All the old staff would be retained, with the addition of Bitte's little clerk to keep the books, and the name changed simply to the Contessa's Palácio. They were about to seal the bargain with a champagne toast when Porfirio stopped and turned his childlike eyes to Savannah. "Forgive!" he sighed. "I have forget to ask permission of the *baronesa*, my lady step-mother."

Porfirio insisted she take Arcadia, standing empty now except for Cicero, who lived there as a caretaker. Dom Luíz had sent Edward and Veronique packing. "Not exactly packing," Madelyn corrected. "He sent them off empty-handed, with a pair of steamship tickets and the clothes on their backs."

Embarrassed, Porfirio explained that his father had confiscated everything St. James possessed because most of it belonged to the Baron anyway or had been stolen from him. Savannah bit her lip. Porfirio said, "I am sorry."

She touched his arm. "Will you try to find them, please? I want them taken care of, an income or something." Porfirio promised. She turned to Madelyn. "Will you live in Arcadia? Then, when the river is secured, Esteban and the rest of us can use it as a base whenever we're passing through Manáos."

Madelyn agreed, just as the cathedral bells began sounding noon. Swiftly Savannah kissed her mother good-bye and waved to the others; but in the doorway she paused and spoke once more to Porfirio. "The last thing your father said was to ask Esme to pray for his soul. Will you do that?"

She ran all the way back to the harbor, where the armada was ready to set out for Óbidos. All the ships had been re-fueled, and while that was going on Tomás had led a raiding party to the Baron's stable. The results stood on the deck of the frigate: six prize horses. And now the small fleet had been joined by the *Paloma*, back from another spell of repairs, still coughing along on spare parts.

As the ships left the harbor, the people of Manáos, no

longer fearful, poured into the streets and massed along the waterfront. The cheering began with the native peoples, but soon everyone joined in, even the European clerks. From somewhere a band assembled and began to play. By the time the fleet lost sight of the city, the people were dancing in the streets.

Below the confluence of the Rio Negro with the Amazon, the river widened so far that its shores could not be seen. The Manconistas passed the mouth of the Madeira that first night; the next day's run took them close to Óbidos, but they turned north into the mouth of the Trombetas and tied up to trees along the shore. Manco summoned his leaders aboard the yacht and went over the attack plans. Then they set off downstream again.

It was a night of vivid moonlight. Glittering canoe paths cut into the black forest rimming the banks. The town of Óbidos lay tucked into a crescent-shaped cliff, its shoreline narrowed by the thirty-five-foot rise of high water. Cutting their engines, they used the powerful current of the narrows to drift in close. Two teams, one led by Esteban and the other by Tomás, climbed the foliage of the cliffs and struck the forts. Manned by bored Brazilian soldiers, most of them dozing at their posts, the installations fell without a shot.

Meanwhile Will and Savannah paid a call upon the town's mayor, who, once he understood the situation, welcomed the Manconistas hospitably. He was a *caboclo* himself, part Portuguese and part Indian, and he very quickly began enjoying the turn of events. He took a rusty antique sword from the wall of his office and formally surrendered to the Liberator. Further, he insisted upon locking up the captured Federales in the town jail. Then he announced a *festa* of welcome for the next night.

Throughout the day the mayor supervised the construction of a bandstand and the stringing up of colored lanterns in the town square, while the Manconistas labored. Using barges, they got the Baron's horses off the frigate and hitched them to the Krupp field guns to haul them up the narrow road to the top of the bluffs. They set them up between the two forts, entrenched in the ground firmly for the recoil and camouflaged with vines. They also covered the forts with foliage, as if they'd been deserted and the jungle was taking them back.

At sundown the band began to play. Townspeople brought furniture into the square so everyone could sit around watching the dancers. The music went on half the night, and the town folk got blissfully drunk on *cachaça*. Savannah danced with Will and MacNair several times. At last, to the applause of the crowd, she got Manco to his feet. Laughing, they clapped and stamped their way through a raucous flamenco; then, while the guitars strummed softly, they turned slowly in one another's arms far into the night.

"There are so many places I want to take you," he murmured against her hair. "I want you to see the Andes. Sometimes I think whatever strength I have comes from there—like the old myth about the son of Earth: touching that ground restores me."

She kissed him. "It doesn't matter where you take me. The forest, the river. Wherever we are together is enough."

He drew back to look into her eyes. "Have I made you happy?"

She smiled. "Even my mother saw it. At the hotel she said she could see it in my face." She lay her head on his shoulder. "All I ever wanted was to be close to you."

"No. I think in the beginning what you wanted was to be free."

That was true. Had she traded freedom for love? No; somehow this love was a form of freedom. Esteban accepted her fully, as she was.

He gazed off into the darkness. "I never had much use for the romantics. I know mankind mates instinctively, to perpetuate itself. Yet—" He looked at her again with what seemed wonder. "With you I feel complete. Perhaps it's like the *yang* and *yin* of Oriental philosophy. A wholeness formed of light and dark, the firm and the soft, earth and sky, fire and water. It's as if together we form something much more than the sum of our separate parts." He smiled and drew her closer. "I can't explain. There are no words for it."

"And it's for always, isn't it?"

"Yes. In Italy I saw the tomb of a Roman couple. I never forgot the inscription. *Hieme et aestate et prope et procul usque dum vivam et ultra.*"

She frowned, trying to remember her Latin. "Winter and summer?"

"Winter and summer, near and far, throughout life, and beyond."

58

Governor Ribeiro had been right: the British didn't like these new developments. It was Raoul who made sure they found out about them. He'd gone to see the British Consul at Pará to explain the situation, pointing out to the Englishman that an Indian nation in the *selva* would be very difficult to deal with and impossible to bribe. The consul conferred with the governor of the state of Pará, who telegraphed Rio and arranged for the British to receive a formal request from the Government of Brazil for assistance in putting down an insurrection. Soon a representative of the Royal Navy's South Atlantic Squadron was steaming to the aid of Her Majesty's esteemed Brazilian allies.

By noon of the day after the *festa* at Óbidos the Manconistas had sighted the ship in the distance and its configuration was clear: a battleship, probably admiral class, and big enough to make the Manconistas' gunboats look like a swarm of gnats. Watching it from the bluffs above the town, Will's heart sank.

He found Esteban hard at work in his command post aboard the *Primavera*. He was dispatching his little fleet with orders to scatter upstream into the side channels and canoe paths until summoned by the drums. Esteban, always restless when waiting, was exultant now that action could be taken. Will stood in a corner of the room watching. Gradually, at least for the moment, his feeling of despair diminished. One after the other, men and women were sent on errands. Produce must be gathered, Brazil nuts, gourds, sweetmeats; Manco wanted a fleet of vendors in canoes. More supplies must be put aboard the *Paloma:* bags of grain, sugar, coffee, crates of chickens, pigs, a cow; he wanted the boat to look like a filthy river trader once again. Tomás was to take an old barge and all the dynamite upstream.

The mayor of Óbidos came aboard. Jerking his head forward apologetically he said, "Senhor Liberator, if the British are coming here, we respectfully request you leave our town. Is this possible, sir?" Manco put his arm around the man's shoulders. "We cannot leave, my friend. Take your people into the forest for safety. When the British are gone we will have another festa." The man smiled uncertainly and left.

Esteban turned to Will. "Go to the town jail and ask the Federales if they want to help us fight the British."

"Fight!" Will said.

"If they do, and you think they can be trusted, send them back up to the forts with orders not to fire until you signal." Helpless in the face of this calm decisiveness, Will complied.

The progress of the battleship against the current was a majestic ten knots. Over three hundred feet long, painted a flawless white, and with elaborate scrollwork on her bow, H. M. S. *Relentless* seemed to fill the narrows. She arrived to find the town of Óbidos enjoying its midafternoon *sesta*. The square was deserted, but in the shade under the trees and on the verandas of the houses, hammocks rocked slowly. Moored to the dock, which was almost awash in the flood-level river, creaked an overburdened paddle steamer, streaked with rust. Nearby, a sleek yacht flew the black and red flag of Rio Mar Rubber.

Esteban had moved his command post to the *Paloma*. There, behind the bales of goods, he and Will studied the battleship with field glasses. Scanning the davits they ticked off the small boats the *Relentless* carried—a thirty-two-foot sailing launch, four cutters, two whaleboats, and a gig. Two great funnels vented her smoke and there were ventilators everywhere. Her deck was a mass of equipment, mostly because her guns took up so much space: four twelve-inch guns mounted in pairs in movable turrets, and between these cannons a complete array of six-pounders, four-pounders, and smaller guns, eight or ten to a side. The battleship slowed as she drew abreast of the town, but kept her steam up, doing just a few knots to hold against the current. Will murmured, "She's flying an admiral's flag! Maybe it's all a show, to cow us into giving up." But even as he spoke they saw the sailors in smart whites uncap the twelve-inch guns; then the turrets turned slowly until the big cannons were aimed at the shore. This was a very real threat.

Now the Manconistas, playing the part of residents of Óbidos, sleepily got up from their *sestas* and began preparing to greet the visitors. Canoes loaded with goods for sale pushed off and headed toward the ship. Immediately an officer with a large speaking-trumpet warned them off, calling, "Don't come close! Keep away!" Then, after hastily consulting a pocket lexicon, he cried, *"Distancial Ausentarse!"* The vendors, looking disappointed, fell back.

Will said, "We can't possibly attack her. The guns on the bluff are useless. She's armor-plated."

"Where?" Esteban asked.

"A belt above the waterline, probably eighteen inches thick. Another twelve inches on those gun mounts."

Esteban asked, "How about the bottom?"

Will frowned, trying to remember what he'd read. "If we aim the Krupps below the waterline at the base of her stacks, we might manage to blow up her boilers."

Esteban watched the British sailors working about on her deck. Most of them were barefoot, like boys at play. He said, "How many men are aboard?"

Will searched his memory. "Admiral class battleships carry a complement of five hundred or so—thirty officers and—"

Esteban interrupted, "And you think we ought to try to sink her in hundreds of feet of water, with the current running . . . what did you say it was?"

Yesterday Will had amused himself by rowing out into midstream and throwing a weighted rope into the water, clocking the time it took the knots to slip through his fingers. "Better than seven feet a second. But you can't declare war and then start worrying about—"

Manco smiled as Savannah came up from the galley. He put his palm-straw hat on her head in case the British caught sight of her hair; otherwise she looked like a tapper. Will bit his lip. "If we could think of a way to scare them off . . . maybe MacNair could go aboard and tell them the town's got an epidemic of some sort."

Manco shook his head. "An epidemic won't stop those guns."

"And unfortunately," Savannah added, "you can't frighten them by blowing up the riverbank." Will agreed that the British were, of all people, the least superstitious; but Savannah persisted, "They must fear something, though."

Esteban's eyes narrowed in amusement. "Women. Well-born women like their queen." He turned to Savannah. "Get dressed. We'll send for something belonging to the mayor's wife." Savannah protested that Senhora Mayor was twice her size; besides, she had clothes of her own, for the Contessa was always packing her a basket. What did he want her to do?

Esteban kept his eyes on the battleship as he answered. "We're going to let the river itself take care of the British.

But we need time. Darkness. The rain. So the Baroness do Rio Mar is going to pay a call."

Will argued with Manco all the time Savannah was getting ready. Esteban refused to let Will go with her; he needed him to direct the batteries on the bluffs. He also refused to send MacNair along; he said, "They'll know how to deal with him, he's one of their kind. But Savannah—they won't harm her, but she'll be very disconcerting."

A few minutes later the *Primavera* moved away from shore, turned, and headed for the battleship. Again the officer called through his megaphone. At the same time the amidships guns were manned. Savannah, all in white, wearing long gloves and a broad hat beneath her ruffled parasol, walked carefully to the bow of her yacht. Ignoring the guns trained upon her she called out, "I say, mightn't I borrow a bit of proper tea? All they've got ashore is that dreadful Brazilian matte!"

The officer with the speaking-trumpet consulted his superiors. The admiral himself stepped to the rail. "Good Lord," he burst out, "it's a girl! Well, don't stand gawking, pipe her aboard!"

The stairway was lowered and Savannah, taking mincing steps in her tight skirt, made her way to the deck. As she reached it, the *Primavera* was waved away and returned to shore. Dismayed, Savannah feigned giddiness and said, looking down at the water thirty feet below, "Heavens, you're so high up."

The portly man with all the ribbons on his white coat said, "Vice Admiral Sir Herbert Beckwith, at your service, ma'am."

She gave him her hand. "Baroness Savannah Saint James do Rio Mar, wife of Dom Luíz Alvarez y Costa—" A scented handkerchief wafted to the corner of her eye. "Recently deceased," she explained. The admiral cleared his throat and murmured something about being sorry. Savannah sighed, aware that some five hundred pairs of eyes were peering at her from behind the chaos of equipment on the ship. "I hope you'll forgive my being so forward, but I haven't had a decent cup of tea since last visiting Broadstairs, the home of my dear friends the Estyns. Do you by chance know Mr. Estyn, M. P.?" Beckwith replied that he hadn't had the pleasure, although he'd heard of him, of course. "His daughter and I were classmates and such dear friends," Savannah said. She took his arm and added, "I miss her so."

The admiral blushed and began bustling about, ordering tea and chairs to be brought on deck, all the while muttering that in this beastly climate it was impossible to go below, it was like an oven. Moments later men in white jackets served tea. "Allow me," Savannah said, and poured with a discreet flourish.

Beckwith, still flustered, drank his tea, and murmured, "Beastly climate."

"One gets used to it, in time." She glanced about the deck. The sailors and their crisply uniformed officers stood about under those huge guns; the ship fairly bristled with them, like an armored porcupine. She said, "Admiral, I hope the lack of suitable society here hasn't made me boorish—" He, of course, denied that vehemently, so she went on, "But I wonder if I mightn't have a tour of the ship? It looks so frightfully interesting."

His brow furrowed. "My dear, I should be delighted to oblige, but we're here on business for the Government of Brazil. It seems there's been some trouble upriver."

"Oh, that! There's always trouble upriver."

He smiled paternally. "I'm sure it's of no consequence, but Her Majesty's fleet . . ."

She poured herself another cup of tea and said, "As a matter of fact, this time it's simply a family quarrel. Two of my stepsons are at odds about the rubber business. I feel it is my duty to side with the legal heir." She touched her waist protectively and spoke in a whisper. "He has sworn to safeguard the inheritance of my unborn child."

"Dear lady! Are you all right?"

"Very well, thank you. At any rate, now that we've gotten that unsavory situation out of the way, mightn't I have a tour of your lovely boat?" They got to their feet and he began leading her toward the companionway. She took his arm. "Admiral, might your assignment take you as far as Manáos? I'd be delighted to have you and your men as my guests at the Palácio Rio Mar."

He chuckled. "My dear, I have five hundred thirty-five men!"

She clapped her hands. "A garden party then, with an orchestra beside the lake." They passed a line of officers who stood at attention, grinning. "And young ladies to dance with. How much I should enjoy introducing you all to my friends: Gaya, Elena, and . . ." She chattered all the way through the tour of the paymaster's office, the galley, the enlisted men's mess and the officer's dining room, along with the crew's quarters, the dispensary, and the admiral's cabin. He, worried about her "condition," felt sure she'd had enough, but she insisted on climbing the ladder to the navigating bridge.

The bridge had windows on three sides, odd devices standing about on poles, and speaking tubes which permitted one to call the engine room. Esteban had told her to keep the British busy until it was time for the sunset storm, and that when she heard the drums she must call for the *Primavera* and leave at once. If she was for any reason delayed, she must get off the ship at all costs when the pace of the drumming increased. Now she saw that clouds were forming on the horizon, still white and far away, but moving fast. Meanwhile, an officer, his eyes trained upriver, said, "Something's coming, sir."

Everyone looked, alert and ready for action, but Savannah laughed and assured them that it was only one of the Amazon's floating islands. "They break off from the banks at high water and head for the sea." The admiral muttered that they must be a menace to navigation, and the duty officer said, "Shall I give the order to blast it out of the water, sir?" The admiral agreed, but Savannah protested. "But the wildlife! Look at those birds!" The admiral relented, but told the man to keep an eye on it and take action if it came close.

By the time they left the bridge the drumming had begun. Savannah clapped her hands. "There's going to be another festa tonight! I must get ashore and change." The admiral frowned toward Óbidos, where a group of musicians were tuning up at the bandstand on the square. She turned to the officer who'd used the speaking-trumpet. "Will you please call my yacht?"

The admiral scanned the town with field glasses. "Not a soldier in sight," he said. "They could have wiped out the garrison. For all we know, they're waiting in the bush for nightfall. Tell you what, my dear. The safest place for you is right here aboard the *Relentless* until we're quite sure what's going on here. We'll have a cabin made ready for you in a trice. Bit unorthodox, I warrant, but our job is to protect Her Majesty's subjects—and friends of her subjects."

In the square the drum tempo doubled. Savannah swayed uncertainly.

He moved closer. "Dear child, are you all right?"

"A little queasy. The motion of the ship and the tea—"
She clapped a hand to her mouth and ran to the rail where,
to the stupefaction of the admiral, his officers and crew, she
ripped open the front of her dress, stepped out of it, and
flung herself overboard feet first in her lace knickers.

59

Watching from a gun emplacement on the bluffs, Will saw
her surface ten yards from where she hit the water. She
began to dogpaddle against the swift current until she caught
sight of the *Primavera* moving downstream to intercept her.
She let the river take her and swam with it until well past
the battleship. Dr. MacNair was at the rail to help her
clamber aboard.

The British had little time to contemplate her actions,
for now the sunset storm burst upon the river with stinging
sheets of rain and battering wind. Meanwhile, the floating
island Will knew to be a dynamite-loaded barge covered
with foliage and tethered birds manned by Tomás, sped past
the *Relentless* on the far side. It seemed harmless until it
neared the battleship's stern; then it swerved sharply in
toward the hull, lassoed to the stern flagstaff. The Manconistas dove clear just as the charge of dynamite exploded,
blowing the ship's rudder clean away.

Upstream on the darkening river the half dozen ships of
Manco's armada hove into view, closing fast and peppering
the battleship with gunfire. The British turrets swung toward
the attackers. Immediately the *Paloma*'s whistle shrilled and
Will signaled the guns on the cliffs to commence firing. At
once the battleship's turrets swung back toward the town,
along with the smaller weapons amidships. Will watched,
anticipating the worst; even so, the first thunderous discharge
of the cannons startled him. However, to his astonishment
he saw that their aim was low; they were lobbing shells into
the rock face of the bluff below him. He let out a jubilant
whoop when he realized that their problem was insoluble:
no battleship is meant to fire at high targets, but only at other
battleships. Unmindful of the din, he shouted toward the
river, "So much for your show of force, you arrogant bastards! You should have sent gunboats!"

Manco's vessels had drawn in close and were firing at the

amidships guns above them, not doing much damage, but keeping the British seamen back from the rail. The *Relentless*'s smaller guns were less and less a threat, for the battleship had begun a rudderless drifting. Will guessed his Krupps had damaged her boilers, for she was no longer making headway against the current. He saw her drop anchor to steady her position, but it took time to hit the bottom, 350 feet down, and in the interim she swung about slowly, as if caught in a sluggish whirlpool. Her twelve-inch guns fired aimlessly; the shells arced over the breast of the Amazon only to fall into her depths. By the time the anchors had caught hold enough to steady her drift, Will had his guns aimed; it took them less than a minute to blast through the chains and set her loose again. The British guns fell silent and Manco's boats drew back to avoid her erratic sideways course. On her deck Will saw frantic activity. The small craft were being readied. At first he thought they were going to abandon ship, but only the steam launches were being loosed, apparently for use as tugs to steer her through the narrows. They were too late. The *Relentless* slammed downriver broadside, veering so close to shore he wondered if she'd run up on the bank and land in the middle of the town square. But then she took another slow turn and headed off downstream once more.

Her smashing wake had caught the *Paloma* and tossed it against the bank, crushing the feeble dock. The steamer's boiler ruptured. The explosion sent gourds, Brazil nut pods, and chickens into the air. Esteban dove low into the water, clear of the blast, but he surfaced at once to watch for Gonçalves and Filomena, who popped up nearby. On the battleship's stern a zealous British officer, ignoring his ship's peril, kept firing a machine gun back toward the town, systematically aiming at whatever he saw moving in the water. Esteban, silhouetted in the darkness against the flaming wreckage of the *Paloma*, made a clear target.

Downstream, those aboard the *Primavera* saw the battleship drift past them harmlessly, although close enough to stop their hearts. Then they went back to their task of pulling Manconistas from the water and giving aid to the wounded. When the battleship passed through the narrows and began to crash about among the islands on the way to Santerem, Savannah looked back toward the town and paused, stunned by the wreckage where the *Paloma* had been moored. She peered at the dark river, still lashed by rain. At last she saw his arm rise from the water in an odd one-sided stroke. She dove in, followed by Tomás. Esteban's eyes were closed; he swam unconsciously as another man might breathe. They got him to the yacht's side, where MacNair waited to lift him aboard. The doctor laid him down gently on the deck. The machine gun had raked across his body. No vital organs had been hit, but MacNair had a half dozen bullets to remove.

They got him ashore and into the mayor's house, where MacNair set to work. The operation took two hours. Tomás, as he'd done before on the Semnome, lay beside Esteban, his body supplying blood to the liberator through rubber tubing. At last Esteban opened his eyes and looked upon Tomás. Tomás said, "They are gone. Their battleship is on a sandbar near Santerem. It will stay there until the next year's rains." And Will, standing with Savannah in the shadows, pictured the headline. "H.M.S. *Relentless* Disabled by Band of Rubber Tappers. Underdogs Triumphant."

Manco whispered, "Our ships?"

Tomás answered, "All well."

"Casualties?"

Tomás grinned. "We lost a lot of chickens."

Esteban turned his head to look around the room until his eyes found Savannah. She went to him, knelt beside the bed, and raised his hand to her lips.

Will saw once more that look pass between them, an instant of utter regard in which time itself seemed stilled. Like being lost in the depths of the *selva*, he thought, where everything real is always fully present and nothing ever changes. Winter and summer, and near and far, throughout life . . . and beyond.

Afterword

The Amazon rubber boom went on for another fifteen years. So did the atrocities. One entrepreneur working on a single tributary (the Putumayo) was at length held accountable for thirty thousand deaths. But that wasn't why the boom ended. After decades of experimentation, transplants, cross-breeding, grafting, and cloning, the British succeeded in getting rubber trees to thrive in orderly rows on Asian plantations. Grown under these conditions the latex cost less and the industrialized nations lost interest in the Amazon. By the time of the First World War, Manáos was a ghost town, its businesses bankrupt, its mansions boarded up, its colorful Governor Ribeiro a suicide, and his multimillion-dollar opera house falling into ruin. The intruders vanished; the *selva* closed over their installations without a trace. And in the end the rubber boom left no mark upon Amazonia, except for the fact that the forest Indians had been decimated.

Four Best-Selling Authors of Sweeping Historical Romance

Stephanie Blake

___ 21005	BLAZE OF PASSION	$2.95
___ 16425	DAUGHTER OF DESTINY	$1.95
___ 16891	FLOWERS OF FIRE	$2.95
___ 16847	SCARLET KISSES	$2.95
___ 16719	SECRET SINS	$2.75
___ 16892	SO WICKED MY DESIRE	$2.95
___ 16785	UNHOLY DESIRES	$2.95
___ 21044	WICKED IS MY FLESH	$2.95

Roberta Gellis

___ 16468	ALINOR	$2.25
___ 16776	THE DRAGON AND THE ROSE	$2.75
___ 16829	GILLIANE	$2.75
___ 16490	JOANNA	$2.25
___ 16814	ROSELYNDE	$2.75
___ 16692	SIREN SONG	$2.75
___ 21043	THE SWORD AND THE SWAN	$2.95

Morgan Llywelyn

___ 16825	LION OF IRELAND	$3.50

Barbara Riefe

___ 16747	BLACK FIRE	$2.75
___ 16444	FAR BEYOND DESIRE	$1.95
___ 16480	FIRE AND FLESH	$2.25
___ 16658	SO WICKED THE HEART	$2.75
___ 16938	TEMPT NOT THIS FLESH	$2.95
___ 16890	THIS RAVAGED HEART	$2.95
___ 16798	WILD FIRE	$2.95

781-1

PLAYBOY PAPERBACKS
Book Mailing Service
P.O. Box 690 Rockville Centre, New York 11571

NAME_____

ADDRESS_____

CITY_____ STATE_____ ZIP_____

Please enclose 50¢ for postage and handling if one book is ordered;
25¢ for each additional book. $1.50 maximum postage and handling
charge. No cash, CODs or stamps. Send check or money order.

Total amount enclosed: $_____

The Best in Historical Romance from Playboy Paperbacks